Ego, THE PEOPLE

A Novel

DONELLA DUNLOP

Order this book online at www.trafford.com
or email orders@trafford.com

Most Trafford titles are also available at major online book retailers.

Front Cover painting—copyright expired—credit Emmanuel Benner

Back Cover photograph—with permission from Don Russel,
former Manager of Canadian Wildlife Service, Yukon College, Yukon.

Printed in the United States of America.

ISBN: 978-1-4669-7973-4 (sc)
ISBN: 978-1-4669-7975-8 (hc)
ISBN: 978-1-4669-7974-1 (e)

Library of Congress Control Number: 2013902144

Trafford rev. 02/12/2013

Trafford PUBLISHING www.trafford.com

North America & international
toll-free: 1 888 232 4444 (USA & Canada)
phone: 250 383 6864 • fax: 812 355 4082

DEDICATION

For my sister, Catherine, without whose inspiration and encouragement this book would never have been written.

Also for the Ottawa Valley Algonkin Peoples

And for my family

ACKNOWLEDGEMENT

I am indebted to the writings, photography and drawings of Canadian archaeologists, anthropologists, and historians, and the Ottawa Valley Algonkins.

My thanks to Don Russell, former Manager of the Canadian Wildlife Service in the Yukon, Yukon College, for his wonderful back cover photo of wintering caribou.

The special maps were done by my much loved and always supportive daughter-in-law, Ruth Wood-Knobel, proprietor of *Rideau Design*.

Finally, I thank my father, Ed Dunlop, without whose fascinating stories of the Canadian wilderness this book would never have been born. I thank also my mother, Kathleen Carmichael-Dunlop, my lifelong inspiration.

CONTENTS

BOOK III

BOOK IV

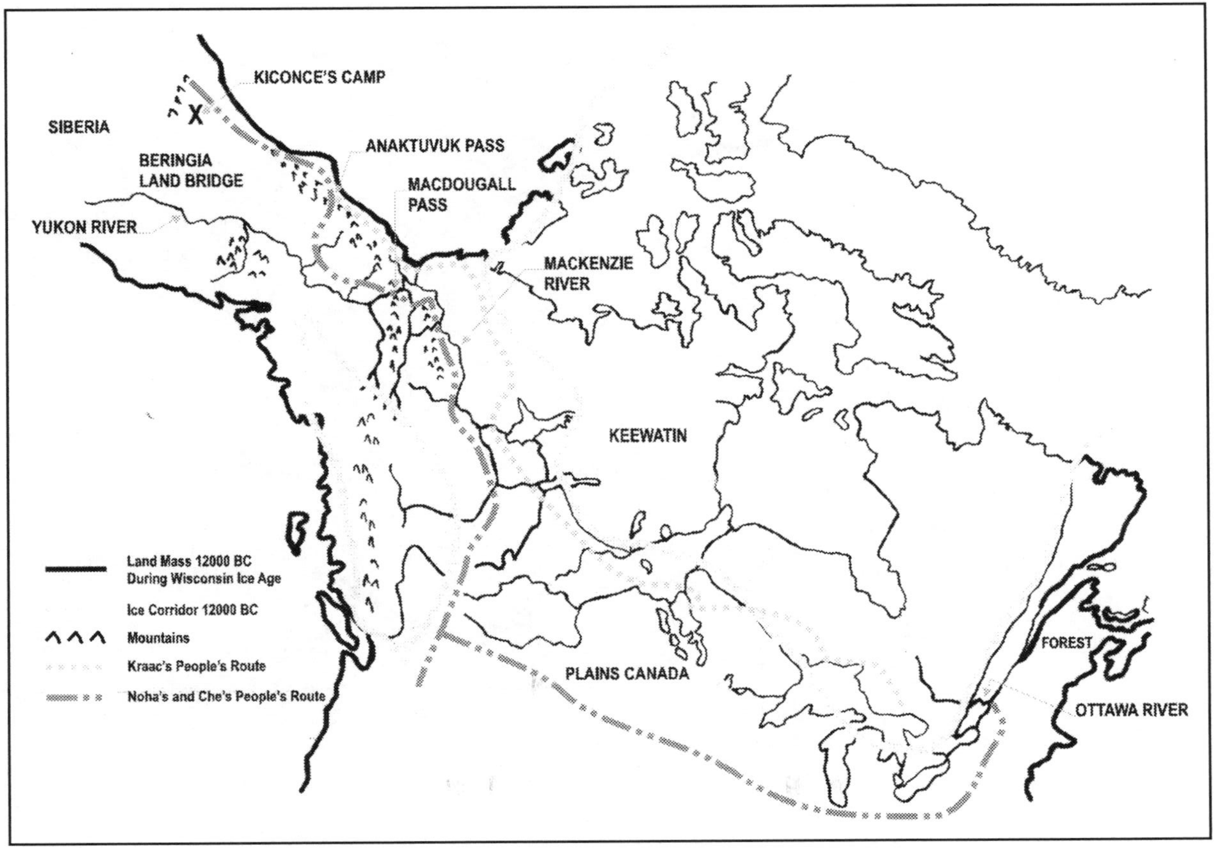
KICONCE'S CAMP
SIBERIA
X
ANAKTUVUK PASS
BERINGIA
LAND BRIDGE
MACDOUGALL
PASS
YUKON RIVER
MACKENZIE
RIVER
KEEWATIN
Land Mass 12000 BC
During Wisconsin Ice Age
Ice Corridor 12000 BC
Mountains
Kraac's People's Route
Noha's and Che's People's Route
FOREST
PLAINS CANADA
OTTAWA RIVER

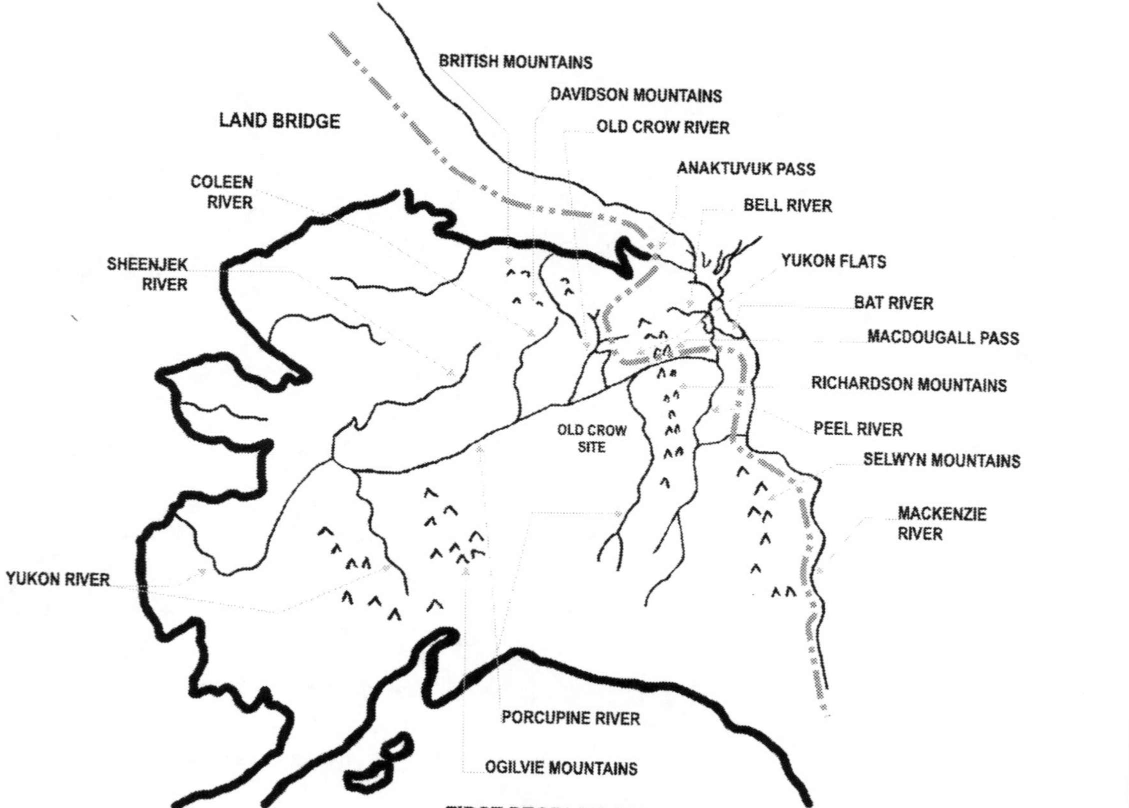

FIRST PEOPLE'S PATH

INTRODUCTION

When I was young and deeply in love with my home, The Ottawa Valley in Ontario, Canada, I decided that I wanted to share the story of the majestic Ottawa River, the surrounding mystic Laurentian Mountains, the cozy small towns and the neat, rustic farms and above all, the tale of the Valley's first inhabitants, the brave Algonkin, and of the adventuresome Scots, Irish and French who mapped and settled the Valley.

My first attempt was that of a novice writer and though the heart and the magic were there my writing skills needed that ephemeral something . . . I put the book aside and proceeded to write the intriguing story of my own ancestors, the Scots/Irish, and of the French missionaries and voyageurs and finally, of the era of my own growing up in the Valley. The books were well received. I think I have shared the story of the valley I love.

Now I travel back to those far off beginnings in the last Ice Age when the ancestors of the Algonkin ventured across an ancient land bridge in Beringia to find the Valley of a Dream. Excitement, adventure, fear, bravery, amazing mountain ranges, walls of blue ice, beautiful and frightening rivers, terrible spirits and myriad animals. All this and more they encountered. And yet they pushed on, Noha and Che and their clan, *the Eyo, the First People*, the first Canadians, the first North Americans. They searched for the Valley of their Dream. And the children of their children—the Algonkin of the Ottawa Valley—would at last find and settle the Ottawa Valley, our home.

PROLOGUE

MAYWISHER, LONG TIME AGO, up over and beyond, during the time of Ice, there lived in Siberia a young hunter called Noha, the son of the leader of the *Eyo*, the People.

Noha's early ancestors had followed retreating herds of long-haired reindeer and lumbering mammoths and led the Eyo across the steppes and into the *mountains of the north-east*. In time, they reached the furthermost mountain beyond which stretched empty tundra and the Endless Lake.

They prospered there, and their bellies were full.

And in that time, there also lived in Siberia a maiden called Che, the daughter of the leader of the Omeeseh, the Owls. Che's early ancestors had followed the retreating herds of long-haired reindeer and lumbering mammoths across the steppes and *into the forests of the north-east*. In time, they too, reached empty tundra and the shore of the Endless Lake.

They prospered there, and their bellies were full.

MAYWISHER, LONG TIME AGO, up over and beyond, during the time of Melting Ice, *Manitou*, the Great Spirit, stretched a land bridge across the Endless Lake and the Peoples of Siberia went forth in search of the Valley of the Dream.

BOOK I

CHAPTER 1

Noha's Dream

Polar cold in the mountain's bowels. Black strokes his eyes as the Spirit of Darkness steals Noha's sight. Bumps rise in his flesh and he gasps though there is air enough in the stone corridor. He almost reaches out for his father but forces his hand down. Black changes with lesser blacks taking shape and Noha sees granite walls bending, curving. Crevices. And his father's bulk. Noha's breathing eases.

A sudden chasm forces him to slide along the cave wall, his toes gripping the precipice edge. Noha shrinks from the confining granite and then emptiness presses him back into its safety. Why does his body betray him? He fears nothing. *Nothing*! He passes the chasm and moves through the final rock corridor. He smells fire.

Hurry, Father.

They approach the deepest cave of all, Boog the Shaman's lair. A sucking sound from Noha.

His father, Kiconce, says, "No need to announce yourself. Boog know's we are here."

Noha's calves tremble; his feet ache to run forward. Boog must listen. Noha is Spirit chosen. Noha has dreamed. He must tell his dream. If the shaman is wise enough to listen, the rest of the People will listen!

His calves tingle as he steps into a volcanic cavity stretched in front, around, and above them. Sparse flames flicker in the rock floor's center. Trapped smoke stings Noha's hazel coloured eyes. Flame sends orange snaking and sliding along the walls, making leap the things represented there. The shaman, Boog, presents his back to Noha and his father. Boog paints on the cave wall. At his side a thin cub wrapped in hare-skins holds a lamp filled with animal fat which spits and sparkles. The shaman wields a chewed aspen wand. Shells containing coloured mineral pastes are scattered at his feet. He dips into blacks, yellows, ochres, browns, and reds. He outlines a dancing reindeer, hooves flashing and many-branched horns and musculature outlined in charcoal. A black spear pierces the deer's side just above its distended abdomen. Above the figure, Boog has silhouetted his ancient hand, fingers splayed and outlined in spattered red hematite powder blown from a hollowed-out bone.

Noha peers hungrily at the sacred drawings. His father has told him that there are more pictures in the shadows. A gigantic cave bear, brown as Mother Earth's clay, displays its belly from which a spear protrudes. There are mammoths, mastodons, aurochs, galloping steppe horses, fleeing hinds, and bison crayoned in black. In places, red ochre deer are superimposed on ibex and bison, the whole surrounded by strange geometric symbols. In the darkest corner,

Boog had once shown Noha's father a cavorting creature with the body of a man, a reindeer's face, a bison's hooves, and a horse's mane.

Noha tosses back his long, brown hair, straightens his spine. To hunt such a creature!

The apprentice peers at the intruders. Boog's arm drops to his side. He is as emaciated as a starvling hawk because he eats only roots and herbs which his apprentice gathers from the sparse forests. Boog's naked shoulders stoop under a grey hare-skin mantle. Similar skins wrap his feet, snail shells wreath his head and beads carved from mammoth tusks and sharpened animal's teeth hang against his sunken chest. A musty smell encases him.

"Why have you come?" Boog's voice is frail and hoarse.

"My youngest son has dreamed," Kiconce says.

Noha pushes past his father. "The reindeer will not come. The Fox Spirit first told me this but the foolish hunters would not listen? Now I . . ."

Kiconce growls deep in his throat and Noha bites down hard on his tongue and moves aside. Show disrespect for Kiconce, the greatest of all hunters? *Never*. And he must not anger the shaman.

Boog turns. "Come closer."

Noha moves into the firelight, careful not to step on his father's shadow.

"Speak."

Noha stares at the shaman. "The reindeer have not come. They are not going to come."

Boog's eyes flash. "The Dream!"

"I . . . I was wandering on the mountain. I was thirsty and I went to a stream which flowed from the glacier's edge. I stooped to drink."

Memory rushes into Noha’s knowing place . . .

The air was soft against his skin and he shed his hides to roam naked but for his spear among the violet gentians and multi-hued rocks. The sun became hotter, sheened him with acrid sweat. He sniffed. Water nearby. A ravine where a cold stream churned cobalt against moss robed rocks and grass spread a rich duck feather green coverlet. He had argued with the elder hunters since sunrise and he was weary. Sleep would help. He lay in the sun, soft grass soothing his back, his spear close to his right hand.

Dozed through the afternoon.

The shadow fell across his eyes. He slowly gripped his spear, carefully parted his eyelids. His innards twisted. A reindeer with horns like forest branches loomed over him.

Do not be afraid. I have come to speak with you.

Noha took a deep, trembling breath, got to his knees. I’m not afraid.

At these words, the reindeer lay aside his grey garment and stood before Noha as a tall hunter draped in robes as bright as the afternoon sky.

Awaskesh, the Reindeer Spirit! Noha had always known he would come. *He has come to me! Me!* He forced himself to wait in silence.

Awaskesh spoke.

The Greatest Spirit, Manitou, has seen your trouble and He has sent me to reassure you. Take heed of the signs He has given. The Eyo must follow the eastern game trails along the Endless Lake. In time, the Eyo shall cross a spirit bridge and come to a new land of mountains where no man-creature dwells and they shall claim it and the people shall eat its many animals, and travel far. There shall be wonders, lakes wider than the eye can see and grassy plains thick with bison. One day, the Eyo shall find a hidden valley and there they shall dwell forever! Do not hesitate!

Manitou speaks!

But what if my heedless People won't listen?

Manitou speaks!

Noha rubbed his forehead into the grass. I obey.

When he looked up, Awaskesh had disappeared.

Boog puts down his wand, approaches the fire, hunkers beside it and gazes into its depths. Bronze light examines the grooves of his face. After much time has passed, he says, "You must speak at the council fire."

Noha quickly controls the grin pulling at his lips.

The apprentice bends toward his master and whispers.

Noha has always thought him a strange cub who was given to the shaman when very young but had not once journeyed to the Land of the Great Spirit. However, he is a docile, willing worker, instinctively knowledgeable about plants and content only when serving the shaman or gathering their food. Boog seems fond of him though he must be worried about whom Manitou would choose as his successor.

Boog twitches his bony fingers and the cub glides to a dark corner and takes a large roll of ibex skins from a stone shelf. He brings it to Boog who carefully unwraps the skins and places them before the fire. Some are ancient and some new. All are covered with drawings. Unlike the masterful paintings on the cave walls, these are cartoon-like figures inked in black. Boog follows a line of figures with his finger and reads disjointedly:

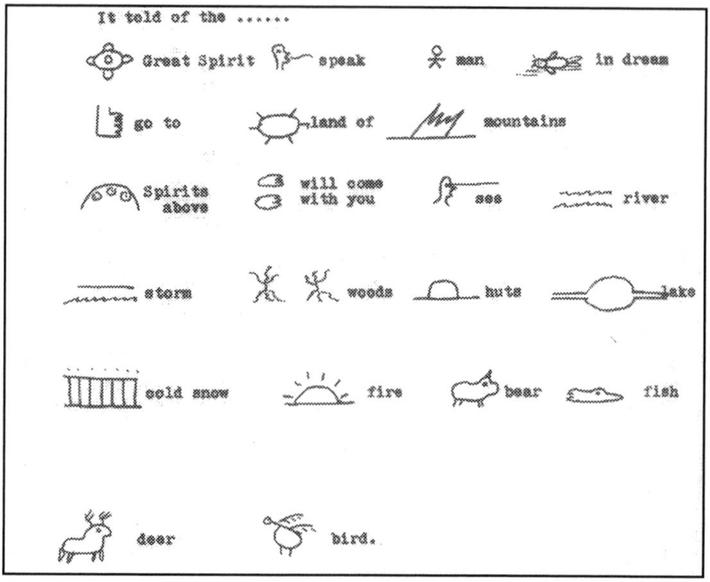

Life sap sings through Noha. Only *Ogima*, Leaders like his father, are usually allowed to see the sacred tale writings of the journey the Eyo ancestors made to the mountains. And only Boog knows how to read the record which is faded with age even though many shamans have painted over it.

Without being told, the apprentice fetches a wand and a shell full of black paint. Boog begins carefully to outline a new addition to the Eyo's sacred story. The apprentice turns and stares at Noha and Kiconce.

It is a dismissal.

CHAPTER 2

Boog's Vision

Noha goes to his mother's rock shelter. Bara sits cross-legged at her cook fire sewing with an ibex horn needle reindeer-hide leggings. She is heavy bodied and pale skinned, a face as plump as a spring salmonberry, her thick hands always tackling endless tasks.

Bara glances up. "I greet you."

"And I you, *Ninga,* Mother. I have a request."

"Speak."

"My leggings are torn and need your needle's skill."

"Give them to me."

Noha unties the offending leggings and lets them fall, hoping she will not notice how small the tear is. Bara retrieves them and putting aside her mate, Kiconce's, leggings, begins work on Noha's. Instead of leaving, Noha squats beside her. Bara's moon-face is expressionless.

"I need the leggings tonight. I shall speak of my dream tonight at the council fire."

Bara plies her needle.

"Didn't you hear me?"

"I heard."

Noha teeters back and forth, glancing at his mother's bent face. Why doesn't she say something?

"Stop fidgeting," Bara says.

Noha bites his lower lip. Bara will abide no disrespect from even her youngest son. She puts down her work and shuffles to a stone shelf where she keeps a bear-cub's skull, a collection of teeth, small horns for making ornaments, bone needles, and a prized possession, a statuette. She brings the figure to Noha.

She tilts her head. "I fashioned it."

Noha's shoulders slump. Female foolishness, but such things are important to her. "For Ecakik's mate?"

Bara laughs. Her laugh slides up from her belly and ripples from her mouth like noisy spring run-off. "No need for that."

Noha's eldest brother, Ecakik, often leads his pretty mate aside and their frequent, noisy couplings have made the babe, Pu. Noha laughs with the dissonance of youth, his head thrown back on its sturdy neck.

"It's for your other brother, Kraac's, mate."

The laughter seeps from Noha's chest, like water into sand. He stares absently at the figure. It is one hand high and made from a mixture of clay and ground bone fired to granite hardness, a naked female in a squatting position. While pendulous breasts, pear shaped, enlarged abdomen and lumped, huge thighs stress the appeal to fertility, the arms, hands, and head are suggested only. There is neither face nor feet but a tapered point at the base for thrusting into the ground or between lumps of clay.

Noha's member swells and he covers himself with a casual hand.

His mother doesn't notice. Bara fondles the statuette. "I'll push it into Mother Earth near Kraac's sleep place. Surely it will succeed." Noha stirs restlessly, his face red. "One day, I'll fashion one for your mate."

Noha leaps to his feet, no longer hiding the member thrust out like a limb from a sapling. "I'll choose a special maiden when the time is ripe, and she'll need no charms!"

"She will be fortunate."

Noha bends sideways to see into her moon face. It is once more placid and her eyes hidden by thick, downcast lids, though he detects a slight twitching of her lips. She must be thinking of Ecakik.

That night, Kiconce kindles a council fire, a lonely beacon on the mountainside. The Eyo gather. Boog has spoken and a delighted Noha is granted permission to relate his dream about the new land. The Eyo listen quietly. Some awed. Some sceptical. A few admiring. Even the shaman shows respect by remaining in the shadows. Noha watches his older brothers, handsome Kraac and hulking Ecakik, who squat on the ground near his father. Ecakik is looking suitably impressed but Kraac seems unmoved.

Silence.

Noha's shoulders twitch. How unfeeling they are! How can they hear such a dream and sit there like deaf turtles?

At the firelight's furthest edge, the females peer from the darkness and in their midst Noha sees Artisan, a gaunt, kindly elder with hair the colour of slate and long fingers always battered and scraped from fashioning amulets and such. Surely Artisan will understand what an adventure it would be to follow the reindeer to a new land! Noha smirks. Most of the females who surround Artisan are timid and though they move their huts in proper season, have never before been asked to leave the Home Mountain and the river country. At least *they* will have to keep their fears to themselves.

Only my *Ninga* won't be afraid of the journey beyond the horizon. She is always first to try a new thing and still robust despite her forty summers.

No one moves. No one speaks. Words rush up Noha's throat and leap from his mouth like rodents from a fire hole. "We must leave immediately for the new mountains!" Amusement lights his brother Kraac's austere face and Noha shouts, "We go or we starve!"

Kiconce stands and stares mildly at his youngest son. Noha closes his mouth, opens it, closes it again, and sinks down beside big Ecakik, his favourite brother.

"You are too impetuous," Ecakik whispers.

"A mere stripling has no right to speak like that to us!" Pak, an axe-faced, round shouldered hunter, snarls from behind them.

Noha feels blood rush to his face and hopes the hunters won't notice in the firelight. Pak never has dreamed, never will. Noha concentrates on his father's superb silhouette with its wide shoulders, narrow hips, and long legs. Kiconce wears bearskin in honour of his rank as ogima of the clan. His leggings are loose but made to fit snugly at the top of the thick thighs. His breech cloth is rabbit and rodent bones decorate his tunic sleeves. Yellowed cave bear teeth, mark of his rank, tremble on a thong around his neck. His musk odour mingles with the fire's pungency.

He says, "I do not wish to leave our good home and plunge our people into the dangers of unknown lands. A stripling's dream is not enough. I must have a sign! And Manitou has sent none."

Noha struggles for control. His father's mouth sculpts a determined line.

Ecakik, neck jutting like a stalactite from his deer hides; wide, kindly face betraying no emotion, rises slowly.

Glancing at his younger brother, Noha, he said, "The tundra is softening."

The hunters murmur.

Ecakik continues mildly, "The blue flowers have appeared between the rocks. Among the trees and on the tundra, the animals are coupling." Another murmur, louder this time. "But where are the reindeer? No herd blackens the grasses and flees from our spears."

"It is so!" Noha interrupts.

Ecakik waits pointedly for silence. "And what about the time of the snows? Where were the countless herds? Why didn't they retreat as always to the western woodlands?"

"They had travelled to the far north near the Endless Lake," Noha again interrupts.

A warning cough from Kiconce. Too late Noha remembers that these ritual questions are not meant to be answered by one alone, especially a young hunter.

Ecakik meanders on. "Why didn't *Awaskesh*, the Reindeer Spirit, lead his charges past our mountain when the snows left? Should we move to the place of bones in search of them?" He squats once more beside Noha.

Noha squirms like a pinioned worm. Why didn't Ecakik remind them that Awaskesh has already spoken to me? What about the New Land? The fools have forgotten already about the New Land.

Noha's father, Kiconce intones, "Each time the snow passes, the Eyo follow the herds to the northeast and build their huts beside the huts of friendly clans at the Place of the Mammoth Bones near the feeding grounds. The hunters pursue and slay many of the grey reindeer so the clan's bellies are full of good meat."

"May I speak, Ogima?" The words squirt out before Noha can swallow them.

Kiconce raises his eyebrows and sighs, "Speak if you must."

Noha leaps up and faces the hunters. His second brother Kraac is looking enigmatic. Axe-faced Pak is staring malevolently at Noha. Some of the elder hunters are openly angry.

He squares his shoulders, tosses back his long hair. "I ran for many suns across the grasses to the bone huts. I searched well and I saw no large herds, only the weak who are left behind. I met Assinbo and spoke with him."

Kiconce says mildly, "You speak often to your mentor, *Assinbo*, Spirit Leader of the Foxes. This is good." Some of the hunters nod.

Noha takes heart. "Assinbo goes to the lands near the Endless Lake where the reindeer have fled fearing the Eyo's spears and He speaks of many other animal spirits who take the same path. Is this not a sign from Awaskesh?" This comes out in a disjointed, unseemly rush, and finally abashed, Noha sputters to a stop and lowers his gaze before his father's calm regard; but not before he notices that some of the younger males are impressed with his boldness and nod their approval, though Pak still stares balefully at him.

Kiconce eyes all of them and again turns purposefully to Ecakik, his eldest son. "What do you say?"

Ecakik screws up his forehead, considers, and says in a voice like shifting scree, "*Mahingan*, Spirit Leader of the Wolves, will go hungry and he will be angry."

Kiconce nods and says to Ecakik, "As Assinbo is Noha's friend, Mahingan is yours, though he doesn't speak to you. You are right. Mahingan will also follow the herds."

"And what about you?" Kiconce asks Kraac. He has left to last his tall son with the haughty hawk's nose and glittering eyes, whose quick mind is a constant unspoken challenge to his father's leadership.

Kraac's tone is respectful if detached. "The one who dreams and captures Awaskesh's spirit on the walls of forbidden places, sees many things lost to hunters."

"You have said it," Kiconce says, satisfied.

However, Pak, who so often criticizes and berates Noha, mutters, "Why does Ogima consult only his blood-kin and not the elder hunters, men of age and experience?"

A sudden hush.

Anikeogima, Second Leader, a squat, big-headed, muscular hunter says coldly to Pak, "Ogima has already spoken with his trusted chief hunters. And we shall abide by his wishes."

Noha hides a smirk behind his hand. Pak hadn't been included among the "chief hunters".

"Enough!" Boog, the shaman, hobbles into the firelight and stands beside Kiconce. Every head turns.

Boog declares, "I have travelled to the land of the Spirits."

The Eyo gasp. Noha smiles. Now they can't think this merely a stripling's dream. The shaman's visions are never questioned but acted upon.

Boog sways before them, his ragged, dusty figure eclipsed by slit eyes flashing orange as if fire itself lives in him. Noha's skin quivers as if trod by snails.

Boog speaks.

I have dreamed. The Spirits killed my body, dismembered and consumed it, but while I dreamed, the parts came once more together and I was strong again. Great Manitou showed me new lands. I came upon a mighty reindeer herd galloping on the tundra, and at their head was Awaskesh, the Reindeer Spirit. They moved to the place where sky and land meet and where hangs Kewadenahmung, the North Star. I pursued them with my spear. I followed for many summers, but always they remained out of reach. Many others followed also, the auroch, the mammoth, the white fox, the bison, the wolf, the great bear, and animals I did not know. At last, we came to a place of New Mountains. I rested and there Awaskesh knelt before me. I pierced his heart with my spear and his blood spilled upon the ground."

Noha lowers his head, bites his lower lip. Does Boog mean they should go to the north? And are his new mountains the same as those of Noha's own dream?

Boog speaks.

"Awaskesh said to me, 'Your destiny is here in the New Land!'"

Boog begins to shake. Muscles snake under his parched skin. He puts a hand on Kiconce's arm to steady himself. Noha holds his breath, but Boog says nothing further. Only the sound of the crackling fire breaks the stillness. Noha gazes at the faces surrounding the fire. What is wrong with everyone? Can't they see what a wonderful destiny lies before them? *Boog has spoken.*

After much time had passed, Kiconce asks the shaman, "Will you capture Awaskesh on the cave walls so he won't escape the Eyo?"

"I have already done this."

Kiconce looks about him. One by one, the elders nod.

Do we follow our shaman's vision?"

"*Éhe*, Yes!" A young voice from the shadows. Noha grins. The striplings are with him. Another *Éhe*. Another! Anikeogima, Second Leader, stands. Most of the hunters are on their feet.

Noha leaps up shakes his spear and screams, *Éhe!* We shall follow the Vision!"

The decision made, Kiconce demands food, and his mate, Bara, and her females scurry to obey. Soon meat sizzles on the fire and the clan gorge themselves as if to guard against starvation on the journey to come. Even the dogs are thrown an extra share. There are three dogs, grey, small-eared, big-bodied, with thick, long coats. Each one answers to a different hunter's call. Noha prefers to hunt alone. The quickest dog knows Kraac as master. Naturally Pak has tamed the most vicious dog and only he can safely approach it. The third dog, a lumbering beast, not nearly as intelligent as its fellows but loyal and obedient, follows Ecakik. They suit each other.

The feasting over, the shaman drones a monotonous chant. He accompanies himself by shaking a rattle made from turtle shell and pebbles, and before long, he has squalled himself into a trance. He leaps vacant eyed to his feet, bounding around the fire, rearing and roaring like the cave bear he mimics. Soon Noha and the other hunters join in the dance. Noha feints with his spear and whirls until he sees a hundred fires. He flounders, falls to one knee and stays there panting until Bara calls, "Come, *Nimi*, Sisters!"

Circling round the hunters, the females and striplings take up the chant, louder, rolling, threatening. Kiconce leaps beneath the shaman's claws and thrusts his spear at his belly. The shaman stills, staggers, stumbles on. Again and again the singing climaxes, and again and again the bear survives the wounds inflicted by the hunters; but in the end, he sinks exhausted to the ground amid his persecutors' manic cries and the females' erotic sighs. Noha's loins ache. He shudders, his eyes on the shaman.

Boog rises and walks through the circle which parts before him like hairs before an ivory comb. Kiconce is immediately at his heels. Noha seizes a brand from the fire and follows, others do the same until a procession forms on the dark mountainside. It winds like a golden caterpillar to Kiconce's rock shelter, not the hidden inner chamber but an antechamber. The hunters crowd together, their torchlight prancing on the cave walls. Noha watches as Kiconce and Anikeogima strain to remove a stone slab which hides a cavity in the floor. Inside the rock-lined hole lie the bones of the Sacred Totem, the skull and horns arranged to face the cave entrance.

Noha whispers to Ecakik, "Are these the holy bones?"

"Yes, they are the remains of the giant reindeer that Ogima killed *maywisher*, long time ago. They say he offered it in sacrificial ceremony to Awaskesh in return for good hunting for our clan."

"I wish I were allowed to hunt for the giant reindeer."

Ecakik clicks his tongue. "Only Ogima is allowed to slay the Totem and only for the first ceremony."

The sacred bones are carefully arranged on a choice reindeer skin. The shaman rolls them, ties them securely, and offers the bundle to Kiconce. He refuses, as is the custom, consigning the bones to the shaman.

Kiconce says to his people, "Rest now. The sacred relics have been removed, the journey is at hand."

Night air caresses Noha's tired flesh as he follows the unmated hunters to a lonely sleeping platform. The thought of a lovely Oomeseh maiden creeps upon him. He tosses his long hair. No true hunter wastes sleep time moon-calfing after a female.

CHAPTER 3

The Trek

Noha had been awake before Paternal Sun and fidgeted as the column formed for the trek. The dawn sky was a clear, pale, pulsing blue, the tundra spongy above permafrost and still covered in most places by dead straw and dun-coloured, wispy grass. However, there were bright patches of virgin green and scarlet bearberry leaves growing from frost-covered lichen beds, sedges, and deep purple gentian. He looked back. Home Mountain's ice-capped, jagged teeth thrust into the sky, oblivious to their departure.

Kiconce said, "My seasoned hunters shall take the lead with the females and young behind."

Near the column's center, the shaman and his apprentice trudged. Boog dragged the sacred bones on a stick-litter and even his apprentice didn't yet dare to offer help.

Noha said to his brother, Kraac. "I hate this crawling. Usually we hunters make a late start and run to catch up."

Kraac sighed. "Perhaps, Ogima thinks it will be good for clan discipline that we learn patience."

Noha, suspecting sarcasm, looked closely at him but Kraac was as enigmatic as ever. Noha shrugged. As the day warmed, clouds of mosquitoes and other pests rose from melt-pools. He steeled himself to ignore them.

Noha saw Kraac watching the sinuous movement of his mate, Narima's, erect spine and narrow hips, and hot blood coursed through Noha. He knew why Kraac was so concerned with his mate. It was because their nightly coupling brought no fruit. He had noticed swiftly hidden pain in Kraac's eyes when Narima fondled Ecakik's son, Pu. Kraac was difficult to understand. He seemed always so cold and yet Noha wondered how he himself would feel if Narima were his mate and had to be put aside as barren. Surely it was the right thing to do, but he had heard Kraac speak against it.

As if sensing Kraac's eyes upon her, Narima looked over her shoulder and smiled. Noha felt an envious pang. He fell back to join his tall friend, Laf, who strolled behind Ecakik. Noha's eldest brother walked with surprisingly light tread for all his bulk. Beside him, his dog kept pace, whining to attract his attention when they passed rodent holes but following obediently when he saw Ecakik's disinterest. Noha punched Laf affectionately on the shoulder and his friend grinned. Noha glanced back at the fair-haired stripling, Dinkka, and the youngest hunters. He was certain it had been Dinkka who supported him at the council. How could he move so sedately? Hatchet-faced Pak brought up the rear of the column, sulking at some imagined injury, his grey dog skulking at his heels.

At this rate, they would never reach the bone village. The Omeeseh might be there already. Noha blundered into Ecakik whose dog growled menacingly. Noha slowed his pace. Ecakik would take note of his brother's awkwardness though he would say nothing. At least Kraac hadn't noticed. Laf grinned and unsuccessfully hid the insult behind his long, skeletal hand. Noha decided to forgive this.

They camped that night on a dry hillock raised above a mosaic of melt-pools and moss spread to the horizon. The females had carried wood for the first night's fires and soon all were eating happily. After the meal, they rolled into skins and slept in the open.

Noha awakens first in the grey hours before dawn. Near him on a willow sprig a redpoll fixes him with a round, black eye. It ruffles its brown and white wings and preens the buff fluff on its chest. Noha stands, letting his deerskin coverlet fall to the ground, and gazes out over the misty tundra. A plump willow ptarmigan, already sporting summer's speckled brown plumage, digs for insects in the hillside's dry soil. It looks up at him, its red combs lifting like two inquisitive eyebrows, and struts away.

In the distance, Noha discerns a vague form moving over the landscape. It approaches quickly and heads directly for the campsite with a runner's purposeful movements rather than a grazing animal's meanderings. As the morning clears, Noha sees that it is, indeed, a runner and that he will soon reach the hillock.

The runner must have seen last night's cook fires and marked the place.

From behind a rise between them, a fox appears, its ears pointed toward the runner. Noha makes a greeting sign to his canine mentor who, like the ptarmigan, is already taking on summer's subdued hues.

Assinbo, the Fox Spirit, has sent one of his kindred. A good omen.

Noha studies the distant runner. He should wake Ogima and report this sighting. Instead, he picks up his spear and leaps down the hillside, springing over melt-pools encrusted with ice sheets, determined to reach the runner and get the news before the others.

They meet at a stream's edge. The runner is panting. Noha recognizes him and his own breath comes unevenly. He pretends to have picked up a pebble in his foot-covering and stoops to examine it minutely. When sufficient time has elapsed for both to gain composure, he rises and with spear-point touching the ground says, though he is certain the runner has also recognized him, "I am Noha, Youngest Ogucen of Kiconce of the Eyo. What news do you carry to us on feet as swift as the reindeer's?"

The runner is short but rugged. He carries a spear whose stone point is larger and less delicate than the Eyo's. He has tied at his waist a stone knife with an ibex-horn handle. He has an oval face, a large nose, and cheerful egg-shaped eyes.

"I am San of the Omeeseh." The Eyo join each year with this Owl Clan and the *Mahantanis*, Mountain Sheep Clan, for the reindeer hunt.

Noha's heart surges into his throat. He had been right; This is the beautiful Fina's brother! But the rituals must be observed.

San says, "I bring news to the Reindeer Clan."

Noha waits but San is silent. "Your presence brings honour to our camp. Come and I'll take you to Kiconce, our Ogima."

They walk slowly to the hillock, for it would be unseemly to race into the sleeping camp. When they reach it, the females are stirring and have lit the cook fires. Kiconce, his Second Leader, Anikeogima, and aged Mizinawa stand together watching Noha and his companion stride up the hill. Kiconce's wide face is stern.

Noha has again displeased his Ogima. He keeps his head humbly lowered and controls himself when he hears Pak snicker.

Kiconce speaks. "In the name of the Eyo, I welcome you."

"I am San of the Omeeseh, and I bring news."

"First we eat." Kiconce leads the visitor to Bara's hearth where meat chunks are roasting.

When they have refreshed themselves, San says, "The Omeeseh are camped at the place of the bones; many runners have been sent to the northeast.

Kiconce nods. Noha leans forward.

San says, "Three lights ago, one runner brought news. A great herd of reindeer has paused in its trek and is grazing on the mosses to the north. The Omeeseh will hunt these reindeer."

"We wish you many blooded spears," Kiconce says.

"The shaman of the Omeeseh has dreamed."

Noha's ears twitch. *Another dream.*

"Will you tell us this dream?" Kiconce says.

"The shaman saw reindeer slaughtered by our totem, the Spirit Hunter, *Omeeseh*, Owl." San pauses. "By his side ran *Awaskesh*, the Reindeer Spirit, and *Mahantanis,* the Mountain Sheep Spirit, who helped them and shared with them the reindeer meat. The slaughter took place far to the northeast where our clan has never before hunted."

The Eyo hunters gather close. "Will the Omeeseh follow the game trails far to the northeast?" Kiconce asks.

"It is so."

"The Eyo also. Do your Owl People wish that we travel together?"

"We wish it."

Noha hugs himself. Now he will surely win San's eldest sister, Fina!

"Good," Kiconce says. "We'll start when you are rested."

"I'm ready," San says.

Kiconce rises, motions Noha to him. "My Ogucen, your mother is no longer young. You will help her with her burdens."

Noha's shoulders slump. Only striplings carry females' burdens, and he has sixteen summers! Now he is being degraded before the clan!

His muscles quivering, he approaches his mother. She hands him a bundle. He takes it and straps across his forehead the chewed sling which secures the hides. He feels Pak's malicious eyes watching. He cuts off all feeling. The camp breaks and the trek begins.

Bara allows him to be humiliated for a short time and then, without consulting her mate, she stalks up to Noha and shouts, "Can't you be careful? You'll let my hides fall into the melt water!" Divining her purpose, Noha bows his head meekly and she snatches the bundle from him.

"No hunter knows how to carry hides well," she snaps, with emphasis on the word, *hunter.*

"Yes, Ninga," Noha replies with downcast eyes.

Bara storms off, leaving a grateful son behind.

Pak makes some sneering comment which Noha ignores.

CHAPTER 4

Che

Che and the other Omeeseh females have built their bone huts at a bend in a grey tributary river which flows into the Endless Lake and near a hill of hulking mammoth bones laid out in a huge semicircle. Che has never seen a mammoth but in times gone by, the hairy elephants watered at the river, and the clans hunted them relentlessly. According to her father's tales, there are still to be found along far off glaciers mammoths as well as woolly rhinoceros, but the numbers are few. Che has draped with skins the ancient bones to make her hut while the clans gather to hunt reindeer.

Che spits out the piece of hide she's been chewing and says, "I wish I could escape all these tedious female chores and go on an adventure!"

Her beautiful sister, Fina, giggles. "Wait until I tell the others what you've said now."

"Tell them. I don't care." Che is used to being made feel an outsider among the docile Omeeseh maidens. And as for the hunters, she serves but thinks little about them except to covet their many freedoms. She has repeatedly begged her brothers to take her on the hunt, and they at first laughed and finally, realizing she meant what she said, scolded her in horror.

Even her quiet father Chetu, Ogima of the Omeeseh, had shouted at her, "Keep to female things!"

Once she stole a spear from her youngest brother, San, and killed a hare. She concealed it among her brother's kills, needing only to prove to herself she could hunt if necessary . . . do *anything* the conceited hunters could do!

"What do you think of Noha of the Eyo?" Fina asks in a languid tone but with a sidelong glance at Che to see her reaction. "Don't you agree that Hun of the Mahantanis, Sheep Men, would make me a much finer mate?"

Che sniffed. "I don't think about such things."

A knowing smile slides across Fina's lovely face. "You will think of such things."

One of the maidens rushes up. "The Eyo are here!"

"I must get my new tunic!" squeals Fina and disappears into the bone hut.

That night Che is drawn on skeins of light to a council fire which burns golden in the clearing before the bone huts. Here hunch the shamans, their old eyes glinting in the firelight. The Omeeseh shaman begins a monotonous telling of the Omeeseh blood-maps. The peoples listen, obedient and silent. Che avidly drinks in the scene, her amber coloured eyes glistening, her thoughts swirling. She jostles as close as possible to the hunters' circle and to Boog who is known to be the greatest shaman. She fervently hopes the Omeeseh shaman will tire soon.

He says, as always, too much at too great length and with too little depth.

She watches Boog.

Boog licks his cracked lips and raises his wrinkled eyelids. His gaze wanders tiredly among visages, slides over them, sucks them in and spits them out. He pauses momentarily at Che but moves quickly on and settles on the council fire. His body contorts in terrible spasms and he topples.

Che's heart leaps in her breast. Boog squirms in the dirt. Blood and foam speckle his lips. Noha of the Eyo takes a step toward him but his father pulls him away with an angry grunt. Boog's spine arches like an ancient bow from which darts might fly even to *Manitou's* lair in the sky.

Noha's mother, Bara, moves toward Boog.

"No!" cries Boog's apprentice. "Leave him! Leave him!"

Bara wails, "Return to us, Old One!"

Che goes to her and whispers, "You cannot help him," and puts her arm around the older woman's thick waist.

Boog stills. His shattered frame trembles, relaxes.

"He is returning!" the apprentice cries. "Help me to lift him!"

Noha and Kiconce rush forward and gently grasp the shaman's limp arms and legs. Boog stirs and groans. They carry him as easily as if he were a dry, rotted tree limb. Bara follows and Che, taking courage from the older female's self-confidence, goes with her. Boog is carried to his hut and carefully placed on skins in a dark corner. The hunters are so fixed on the shaman that they don't notice Che and Bara enter the hut and stand hidden in the shadows.

The shaman mumbles, "*The new mountain . . .*" He drifts off. But once more, "*fire . . . darkness . . . headless . . . my people . . .*"

The old eyelids slit, the black glance rests on Noha; however, the young hunter is backing gingerly off, making room for the apprentice who kneels beside Boog. Noha is now so close to Che that she might touch him, his smell as pungent as a fox pelt but with an underlying hint of musk and brine. The muscles on his back glisten with sweat. Tingling awareness caresses the nape of Che's neck and creeps into her skull making her light-headed. She clasps her hands behind her back. She angrily shakes her head and moves closer to Bara.

Bending over the shaman, the apprentice places his hand on Boog's grizzled head. "You must take nourishment. Your manitu is once more within you, but you are weak."

Boog gasps, "I have been to the land of the manitu. I have dwelt once more among the ancient ones and I saw the old ones." His rheumy eyes close and Boog drops into natural sleep. The apprentice hurries to the hearth and mixes a brew of herbs, roots, and water.

Che whispers into Bara's ear, "Will the Old One speak of what he saw?"

Bara puts her big hand across Che's lips.

"We must leave him to the cub."

Che follows her out and would speak further with her but Bara hurries into the night.

The following day, the *Mahantanis*, Clan of the Mountain Sheep, arrive to join the annual reindeer hunt, and Fina is soon surrounded by big hunters with pale skins, curly black hair, and matted chests, arms, and legs. Che, hovering nearby, has already decided that the Omeeseh and Eyo hunters are preferable to these ungainly, hairy males who subsist mainly on high mountain sheep. They even smell of mutton. The Eyo and the Omeeseh, on the other hand, have scanty hair on their muscular bodies, and their males' dusky faces are beardless. A remembered smell of musk and brine invades her nostrils. She rubs hard at her nose.

Che sees Noha gazing with mouth stupidly agape at the largest Mahantanis. It's Hun, the hunter whom her sister Fina mentioned the day before. Everyone knows Noha can run like a reindeer, some say even faster. He is far superior to this slow sheep-man. So why does Noha stand gaping like a dying salmon? Could it be because of Fina? Is he jealous? The top of Noha's head comes barely to the giant's shoulder and Hun's spear is as tall as the young Eyo hunter.

Che goes to stand behind Noha. She is not going to miss this exchange. Hun makes some deep-voiced remark to Fina and Noha stiffens and whirls, tramping on Che's instep. She bites back a yelp and he instinctively grasps her forearms to keep her from falling. His hands are strong and warm on her skin. He steadies her and quickly removes his hands as it is unseemly for a hunter to touch an unmated female. A high laugh from Fina. Noha turns back to the group. Che can still feel his touch on her arms. Suddenly she wants to hurt him.

"He's very handsome, isn't he?" Che says to the back of Noha's head.

"Who?" Noha turns to stare at her, although he knows full well who she means.

"Hun of the Mahantanis. He's also very strong and so big." A stricken look in Noha's eyes. Che feels shame and adds. "But the maidens say he moves slowly and takes prey only from ambush or when the striplings and the swiftest hunters have tired it."

"Cub, it's not your place to say such things about a hunter!"

Heat surges in her. "I am no cub. I have fourteen summers!"

He isn't listening. Ungrateful, stupid male. Just like all of them! As shallow as streams!

Che marches to a bare spot near the river where some chattering females sit sewing hides with their reindeer-horn needles. Bara and two younger Eyo females, a delicate pretty girl and a tall nervous one, sit nearby. At their feet, a pudgy boy-babe rolls naked in the grass, playing with fistfuls of small stones. He put them tentatively between his lips and spits them out. Che laughs.

Bara looks up. "You're the youngest daughter of Chetu, aren't you?"

Che nods. Her brothers say the peoples think Bara wise and Che would know more of her.

"It was you who comforted me last night, wasn't it?"

Che nods again.

"Will you sit and work with us?"

"I'll get more skins." Che runs off, humming through her sharp little teeth.

As she passes the hunters grouped around giggling Fina, she sees that Noha has finally got her sister's attention and Fina is moving towards him, an inviting smile on her sensuous lips. Hun towers behind Noha and Fina's smile shifts to him. Noha's face reddens and he glances around like a cub who has been shamed. He stalks away.

Che shakes her head. How could he be such a fool? Should she go after him and praise his speed and his skill in the hunt as she would her father or her brothers when they are downcast?

No. Che crawls after no hunter!

CHAPTER 5

The Hunt

Che is miserable and taking pains to hide it.

The clans have followed the reindeer spoor. They struck camp, the hunters going ahead unencumbered except for their weapons, the females following, bowed under heavy loads of poles, skins, cubs, and drying salmon. Fishing has been good at the river camp and their nets captured many fat char who were making their fourth year journey to the Endless Lake.

Che tries not to inhale the rotting smell that encases her.

Seeking distraction, she manoeuvres closer to the shamans, hoping to overhear Boog converse of things beyond her ken. Boog is silent. In fact, none of the Eyo hunters are ever communicative. She likes Artisan, though. He is always hoisting some straying, querulous cub to his shoulders where it rides grinning, and he doesn't overlook the girl-cubs.

For several wake times they slog through wetlands, skirting shallow, sluggish streams choked with mosses and marsh plants, following high ground where they can. Fina complains incessantly but Che takes her cue from Bara and bears it all stoically. What a wonderful clan mother Bara is. No wonder Kraac's mate, Narima, is so efficient and Ecakik's pretty mate, Inik, so cheerful! One can't help liking Inik.

The clans erect camps near shrub willows and sedges as often as feasible, but most camps are fireless. They skirt temporary shallow lakes edged with yellow water buttercups. Che picks one and puts it in a girl-cub's hair. As they move steadily to the northeast, the land becomes less marshy and the air drier, though the night still spreads thin ice-sheets on the ponds. The flies hover in hordes around their heads.

Che mutters, "The insects will drive me mad!"

There is nothing she can do to relieve her misery. Fina weeps and Che ignores her. Perhaps Fina weeps for Noha who has volunteered as forward scout along with their youngest brother, San, and a woolly-skinned Mahantanis. Noha certainly left at the first opportunity. No smelly fish bundles for him.

The scouts have fanned from a central point on the tundra, San skirting north, the Mahantanis scout trudging south, and Noha moving straight ahead to the east. There is much reindeer sign, trampled paths along dry ridges and large, devastated areas of moss.

Noha sights the river flowing to the Endless Lake which spreads forever under Kewadenahmung. Ice islands float there, monsters haunt its waves, and no hunter ever ventures too near it. Noha has no intention of being the first. A fox skitters across his path, turning to smile at him. A good omen! Assinbo has sent one of his brothers to bless the hunt.

Noha comes to an escarpment and gazes into a shallow valley where meanders a grey-blue river rippled at the edges with deeper blue. A similar escarpment overhangs the valley's far side, some three miles away, making the valley a safe oasis sheltered from tundra winds. Stunted pine, birch, and willow grow here and there. Straw coloured grasses stand knee high along the pebbly riverbanks.

It isn't the river that captures Noha's attention. For hours now, he has followed fresh spoor. Clouds of mosquitoes and gnats attacked him and he is grateful for the snug hides Bara has insisted he wear, but these insects are on the trail of larger game. He surveys the river and sees a distant brown and white puddle, a puddle whose edges flow relentlessly to the riverside.

Reindeer!

Several hundred deer wade shoulder high in the sluggish current; others stumble to shore or are already dispersing among the trees and grasses of the opposite bank.

Noha's manitu sings. These are his natural prey, these swift beasts with their shaggy coats of coarse, compact hair, each strand a hollow cylinder for warmth in the time of snows. They are deceptively ungainly looking, with broad, flat feet that click as they walk. Some females have already calved and their pale coated young run with the herd. The males are still wearing branched, velvet-covered antlers with brow-tine pointed forward over their stolid faces. They will soon shed these tines. But not before they meet Noha of the Eyo!

Grey shapes move behind the reindeer.

"Greetings, friends of Ecakik!" Noha calls to the wolves.

He takes time to watch as the wolves wait for old deer to falter or a calf to stray unprotected. They circle the herd at a slow trot until downwind and then lope toward the migrating deer, searching for weakness. The reindeer make an instant turn into full gallop. An old one stumbles and the wolves fly after it with the silent, desperate pace they can maintain only for minutes. A sudden leap, jaws grip flesh, a wolf is thrown tumbling through the air; but there are too many, the reindeer is down.

Noha hovers as the attack becomes a series of feints and retreats until the pack seizes the deer's vulnerable neck, converges and gorges. It is a lean and difficult way to live. Mahingan hunts like Ecakik. No wonder Noha's *Nisages,* Elder Brother, admires the fanged ones; he too is patient and brave rather than fleet.

This is not Noha's way. He sometimes thinks he knows the reindeer better than he knows his own manitu. This herd, guided by Awaskesh, has chosen summer feeding grounds far to the northeast of their usual haunts, *just as the dream predicted*, and will certainly continue to move east with the seasons. The clan has done a good thing in setting out to walk these trails. They will follow Awaskesh to the new land. Noha's dream and Boog's vision will be realized.

"But I must to the clans!" he shouts into the wind.

With a last, yearning look at the herd, Noha turns and with loose-kneed lope eats the miles to the trekkers' main body. The other scouts arrive only hours behind him. They, too, have seen deer.

The hunters are ecstatic. Che is too tired to care.

Kiconce addresses the council. "We should set up camp at the shallow river crossing. From there, the scouts and striplings can search out the main herd."

Che's father, Chetu, says, "We'll leave the females at the river. It's the warm time. There will be no deep darkness and a hunter can stalk his prey when he wishes. Only exhaustion need halt him. There will be many kills."

Che sighs, but she is distracted by the desiccated Mahantanis shaman who warns, "It is said that during the cold time, the far north-eastern lands are clothed in perpetual darkness. We should remember this."

"Surely that can't be true," Che says to Fina. "Perpetual darkness?"

Kiconce says, "We'll test this in good time. At present, we must follow the herd migration or starve!"

Che sees Noha leap into the air and then hug his lanky friend, Laf.

"He certainly doesn't seem broken hearted over Fina," she murmurs.

"Did you say something, *Nici,* Younger Sister?" Fina asks, her face drawn into a deep sulk.

"I? Of course not." Che sees Bara shrewdly watching her and feels colour rise to her forehead.

At least the hunters had chosen a good place to camp. Although the beach is gravelled and difficult to dig, it is dry and wide. Che goes quickly to her tasks, noticing that Bara and her daughters place their huts near the water's edge in a semicircle, while the other Eyo females take up positions behind them.

These Eyo like to be close together. She looks around her. My people are strung along the beach as if avoiding one another, and the Mahantanis stay near the sparsely treed escarpment, perhaps because it reminds them of their former mountain home. How different we are.

She collects green branches, strips them with her notched, stone hide scraper, and erects them in a circle bent over and tied with hide thongs at the center where she leaves a place for hearth smoke to escape. She covers this skeleton with hides, leaning treasured forest pine poles against the outside to keep them from blowing away.

She has her hut up first of all. And it is a fine hut, too!

She cuts long grass and drags it into the hut for sleeping platforms. Over her own, she suspends her few treasures, some rodent bones for her tunics and some duck feathers she is saving to decorate her hair on her mating day.

Where is that lazy Fina? Probably doing the lightest task possible as usual.

When Che has dug the hole for her inner hearth, she goes outside and calls to some cubs, "Will you gather wood for my fire?"

The female cubs run willingly to do her bidding but the males hesitate, scuffing the ground.

"Well," says Che, looking at them from the corners of her eyes, "if you have not enough strength after your long trek . . ."

She smiles to see them scamper immediately off, outdistancing the females and vying with one another to be the first to stagger back under huge loads of driftwood. She thanks them gravely but is careful to show equal gratitude to the girl cubs when they arrive with their smaller loads.

She pauses to examine the other Clans' huts. Except for the shamans' huts, they have pointed shapes. Easier to construct, of course." She enters her own.

Shortly afterwards, Fina wanders in to spread a doeskin on Chetu's bed and to hang above it his strings of precious owl feathers.

"It's good of you to help," Che says, but sarcasm is lost on her sister.

"I wish our Ninga were alive," Fina sighs pitifully. "Or our Nuse had chosen another mate." Their mother had died of lingering cough when they were cubs.

"Our Nuse has forty-nine summers! He doesn't even join in the chase anymore. Surely he is beyond mating."

Fina's only response is a superior smile.

"Don't look so smug. Our Ninga may be dead, but we're lucky to have been born in summer when there was plenty of food or we might have been smothered. What hunter needs two daughters when he already has sons?" Che knows she is being unfair. Her father valued his mate and on her passing, had looked to his daughters, to Che for comfort, to Fina as the ornament of his last days. He is kind enough to them.

Fina hasn't been listening anyway. "I shall rejoice when our nuse returns," she says as she patted into place the bed skins.

Che longs to say, "It's the attentions of Noha, Hun, and the other young hunters you miss so sorely."

Fina chatters on. "Come sit, Nici. You sweat and stink from much work."

Work which could be shared, but Che says only, "The hut must be prepared."

"But I have need of your counsel."

What mischief is Fina planning now? "A nici's counsel is a small thing."

"That's true. Nevertheless . . ."

Raising her eyebrows, Che, glad in fact to rest for a time, squats beside her sister. Fina hums a tune and runs her finger teasingly across Che's hand. Che snatches it away and Fina laughs.

"I'm sorry," she says insincerely. "I know you don't like to be touched."

"I do not."

"Not even by a hunter?"

"I allow no hunter to touch me." Tingling awareness on her forearms, remembered a smell of fox and sweat.

"When you are mated, you must allow yourself to be touched."

"It's not seemly to talk about such things."

"What things?" Fina grins.

Che feels her neck muscles tighten. She shakes her head and begins to climb to her feet.

"Don't go, Nici!" Fina pleads, immediately contrite.

"Our Ninga is in the land of *Manitou*. So whom shall I ask?"

Is there a hint of fear in Fina's voice? She might like hunters' attentions but Che suspects she secretly fears their domination. "Perhaps one of the elder females?"

"I have already spoken to them as is the custom in my time apart. They say that our mates will examine every part of our bodies, even to the most secret. They say that his member will swell and throb and the he will thrust it . . ."

"Stop!" Che jumps shakily to her feet. "When my time to be mated comes, I shall learn these things. You shame me, Nimises!"

Pursing her lips, Fina sighed. "Forgive me. It's just . . ."

Che runs from the hut.

It is the fifth sun and Che is busy with endless chores when her brother, San, splashes across the ford.

He wipes water off his nose and shouts to the quickly gathering females, "The main herd has been sighted. You are needed. I shall guide you."

Che is pleased until she sees Fina's beaming face. She says sourly, "I suppose you just can't wait to muck about in blood and offal?" Fina stares, surprised. Che looks away. What is the matter with me? Why am I so sarcastic? Fina can't help what she is and it has never bothered me before that she can think of nothing but hunters, hunters. It must be the work. No! I have always thrived on labour. I must stop this inner carping!

Leaving behind the old, the babes, and the very young, the females gather their stone cutting and scraping tools and pouches of dried food and prepare to follow San.

Che says to Fina, "I'm looking forward to seeing the new territory beyond the river valley."

"Soon we'll join in our hunters' success," Fina says happily.

Che tries a smile. Fina is right. The clans must eat.

A happy group follows San across the ford. Bara is first to enter the river and Inik and Narima are close, chattering and laughing. Not far away, overly eager Fina trips on a stone and rises dripping, her soft tunic moulded to her breasts and belly. Behind her, Che stubs a toe. A pretty Omeeseh maiden, called Mirra, grabs Che's arm to keep her from falling into the water with her precious pack. Che thanks her absently. She is wondering if Noha has rejoined the other hunters.

Noha and the younger males are huddled behind a hillock. Beyond it spreads an area such as they had never before hunted, mile after mile of rolling, grassy plain shaded delicate green under a cloudless sky. The plain is dotted with myriad freshwater lakes and ponds, and best of all, as far as Noha's keen eye can fathom, is an undulating forest of reindeer antlers, thousands upon thousands of the beloved beasts moving purposefully, relentlessly eastward; mowing down the grasses as they go; skirting the lakes and rivulets; rubbing against scattered clumps of dwarf birch, willow, and alder; sampling heath moss.

On the hillock's far side, Noha's father, Kiconce, Chetu of the Omeeseh, and the Mahantanis leader squat with their elder hunters. Among them are stocky, grizzled Anikeogima and old Mizinawa sucking on his pebbles.

"Oh, hurry! The deer await us!" moans Noha.

His friend, long-faced, long-nosed Laf says complacently. "They won't be long now."

Noha glances around at the other young hunters who usually follow in his wake: the twins, Tuk and Megi, a comely pair, big as bears but not as quick witted; and the stripling, Dinkka, who admires Noha for his speed and his friendship with the Fox Spirit. Noha smiles, remembering that Dinkka had called out the first *Éhe* in Noha's favour at the council.

His brother, Kraac, is staring about him with self-contained aloofness. Noha imagines Kraac stung by a cloud of bees, hopping on his long legs and screeching. He grins widely.

Ecakik seems engrossed in tying thongs, pretending not to be just as anxious as the rest. Behind him, Pak examines the Eyo group with jealous, watchful eyes, looking as usual for rivals among his own rather than among the other clans. The brothers, Tiga and San, are the center of a nearby Omeeseh group and Hun towers over the Mahantanis. His heavy spear with its round shouldered tip is a willow wand in his big hand.

Noha sniffs. "That Hun will fall over those big feet in the chase."

Finally, Chetu makes the long awaited announcement.

"This day, the mighty hunters of the Eyo, the Omeeseh, and the Mahantanis will join together in the hunt. Swift will be our hunters' legs, keen our hunters' eyes, straight and true the flight of our spears. The Great Manitou will instruct the wily spirit of the mountain sheep, the courageous spirit of the giant reindeer, and the swift spirit of the owl to enter into us and guide us. Huge shall be the slaughter!"

"At last!" cries Noha, but silently, for he has no wish to incur Kiconce's wrath.

Nevertheless, the bear-like Eyo twins, Megi and Tuk, and some other striplings who are standing far to the rear let out unseemly yips and are quickly subdued by the more mature among them, like Dinkka. Noha leans on his spear, trying to appear unconcerned. His calves twitch spasmodically.

Kiconce says, "The Mahantanis will make a wide half-circle into the herd's body. The reindeer will divide at their approach, leaving a goodly portion between the Mahantanis and the Eyo. The Mahantanis will then conceal themselves at some distance among the grasses at the edges of lakes and streams in hopes that the Eyo will succeed in driving the reindeer in their direction. This will give them a close-up chance at the prey as it struggles in the water or on the pond's marshy edges; they will down the beasts with single blows."

"After we've done all the work," Pak snickers but softly so Kiconce will not hear him.

"The Omeeseh will also circle but in the opposite direction, where they will cut off the isolated reindeer section's retreat. Finally, the striplings of all three clans and the Eyo hunters will attack the herd from the front, killing what they can and driving the rest through the lines. All will then pursue wounded deer to their strength's limit. Those who have dog companions will cut out single reindeer from the herd's edges and hunt on their own."

"It's a good plan!" Noha says to Laf. His speed and stamina will be well used. He gathers his spears and ties them across his back.

The previous day, each hunter pursued, killed and skinned one straggler or lost calf, then worked through the sleeping hours at scraping the hides. Some retained the hollowed-out skull coverings and now put them on their heads in hopes of being able to approach the deer without frightening them. Others, like Noha, were content to mask their man scent with hide strips.

Soon all are prepared. Chetu's hunters move to the north, leaving their Ogima to watch from the knoll while Hun's people circle to the south. Around them for miles, shallow valleys and hills hold undulating masses of reindeer. As they move among them, they cause as little worry as if invisible. The animals simply part and flow around them like a muddy river flows past an island; however, the reindeer at the edge are somehow always beyond spear's thrust.

"Will you run at my side?" Laf asks Noha.

"Not this time, my friend. May Awaskesh be generous with you."

It takes the Omeeseh and the Mahantanis many hours to manoeuvre into ambush, and Noha grinds his teeth. Laf gives him a playful poke in the midriff but is rewarded with a hot glare and, shrugging good naturedly, he moves away. At last, Kiconce gives the signal and the striplings are off! Their brown legs flicker through the grasses. Hair flies and hands bare of weapons swing close to their sides. They skirt the herd's edge cutting out small groups of deer who mill confused and are driven on to the next fresh stripling who repeats the process.

Noha notes with approval that Dinkka is the fleetest.

The Eyo hunters lope steadily along this ordered chaos's edge and are eventually able to match the tiring deer's pace. Kraac, Pak, and Ecakik are among the first to bring down reindeer.

Noha runs effortlessly and each time he approaches a group of exhausted deer, they are slower to retreat. Finally, he wills his legs to knife through the grass as nimble-footed as the fastest prey. A dozen reindeer fly before him, hooves clicking in deafening uproar, graceful antlers swaying, eyes rolled back in panic.

Then he is on them.

The largest turns to face him, a male, furious. Behind him, a doe protects her calf. Noha's arm lifts, his fingers tense, thrust, and the spear zings to the male, pierces and holds in the white neck ruff. The head jerks sideways, the animal turns, staggers, recovers, and runs. Blood spatters into the breeze.

Ignoring the doe and calf, Noha bounds after the buck. Dinkka trots to his side, eager to join in a relay chase. Noha motions him away.

His first kill will be his alone!

He pursues the dying beast for three miles before the animal stumbles to its knees. Noha dispatches him. "Forgive me, Awaskesh." With a victorious yowl, he resumes the chase.

He stampedes some does onto Hun's spear. The Mahantanis are hidden in reeds near a small lake.

They leap into the very faces of the frightened animals, killing them in twos, threes, and dozens. Noha, instead of joining them, waves his spear above his head and dances. Hun lays about him like a cave bear.

Noha screeches, "Here is a fine killer of beasts!"

Quickly losing interest in this stationary slaughter, Noha spies a large herd on the opposite shore. It is already besieged by tireless striplings. With new energy, he gallops around the lake's shore. He, the striplings and some younger hunters, including Laf and the sons of Chetu, chase the herd for three sleep-times, working in teams with Noha doing much of the slaying, although after his first kill, he shares his extra spears with Dinkka. The hunters leave behind them a trail of blood ten miles long.

Finally sated, they make rough camp near a wandering stream. Kiconce thanks the Reindeer Spirit for His generosity in the kill. They build a fire and feast, laughing and shouting as blood juice runs down their chins, telling over and over again to their heedless companions the story of the hunt. At one point, Noha catches Fina's eldest brother, Tiga, examining him speculatively, and the maiden's face flashes into his knowing-place.

Tiga looks at him and not at the big Mahantanis. Noha turns away to hide his pleasure.

Pak approaches Chetu's sons.

"The Eyo have been privileged in this hunt," he says.

"How is that?" asks Tiga, a narrow shouldered, long waisted hunter with a sagacious air.

"To hunt in the shadow of Omeeseh is a great honour," Pak replies unctuously.

"I thank you in the name of my people."

"Many were the Reindeer Clan's victims," says the cheery-eyed scout, San.

"We have been fortunate."

"It is said that your clansman, Noha, is the swiftest of all hunters," says San ingenuously.

Noha pretends not to be listening.

"His feet have wings," Pak agrees and is silent for a time before he adds, "It is said that Noha's humours are as swift to rise as his legs are to run."

Noha freezes.

"How is that?" San asks, curious now.

"Only that he is often chastised for lack of control in council," Pak claims then quickly adds, "However, he is much liked in the clan."

"What about the tall one?" the boy asks, referring to Kraac.

"A great hunter and clever. Kiconce looks to him already for advice."

"I have heard this. A pity Kraac has not sired a son," Tiga comments acidly. "What about the eldest? The big, quiet one?"

"His silence conceals much wisdom."

Tiga asks archly, "And what about you? Many reindeer have died on your spear."

Pak smiles, bows his head and leaves them, shooting a look full of venom at Noha as he passes.

Laf leans over and says quietly into Noha's ear. "You should keep watch on Pak."

Noha laughs. "Nobody listens to Pak."

"He means you harm."

"It's unseemly to speak ill of one of the clan. Pak has a nasty tongue but he's a fine hunter. That's all that matters."

"Is he a fitting mate for Fina?"

Noha chuckles, burps, sputters and then dissolves in helpless laughter, rolling like a cub on the moss.

Pak with his Fina?

CHAPTER 6

The Time of Mating

Vomit rises in Che's throat. Steeling herself, she bends to her ugly task.

It takes many suns for the females to find and butcher all the reindeer. At first, they dry meat over moss fires; by the time they reach the last carcasses, the meat stinks and crawls with maggots. The Mahantanis females fall upon the rotting reindeer, pulling brains from skulls and licking blood and gel from their fingers.

Che averts her eyes. This meat is useless, but she must salvage what is valuable.

The Omeeseh and Eyo females pile antlers in huge clumps so the hunters and the Artisan can choose horn for knives, needles, and ornaments. They remove the hides in sections and carefully scrape off the fat. They dry on bone racks sinews and gut for thread. At Bara's suggestion, Che saves some leg skins intact.

If the new land is as cold and dark as they tell us," Bara says, "the hunters will need extra foot coverings. I'll show you how to sew leg skins into winter *mackasins* using hide strips which will swell and fill the needle holes. Lined with fur and grass, the *mackasins* will freeze on the outside to foot shape and make excellent gear for travelling across snowy tundra."

She watches Bara. A clever woman. Proud, too, though she has just as many irksome responsibilities and just as few freedoms as anyone. The other Eyo females also seem unfettered in their manitu, while the Omeeseh hunters dominate their females. True, there are a few spoiled ones like Fina, but isn't that, too, a form of subservience?

Che feels kinship with the Eyo that she has never felt with her own people. Perhaps her Ninga was independent. If only she had known her.

When she mentions her observations to Fina, her sister snickers and said, "What about Jag?"

True, an unfriendly Omeeseh widow, called Jag, goes her own way. But the others disapprove. They disapprove of Che, too, for that matter and she retreats more and more into loneliness feeling true kinship only with striplings and cubs.

She remembers how young Miira had helped her cross the river. Miira is a kindly maiden, even if she never rebels. Che bites her lip. Am I being too intransigent?

Bara, Narima, and Inik labour nearby and Che notices that Kraac's mate moves more slowly than the others. Both Inik and Bara do part of her tasks. Che now knows the three better. Bara she admires without reservation and she likes Narima in an offhand way, though she prefers Inik who laughs a lot and isn't so critical. She watches the tall, graceful Narima.

If she sickens, her clan will cast her off and she will die. Not even Bara can save an unwanted barren woman. If I help her, too, maybe no one else will notice Narima's laxity. Che slips some of her own cullings into Narima's pile and looks up to see Bara watching.

Even Fina has to work hard and complains continuously to Che.

"How I hate the smell! She moans, thrusting away suppurating entrails and wiping sticky hands against her thighs. She is near to sobbing.

Che despises the task just as much as her sister does but she says, "The people must live." Fina will shame the Omeeseh in front of Bara.

"Nothing disgusts you! You're without feeling!"

"That's not so," Che's voice catches in spite of her. "I'm about to lose my stomach's contents, but if we don't think about it, it will be easier. Besides," she adds, knowing what ploys to use in an argument with her sister, "Bara's eye is upon you. Look to your work or she will think you unworthy of her son."

Che regrets the words as soon as they leave her lips. Fina needs no such encouragement.

Fina's head whips around. A sly smile splits her mouth and she calls out, "Honoured mate of the Ogima of the Reindeer Clan! You sons have provided well for their people?"

Bara straightens, her sinewed hand supporting her spine's base, and looks across the piles of bones, hides, and offal. "As have the hunters of the Omeeseh."

"I thank you, Ninga of Noha." Fina's face is vibrant with pleasure.

Beside her, Che hacks viciously with her own hand-axe, her stomach seething into a twisted knot. She murmurs, "*Mother Earth, please don't let me shame myself by vomiting.*"

Bara chooses the new camp-site near a beryl coloured lake nestled in a circle of grassy mounds. From it, a meandering stream winds its way to the north. The lake swarms with fish and wild fowl. Flocks of dabbling ducks feed on its submerged vegetation. Red-necked phalarope eat its aquatic insects and loons dive beneath its waters. White-necklaced geese arrive in chevrons to feed and raise their young. Che loves to watch the birds and to help the apprentice, whom she has befriended as she does all striplings, gather goose eggs for Boog.

The old man, always wizened, has dwindled. He walks now leaning on an alder stick, his keen eyes folded into tortured skin as if he misses his secret cave's damp darkness and is blinded by the sunny, rainless land they wander. He now allows the striplings to carry the sacred Totem bones. Even the novelty of conversing with the other shamans has palled, and he tolerates only his apprentice who follows him like a silent hound. He doesn't eat the eggs the apprentice and Che gather. Instead, he leads his servant and the young female to a knoll, indicating the fair land stretching before them.

Che hangs back.

Even the apprentice doesn't know how to react. He says, "It's a land of lasting summer, isn't it, Master?"

Boog's mouth twists in sorrow. "Summer we have with us, but take care lest you become complacent. *Meequorme,* Ice, always was, always is. At times, he sleeps, but when he wakes and thunders forth, his breath howling before him, even Mother Earth cringes beneath his tread."

Sensing a tale's beginning, Che holds her breath.

Thus speaks Boog.

"Maywisher, Long Time Ago, up over and beyond, Meequorme opened his terrible eyes and rose from his sleeping platform in the sky above the Endless Lake. The Paternal Sun watched jealously as Meequorme stalked his mate. And Mother Earth fought bravely as Meequorme's icy touch mutilated her flesh and his breath froze hard her veins through which the water of life flows. She called piteously to her mate and the Sun heard her call and reached out with flaming fingers to free her.

Che shifts uneasily. Surely the Paternal Sun is more powerful than Meequorme.

Boog continues.

"Time and time again these three struggled. But Meequorme grew even stronger. He ravaged again and again our Mother Earth until she fled vanquished into the land of dreams. And soon Meequorme's seed lay in white mounds that did not melt, and the Eyo and the animals fled Meequorme's wrath, seeking out hidden places of safety."

Che trembles. Boog is talking about our ancestors! In a frozen world. How terrible!

"Yet Meequorme's seed didn't vanish but thawed and froze again and once again until it lay like white pebbles on Mother Earth. Meequorme forced Mother Earth from the land of dreams. With cruel hands and spirit strength, Meequorme kneaded his seed, pounded and packed ice, rubbing it into Mother Earth's flesh until the heat of her suffering welded his seed into a giant crust which weighed on her mightily. Finally, sighing she sank into the abyss and slept.

The white crust crept over the lands. Paternal Sun hid his face in shame from his own reflection in the shining ice and, in impotence, cried out for his mate. But Mother Earth slumbered on while rivers of ice crept down from her mountains, rivers in which no fish could swim. The Eyo starved, wept and survived as best they could."

"But how could they survive?" asks the apprentice.

"Ah, Little One, even Meequorme must rest and when, in time, he did so, the Sun destroyed his seed and took once more to himself his mate." The shaman pauses, staring out over the land. His voice gentles as he say, "It is such a time now. Meequorme rests. The ice retreats. The way is open to us. We must go forth to seek the land of the New Mountains and the Valley of the Dream"

"Where you lead, I follow, Master."

And I! Che dares not say it aloud.

Boog places his clawed hand on his apprentice's narrow shoulder. "Come, faithful one, lead me to my hut. I shall take food from your hands, for ahead is a long journey."

With a happy smile, the apprentice leads the shaman toward the camp. Che watches them go. Had

Boog spoken also to her? No. She presumes too much. She isn't even of his clan. She runs down the knoll's opposite side.

The clans remain together for the time being, their huts within hailing distance along the grassy lakeshore, but already many miss the mountains. Reindeer herds pass in endless tide going east. One day, Noha sights a small group of mammoth.

"May I hunt them?" he asks Kiconce.

Kiconce shakes his head. "Do we not have meat in superabundance? There are berries to gather in the grasses; rainfall is light and the days pass pleasantly, the bright nights in dalliance."

Noha turns away to hide a bitter grimace.

The unmated hunters wander back and forth to exchange yarns and bone trinkets in the neighbouring camps. The true reason for these visits becomes apparent as one by one the hunters build huts apart from their parents. When the structures are completed and furnished with earthen hearth and grass bed, the hunter visits his chosen mate's father, and if he finds favour there, pays the bride price and guides a soft-eyed maiden back to the hut where they lie entwined on the bed he has fashioned.

Even an ugly Eyo hunter, rat-faced Fuum, wins a lovely maiden, Lara of the Mahantanis! Though he merely follows the lead of his gigantic shadow, stupid Quork, who somehow convinces a tall, garrulous female, Whea, to allow him to build a marriage hut.

Not that Noha, too, can't mate if he wishes. However, it isn't that easy. Suitors beset Fina and it is understood that as Chetu's daughter, she need not choose immediately.

Che sits nervously by and eavesdrops as Fina listens to her brothers' pointed stories about Noha's swiftness and bravery and the many reindeer he has slain or driven on others' spears; stories of Hun's strength.

Bright-eyed San says, "Once Hun's spear pierced a fat deer and reappeared on the other side, impaling the beast!"

As usual, Fina uses Che as a core stone to test her own emotions. Che chafes under her insensitivity but as *nici*, she knows she must swallow her words, listen patiently.

"Hun has visited our Nuse," Fina says smugly as the two maidens sit mending their fishing nets on the lakeshore.

Che nods.

"Noha has also visited our hut."

Che's shoulders and back stiffen. Her fingers still on the hide thongs. Chagrin and sudden realization tighten her chest.

"I believe both hunters have offered spear-points for me," Fina babbles on, oblivious.

"Has Nuse spoken to you about these things?" Che asks hoarsely.

"Not yet. But he will. I saw them come and there were others."

"Which hunter will you choose?" Che gulps in air and holds it in her throat.

"I admire both hunters. But Noha is too slight of stature, and the thought of lying in his arms does not stir my loins," Fina said lazily.

Che releases her breath in a noisy rush.

"Why do you puff so?"

"I am weary."

Fina's annoyance passes quickly as do most of her moods. Her mouth curves in a secret smile. "Hun could if he wished, crush me with his strength. He is not puny."

But he is so stupid! There is fire in Noha! Che bites back the retort. *No! I bow to no hunter!* Does she want Noha for herself? The answer knifes through her. *Nonsense! But is it?* If she defends Noha, Fina will suspect and want him, too. Why is she so ugly while her silly sister . . . ? Anger rises in her. How can she be so weak, letting a hunter affect her so? The last time he visited her brothers she had served him and stifled an insane desire to touch his skin, to lick salt from it as she did her own on hot summer days. There is a stirring between her thighs at the memory.

She clutches the net as she says, "Others have also come to our hut, you said?"

"Perhaps they came for you," Fina teased.

"Perhaps they did." Surprise in Fina's dark eyes.

"Ah well," Fina says snidely, "I don't consider them worth notice, they are not ogimas' sons."

"None of them?" The need for a cleansing quarrel rises in Che.

Fina simply says, "None of them."

Che watches Fina's face as she says it and guilt crosses it. It is unmistakable. She even lowers her eyes. Che knows very well that no compunction at her nastiness grips Fina. There is something else. What new mischief can she be plotting? I should ask. This isn't the time for Fina to disgrace herself. But why bother? Let her handle her own life, and if Noha is blind enough to choose her, he deserves her!

Che keeps her resolve until she sees venomous Pak watching Fina.

His hot eyes follow her everywhere and he doesn't look away when Fina notices, as a seemly hunter would. He holds her mesmerized. One day Che sees Fina slip alone along the path to the lake. Pak looks about to see if anyone sees and follows Fina. Che goes after them avoiding the path and creeping silently through the scrub willow. She discovers Pak openly watching Fina from shore as she swims naked and alone in a bay. Che bites her lip. Should she interfere? Fina stays in the water for a long time possibly hoping that Pak will go away, but he is there when she emerges, and his quick hands reach out to caress her. Che feels her own flesh contract along her bones. Surely Fina will berate him and run away. Fina hesitates, but when hard fingers try roughly to enter her, she breaks away, snatches up her tunic and runs like a startled fawn to the camp.

If Che tells her brothers as she should, Pak will be warned off, for both clans frown on mating before choosing, though she knows bolder hunters sometimes coax a chosen maiden to sample their prowess before building a marriage hut.

Perhaps Pak means no real harm, and Fina has said nothing.

The next day, as Che rests in their hut and Fina sits outside chewing a piece of cod fish, Che hears Pak say to her sister, "Come to the hillock where the ground squirrels have their dens when all are sleeping." His voice is as dangerously enticing as a storm's approach. Fina goes and Che follows. She circles far to come upon the hillock from above and behind. She crawls the last few feet and peers over a rock.

Fina and Pak stand below. One of Pak's hands explores her and the other is clamped over her mouth. Fina struggles half-heartedly biting at him, but he merely laughs and bends her to the ground where he mounts her. At first Fina gasps as if in pain but soon she begins to squirm under his thrustings.

Che's own hands go to her lips. She jumps up expecting Fina to call for help but she sees only writhings and hears guttural sounds. A horrible, guilty excitement mounts in her. She cannnot tear her eyes from them.

When he finishs rutting, Pak gentles Fina, sucks her and fondles her, and she doesn't try to crawl away. Then he works on her until, with kneading and whisperings, he arouses her again and brings her shuddering to climax. Then he mounts her again.

Che turns and flees.

She waits anxiously for Pak to speak to Chetu. He doesn't nor does he again invite Fina to the hillock. Che cringes to see Fina seek him out, stare brazenly, push out her teats, wiggle her hips, and sway across his vision whenever she can. He shrewdly waits for three sleeps, while her desire for him grows, and then he goes to Chetu.

Fina doesn't bother to find out how he is received. On the following morning, she announces, "I shall mate with Pak of the Eyo!"

Che dithers. Fina is heedless and often lazy and unkind. Nevertheless, the lot of females, even beautiful ones, is hard, and a good and helpful mate could ease her burden.

"Why don't you choose Hun? She cries in dismay. *Why can't she say Noha?* "He would have treated you well. I don't like this Pak!"

"It's not required that you like him."

Though Chetu, who always indulges Fina's wishes, is silent, his sons add their entreaties to Che's. Pak has flattered them on many occasions; but they, too, feel uneasy in his presence. Even the inexperienced San would choose the forthright Noha for his sister.

Fina silences them with the one claim that they cannot gainsay, "Pak is a fine hunter!" And is not hunters' prowess the rock upon which the clans' survival rests?

Cunning Pak has read his victim well.

At first, Noha feels nothing. It is as if a boulder has rolled from a cliff to crush his chest and the pain is so great that his knowing-place dares not recognize it. Slowly humiliation seeps through him. After that comes anger's blessed relief. To kill! To kill that devious Pak! Laf warned me. Why didn't I listen? But who would have thought? Hun would have been better. There would have been no dishonour in that. Yes, Hun is worthy of Fina despite those slow ways. But Pak? That hatchet-faced, sly, untrustworthy, sneaky . . . How *can* she? When I, Noha, Ogucen of Kiconce, had already asked for her? I'll never understand it!

And then comes the shame, the embarrassment, the disgust at the thought of Fina's sensuous body straining under Pak's. With his face blazing, taking nothing but his spear, Noha strides from the camp towards the old hunting grounds.

Pak constructs a big hut for his mate. He gathers smooth stones from the lake bottom for a hearth and places the finest chewed reindeer skins on the nuptial bed, but there his efforts cease. Fina is his belonging now and as such, she must face alone a mate's numerous tasks. He demands the most meticulous tailoring in his tunics and leggings, criticizes her attempts to prepare meat and often casts it away in anger. When, trying to please him, she pierces white shells gathered at the lake and strings them on a thong to hang around his neck, he rejects her offering, calling her handiwork, *females' toys!* and shakes in her downcast face the string of woverine teeth that he habitually wears.

He doesn't beat her. He doesn't have to. One look at his heartless, axe-edged countenance sends her scurrying to do his bidding.

Che watches, dismayed. Fina might be flighty and a vain fool, but she is of Che's blood! Resentment rises like phlegm in Che's throat but custom forbids her interfering or even offering help.

She asks her brother, Tiga, "Can't you do something?"

He replies sadly, "Fina is no longer Omeeseh, she is Pak's possession."

She gets the same reaction from her father, Chetu. "Fina is now of the Eyo. I can do nothing."

When Noha returns, be brings with him the tusks of a long-haired mammoth.

During the first days of his wandering, Noha ran relentlessly, disregarding the need for food and water, ran like the spirit-pursued until he dropped and slept where he fell, twitching in dreams of revenge. In lucid moments, he asked the spirits to forgive him. It was unthinkable that a hunter should so debase himself because of a mere female. In fact, he began to realize, as time went by, that his pain came not from losing Fina, although she was very desirable, but because she had chosen the inferior Pak.

Pride ate at his manitu, not the feeling for which there was no name, the feeling his Ninga and Nuse shared. He must kill this pride, or better still, harness it! But how could he drive this demon from him? Perhaps he should consult Boog. No! He must do it himself with Manitou's help.

He knelt. He prayed. He fasted. But he could not bring himself to return to the camp and look into Pak's face.

Manitou heard Noha's prayer. After five sleeps, the young hunter came upon the small mammoth herd in a green valley scooped from the plain. It was not unknown for such herds to be sighted, though unusual to find them so far away from the glaciers.

He spied upon them.

The beasts had lost most of their grey shaggy coats and each had something wrong with it—an injury, a broken tusk, deformity, weakness, disease. They must be the remnants of a herd that had travelled from the west in the dark winter and they had dropped behind, surviving on what they could scrape from the ground and remaining here to enjoy the time of light.

One old bull was blind. He was a gigantic beast, standing eleven foot-lengths at the shoulder, a towering slope-backed mammoth with extravagantly curved tusks scraping the ground. This creature turned to face the approaching hunter, his trunk lifted to test the air. The breeze had brought to him a dreaded enemy's scent. *Man!* The crippled herd formed a rough circle, rumps inward. The old bull, however, charged Noha without warning, trumpeting his rage.

Noha reacted instinctively, dashing to the side and weaving a wide circle while the bull, confused in his blindness by the shifting breeze and the elusive hunter, searched for fresh scent. Around and around Noha flew, watching the animal stumble in his sightless search for him. The other elephants didn't come to the bull's aid but trumpeted encouragement to him.

The ancient animal suffered from more than blindness, for it took only two hours' feinting and running in circles to exhaust him. Noha galloped up behind him and grabbing the mammoth's short tail, swung himself onto the beast's back. A few lightning steps along the spine and he reached the head and thrust his spear into the vulnerable spot at the skull's base. It took three mighty heaves to embed the spear, and all the fury in Noha's heart went into the blows.

Dancing along the mammoth's ridged back, he leaped to the ground. When the old bull finally succumbed, Noha squatted beside his head and ran his hand along his trunk, feeling the deep ridges.

"I thank you, Old One," he whispered.

"Hear my vow. Never again will I let a female weaken my manitu!" He cut free the tusks and returned to camp.

The other hunters act as if he has simply been on a hunting expedition and listen attentively to his story. He sits with them after the evening meal, describing once more to Laf how he slew his first mammoth when Pak, until then conspicuously absent, approaches. Noha tries to take no particular notice as he continues his tale, but Laf and the other hunters tense; they know Noha's volatile temper and Pak's pitiless tongue. When Noha shows no sign of ire against Pak, they begin to relax.

Pak says, "I am told that you have had success on your . . . hunt."

"I did," replies Noha courteously.

He sees Kraac watching him narrowly. Noha must not raise his spear against one of his clan!

"What is your kill?"

"A mammoth," Noha says and cannot keep the satisfaction from his voice.

Pak smiles superciliously as if he doesn't believe the polite answer, a terrible insult to Noha, since an Eyo hunter would suffer death rather than lie to a male of his clan.

"Where are the tusks?" Pak asks, as if demanding proof.

Laf moves to intervene but Noha sees Kraac put a steadying hand on his arm.

"I have given them to ogima," Noha says quietly.

Pak again smiles derisively and looks about at the hunters. His smile fades, though, when he sees the hostility there and meets Kraac's calm, cold gaze. He says patronizingly to Noha, "You are to be congratulated."

A long silence. All held their breaths.

Noha says, "I deserve no praise. The mammoth was old and blind."

The hunters begin to grin and look meaningfully at one another. Even Kraac's handsome mouth curves. Noha looks into Pak's black as onyx eyes and what he sees there un-nerves him. A demon gazes out at him. Such enmity is impossible to understand. Surely Pak is possessed!

Laf breaks the spell. "Tell us once more the story of your hunt, Nijkiwe, Brother," he says to Noha, deliberately turning his back on Pak.

When the tale has been retold almost to absurdity and the hunters have begun to drift away, Pak chooses that moment to throw his most cruel dart. "You have not yet congratulated me," he said to Noha.

Noha feels his face freeze, his gesticulating hands halt in midair.

"How so?" he says softly. "Have you, too, slain a mammoth?"

His adversary controls himself with a visible effort. "Not I," he admits. "I spoke of the new hut I have constructed." This is the oblique way among the hunters of referring to mating.

Laf gulps.

"Have you chosen a mate?" Noha asks carefully.

"I have. Fina, the daughter of Chetu." Pak spews the words at him.

Noha says, "She is a fine maiden. I congratulate you, Nijkiwe, and I wish you many male offspring."

The tone is perfunctory but Noha has managed to say it. He is beginning to believe there are more important things than females and, anyway, once he accepted the fact that he could not have Fina, she lost all of her appeal.

"I thank you," Pak mutters resentfully after a brief, stunned silence. Then he turns on his heel and strides off.

Laf lets out a long sigh. "You did well. I was tempted to strike him myself."

"You?" Noha laughs. "Pak has no quarrel with you." He is to remember and regret this comment, for Pak will not forgive Laf's defence of Noha.

Anxious to change the subject, Noha asks, "And when shall my companion build a marriage hut for a fair maiden?"

Laf pushes out his long cheek with his tongue and scuffs the ground with one big toe. "I have not decided," he says. "But there is a pleasing maiden who looks at me with melting eyes, and I suppose it's time I thought about fathering sons."

Noha suddenly realizes that Laf likes this maiden.

"What's her name?" It is a bold question but since they are companions, the easygoing Laf allows it, even replies. "She's called, Miira. She's of the Omeeseh."

Noha remembers Miira. Another pretty one taken, he thinks and finds that he doesn't care. For, from his moment of conciliation with Pak, his desire for Fina and his agony of rejection cease to exist. He ignores her as is proper for a hunter to ignore a mated female unless she is his mother or sister by blood or mating. Pak and Noha kept their distance from one another and peace reigns. The people are grateful, for nothing is more repugnant to them than serious quarrelling within the clan. Each member lives on the others' sufferance and survives on their work, sharing, and bravery.

The unmated Omeeseh and Mahantanis maidens try to catch Noha's eye but he seems not to notice any of them. At sleep time, Che lies in her father's hut, her aching head buried in skins. She has finally admitted that she wants to mate and that Noha is her choice. No other will do. However, she will never humble herself by pursuing his friendship.

The long daylight remains warm and dry for the most part. The sky is cloudless and there is good hunting, much stored reindeer meat and berries to chew with wild roots. The people are content. The females spend their leisure fashioning handsome coverings for their mates and tunics and leggings for their own use in the coming dark time. They even find opportunities to sew shells and ground hog bone amulets to their tunic bodices. The Artisan is kept busy carving horn pendants for everyone and helping Bara make fertility statues for the newly mated maidens. Kraac's mate, Narima, is finally with cub and the envy of all the young brides except Fina whose belly also swells.

Kiconce and Boog pass long hours locked in discussion. It seems that Boog's rest and even his waking hours are disturbed by visions and portents in all of which he sees the new mountains of the first prophecy.

Che overhears Kiconce say wearily to him, "The Eyo are happy. Perhaps we have found a land where winter and night never come."

"Not true," Boog hisses. "Night will come, and it will be long and very cold, and the people could sicken and die. We must leave this place and journey to the land which the great Manitou has ordained for the Eyo."

To Kiconce's chagrin, the Mahantanis ogima calls a council and informs him and Chetu that he intends to lead his people back to the home mountains from whence they came. There they will feed on the mountain sheep, who give them their name, and travel in the summer to the great forest in the west.

"My people dislike this bright, grassy plain," he tells them, "and yearn for their homeland and the cold, clear air of the mountain peaks. Also our shaman has dreamed and in the dream, the Giant Reindeer, the Owl, and the Mountain Sheep pause in their travels. Our Totem bids farewell to his companions and retraces his path. No longer shall the three clans journey together!"

At this saying, a great sigh rises from the peoples.

"So be it," say Kiconce and Chetu. The peoples feast the Mahantanis. Many dances and songs tell of the mountain clan's strength and courage, but the people are saddened.

Noha seeks out Hun as the big hunter smooths his spear shaft with a cutting stone. Noha squats near him and Hun acknowledges his presence with a friendly grunt.

"Your spear will be missed in the hunt," Noha says.

The mountain man answers with a slow smile. "And who will chase with flashing feet the reindeer upon my spear?"

Noha smiles in turn. "There are many who run as fast as I," he claims, not meaning a word of it.

Nevertheless, Hun, not as slow witted as he seems on the surface, says softly, "There are times when it is better to move slowly."

Noha's head goes up. "And there are times when a quick wit cannot be replaced."

"That is so," Hun agrees, unperturbed.

Noha inwardly chastises himself.

"I shall miss you," he says simply.

Big Hun doesn't reply but hunches over his work with satisfaction on his bearded face.

When the Mahantanis have departed, Noha meanders restlessly along the lakeshore. He watches a flight of dappled geese wing their way southward, indication that the time of darkness will soon be upon them.

My father should long ago have heeded Boog's arguments and pressed eastward to the place of the Stranger Mountains.

However, Noha now keeps his opinions to himself. If he can't tame his yearnings, he can at least keep them twisted in his tongue.

It is still pleasant by the lake, even though the days are increasingly short and cold and more and more hunters don tunics during the waking time. He comes upon a grassy point which thrusts like a finger into the lake. It is raised above the shore and rodents have built dens in it sides. They chatter and flit into hiding as he climbs the bank. Beyond it is a small, sandy cove. The sand is a pleasant brown, and he knows it will be warm to the touch. However, the beach already has an occupant. Even though the air is chill, a maiden kneels in the sand drawing upon it with a stick.

Noha is about to turn away when he recognizes small, sturdy Che of the Omeeseh. He has not really noticed her since courting time. On impulse, he climbs down to the bay and circles to come to her from the front. Che continues to draw pictures in the sand.

"What are you making?"

She glances up, her pointy-chinned face a mask. "I dreamed," she says simply.

As she doesn't invite it, he doesn't ask to look but averts his eyes as she wipes away with her compact nut brown hand the lines she has drawn.

"You don't visit my brothers in the huts of the Omeeseh?" she asks.

"I have grown lazy," he replies, laughing. "But how is it that you are still among your people? I thought that so *aged* a person would have mated by now with the great Mahantanis and have gone to live with them on the mountain."

"I'm not a cub to be mocked!" she draws up her small body.

"Forgive me," Noha says unconcernedly. "I meant no harm." In fact, he had been remembering with amusement their first meeting when she angrily claimed fourteen summers.

"I haven't yet found a suitable mate," she says candidly, looking uncustomarily vulnerable as she admits it.

His heart softens with pity for this tiny female. "Any hunter would be honoured to build a hut for you," he exclaims unthinkingly. "Why even I . . ." He stops. This time he must leash his wagging tongue before he hurts this cub.

"You?" she asks boldly, and he is shocked at the hope he thinks he discerns in that single word.

He takes a deep breath and looks again into her amber coloured eyes. Why not? She is the daughter of Chetu and a good, strong, and sensible maiden and not ugly, if a little touchy. He has often seen her with his Ninga. There is no fire for her in him, but he would be kind. She would surely be grateful

"Yes, I," he says aloud. "If I were to visit Chetu, would you come to my hut?"

She bows her head to hide whatever is in her eyes. "I would be honoured, Ogucen of Kiconce," she replies formally.

Thus it is settled.

Noha builds a fine hut for Che, using pelts which Bara has saved for him and the best of his own pelts. He even goes so far as to ask Bara to place extra comforts within the hut. On her suggestion, he hunts with his bola for hare and ground squirrel and from their soft hides Bara sews a square wrapping that will make a warm winter cape for the bride. Bara, Inik, Narima, and Fina go for Che at the appointed hour and lead her to the hut where Noha awaits her.

Che feels a momentary compunction when she sees her sister's lovely face. However, Noha doesn't even look at Fina but stands aside and with a courteous motion conducts Che into the hut. She notes the care with which her new home has been prepared, not realizing that it was mostly Bara's doing. She is overcome with trembling when Noha offers the robe he has procured for her.

It is lovely! But she must not deceive herself! As yet, Noha doesn't value her as he should. Nevertheless, some day he will have for *her The Feeling For Which There Is No Word*. This thing she vows. Some day.

Noha is gentle with her, as one who experiences no passion but only respect and release, and if Che is disappointed, she doesn't show it but sleeps curled in his arms like the fox pup on the vixen's breast.

The fire dies and darkness is in the hut with them.

The long night descends.

CHAPTER 7

Debbikat—Night

The trek began well.

Kiconce cried, "Bundle your hides, pull your hut-poles, and take up your burdens. We go to the east!

"Boog's vision has triumphed," Bara said, biting her lip.

"Noha will be pleased." Mischievous Inik looked coyly through her eyelashes at Che.

Che laughed. "Pleased? Laf will have to tie him down!"

"Not everyone will be so happy." Narima stalked off, hand protectively on her distended belly.

Che bit he lip. For once, Narima seemed justified because *Debbikat,* Night was upon them.

Debbikat had given good warning before he enveloped the land. Early autumn had brought the first short, cold nights when the sun stopped riding the horizon during sleep-time and dipped out of sight behind it. These periods of darkness became longer and longer until day and night were equal. During this gradual glooming, Kiconce finally heeded Boog's insistent counsel and after many meetings with Chetu and the elder hunters, instructed his people.

He told Bara and Che, "You must abandon most of your dried meat. Tell your nimi to carry as much as they can and not to forget berries and roots. I'll send scouts ahead and you'll follow. Our hunters will stay near you, killing as they go. This will save your supplies."

As the first snowflakes brushed her cheeks, Che hoped he hadn't left the trek too late.

Back in the valley where Noha had killed the elephant, the surviving mammoths were growing protective hair. Overhead, the last geese wedges honked their way south and, beneath the peoples' trudging feet, ground squirrels burrowed deeper into the tundra and lemmings in white winter tunics dug tunnels in the still warm earth. Long-eared hare wandered freely but established high ground shelter. Some of these creatures helped to fill the hunting pouches but for the most part, the hunters depended as usual upon the reindeer.

Mahingan also followed the reindeer herd further and further to the east across the spirit bridge, trapping them between the seas to the south and north, and Noha's canine brothers, the foxes, now snow white, stowed rodents in rock crevice larders.

Che overhears Noha tell Ecakik, "I met Assinbo on the plain, but he didn't speak to me." Noha never talks to her about these things. In fact, Noha seldom speaks to her.

On the fourth day, the sun doesn't rise but appears only as a pale reflection along the dark horizon. It is suddenly achingly cold.

Narima cries, "The demons of darkness have overcome the world."

"Our mates will protect us," Inik says and hugs her son, Pu, close to her and shivers. Bara puts her hand on Narima's shoulder. "Remember Boog's prophecies! Though you are cold, your stomachs are filled daily and none sicken."

Che feels her own taut stomach muscles relax. When she and Inik are alone, she says, "My respect for Ninga grows every day. I like Ogima, too. Both of them make me feel welcome in the clan."

"Why not?" Inik smiles. "They were lucky to get you."

To hide her pleasure, Che fixes her gaze on some chatty little snow buntings with fat white breasts and brown-tipped wings, who are culling grass seed from dead stalks and picking patiently through snow dust for food.

"I admire birds. If they can toil and survive in the darkness, so can we."

Che is happy enough, feels safe and accepted as never before. But she wishes Noha would talk to her. Does he think her incapable of understanding? He shares his manitu with Laf and Dinkka. But what does she expect? To be another Bara? Even Bara behaves humbly when hunters are about. Che finds some comfort in the warmth and closeness of bedding with Noha and though she experiences no loin fire, decides that such feelings must be one of Fina's exaggerations, forgetting the rutting scene between Pak and Lara on the summer sands.

She watches the bunting wing across the darkling plain. "It's strangely lovely here, isn't it? So mysterious," she says to Inik.

Che soon has little energy left for looking about. The two clans move quickly, not wishing the herds to outdistance them as the dim days grow shorter and bitter winds batter the browned grasses, bringing light drifting snow. Che struggles gamely and inures herself to ordinary suffering. Inik wraps Pu in fur and totes him in a sling against her breast.

She tells Che, "I am worried about Fina and Narima. Kiconce will allow no respite even to pregnant females, except an early morning head start on the trail that robs them of much needed rest."

"I know."

Che helps surreptitiously as much as she can but, being both strong and cubless, she already carries more than her share. Narima's abdomen is more distended than Fina's and Che often sees Kraac watching his mate from a distance as if waiting for a sign. As Che trudges over prairies patched with snow pellets and over solid ice ponds, she thinks about her new brothers. Though Kraac has welcomed her formally to the clan, he seems oblivious to her. He is attractive but distant. She decides to reserve judgement of him, but she likes Ecakik. No one can help liking Ecakik.

The following night, the people come to a valley where many reindeer have sought refuge, scratching in the shallow snows for forage. On the valley's gently sloping side is a copse of runty trees.

"We can go no further," Kiconce tells the females. "Build your winter huts here and build them well."

This time, most of the hunters help. However, Noha is, as usual, off scouting the terrain. Che finds a sheltered spot and putting her burdens on the ground, selects a flat-edged stone scraper from a pack. Kneeling on the frozen earth, she draws the hand-axe toward her. The axe slides uselessly across the hard surface. Her back throbbing from the long trek and the frozen earth ruts digging into her knees through her leggings, she murmurs, "Give me patience, Mother Earth," and uses a chopping motion. Sometimes the axe bounces but at other times, it bites shallow chips from the ground.

Che labours on, ignoring the cold and the pain. Inik, noticing her predicament, approaches but Che sends her away. "You must help Ninga."

"She sent me. Besides, my mate and Kraac share the task."

And where is Noha? Che immediately chides herself for the thought.

"Nevertheless, you'll be needed." Still obstinate. "Go to help Fina. Pak won't let me go near her. I'll prepare my mate's hut.

Inik leaves, shaking her head.

Che achieves a pit and an entrance passageway. Staggering to her feet and wiping her bloodied hands against her tunic, she slowly unties her hide bundle and selecting the thickest skins, lines the cavities with them. She extends her hut poles across the pit and crawling out on them, piles more hides to form a roof. With a sharpened pole, she levers large stones from the earth and scrabbling once more on her protesting knees, rolls them onto the roof.

"These hides will not blow away," she gasps. "Noha should be pleased."

Drained, she wriggles into the dark pit through the passageway. She slumps to the hide floor, buries her head in the furs and sleeps.

Hunger wakes her and cold drives her from the hut. She ignores her discomfort while building a fire; cooks some hare strips; chews gratefully; squats near the blaze. Scarlet juice runs down her fingers and chin. Her hands sting so much that she pauses to examine them and shrinks from the sight of pulped flesh and crusted blood. She closes her eyes and slowly opens them. Swaying to her feet, she finds her digging pole and wanders a little way to gather more stones.

She digs a round earthen hearth in the hut and into one corner, she carts baskets of half frozen soil wrenched from Mother Earth and makes a raised sleeping platform. She regrets her obstinate refusal of Inik's help because she has still to dig a food storage pit, pile in the supplies, and cover it with grass mats and stones. The Omeeseh never waited so late in the season to build winter huts and always before, she'd had Fina's unwilling help.

She catches herself. Noha will be unhappy and shamed if she can't do her work.

"Mother Earth," she whispers, kneeling by her new hearth. "Where shall I find the strength for these tasks? My body cries out for rest. I'm as an old female! Help me! However, Mother Earth sleeps deaf to her daughter's prayers.

Noha finds her there, weary tears glistening on her cheeks. He kneels by her. "Ninitegamagan," he asks. "What is this?"

"I have dirt in my eyes." Che stumbles to her feet, wiping away the betraying tears with the back of her hands. This exposes her palms.

Noha draws her hands to his chest. "You have laboured much," he says quietly. "I shall dig the food pits. Go to your sleeping platform and rest."

Now grateful tears spring to her eyes. Perhaps he does feel something for her. Perhaps!

"I wanted to build a fine winter hut for you." Her lips tremble.

He says, "And you have done so. I've chosen well in my mate." Che's heart fills. "A hunter values a mate who is strong above all else."

She flinches. *Strong?* Pulling her hands from his, she turns her back on him and crawls to the sleeping platform. She lies upon it, facing the dirt wall.

Noha, nonplussed, says, "I'll go to dig the food pit now."

She can't answer. Noha gets to his knees and crawls down the entrance passage, mumbling as he goes, "What wrong have I done? I'll never understand this mate of mine!"

However, after sleep time, Che forgets her pain and when Noha comes to her with fire in his loins, she opens her thighs. In the other huts, too, the drained people seek solace and settle in to wait out the long night as *Meequorme,* Ice; *Pepoon,* Winter; and *Keewatin,* North Wind, stalk the land.

Narima bears a daughter with a thick thatch of dark hair and long bones like her mother. Since, thanks to Kiconce's foresight, there is much meat in the pits, the older females don't have to kill the winter girl cub because she will take no food from the hunters.

Che is glad.

Although her prayer to Mother Earth for a son has been refused, Narima seems well content when Kraac does not chastise her. In fact, he seems to take pleasure in fondling his offspring and often stops to watch her suckle at her ninga's pale breast. There will be, however, no naming feast for a female cub, so Narima decides to call her *Drilla* and Bara sanctions the name.

Other babes are born that long winter's night, among them a boy-cub to Fina and Pak. They name him Koo Koo Kooh for the snowy-owl's call which Pak heard at the moment of his son's birth. Fina nicknames him Kooh. He has his mother's high colouring and handsome features. After his birth, the relationship between Fina and Pak improves and the cub's presence seems temporarily to soften his nuse's nature, though he still allows Fina little freedom.

As for Noha and Che, they go on as before, their only communication upon the sleeping platform. Che consoles herself. Though he doesn't feel deeply for her, he treats her well and supplies her with fine pelts. During milder wake times, the hunters go upon the tundra, and blood often stains the shallow snows. However, the summer's wholesale slaughter is not repeated because reindeer are few and butchering has to be done quickly so the meat can be cast into pits to freeze.

Often lonely, Che visits Inik's hut and is warmly greeted. Pu always holds out his chubby arms to her. He is now a staunch cub who stomps about the hide floor on sturdy legs encased in fur. He sits quietly, intelligent, round eyes agleam with interest, as Ecakik describes his forays. How happy those three are. A coldness grips Che's chest.

There has been a change in Boog. The journey's resumption cheered him. He eats well and he travels less often into the spirit world. Instead, he reaches out for companionship.

Winter is the traditional time for storytelling and Ecakik and Inik often take Pu to the hut of the shaman who can be relied upon to fill the darkling hours with the history of the Eyo and the Spirits. Che accompanies them because she loves these stories just as much as Pu does. Noha prefers to remain in his own pit-hut with the younger hunters and recount killing tales. Narima stays away, too, though Kraac comes to sit near Boog and sometimes Che feels his black, cognizant glance upon her and wonders what lies behind that handsome face.

She listens fascinated as Boog tells them how the earth was created and how the animals got their names. He tells them about the Great Spirit, Manitou, and of the Sun Spirit, the Moon, and the Morning Star. He tells them of the Giant Reindeer whom Kiconce slew and how it became the Totem of the people, and how they bear a special kinship to Awaskesh and live under his protection, sharing in his strength and cunning forever.

One story, a favourite with the cubs and indeed with many adults, particularly pleases Che's fertile imagination and gives her new understanding of the land they now occupy.

Boog speaks.

"North of our ancestors' country lay a great Cold Land, the land where the giant Pepoon, W inter, has his hut. As it happens, it is this very land which we now cross. But Pepoon was unhappy with his dark land and once every year, he travelled stealthily

south-west and built another hut in the land of the Elves of Light, intending to dwell there always."

Our old land, Che thinks wistfully.

"Pepoon brought with him Keewatin who was cruel and noisy and attacked every person, shaking and buffeting him and nipping at his nose and fingers. At times he buried people entirely in snow, killing them."

Che watches Pu's eyes grow round. He might well be scared, for Keewatin howls and shrieks about the very hut where they sit.

Boog continues the tale.

"The little Elves of Light were, at first, frightened of Pepoon and Keewatin, and so they scurried away to hide. The southern land became dark and very cold, and the Eyo hungered. Even the animals hid themselves.

As for Pepoon, he was quite content in his hut."

"Did the elves die?" Pu cries out and is quickly shushed by Inik.

Though he pretends to ignore the cub, Che sees Boog's rheumy eyes soften. He continues.

"The Elves, though small, are very brave and very kind and when they saw the People's plight, they were angry and came peeping by twos and threes from their hiding places. Keewatin swooped down upon them, sending them scrambling back into hiding."

He casts a sidelong glance at Pu and says, "*They were not hurt, for it is not in Keewatin's power to hurt the Elves. Also, Keewatin found that this southern land sapped his great strength and he was weaker every day. When the Elves saw this, they tormented and teased him with their light until he went flying back from whence he came.*"

Pu chortles loudly and Che smiles. She sees Kraac watching her and bends her head.

Boog continues.

"*With Keewatin gone, the Elves were free to gambol around Pepoon's hut, calling him and daring him to emerge. Pepoon, who hates light and warmth, escaped their tortures by retreating further north. However, the Elves were not content with this and they pursued him relentlessly all the way back to the Great Cold Land.*"

His audience grunts satisfaction and Boog's eyes narrow.

"*However, the Elves again encountered Keewatin who had gathered strength in his native land, and he drove them out once more.*"

At a worried gasp from Pu, he adds, "Do not be afraid. Every year the Elves of Light journey once more north where they dance on the soft tundra grass, little people with beautiful bright faces and glistening hair and garments as many hued as the tundra flowers. With their advent comes blessed light and soft breezes and, in their midst dances their queen *Menokomeg, Summer* and as she dances, ice and snow disappear; the air softens; the grass and tundra mosses become spongy; among the rocks the gentians and buttercups and bearberries show their smiling faces."

At story's end, Pu always asks, "Will the Elves of Light visit this dark land, O Shaman?"

"I have said it," Boog replies and regards the cub with interest.

He asks Ecakik, "Which is Pu's Wisana?"

Bara had explained to Che this strange word *Wisana*. Boog referred to the Eyo belief that a Spirit-guide or wisana, in the form of an animal or bird, sometimes came to the place of birth. A wolf had invaded the camp on the night of Ecakik's birth, sniffing but not harming the bloodied infant as Bara cringed in fear at this powerful sign. Mahingan was then considered to be Ecakik's wisana, as Assinbo was Noha's. Mahingan and Assinbo would help them always and in return, they would never seek to kill their Wisana.

"At Pu's birth, a fox came to the camp," Ecakik replies quietly to Boog's question, but with concern in his eyes. "However, it was not a good happening because the fox's fur was white, although it was summertime."

"Why was I not told about this omen?" Boog frowns.

"You were in the inner cave and would not be disturbed."

The shaman's old face twists in troubled thought and he moves to a cluster of pouches which the apprentice has suspended on a hut pole along with the other accruements of his calling. From one pouch he withdraws a fox tooth and, with many incantations, places the tooth back in its small pouch which he hangs on a thong about the cub's neck. Inik, silent through all of this, breaths an anxious sigh. Che wants to console her but knows no way.

"Pu must wear this always," Boog orders.

"As you wish," Ecakik replies.

Despite the shaman's tales, waking times are long and often tedious for Che. She doesn't fear darkness but can find little respite from the hut's smoky interior because of the savage tundra winds. For this reason, the females and cubs begin daily to congregate in Bara's large hut when the males are hunting.

Che, Bara, Inik, Narima, and Fuum's and Quork's new mates, beautiful Lara and ungainly Whea, spend many hours together. Fina doesn't join them. Pak would punish her for wasting work time. Che, formerly starved of congenial female companionship, sits contented with her new sisters, sewing tunics and leggings and momentarily forgetting her growing knowledge that Noha wants only to find comfort in her and to mount her. Often she watches spellbound as Bara fashions a fertility figure. Che, herself, has one thrust into the earth at the head of her sleeping platform. There is no sign of quickening in her belly.

Sometimes, Bara tells them stories about when she was young and their mates were babes. Che loves especially the much-repeated tale about how Kiconce slew the Giant Reindeer and how the spirit deer, instead of punishing him, admired his bravery and took the Eyo under his protection.

"If I were a hunter, I would do such things," she declares.

All but Bara look shocked and Narima snickers.

Che ignores her. She means what she says, though the ninga in her loves to cuddle the sleeping Drilla or to play with the delightful Pu. She makes for him a small hunter doll with a face drawn with paints begged from Boog's apprentice, and a tiny spear to place across its shoulder.

Someday she will have a son like Pu. Then perhaps Noha . . .

Pu is infinitely careful with Drilla and will sit with her propped in her moss-bag between his fat legs, humming an unintelligible cub song to her. He seems to regard her as a personal possession and is always angry when Narima takes her away to Kraac's hut.

One waking time, even the homely pleasures of Bara's hut do not tempt Che. She yearns with no respite. She suspects that her relationship with Noha is robbing her of the satisfaction and fulfillment she craves. Was she wrong to think his absentminded respect would grow into something else? Wasn't it, after all, more than any female could expect of her mate? She tells herself this, but she doesn't really believe it.

Once when Noha is hunting as usual and when the restlessness becomes too much to bear, when the hut is quiet and even Wind is silent, Che wraps herself in the hare blanket, her bridal gift from Noha, and steps outside. She walks through the copse and climbs the valley's sloping side. The arid air numbs her face. Her breath hangs before her in patterned, white wreaths, and the cold penetrates her throat making her cough. She puts a fur-mittened hand over her lips to protect the breath of life and climbs to the plain's edge.

The tundra stretches empty before her, dead grey moss and brown grass patched with powdery snow. Frosty fronds crackle and snap beneath her foot-pelts. Along the horizon, yellowish haze gives a twilight glow to the land and the stars blink dimly. Without thinking but simply following her feet wherever they lead, she strides over the plain, her long blanket trailing a strange, wide spoor. She knows not how long she walks but when she finally tires, she is several miles from the camp; the cold has stolen through her grass-stuffed *mackisins* and her face is stiff. She realizes with a pang that she has been dangerously stupid to wander like this. She guiltily retraces her steps, hurrying on benumbed feet. It is then that the little reflected light which the hidden sun provides disappears below the horizon. Che plunges into darkness.

At first she stoically ignores this new hazard and trudges in the direction in which she thinks the camp lies. She struggles for a long time before suspecting that she should already have reached the valley. She sees only black-on-grey tundra stretching on all sides. Her throat tightens as she fights gathering panic. She must find a sheltered spot.

An icy wind now rises to complicate her peril.

Surely the Eyo will search for her. She is a newly mated female of cub-bearing age and not to be left to freeze in the darkness. Surely Bara will plead for her. Surely Noha . . . At the thought of him, her heart twists. Will Noha search for her? Her sudden terror that he will not is even greater than her fear of dying alone in the frozen wastes.

There is no willow stand or rocky indentation into which she might crawl like a burrowing vixen, no hillock to shelter her, though Che hunts for as long as she dares. Finally, she curls up behind a large rock, drawing her blanket around her, a small patch of grey against the darkness. The wind moans. She wills herself to remain awake.

She sleeps. She doesn't hear the animal creep stealthily upon her. It is a wolf, almost as tall as a steppe pony, a powerful beast, leader of his pack who on this night has chosen to hunt alone. He pads across stem grass on large, hairy paws, sniffing the freezing air. Suddenly a scent fills his nostrils. It is Man, an enemy he has lately learned to respect and fear. However, his nose tells him that there is only one creature and he decides, from the quality of the scent, that it is not a hunter. Added to this, the bitch is far away from her lair. And she has no fire.

Intrigued, he pads to the huddled form behind the rock. He moves closer, having never before been so near a human. Che awakes with a start, sensing an alien presence, and awkwardly pulling the stiffened blanket from her face, she peers into the darkness. A big, grey head looms above her, eyes glittering yellow, foul breath panting from jaws lined with fangs.

Che screams only once. "Napima, Husband!" she cries knowing that she will never again see Noha.

Kraac hears the cry from where he kneels sniffing the wolf's trail. He has been tracking it for many miles, not intending to harm it but since it is his brother's totem, he hopes to encounter it on the chance that it might shed its animal flesh and speak to him in its spirit-form and tell him what the future holds. Kraac has no wisana. He was born unexpectedly when Bara and Kiconce were alone and away from camp, and no animal or bird came to bear witness. On his back, Kraac carries a large hare which he means as an offering to the wolf.

He stiffens. The sound on the wind is human, female, and originates from a spot far from camp. He begins to run, his spear jouncing by his side, the hare jiggling on his back. He comes quickly upon the female and the wolf. The female cowers against a rock the wolf standing over her like a hunting cur on point.

"Mahingan!" Kraac calls softly.

The wolf's great head turns to regard this new phenomenon.

"Mahingan!" Kraac calls again and, raising the hare high above his head, casts it aside, away from the female.

The wolf puzzles over this odd behaviour and awaits further developments. However, the hunter stands still and doesn't raise his spear. The wolf takes a tentative step toward the hare. Still the hunter doesn't move. With a switch of its tail, the wolf turns and walks over to the carcass. Still the hunter doesn't move. Bending, the wolf snatches the hare in its jaws and with one more curious glance at Kraac, trots into the darkness with its unexpected prize.

Kraac plucks Che from the rock as if she were a cub and holding her against his body turns and lopes toward camp. She clings to him, her soft breasts pressed to his chest. Kraac goes directly to Noha's hut. It is empty. He carries Che to the fire and kneels to place her near it. He would rise but Che tightens her arms on his neck. She tries, in a trembling voice, to thank him. He listens courteously so she might rid herself of her burden of gratitude.

Noha finds them kneeling before the fire, clasped in each other's arms, their faces close together. Che sees him. Her arms drop. Noha's face is a mask of disbelieving horror. He snarls. *"Like Fina! She snake! My Che? No! How dare you hold her? My blood brother!"*

If what he suspected were true, a mature hunter would leave quietly and the following day send the female packing to her birth-clan, keeping for himself any male cubs of the union and taking another mate. But not Noha. All his carefully acquired dignity drops from him in an instant and he seizes Kraac by the shoulder and Che by the hair and rips them apart.

Then as suddenly as it rose, his sustaining anger desserts him, leaving him limp. Che gazes at him from the hut floor. He is looking at Kraac who has regained his balance, eyes glittering menacingly, hand gripping his spear, face hard.

Noha whispers low, "She is mine! And no one, not even my Nisages, will have her!" His spear begins slowly to rise.

Kraac hears him but pretends he does not. "Your mate needs attendance," he says in an even tone. Bewilderment leaps into Noha's eyes. The spear stills. "She was lost on the tundra," Kraac explains conversationally. "A wolf frightened her and she suffers much from the cold."

Realization dawns in Noha's eyes. Then mortification takes hold and his face blazes. He tries to apologize.

Kraac forestalls him and, as if nothing at all unusual has happened, he says, "You must have been worried about her. I'll fetch Narima to tend her."

"I shall always remember what you did for me this night, Nisages," Noha says.

"As will I," Che adds in a small voice.

"I'll fetch Narima."

No need," Noha says, looking at Che. "I'll take care of my mate."

And so he does, holding her frozen hands and feet against his body lest the fire thaw them too rapidly, wiping away the involuntary tears, giving her heated nourishment and wrapping her finally with infinite care in warmed skins, watching over her until she sleeps.

Many hours later, Che awakes to find her mate yet sitting near, gazing into her face with a strange look.

"Will you forgive me, Napima?" she asks, lowering her lashes from his look. "I was stupid. I deserved to die."

Instead of answering, he reaches for her and moving her back among the skins, lies beside her. At first, his explorations are as gentle as always but after a time, he demands more and joyful Che responds. Through the long hours they caress one another, going from height to delicious height, to peace and back again to delirium.

I'll hold him, Che exults. Surely, with this body I shall hold him!

During that long winter's darkness, the cub, Rin, is conceived.

CHAPTER 8

Nerockaming — Spring

Noha is in a talkative mood.

"This is a time of good fortune for me. Lemming, ground squirrel, and hare scamper over the tundra. Fox pups feast on them until their bellies scrape the ground when they tumble at their den doors. Assinbo has leisure to sit in the sun and fondly guard his cubs at play.

"Best of all, your belly is big with my cub!"

Che smiles indulgently. She should be delighted, too. The tundra leaps with life, one vast wetland of grass, algar moss, lichens, sedges, and rushes. Willows and birch swell tender with gently folded leaves. Pert ptarmigan build their nests among the rocks. The skies darken with geese, ducks, and waders returning from their winter journey to the Land of Light. The flying bugs are voracious but, as if to compensate, warm air promises cool dryness to come. Before long, day and night will hold equal balance over the clans' new home.

Why does she feel so on edge? Is it natural when with cub?

It is also the time of Awaskesh. Winter larders are almost empty and the deer gather in vast herds for their spring trek to the east. Discarded antlers litter the tundra and frenzied males mount their mates. Hunters strut about the camp as if they, too, have just come to life. Noha is abrupt with Che during the day, nagging her about the dried food bags he will carry for the hunt's first days, but at night he is insatiable for her body. And she for his.

And still Che frets.

For one thing, Boog is unhappy.

While everyone else scurries about, Boog remains sequestered in his hut. The shaman has deteriorated during darkness and sometimes when he goes to the land of the spirits, Che fears his trance will turn into cold death. She asks the apprentice if she can help.

He smiles but replies, "My Master wants only me."

The apprentice squats before Boog's hut, keeping off all who dare to approach and supplying his master's needs when Boog's spirit returns for short periods.

Noha loses patience. Che hears him ask Laf, "Why doesn't Boog just send us on our way with predictions of good hunting?"

"When the proper time comes, the shaman will tell us," Laf replies.

Days pass, and Boog does not emerge, and they dare not disturb him.

Kraac and Ecakik seem unperturbed. They lounge by their fires with Kiconce, Anikeogima, and the elder hunters while the younger males such as Noha, Laf, Dinkka, Che's brothers, and the striplings chase hare over the tundra, spearing them on the run.

Pak joins neither group but stays close to Fina with an anxious eye on little Kooh who is ailing.

Che offers to help but Pak yells, "Get away from here! We need no help from the likes of you!"

Che holds her temper and turns to Fina, hoping to find support there. It is her right to help; Fina shakes her head and lowers her eyes. Che leaves reluctantly, brimming with anger at Pak and contempt for Fina.

One day, Pak chokes down pride and goes to Boog's hut. Che squats outside it talking with the apprentice. She sees terror on Pak's face and pity stirs. The apprentice stops Pak at the hut entrance.

"I must speak with the shaman!" Pak cries.

"You cannot enter here. My Master can see no one."

Madness shines in Pak's eyes. "I must see him. A jealous enemy has wished a *matchee manitu,* evil spirit, upon Kooh."

"Surely not!" Che says, dismayed. "There's no sorcerer among out peoples!"

"Silence!" Pak shouts. "What do you know about such things? Laf is the sorcerer. I have always distrusted his good humour and his easy ways. He walks through the world protected on all sides by a host of friendly spirits. He doesn't deserve it! He's a poor hunter and he pretends not to envy those who are superior. He has everyone fooled. You all respect him even though he has only sixteen summers and has not even taken a mate, though I saw him sniffing after one of the Omeeseh maidens, that Miira."

Che raises her eyebrows. *And he takes Noha's side against you.*

"No one is as good as Laf pretends to be," Pak growls. "He's a sorcerer! Let me see Boog!"

"It would be useless to try," the apprentice says calmly.

Cunning replaces the anger on Pak's narrow face and insincere diffidence oozes in his voice as he says, "Will you, then, who are learned in the arts of healing, come to look at my ogucen?"

The apprentice goes willingly enough and Che follows, ignoring Pak's menacing scowl. The apprentice examines the babe, pressing its abdomen and putting his index finger in the babe's tiny armpit to test its body heat. He lifts the drooping eyelids to see if any alien spirit looks out there.

"Your cub is possessed of the Spirit of *Scouté*, Fire," the apprentice says.

"What can we do?" Fina asks fearfully.

"You must force him to drink to quench the fire." The apprentice selects a pouch filled with pine needle powder from the many hanging on his belt. "Heat stones. Wrap some in skins and place them near the cub. Heat other stones and put them in a pouch full of water, birch tree sap, and this powder. Keep replacing the stones until the liquid is warm. Then take a reed and suck up the juices without swallowing them. Place the reed's end in the cub's mouth and blow the liquid in. Take care not to choke him."

"These are womanish remedies! Why don't you cut Kooh's belly to draw out the matchee manitu?" Pak snarls.

"My Master has taught me that there is much danger in such a thing, especially with one so young.

Often the knife's touch is more than a small manitu can bear and it, too, flees the body or sometimes the cut becomes enlarged and angry and doesn't heal and the whole body rots away."

"Still I think it would be best," Pak says in a tightly controlled voice.

The apprentice shuffles his feet but says obdurately, "Only Boog can decide this. Only Boog cuts the body of an Eyo, no matter how young, and Boog is in the spirit land."

"He must see me!" Pak shouts and the apprentice quails. "I must tell him my suspicions of Laf." Pak lowers his voice to a whisper; his eyes glitter insanely.

The apprentice raises a quivering hand to stop the denouncement. "You must express such accusations only to Boog. It is the law."

"I will deal with the sorcerer myself then."

"You dare not. I warn you!" Though the apprentice is probably doubly frightened now, he hides it well.

"Perhaps I could take Kooh to the Omeeseh shaman?" Fina suggests timidly. "He might help."

The apprentice shrugs to show that he has no objections to this idea but Pak growls at Fina, "You are of the Eyo now, you will not crawl to the Omeeseh shaman!"

Through all this Che says nothing. Her only hope of helping Fina is to be as unobtrusive as possible. With a compassionate glance at Fina, the apprentice shrugs and leaves. Fina quickly begins to apply the remedies he has suggested.

Pak's glance falls on Che. "Leave us!"

"Nimi?" Che asks.

"Please go," Fina begs. Tears run down her face.

Fury surges in Che, but she quells it. If she interferes between them, Fina will suffer and no one will raise a hand to defend her. Not even Bara can intercede in this.

With a defiant look at Pak she leaves but not before saying, "I'll send the maidens to help."

The camp sleeps because dawn might bring the long-delayed summons to the hunt and, at any rate, it will bring toil for the females. Only Che lies wakeful listening to the stirrings and struggles in her womb, her eyes wet and worried in the darkness. Noha sleeps at her side, curled in a ball like a cub, his fists tight, his legs jerking as he dreams about the hunt. Finally Che rises and goes to stand under the stars.

In the darkness near the huts, a tall shadow moves silently through the trees. Another shadow, slight and graceful, detaches itself from the trees and runs to him. The two melt together and sink to the ground while dark clouds hide the moon's face as if to shield the lovers from its knowing gaze. The girl is Miira, the hunter Laf.

Che smiles and creeps back to Noha's side.

At the darkest hour, when all but the sick and lovers sleep, the evil spirit which seethes in Kooh, instead of leaving the cub, spreads its tentacles to snatch Fina's unresisting body.

The Peoples have, as a rule, been healthy, dying not from disease—almost unknown to them—but from wounds received in the hunt or in difficult cub-birth or just from premature aging caused by hardship. Very few live beyond forty summers. However, this new, virulent sickness comes on them like tundra fire. Fever sweeps through the huts. Many die despite the efforts of Boog and the Omeeseh shaman to drive away Matchee Manitu. In vain they paint their bodies and dance about the stricken, chanting prayers to Manitou and shaking their turtle shell rattles. First one then another Eyo falls. *Scouté* seizes cubs. Some perish, some recover seemingly without reason. Among the first to die is Kooh, followed shortly by Fina.

Che is frantic. "I should have helped her! I should have challenged Pak!" she cries to Bara.

"You have done nothing wrong. You could not interfere. Believe this or it will go ill with you."

"Why couldn't I interfere? I should have spit in Pak's face and gone to her! I hate him! May he sicken and rot! I should not have bent to that . . . that hunter!"

"Enough!" Bara whispers. "You go too far!" She relents. "You had no ninga to teach you. Even though our hearts rebel, we females must bow to the hunters' wishes. Can't you see that without them we would all die?"

I killed the hare. I can hunt! But Che doesn't say it.

Bara goes earnestly on, "Fina had help. And what if you had gone to her and the Matchee Manitou claimed you?"

"I don't care."

"Ah no. For yourself you do not care. But what about my Ogucen?"

"Noha doesn't need me. He would quickly find another mate on whom to rut." The bitter words are out before Che can bite them back. She puts her hand over her mouth, too late.

Bara pales. "You wrong him. But that's not important. The most important thing of all you have forgotten. You have forgotten the babe in your belly."

Within her, Che's cub flutters as if to support Bara's words. Terror for it grips Che's throat. She stares at Bara who puts a motherly hand out to touch her cheek. At this, Che crumples.

"Ninga, forgive me. My Elder Sister is gone. She's gone! You see, we quarrelled so much! Always we walked different paths. And now I can walk with her no more. And . . . I never told her that I held her in my heart . . . I never told her."

"She knew," Bara says. "She knew."

Kiconce finally sends the Eyo hunters away when the males begin to sicken.

"Maybe the matchee manitu will not note their passing and follow them," he says.

In one light both of Che's brothers are stricken and die, their bodies racked with fire and convulsions, their eyes staring and bulging from their skulls, their mouths lined with loathsome green fur. Shocked Che mourns her brothers' deaths as she had Fina's and tries to control mortal fear for the babe in her womb and for Noha.

At first, Noha refuses to leave the camp for the hunting trails. Kiconce, his face grey with grief for his and Chetu's people, visits his son's hut. Soon Noha emerges, spear in hand, provision bag at his waist, and trots to Laf's side.

Che watches him go with relief. "If I am to lose him, may it not be to such a scourge."

She sees the maiden Miira standing beneath a tree. Her dark eyes follow Laf and tears trickle on her cheeks. Che approaches her.

"Come, Nimi. We must prepare some of the finest skins for your mating."

Miira blushes and stammers. "I am not yet promised."

Che grins. "I have eyes in my head and I see the way Laf looks at you. Best to be prepared." She takes the maiden's tiny hand and tugs her along the path to her hut. Miira comes willingly and immediately confides in Che that she holds in her manitu the feeling for which there is no word.

"Hold it with care, Nimi, for it is precious." Che turns away so the maiden will not see the pain in her eyes.

Pac has also watched Noha and Laf leave the camp, his mad eyes cold. He will remain at his hut for the burial of Fina and his son before following.

Mother Earth takes pity on her Eyo cubs. She stirs gently beneath her spring coverlet on which the many coloured faces of sprite flowers gleam. Sun's fingers caress her brow. With a contented sigh, she rises and from her breasts flow the juices which bring to life the trees. Mother Earth gathers in her arms many animal spirits and guides them from the old land across the Spirit Bridge to the new world beyond. They are mostly creatures of her grassy plains and forest edges because the other animals have already preceded the people beyond the land bridge.

The Matchee Manitu flees.

Scout after scout returns with tales of countless herds of reindeer, elk, and steppe antelope. They exclaim, "Never before have we seen such multitudes spread on the tundra!"

All of Mother Earth's cubs are not so happy. Che and others are left behind at the camp to bury the dead. Ordinarily, the entire clan would be present at the burials. As it is, with Kiconce's edict that hunters not immediately affected should leave the campsite, there remain to mourn the pitiful victims only their parents and mates, the females and cubs, elders, the Artisan, and the shamans.

Che dresses her brothers in their best leggings, tunics, and *mackisins*. She hangs carefully about their necks medicine-bags containing wooden and bone images of sacred objects which had been revealed to them in visions. She removes Chetu's hearth and digs a pit on the spot. She lines the pit with stones.

She calls to Chetu, "Nuse. All is prepared."

Her stricken father places in the pit his sons, their stone axes, awls, and other tools and near their hands, their hunting spears.

Che fills containers woven of lake reeds with dried meat and berries and puts them in the pit with other possessions saying softly, "They shall need these on their journey."

Boog sprinkles the corpses with red hematite and iron oxide powders and he sings and dances about the grave calling on the Great Ruling Spirits of the Land of Spirits by all their names: *Manitou, Nanabush, Nanabozho, Glooscap, Wisakedjak."*

Grieving Chetu says to Che, "My unfortunate Ogucen are taken so young, never mated. You are all that is left of my loins' fruits. Would that you were male."

Anguish sears through Che but her father has already turned away.

All about them, females wail pitifully and cast from them their most prized possessions, while the striplings throw handfuls of tundra flowers on the bodies. Che sits silent and still, trying to conceal the pain her father's words have added to the grief she already bears.

At length, they fill in the graves and return the hearths to their places. On her brothers' grave, Che kindles a fire and tends it for four lights, the required length of time for Nanabush to guide the hunters to the happy land where they will once more dance and pursue deer.

She finds some comfort in these ceremonies.

But not so Pak.

As he gazes down at his mate's body in the pit, Kooh in her arms, he loses all control and rails loudly against the sorcerer who has caused it all, vowing vengeance on Laf's head. Boog glares angrily at him but he is too distraught to notice. He throws himself into the pit, screaming, "Ninitegmagan! Ogucen!"

In disgust at such a display, Boog leaves the hut followed by his apprentice.

Moved by reluctant compassion, Che, whom Pak has forbidden to enter the mourning hut, puts aside her dislike of him, marches determined inside and tries to reason with him. "Do not grieve for Kooh. He is fortunate. When he completes the journey to the land of souls, he will find there his loving ninga to feed him and care for him. He will grow to be a great hunter, as you are, Nidjkiwe." It had takes great effort to address this intransigent man as *brother.*

Pak pays her no heed and at length she, too, leaves him there with the bodies.

When morning comes and all the other burials have been completed, Che returns to Pak's hut to find him gone. Quietly, she straightens the disarranged corpses and covers them with earth.

She whispers, "May you find a kindly land, Nimises."

The Artisan finds her there and helps her with her task. He had loved Kooh, as he loves all cubs with his tender artist's heart, and he tends the hearth fire for the requisite four days by Che's side since Chetu is too overcome by his sons' deaths to sit with her.

Seeing Che's misery, the Artisan murmurs, "You felt for your Nimises the feeling for which there is no word, didn't you?"

Che doesn't reply.

"You will miss her."

Tears spurt from Che's eyes. "She was only a female!"

"And therefore of great value to the clan," says the Artisan, unperturbed.

Che turns bitterly on him but hesitates when she sees the sincerity in his lined face. Each groove has been carved by good humour, kindness, and endless patience.

"Do you really believe that?" she asks.

"I know it."

"Then you are one only among many."

The artisan regards her shrewdly. He says, "Little One, you are different as only our clan mother is different but don't shame your nimi be robbing their toil of its value. As for the hunters, let their actions and not their words show you what they carry in their hearts."

The hunters gone and the dead buried, Che has no more time to think of death and fire spirits for everywhere about her life teems and offers her riches. Bara sets the cubs and the three Eyo maidens to gathering birds' eggs in the grasses and duck and geese eggs in the lake reeds. She then instructs them in the digging of roots and lichen bulbs while Che makes tightly woven grass cups to catch the sweet sap of the scrub birch which grows around their underground shelters and others make nets for a coming fishing trip.

Miira makes excuses to join the Eyo females just as Che had once done.

Their tasks completed, the females come together to strip down their pit homes, packing away the hides and their personal possessions and tying the old hut-poles together to be used for weir building at the fishing places. The Artisan distributes among them horn hooks to be used for jigging.

He said, "I'll watch the younger cubs. The striplings are needed for more important tasks."

"He is a good man," Che says to Inik.

"Did you know that the apprentice is his ogucen?" Inik asks.

"How can that be?"

"He had a mate once but she was killed in a rock fall. The apprentice was only a cub but the shaman wanted him."

"You mean that the Artisan gave him up, just like that?"

"It hurt him dreadfully. You know how he adores cubs. He saw the clan's need and bent to it."

"I could never do such a thing."

"Nor I. If I lost Pu, I would die."

Che and Bara are the first prepared for the journey to the lake's end, where they will go to a spot Kiconce discovered on a river leading to the endless lake in the north and build their weirs for spawning salmon. They are also first to arrive at the new campsite and while they wait for the others, they use hooks, dip-nets, and gaffs to catch whitefish trout. In the meantime, the youngest striplings set snares for muskrat and porcupine and break into the beaver lodges which are gradually appearing on the ponds.

Che says to Bara, "After the long heartbreaking winter, this work seems play!"

She now feels one with the Eyo females and little Miira tempts her to good humour with her innocence and ready laughter.

Che says, "I am glad we shall spend a long time catching and drying fish on racks and over open fires until a scout comes to lead us to the place where the hunters decide to camp. I like being alone with the females."

"Don't work too hard," Bara says. "Remember your babe. Narima, come here and help Che."

Che wonders at the sour look which Kraac's mate gives her.

Pak wanders mad upon the tundra and none know where he goes or what demons he seeks. He returns to the Eyo only when the hunt is finished, the fishing and slaughtering completed and a new lake campsite chosen two days to the east. He is a wraith who speaks seldom, who seems calm but whose eyes bulge with outrage. Nevertheless, they accept him back among them, as words spoken in grief are soon forgiven.

Che doesn't forgive him.

She says to Inik, "I don't understand why Laf, though he knows what Pak has said about him, takes pity on the wretch. He actually went to his hut to offer him a new spear he had fashioned."

Inik replies, "Pak treated him cordially enough and accepted the spear."

The people sigh with relief at this reconciliation and are deceived by the bereaved hunter's subdued exterior.

"Laf will be sorry he was so soft," Che predicts.

That night Chetu calls council. Males having fourteen summers build a huge fire in the clearing's center. The Ogima, Kiconce, and Chetu of the Omeeseh take honoured places on either side of the shamans. Beyond them sit Anikeogima, Mizinawa, and the elder hunters of the Omeeseh and the Eyo and opposite these the younger males of both clans mixed together. Many hearts mourn the absence of Che's brothers, the noble hunters Tiga and San. The Artisan with male striplings clustered around him stands back from the fire and in the background shadow, the females stand where they can listen but not be seen.

Che has a feeling that she will not like what she is about to hear.

Kiconce begins, "Manitou, bless your people and guide them. Spirits of Awaskesh and Omeeseh, look on your Totem bearers and reveal to them your counsel!"

Chetu rises. "A time of decision is upon us," he intones, looking about at the hunters' faces reflected in the fire. "The shaman of the Omeeseh has dreamed and, in his dream, he has seen what is to come."

"We would hear this dream," chant the hunters in unison.

Chetu turns to the place where his shaman sits. He is even older than Boog and his body is creased and leathered until it resembles the shrivelled surface of the Kara root. Wispy, white hair hangs in patches from his egg shaped skull and his eyes alone gleam like blue-black quartz. He doesn't move at once, but finally struggles to his feet and speaks. His voice is as thin as a lake breeze singing through cat-tails.

"I have dreamed," he says.

The clans wait.

In the dream, I saw a great land, a sea of grass on which wandered a multitude of reindeer and other animals."

It sounds to Che like the land where they presently squat. Surely they won't be asked to move again.

"It was a land of plenty with a goodly supply of water and fish for the females to catch. Berries grew there and edible roots. In that land dwelt the Giant Reindeer."

They Eyo hunters stir.

The Great Reindeer wandered the land and thrived. Above his head swooped the Owl and they were nijkiwe."

Murmurs of brotherhood and friendship from all assembled.

Che smiles. *And I found nimi.* She looks at the females, singling out Bara and Inik and little Miira. Lara, too, has earned her friendship for though she is just as lovely as Fina had been, she is patient and sensible. She would have to be, living in Fuum's hut, thinks Che with a little grin. She finds that ugly, diminutive hunter aloof and unfriendly. She notes that the faces of Kiconce and her father remain stiff and serious and so also Boog's inscrutable visage. Her unease returns.

The Omeeseh shaman speaks.

There came a time when the Giant Reindeer looked to the east over the grasses and spoke to Owl. 'There are no new mountains in this land, My Companion, and I must see mountains before I die.'

Omeeseh replied, 'Will you leave this place?'

'I will,' said the Reindeer."

Che feels a sinking in her belly.

"Reindeer said, 'Come, Nicimec, Younger Brother, and travel with me.'

"But the owl was saddened. He did not wish to leave the goodly land nor did he desire to wander to the far mountains. Owl said, 'Forgive me, Nisages, Elder Brother, but it is my fate to remain here among the grasses and to hunt the rodent and the hare.'

"Giant Reindeer looked with grief upon his brother.

'Must I journey on alone?'

'You have said it.'"

The shaman stops abruptly, drops to his haunches and drones a sorrowful chant. Boog immediately joins in and the hunters look at one another in despair, the knowledge of coming separation and severed friendship on their faces. Only Pak watches all through eyes veiled in sly malevolence.

Che bites her lip. I will lose my Nuse, too! The rock of resentment that has dwelt in her chest since the day of her brothers' burying shatters. Chetu is a good nuse.

The chant completed, Kiconce rises. He addresses Boog. "Have you also a dream to relate, O Shaman?"

Boog's voice is harsh as he replies, "Always my vision remains the same. It is as the Giant Reindeer told it to young Noha in the old mountains, and as I have dreamed. Always the Eyo must move to the east in search of the land of the New Mountains and the Valley of the Dream."

"The Peoples must part?" Kiconce asks formally.

"It is so."

Melancholy engulfs Che. She feels the cub in her belly move and is reassured. She is now of the Eyo. She belongs to adventurous Noha. Where he goes, she must follow. It is the way of the clans.

But to whom can she run if Noha turns her out?

From the shadows around her comes female wailing but the hunters bow their heads in submission. Beyond the fire, Miira looks hopefully at Laf. Pak's evil eyes are also on the young hunter.

CHAPTER 9

The Outcast

Bara and Kiconce don't seem to notice Che half dozing in the shadows.

"I'm frightened." Bara's voice trembles.

"Not you!" Kiconce gasps. "My brave one?"

Che's eyes open. She looks at Kiconce's suddenly vulnerable face. If Bara fails him, where will he find his strength?

Bara shrugs her big shoulders, "It's just female foolishness. It will pass."

He is not yet convinced. "The Peoples cannot, dare not defy the sayings of the shamans. And what about our ogucen's dream?"

"I know. I'm silly. For a moment I forgot that I have my Napima's arm to guard me."

"I'll let nothing hurt you."

"I know."

But many feel like Bara as with heavy hearts the Eyo take down their huts and gather provisions for their solitary journey into the unknown land. Wind gambols ahead, combing through the grasses as if to make a pathway. The first march takes seven waking-times and during that period, young hunters of both clans construct temporary marriage huts because it might be many suns before either the Eyo or the Omeeseh come across other nomadic clans or meet with the peoples of the new land.

There is, at first, consolation for Che.

Chetu comes to her and speaks words which she will carry always in her heart, "I bid you farewell, Little One. Your Ninga's manitu dwells in you. When she left us for the spirit world, I took no other *ninitegamagan* because there was no room in me for another. Now I lose you who have her visage and her ways, and I am bereft. May you walk in grace as did your Ninga and may your loins bring forth another such as you."

Che can only tremble and bow her head. *He values me! Why did he never tell me?*

One among the Eyo agrees with Boog and looks only to the unknown horizon. It is Noha.

He, too, has a visitor. Laf approaches from the direction of the Omeeseh camp and stands awkwardly before him. "Nidjkiwe, I crave a gift of you."

"Whatever I possess is yours."

"I'm to mate with Miira of the Omeeseh."

"I'm glad for you. She's a comely maiden and strong and has a gentle manitu."

"I'm blessed. I want to prepare a gift for her."

"A fitting thing." Noha remembers the hare blanket that Bara made as a mating present for Che.

"I want this gift to be a fox pelt robe."

Noha waits.

"Assinbo has always been your friend and mentor. Will you come with me on a hunt to speak for me so Assinbo won't be angry when I take his life?"

"I'm honoured to be chosen." They set out that very day on their quest.

While they are gone, Miira works tirelessly preparing bridal things and enjoys the other maidens' scarcely hidden envy, for her tall, lean betrothed is much admired. If she notices Pak's insane eye often upon her, she gives no indication. She is a modest girl and her submission to Laf is born of admiration rather than lust. He, in turn, has been so considerate with her that the brief pain of their one union is superseded by his deliberate gentleness. Now that Miira is to be his mate, she is proud and joyous.

Che and Bara discuss her suitability.

Bara pulls her earlobe. Looks wise. "Mirra is small, like most of you Omeeseh females, delicate and narrow of shoulder and hip."

"Like Inik?" Che asks innocently, knowing that Bara once wondered about her, too.

At Bara's amused smile, Che continues lyrically, "Ah but the Long-faced One finds her skin as pale as the morning sky and admires her smooth, black hair drawn back from a white brow where delicately winged eyebrows frame almond shaped eyes . . ."

Bara's own narrow black eyes fix Che with mock annoyance.

She clucks her tongue. "But is she strong?"

A sober pall falls over her daughter's face. Che replies defiantly. "I told Noha she is strong but actually she's merely willing and bright. Nevertheless, lately I have come to like her a great deal and to feel almost motherly toward her. I'm pleased that Miira will soon be of the Eyo."

"If you are pleased, so am I," says wise Bara. And it is settled.

And it is to Che that Miira turns for counsel, for the clan sickness has taken her ninga. She is dithering about her shortcomings and Che tries to comfort her.

"If you can't do a mate's hard work, Laf must find a second wife to help you. Perhaps Jag?" meaning the strange, antisocial Omeeseh widow who walks alone.

Taking a second mate is not common practice among the peoples but not unknown in certain circumstances. However, Che can't help but smile in sympathy at the dismay on Miira's face. Would I willingly share Noha with a second wife? She asks herself and grins even more widely.

"Don't worry, Miira. I shall always be nearby to help you as will the other Eyo females."

Che is not to be allowed to protect her friend.

On the second day of her mating preparations, when Laf is off hunting foxes with Noha, Miira sees soar over the camp a sleek big bird with glorious green and blue wings.

She murmurs, "If only I could creep upon such a bird on its nest and pluck those feathers to adorn Laf's spear . . ." She inquires among the Omeeseh maidens if any know where these birds nest.

"I've seen them sitting on their eggs among the reeds on the opposite lakeshore," one plump maiden tells her. But when asked if she will accompany Miira there, she declines. She too is busily preparing for mating with an Eyo hunter.

Miira searches out Che who is tailoring new leggings for Noha. "Leave your work, Nimi, and come with me on an adventure."

Che smiles ruefully and says, "Soon you will learn that such as I have no time for adventures. I must remain here but you may go. However, you must not wander far; there's much work to do."

"I won't," Miira promised as she runs like a laughing fawn across the clearing.

Neither of them notice the scrawmy figure which detaches itself from among the trees near the campsite to dog her footsteps.

Miira has wandered several miles along the curving shoreline, stopping to pick and eat sweet smelling, lake coloured berries on the sandy banks. It is a gentle morning and the sun's fingers smooth a golden glow across Mirra's high cheekbones and black silken hair. However the sun is also hot and her mackisins' soles burn her feet. Coming on a quiet inlet, she sits on a water sleeked rock, removes her mackisins, lifts her tunic and wades into the cool waters.

From behind a sand ridge, crazy-eyed Pak stares with blood lust on the maiden's limbs, imagining her naked and helpless beneath him. Miira, completely unaware of his presence, wades deeper into the water, a happy humming on her lips.

Suddenly cruel hands grab her long, black hair, yank her on her back and drag her through the water to the shore. She screams then chokes on water splashing in her face, her nose, her mouth. Birds flee from the grasses at the sound but no human ear other than Pak's hears her frantic cries. Ruthless hands are everywhere, ripping away her tunic and pummelling her face and breasts.

Tiny Miira fights, scratching and biting, but this only adds to the attacker's frenzy. A mackisined foot strikes her a jolting blow in the stomach and she doubles over retching. He flings her backwards once more, straddles her, and touches his sharp, reindeer horn knife to her throat. She looks up into Pak's pitiless eyes.

When he has finished with her, Pak wades into the lake, washes blood from his body and the knife. He slowly rinses his leggings, puts them on wet and returns to shore, ignoring his victim. He strides off to the campsite.

When sleep time comes, Che looks for Miira among the huts, ready to share the tale of her adventure. Unsuccessfully. She asks Bara who always knows everyone's whereabouts.

"I have not seen her." Bara frowns.

Alarmed, Che says, "She begged me to go with her on an adventure and I let her go alone!"

"Calm yourself. We'll ask the others."

They do so for some time without success until they come at last upon the fat maiden to whom Miira first spoke about the bird. "She went to search for the big bird with feathers the hue of grass and sky. I told her the nests are on the shore opposite." She points across the lake.

Che stares out over the water. "It's a far journey to the other side," new possibilities springing to mind to assuage her ominous guilt.

Practical Bara says, "It's possible she decided to build a shelter and rest. She will return after sleep."

Che is not convinced. "I think there's something wrong. May I go to look for her?"

"And have two of my nimi lost?" Bara chides. Then seeing the frozen look on Che's face continues, "When the hunters return, they shall search out the wanderer. And may her new mate scold her heartily. Come, *Nindanis*, Younger Sister, there is nothing more to do here. Let's return to our tasks."

Che reluctantly obeys.

Noha finds Miira.

When he and Laf return to discover Miira's nuse readying himself for a search, Noha wrenches the tale of the bird plumes from a deeply worried Che.

She begs to go with them but Noha clicks his tongue and says, "Stay in the camp."

Kraac and Ecakik join the tracking and all converge on the inlet to find Noha, as usual ahead of everyone else, kneeling beside Miira's ravaged body. He tries to shield his friend from the pitiful sight but is thrust aside. Laf looks long. Colour drains from him. The homely face with its ready smile and laughing eyes is suddenly old. A rumble begins in his throat, surges upwards and spews out in one word, "PAK".

He turns on his heel and sprints for camp.

Noha hesitates, reaching a consoling hand to Miira's desolate father who is now kneeling beside him, but Kraac put his own hand on the elder hunter's shoulder and motions Noha to follow Laf.

Noah's thoughts run as quickly as his feet. Laf must be right. Only Pak would rape and kill. He is the only hunter who is eaten with enough mindless hatred to do such a horrendous thing. The Eyo don't shed the blood of their kind under any circumstances, no matter what the provocation! If that were permitted, the clan would long ago have wasted away to nothing. Unthinkable crime!

Noha flies along the lakeshore, his mackisins barely skimming the sand but Laf, inspired by his awful purpose, outdistances him and reaches the campsite before him. Noha finds the two hunters facing one another across the council fire. Laf stands taut and proud, his face calm, his eyes relentless. He has cast aside his spear and he clutches a reindeer-antler knife, the same kind of weapon that must have torn away Miira's life. Facing him across the fire, Pak crouches, back humped, legs bent and ready to spring. His eyes are now completely mad, his teeth bared and saliva dripping from his lips in long, silver ribbons to the ground.

Noha flinches. Surely Pak is possessed by a matchee manitu.

He hovers, not knowing what to do. News of the confrontation has spread quickly through the encampment and the people are gathering in a wide circle around the two figures at the fire. They don't know what has happened but they know that Laf and Noha have been searching for Miira and that Laf has returned without her and now stands like an avenging manitu, a hunter facing a demon. Miira's nuse thunders into the clearing, followed by Kraac and Ecakik.

Che runs to Ecakik, pulling at his massive shoulder. She breathes, "Miira?"

He looks compassionately down at her, "Dead. We think it was Pak." He turns away to grab the arm of Miira's nuse. Kraac takes the other arm and through what follows, they hold him fast.

"Dead? Miira? No. No! NO! I should have gone with her!" Che wrings her hands, looks wildly about. "She can't be dead!"

Inik, then Bara, run to her and put their arms around her. "What is it, Nimi?"

But Che can't speak.

The shamans suddenly emerge from Boog's hut where they have been discussing the Eye's coming departure. They stand just outside the entrance, two ancient figures of power, but the adversaries at the fire pay them no heed. A rattling noise dribbles from Pak's throat as he edges his way around the flames. His obvious purpose is to kill Laf as he slew Miira. Laf is still, his eyes following Pak.

Noha can bear it no longer. He calls softly to his friend, trying to reach through his agony without distracting him from the deadly threat of Pak.

"You must not slay him, Nidjkiwe. It is the law!"

There is no response.

Noha looks at the shamans but they are silent. He turns helplessly to Kiconce, who has emerged from his hut, and to his brothers. All seem to understand the situation, but they make no move to interfere. Noha knows why. This is too inconceivable a thing. Not only has a hunter shed a maiden's frail blood but her lover is about to compound the evil by killing her slayer. No one can doubt that Laf is more than a match for the cringing, evil Pak. But Laf changes that. Suddenly, his right hand unclenches and he throws his knife into the grass. Both of his palms open upward as he turns toward Pak. It is not a gesture of peace but of contempt. He will face Pak as Miira had, weaponless. With an unearthly screech, Pak springs on him, stone knife raised. Noha begins a lunge toward them but a sinewy hand grabs him and swings him off balance.

Kiconce growls, "Don't interfere!"

Laf's hands raise instinctively to Pak's wrists, stopping them for a second in midair, but his adversary is possessed of mad strength and he squirms like a serpent in Laf's grasp. A foot darts out, hooks Laf's ankle, and the hunter falls backwards with a thud. Pak is immediately on top of him.

However, Laf is no weak maiden and he doesn't panic or lose his grip but, completely ignoring Pak's mad threshing, he concentrates all his strength on the arm that holds the knife, pushing it away from him slowly, inexorably; he forces it down and back until Pak's wrist bends at an unnatural angle.

A sudden loud snap.

Pak shrieks.

The knife falls to the ground and Pak rolls away and lies cradling his shattered wrist, sobbing like an injured cub.

For a full minute Laf stands over him, the retrieved knife in his fist. He seems impassive, dead. Noha holds his breath and, when Laf finally throws away the knife, a relieved sigh gushes from the spectators. Noha runs to his friend but Laf walks past him, unseeing. The people move aside as Laf strides towards the spot where Miira lies. Noha snatches up a skin blanket and runs after him.

Che pulls away from Bara and follows.

As she trots along, her thoughts whirl. Why didn't I go with her? If only I had listened. All she wanted was to go on an adventure. I could have; I should have . . . He wouldn't have dared attack two of us. I would have scratched his eyes from his head! Poor little nimi. So sweet, so happy, so full of innocence. I should have known that Pak would do something like this. There is a demon in him. I knew it! I knew it! May he rot!

Poor little maiden . . . Che clamps a hand over her mouth to stifle her sobs.

Noha will not let her near, but she sees. She smells the sickly sweet odour of the blood. She sees the gaping wound in the pale throat. She sees Noha tenderly drape a blanket over the ravaged body. She sees the small brown hand trailing in the sand as Laf lifts his bride. Once more Che trots behind them as they return to camp, breathless now but determined to keep up.

Laf and Miira's nuse allow her to help with the burying beneath the hearth of the marriage hut.

As for Pak, possessed of a demon or not, he has committed the unspeakable crime and must suffer the only punishment terrible enough to eradicate it from Eyo memory. He is stripped of all but his breechclout. One spear is placed in his hand and his medicine bag hung around his neck. He stands near the council fire, a forlorn figure, quiet now, the demon seemingly at rest. The Artisan has tied around the wretch's wrist a makeshift splint of sticks and thongs; he now gently hangs a small pemmican sack about Pak's neck.

Boog approaches the criminal.

Pak shrinks away.

Boog pronounces the sentence sadly, quietly. "You have done the unthinkable, unforgivable deed. You have shed the life blood of the People. Henceforth you don't exist. Go from this place. Let the eyes of mankind never more rest upon your face. Let your name never again be spoken."

At this, he turns his back on Pak and all of those present, hunters, females, and cubs do likewise.

Che feels a moment's compunction but hardens her heart. *Let the female-killer be gone!*

Pak stands very still and then turns on his heel and walks slowly from the camp. His dog slinks from a hut. It senses this is no ordinary expedition but with tail wagging, it begins to follow its master. Old Mizinawa, infuriated, trots over to restrain the animal.

The Artisan's voice breaks the stillness. "Are the Eyo so lacking in compassion even to such as this? Let the cur go! And none contradict him, not even the shamans.

Che and the Artisan come accidentally upon the outcast, after three suns. He hangs by his neck on a hide thong from a rock outcropping. The Artisan kicks away the growling dog and cutting down the evil smelling corpse, buries it at the rock's base. The dog lies on the grave and will not come away.

Che watches.

The Artisan says to Che, "Tell no one what has passed."

CHAPTER 10

Menokemeg — Summer

Noha and Che are not the only ones watching Laf.

Laf is much changed, Kraac thinks privately. The spark of happy humour that always lit his face and heart is gone, extinguished with Miira's life.

He hears Noha say, "I feel sorry for Laf but he is unwise to carry a burden of grief for so long, especially when it concerns only a maiden not yet possessed. After all, The *One Whose Name Shall Not Be Spoken* once stole an intended mate from me and I didn't languish!"

Kraac sighs tiredly. Noha chooses to forget how he raced wildly from camp when Pak won Fina and returned only because he killed the old mammoth.

Menokemeg, Summer follows the Eyo on the journey through the south-east grasslands after a melancholy parting from the Omeeseh. They move among soft winds and long, bright nights. They move steadily, finding always before them the grasses, the wetlands, the lakes, and a good supply of animals and birds to fill their stomachs. They hastily construct huts on two occasions but move on soon, driven not by the search for sustenance but at the instigation of the shaman and of a few, like Kiconce's three sons, who feel stirrings of a new feeling, a desire to see what is new for its own sake. The Eyo majority follow out of obedience and because it is their way.

One day, young Dinkka runs into the hunt camp shrieking, "Rhino! Rhino!"

Kraac has heard of this dangerous, grey, woolly beast with a horn protruding from its brow and a second and larger one from above its big snout, but he has never seen the creature.

Noha pounces on Dinkka. "Tell us!"

Dinkka quickly explains and with great uproar the hunters are off! However, the animal proves almost impossible to slay on the open plain and charges anything that moves.

Kraac says to Ecakik, "It's really a waste of time to hunt him."

"Yes, but it makes them happy. I even saw Laf show some enthusiasm."

"Then we hunt!" cries Kraac, grinning.

They stalk the rhino but he is too wily for them. As they track him, the land stretches changeless before them, except when they journey north almost to the area where the mouths of rivers suck up silvery fish from the endless lake.

"Am I wrong or does the endless lake seem closer now?" Kraac asks Ecakik. "Could it be that our way is narrowing, or the seas rising across the spirit bridge?"

"I don't know," says the bewildered Ecakik.

Kraac doesn't discuss his suspicion with the others because they are afraid of the Endless Lake, thinking that, were they to be swept out on it, they would never return; and that slimy evil beings of the deep would drag them down and grind their bones; and worst of all that their spirits would be forever trapped beneath the sombre waves. The hunters do go within sight of the lake but always direct their females to set their fishing nets well up on the rivers away from the endless lake's dangers.

But Kraac isn't so sure. He finds himself more and more curious about the lake.

Before the clan separation, Laf chose a second Omeeseh female because the Eyo have no way of knowing when they might again encounter other peoples. To Che's chagrin, his odd choice is the nondescript, aging widow, Jag, who seldom speaks and never smiles—the very one Che teased Miira about. With her greying, unkempt hair, her flat chested body, her long, sharp nose and heavily lidded eyes, Jag is unattractive indeed.

Bara says to her daughters, "Jag is skilled and shows particular facility with her bone needle but she avoids our friendship."

Lara lifts her hauntingly lovely face from her work. She is dark skinned like many of the people and her eyes seem almost opaque so black are they. She says, "Che, Inik, and I have all approached Jag at various times, as did Laf's ninga, and she received us with mute courtesy, but she doesn't seem to enjoy our company."

Gradually they leave Jag to her own resources. Bara alone persists in her efforts to reach her. One day, Che hears her ask Jag, "Would you help me to gather herbs for medicines?" and seems pleased when Jag agrees.

Che observes them as they wander over the plains, digging and plucking.

"You have done this before," Bara says to Jag.

"I used to watch the Omeeseh shaman," Jag replies shortly.

Che says to Bara when they are alone, "Should we tell the apprentice about Jag?"

"A good notion, nimi." They make sure that the apprentice, now a tall stripling, is told.

"Maybe she could help you select herbs. She knows more than I do," Bara says to him.

"She's almost uncanny," Che adds.

They are well rewarded for their trouble when the apprentice seeks out Jag. Soon the two are inseparable, spending long periods away from camp in their search for medicinal berries, poplar bark, roots, spider webs, and the puff balls used to stop bleeding. Luckily for Jag, Laf doesn't resent this, as he has already learned that Jag is not really interested in males or copulation, although she is willing to open her legs to him as befits a mate.

Nor does he really care, Che decides. He'll never again feel for anyone what he felt for Miira.

Amazingly, Boog also takes an interest in the strange female, perhaps seeing in her a possible successor, as it is not unknown for a female to be a shaman, and this gives further sanction to the relationship between the apprentice and Jag. Before long, she is being admitted alone to the shaman lodge, the only female other than Bara and Che to be so honoured, and she spends much time there.

"I wonder why the Long-faced One chose that ugly creature," Narima says one day to Che.

The females are gathered together at the hide scraping, a task always made lighter by being shared. Jag is, in fact, the only one who hasn't joined them..

Annoyed as much at Narima's critical carping as at Jag's laxity, Che nevertheless speaks quietly so that the others may not hear. "She's a good enough mate," glancing at Inik and Bara who are the only ones nearby. Inik looks up with interest but Bara's moon face displays no reaction. "She doesn't neglect her hunter," Che continues. "She sees to it that his leggings and tunics are mended and that there is always a new set of foot coverings ready for him when the old ones are worn out in the chase."

Now Che is saying only what she thinks fair and seemly, a habit she had recently acquired which makes her life easier. But privately, she pities Laf. She knows how it feels to have a detached mate and she is interested to realize that even a hunter can suffer that fate.

Pretty Inik moves closer and surprises Che by also defending Jag, though Che knows that she likes her no more than most of the others, indeed than Che herself.

Inik says, "She keeps his hearth fire burning." But then she asks archly, "I wonder if she shares his sleeping platform and heats him in other ways."

"Of course she does," Che says, laughing in spite of herself. She always finds it hard to resist Inik's innocent mischief though she pretends to disapprove. She notes that, since Inik hasn't found it necessary to keep her voice low, lovely Lara has overheard them and edges closer. Che gives a hide a vicious scrape. That hateful Fuum should have mated with Jag and left Lara for Laf.

Scrawny Fuum has proved to be the most ugly little man whom Che has ever known. And he is extremely hard to get along with. Only big Quork follows him like a dumb shadow, and there is something distasteful to Che about the two though they are good hunters and are often included in Noha's group.

"But Jag speaks to the Long-faced One only when necessary," Narima interrupts Che's thoughts, making her dislike of Jag quite plain in her tone.

"It's true that she shows Laf no affection," Inik agrees.

Knowing how important such displays are to Inik. *And would be to me if I received any . . .* Che replies carefully, "Laf seems to prefer that arrangement. And Noha told me that he's proud of the friendship between his mate and the shaman."

"He may be proud of her but how does she feel? If she feels at all!" Narima, whose emotions are quick to rise if not always long lasting, challenges.

Bara has joined them unnoticed. "Enough wagging tongues," she scolds.

The others start and look with guilty eyes at the ground, the sky, their work, everywhere but at their clan mother's round face.

Bara speaks again, "Remember that the Eyo don't consider *the feeling for which there is no word* to be a necessity between mates. Some enjoy this kind of attachment. Some don't."

Che's hands tremble against the reindeer hide that she is cleaning on a flat rock. In her womb, the babe stirs.

"Some of us are pleasured when our mates fill us with life-sap. Some aren't," Bara preaches.

Inik giggles and is quickly silenced by a nudge from Che, for she will countenance no disrespect, even if unintentional, of Bara.

The latter ignores this side play. "But let it be known that among the Eyo, if your mate doesn't satisfy you, you may leave him and return to your Nuse's hut," Bara says.

Che squirms. Why does she keep looking at me? Besides, my Nuse is far away.

"What about cubs?" Inik asks curiously. "What would happen to them?"

"If they are male they belong, of course, to the hunter—to give or not to give. A girl cub, the female may take if her Nuse and new mate don't object and there is plenty of food."

"Such a thing couldn't happen to us," Narima claims, looking scared.

Bara doesn't answer Narima's comment but eyes her narrowly. However, her gaze then travels to beautiful Lara who is listening intensely, her work idle in her hands.

Che sees this. Bara is worried about Lara and Narima is too self-centred to notice.

As if to prove this, Narima asks, "Why is there no word for the feeling I have for my mate and my cub?"

"Who knows?" Bara replies mysteriously.

Inik grins impishly and said, "There are many words for the other thing."

Big Whea, Quork's officious mate, guffaws. The others titter. Even Bara smiles but Che bites her lip and avoids their eyes. Though Noha still mounts her often and can be helpful when he wishes, it needs only the presence of a hunter, any hunter, or the sight of some animal in the distance to wipe her completely from his notice. Sometimes she wishes he was more like Kraac who seems frigid but is not if one listens to Narima's innuendoes, or even like Ecakik who adores his Inik almost foolishly. Even huge, belligerent Quork acts like a steppe stallion in heat around his unattractive Whea with her knot of a nose, her unruly hair, and massive arms and legs.

Che tells herself, "At least Noha isn't like Fuum who obviously can't bear the sight of Lara. And she such a beauty!

There is something sadly wrong with that Fuum, she decides.

During that long, peaceful summer, a cub is born to Noha and Che. When her travail begins, Che goes, accompanied by Bara and Inik, to a separate small hut which she has built.

At first, the wrenching, grinding pain makes her groan. "I'll be torn to pieces!"

"Not so. Not so," Bara says calmly. "Here, bite this." She puts a shard of clean wood between Che's teeth.

Inik bends anxiously over Che and bathes her face with cool water. "Courage, Nimi. It will pass."

"What about the cub," Che grunts. "How can it survive?"

Bara reassures her. "It will survive. And so will you. The spirit of pain will issue from your mouth if you scream. Scream lustily. Your hips are wide. You are made to be a ninga."

But the wrenching agony has Che once more in its grip and she is too occupied with recognizing it and realizing that she can't run from it to cry out. She snorts and storms and threshes, determined now to deliver this cub with valour no matter what happens.

Bara examines her quickly. "It comes!" she says. "Here, Nimi, help me to hold her!"

Between them, they haul Che to a squatting position over a clean piece of hide and supporting her with their strong arms, hold her upright as she strains and pushes, her breath coming in gasps between animal-like yowls.

"How unseemly it is!" she cries idiotically and the others chortle as the cub shoots suddenly from her body. They place Che gently on her back and Inik takes the cub and clears its mouth of mucus and examines it carefully.

"It's perfect! It's male!" she squeals.

Tears rivulet Che's face and she says, "He will be pleased." Her companions know to whom she refers.

Che sighs as Bara places the wet babe on her stomach. *Now surely Noha will have for me the feeling for which there is no word.*

There is a sound and a movement at the door of the birthing hut and they turned to stare at the creature who appears there.

Noha is away from camp, a new one on a lofty outcropping of flat grey rock beyond which spread miles of beryl coloured grasses sprinkled with dark spruce tree groves. It is the highest land-point yet encountered by the Eyo. The shaman and Kiconce think it a good omen for the discovery of the new mountains. It is late afternoon when the hunters stride up the hillside, wading through the knee-high pungent grass and cup shaped crimson flowers. The hunt has finally been successful and they are in high spirits and eager to relate the story of their rhino kill. Laf carries the tusk trophies because he was the one to deliver the killing blow.

Noha is so excited that he doesn't know whether to be envious or not, for they had finally trapped the elusive rhino due to Laf's ingenuity.

One night they had been gathered morosely around a yellow licked campfire when Laf said, "Why don't we dig a pit, concealing it with branches of larch, spruce, and alder intertwined, and drive the rhino into it?"

"That could work," said Kraac approvingly.

"But we have no branches," Dinkka said.

"You striplings could gather them while we track and we could meet you at a prearranged spot before the rhino hunt," Kraac suggested.

"We will do it!" Dinkka cried.

And they did.

There were now nine striplings and Dinkka was their accepted leader. They gathered the branches and, when the cinder grey rhino was sighted, dug the pit, placed the willow covering over it, and enticed the rhino into chasing them by walking downwind of the beast. Since the animal was too blind to see even them among the tall grasses, it was a simple matter to lure it into the pit. There the hunters attacked it with spears and finally slew the brave creature. Since it had been Laf's idea to dig the pit, he was allotted the honour of the final spear thrust.

As the hunters now walk up the hill to the main camp, cubs come scrambling to meet them.

Noha sees Pu among them.

Pu has grown much in one summer. His head sticks up like a brown ball from the grass as he thrusts the fronds aside with tanned arms already losing their baby fat. Although Ecakik, a year before, would have scooped his son into his arms, this would not now be seemly, so he allows the cub to walk beside him, his shoulder brushing his thigh, and to carry his blooded spear. Pu keeps glancing back at Noha.

Suddenly a delegation of females appears over the hill's crest. They are dressed in their finest tunics and have bedecked themselves with bright necklaces of shell and rodent bones and bird claws. In their midst is Bara's bulk and, at her side, sturdy Che. And in Bara's arms lies a naked infant, its skin still wrinkled and red, its small face topped with a thicket of long, fine, black hair!

Noha stops in mid-stride and then hurries toward the group, his ardent gaze on the infant. He stands before Bara, breathing heavily, his face flushes with pleasure. Bara offers the cub to him.

As he reaches out to take it, he sees the tiny organ between its legs.

A male!

He is consumed by pride and tenderness as the cub squirms in his arms and he looks sideways at Che's bent head. *Surely she knows how grateful I am.* But he says nothing directly to her and doesn't notice the stricken look on her face.

Some days after the feasting on rhino meat and the ritual dancing in which Kraac plays the part of the rhino attacking and being slain by Laf, the Eyo gather at the council fire on a summer's light night. Quiet mantles the people and the females draw close to the hunters' circle. Kiconce stands with ceremony, awaiting Bara. In time she comes to him bearing once more the newborn cub. She stands before Kiconce, as the grandfather of the infant rather than as Ogima, and places the sleeping infant in his arms.

Kiconce speaks. "Let the ninga of the cub come forth."

Che steps into the fire circle and modestly bows.

"Nindanis," Kiconce says, "you have brought forth a male cub of the bloodline of the Giant Reindeer's people. You have done well. Tell us, has *Manitou* sent *Wisana* to bless the infant's birth?"

"Yes, Ogima."

A relieved sigh from the onlookers.

"Tell us of the Wisana."

Che raises her head, her eyes on Kiconce. This is the proudest moment of her life so far and she savours it. *Listen, Noha, listen and hear what a mate you have!*

"When my time came," she says, her voice shaking, "I retired to the birthing hut. With me went the mate of Ogima and my Nimi. When I had laboured for a time, I brought forth a male cub and as he lay, still attached to my body by the life cord, there was a noise outside the birthing hut." She pauses then says triumphantly, "It was the bark of the she fox!"

The clan murmurs.

Che continues, "We awaited the will of Manitou with fear and longing. Through the hut door, the vixen came. She had long since discarded her snowy winter's fur and wore a yellow, brindled coat. In her mouth was a pup, still blind, no larger than a mouse. She bent to my infant, looking at it with her amber eyes and then she laid the pup on the hearth near my cub and licked some blood from my cub's flesh. I was anxious for the infant's safety but this changed to joy as the vixen spoke."

She said, 'The Great Manitou has sent me as the Wisana of your cub. Always will I help him and give my friendship to him, as I have to his Nuse before him. In return, he must never hunt or harm one of my kind.'

'It shall be as you wish,' I told her."

Satisfied, the vixen once more picked up her pup in her jaws and left the hut."

A delighted muttering rises from the Eyo because this coming of a summer fox as Wisana is a wonderful omen indeed, since Assinbo has always been Noha's mentor and through him, mentor of the clan.

Noha grins. Ecakik puts a congratulatory hand on his shoulder. Even Kraac lets his approval show, though he is not looking at Noha but at Che as if noting how small and thin she is and yet how very gallant.

"You are blessed," Kiconce says to Che.

Che then retires to the shadows and Noha steps forward.

"Have you chosen a name for the male cub?" Kiconce asks him.

"I have, Ogima. He will be called Rin," Noha replies and then steps backward.

There is a short silence and then Kiconce with studied dignity lifts the cub toward the sky and the pale dancing stars and intones a prayer.

Great Manitou, *Father of all things, impart your blessing to this male cub, Rin. Spirits of the* Wejig, *big dipper; the* Binesemikan, *milky way; the* Ahnung, *starry heavens; the* Waté, *northern lights; the* Kewadenahmung, *north star, light his way in the long night. Spirit of* Keewatin, *have pity on his man weakness at the time of snow. Spirit of our land,* Bdakim, *feed him. Great Creator of the Earth,* Nanabozho, *fill his loins with the sap of life."*

He calls one by one upon all of the powers of the spirit world to give their blessing to the name, *Rin*, and to the cub on whom it is bestowed and, when he has completed the prayer, he hands the cub to the nearest hunter and stands, arms upraised in silent supplication, as the naked babe is passed from one person to the next until every adult member of the clan has held, examined the babe and called it by its name.

When the ceremony is complete, the Eyo return to their huts. Noha and Che, whose time apart is completed, walk side by side to theirs, the cub in its ninga's arms. When they have reached their own warm hearth, Che wraps Rin in the hare blanket, her mating gift from Noha, and places him on a bed of boughs between the sleeping platform and the fire.

Though Noha seems exceedingly pleased, he says nothing of it to her. She lies down beside him and turns to him when his hands began to search her body.

Her heart says, "He is the same. I have given to him the greatest gift, and he is the same."

But as usual his hands bring to her such great release that she swells moaning to their magic.

The Eyo remain in the camp for the summer. It is a long, pleasant summer not, however, without its shadows. It is during those days that Anikeogima, Second Leader of the Eyo, meets his sad fate.

Kraac finds his remains and reads the signs.

He must have been caught alone on the open grasslands with no rock or hill for shelter, when yesterday's sudden thunderstorm sped from the south. Perhaps a chance lightening bolt panicked nearby reindeer and the beasts came down on him like a swarm of wasps. His spear would have been useless.

Kraac finds the splintered spear where Temia dropped it. He examines the death scene. Temia had leaped on the nearest deer, grasped its branched antlers and twisted its neck back until the animal flipped on its side so he could shelter behind its body, then he cut its throat and crouched as near the ground as he could.

Kraac conjectures that for a time, the spirits protected the hunter but at last a flying hoof struck him in the temple and he fell unconscious. By the time the herd had passed, Temia was what now lay at Kraac's feet, a wreckage of broken bones and flesh, hunters' blood mixed on the ground with that of the reindeer behind whom he had sheltered.

So many hunters lost to disease! And now this! Tears stand in Kraac's eyes as he carries Temia to the camp where he is buried with special ceremony. In due course, Kiconce calls a council to choose the next *Anikeogima*, Second Leader. Several names such as ancient Mizinawa's are put forward and all are considered but it is finally decided by everyone that, since the elder hunters are getting very old and slow, Ecakik, with his youth, his silent patience and great courage, will be the best choice as advisor to Ogima. And so Ecakik is named *Anikeogima.*

Narima says meaningfully to Kraac, "Ecakik will not now be considered for the place of Ogima when your Nuse, in his time, shall pass over to the land of the spirits," then sulks when Kraac looks disapprovingly at her.

With characteristic placidity, Ecakik shows neither pride nor disappointment at the decision.

However, others are more mindful of the future.

CHAPTER 11

Pu and the Ptarmigan

Ecakik has given Pu his first spear with a sharp stone chip resined to its tip. It is to replace the pointed sticks Pu and his friends use to pierce targets of rabbit-skin filled with sand and tied to low willow branches. Pu is holding the tiny spear when he steals off downhill from camp.

He smiles mischievously. My first hunt. Ninga will think I am with the Artisan or listening to Boog's stories or even gathering reindeer moss to dry for her hearth. But I'll be hunting ptarmigan.

He considers the ptarmigan a handsome bird with its snow-white winter plumage and black tail feathers. Above its dark eyes it displays vermilion, wattled combs like inquisitive eyebrows. And it struts proudly as it wanders along digging with feathered feet for seeds, insects, and plant shoots.

Pu's walk is much like the ptarmigan's.

It is a fine morning with a clear azure sky and sun warm on the skin. The plain is dry above permafrost and the grass had not yet turned brown but stretches verdant into the distance. Pu holds his spear at arm's length and shoulder height, for there are thickets to circumnavigate and rich meadows to cross; a small copse of birch and willow near a burbling stream; cotton grass already in flower, looking like white miniature clouds fallen from the sky and speared on stalks.

Pu runs his tongue over his upper teeth. This should be a good place to flush waders who feed on water insects. However, today I shall kill a fat ptarmigan.

He knows that if he waits until autumn, he will see many ptarmigan in the brilliant, deliciously perfumed berry patches.

But now is his time.

He comes suddenly on the ptarmigan in an open area on a herb slope where rose coloured saxifrage and arctic bluebells grow among the bare rocks. A cock sits on a stone near its mate who squats concealed in its nest full of reddish yellow eggs under a dwarf willow bush. The cock sings a strident song. The hen's speckled, umber and brown summer cloak blends perfectly into the vegetation but the cock . . . as Ecakik has told Pu that Nanabozho intended . . . stands out like a white swan on a lake, a target to attract enemies away from the nesting hen.

Pu chortles quietly.

Slowly he lowers himself to his belly and crawls, taking advantage of every rock, every tuft of grass and flower. The ptarmigan sings. It takes Pu a long time to come within throwing distance but the male ptarmigan is still on the rock. Finally, with infinite slowness, Pu comes to his knees and at last to his feet. The bird's head turns, globular eyes flickering. Pu raises one hand to his fox-tooth amulet and hurls the tiny spear.

He misses.

The cock is instantly upon him, buffeting him with its short, powerful wings, clawing and screeching as Pu waves his arms ineffectually. If the bird flies off now, it will escape, but the cock, mindful of its mate's danger, presses the attack again and again until Pu manages to get hold of its neck and twist. The bird jerks twice, goes limp.

With an ecstatic shout, Pu scoops up his spear and runs, runs, runs; when near camp he slows and slings the dead bird carelessly over his shoulder. The moment he enters the camp he is surrounded by admiring cubs and adults, for a male's first kill is a special event in clan life. Inik receives the ptarmigan with much ceremony, pretending not to notice Pu's badly scratched face, arms, and chest.

To his relief, she doesn't scold him for going off without permission but says, "I shall pluck your kill and clean it, reserving the claws, beak, and a few of the prettiest feathers for your amulet-bag."

Pu watches proudly as she cuts the meat into strips and puts them, along with all the bones, into a pouch full of water. She heats stones and drops them one by one into the container, adds herbs and says, "It's ready."

By this time all the Eyo have gathered, from the smallest infant, Rin, to Boog himself. Boog prays and self-conscious Pu does a brief, awkward dance describing his hunt. Mizinawa passes around the ptarmigan stew. Everyone eats a tiny morsel until even the bones are sucked, crunched to powder, and swallowed. They pour the juice into shells and consume it to the last drop.

Che says crossly to Lara, "Such a fuss. Someone should have punished him for going off like that. He might have been lost or hurt. He might even do it again."

However, now that Pu has proven himself, he seems satisfied. He returns to his first loves, stories and bone carving.

The Artisan confides to Che, "That cub has an artist's manitu; he already produces fine fishhooks."

Suspecting that he might have found, in Pu, a substitute son who matches his own skill, Che agrees.

The Artisan rambles on, "I hope to mold this talented cub. He has a loving, brave heart and is the darling of all the adults. Even Boog has taken an interest in him. Think what a leader he could become, a man combining Ecakik's bravery with Kraac's keen mind and your mate's bottomless eagerness and curiosity. If along with this he is an artisan, all the better!"

Che wants to say, "Isn't this a heavy burden of expectation to place on one so young?" But she forbears.

So the old man sets about his task, answering the cub's endless questions and watching satisfied as his dreams for Pu sprout like wet tundra in spring. Meanwhile, Che tries to ignore uneasiness when she looks into Pu's bright eyes. The day after Pu's adventure with the ptarmigan, Che sits with the Artisan as he tells the cub the tale of the world's beginning. He speaks to him from waking time to sleeping. He tells him about the Great God, *Manitou,* whose home is the sky and who keeps a watchful eye over every star and whose voice can be heard speaking in the breeze or howling in the tempest.

Manitou appointed the greater spirits as guardians of the lesser and sent some to earth to dwell with men," says Artisan. "*One of these, Nanabozho, possessed great power. He dwelt near a lake of evil monsters and with him dwelt a son, Wolf.'*

Pu grins. His nuse's Wisana is the wolf.

"Nanabozho had warned his son not to venture on the lake when it was covered with winter ice but his son disobeyed him and the monsters of the deep broke the ice with a mighty cracking and swallowed the boy!"

Pu gasps and then looks ashamed.

Time he learned he isn't invincible, Che thinks tartly.

The Artisan puts a hand on Pu's.

"Nanabozho waited until summer for his revenge and, when the monsters came on the shore to sun, he transformed himself into a giant tree and wounded one of them."

Pu smiles smugly but the Artisan's face is stern.

"Their anger was so great that they plunged into the waters and raised such a storm as was never before seen. Even the mountain peaks were inundated!"

Pu's eyes now round with dismay and Che is beginning to feel sorry for him. The Artisan relents.

However, Nanabozho was not to be destroyed. He floated on a giant hollow log and sent his servant, the muskrat, to the lake bottom for a paw full of mud. From this, Nanabozho created a mud cake which grew and grew until it had grown into a new world. And when he returned to his home among the stars, Nanabozho lit fires in the heavens to remind man of his watchful care. These are Waté, the lights in the north."

"Are there many spirits?" Pu asks.

"Countless. Everything seen or unseen possesses a spirit and the spirits of all things are one. Even the rock upon which you sit has a spirit within. And of these, Man is one of the least. So we must always remember this and offer prayers to spirits disturbed by our actions."

"Like when you kill an animal?"

"Yes."

"Who is the greatest of the spirits?"

"Our clan believes that Manitou is the nuse of all."

"Will the spirits speak to me?"

"When you come to manhood and the time of fast, perhaps they will, if you are worthy."

"Do the spirits guard me?"

Che feels the old uneasiness fill her. A shadow crosses the Artisan's kindly face. "At birth some are visited by Wisana who will ever after guard them."

"Did this happen at my birth?" Pu persists.

The Artisan's face closes. "I do not know," he says, smiling reassuringly when the boy shows his disappointment. "But did not the shaman, himself, present you with your amulet bag? Is this not enough honour for such a hunter?"

The boy grins at the word *hunter* and fingers the amulet bag which holds the fox tooth and the ptarmigan things. He begins, for the hundredth time, to describe the killing of the ptarmigan, as the Artisan knew he would.

Che wants to take Pu safely into her arms as she used to do but she knows that he would no longer permit it.

The third summer of the Eyo's journey is, for the most part, a peaceful, happy time of abundance. Even inevitable winter is neither harsh nor cruel. No evil spirits visit sickness upon the clan and their bellies are full, their hearth fires warm. More cubs are born; a narrow bodied babe with big hands and feet to Narima and Kraac. It is the long awaited male. They call him *Cickive* or *Cici*, Rattlesnake, for his long body and the loud rattle of his cry.

Now all three nidjkiwe—Noha, Ecakik, and Kraac—are blessed with ogucen by Mother Earth, and it seems that the Eyo are destined to become fitting residents for the fabled land of the New Mountains.

Whea has twin boys!

Only Jag and Lara remain barren.

During these months, Che sees a further difference in Noha. This began with Kiconce's wise discipline. His abortive love of poor Fina, the singlehanded killing of the old mammoth, Miira's death, Pak's banishment, and the change in Laf have also contributed to his newness.

Che frowns. I wish his feelings for me would also change.

The birth of Rin and of a daughter, Ra, during the following winter continue the transformation. Noha is now, instead of an unpredictable stripling, a male of stature, though still retaining his love of the chase and his joy in the physical.

But for me, Che thinks sadly, he still shows only lust and approval of tasks well done.

Consequently, there is a growing emptiness in Che, a place no male's member and no growing infant can fill. She turns to her Nimi and finds respect and affection, especially from Bara, Inik, and Lara.

But it's not enough, she sighs.

Noha, too, recognizes in himself a new inquisitiveness about things that are not of Mother Earth or her animals. He often wonders, Why is each person so different and how could the same clan produce the gentle Artisan and the One Whose Name Is Never To Be Spoken, not even in one's thoughts?

Having asked himself this question—WHY?—Noha thinks for the first time that the future is to be planned for, to be influenced by his actions. He muses, When I make fire or chip a spear-point from a rock's heart or indicate the number of kills in a hunt to another by holding up a chosen number of fingers, I feel special. But he doesn't speak of these things to Che for she is, after all, a mere female incapable of understanding a hunter's thoughts.

He watches the animals of the plain, the birds, the insects and muses, None of these can perform such feats, only the peoples. Surely our manitu are superior to the animals', the trees', the rivers', and the rocks'!

This forbidden thought scares him.

The Great Manitou, from whence all spirits come, will know what I am thinking. The shaman's teachings say that Man is just one more spirit encased in earthly matter and in no way different from his fellows.

So Noha tries to suppress his ideas and never speaks about them. Little does he know that his mate has long before come to the same conclusions though she thinks Man's mate equal to him, a notion which Noha would never entertain.

As summer fades, the Eyo reach the end of the spirit bridge which joins the old world to the new.

The time of discovery is at hand.

CHAPTER 12

The New Mountains

Noha and Kraac are the first to sight the New Mountains. The brothers are scouting. They have tracked a mammoth herd whose trail suddenly swerved north. They make temporary camp on a hillock and when they have gathered willow sticks for a fire and are about to take dried reindeer meat from their pouches, Noha sights on the horizon what looks like huge cloud mounds. He watches the clouds with interest, since rain is an unusual phenomenon in this land where moisture comes each spring from the lakes, streams, and morasses caused by melting layers of permafrost but where the upper air is dry.

Strange to see such clouds.

The brothers sit silently. Noha knows that for Kraac thoughts are private things and he forces himself to practice the same reticence when alone with his Nisages. So Noha says nothing when he first begins to realize that the clouds aren't moving with the wind and they have a peculiar, angular outline.

The possibility that the white shapes might not be clouds but distant mountains doesn't come immediately to him. However, as he gnaws on dried meat from his pouch, he keeps his gaze upon the eastern horizon. Finally, he looks at Kraac to find that his brother is also watching the shapes.

Noha waits another long, restless hour under the midnight sun before he ventures, "Nisages, you said we must return to the main camp before the next sleep."

Kraac nods.

"I want to travel further towards the distant clouds on the horizon."

"Our Nuse waits for news of the mammoth herd."

"You could carry news to him."

"What about you?"

"I think the clouds aren't what they seem."

"I have been thinking this, too," Kraac says and is silent for several minutes before deciding. "You travel to the horizon and bring news to the Eyo."

Noha's voice remains still, his face expressionless, but his eyes glisten at Kraac's generous decision; for as the youngest Noha must abide by his brother's will no matter what it entails. This is the way of the people.

"May you travel on feet as swift as the reindeer and may the fox guide your path," Kraac intones.

"Thank you, Nisages."

Noha is not only pleased but surprised at such confidence shown in him by this brother whom he most envies but also whose respect he most desires. He says nothing of this to Kraac nor has he ever told him how he feels. After all, one doesn't express feelings which might be construed as weaknesses.

Enthusiasm and eagerness for adventure are things to be shown but never fear or pain or even gratitude except in a ritual way.

The brothers part after rest and Noha strings his food pouch and knife on thongs at his waist and carries his spear loosely in his right hand. Otherwise, he is naked except for mackisins and breechclout. As he runs eastward, grasses whip his legs and spongy earth springs beneath his feet. He is unaware that never before have the feet of man travelled this path.

Noha is the first.

He runs without rest for one wake-time and on into sleep-time without stopping and his brown eyes fill with the marvel that lights all explorers' eyes. Another waking time slides by before he stops to scoop from a clear stream a mouthful of water. At time he puts dried meat on his tongue, sucks it, and spits out the residue.

The shapes on the horizon are gradually taking clear form and expanding north and south as they grew larger. Those directly in front of him are still white and glistening in the sunlight but those shapes to the north and south are white at the peak and dark at the base. Myriad streams grow into ponds and small lakes and the ground is soggier than Noha has ever seen it. Although mosquitoes swarm, he ignores them. He has to make many detours now around larger lakes and often sinks to his shins in sludge but he keeps on weary now and slower.

Birds rise everywhere at his passing and he leaps over she fowl on their nests. Soon it seems that the water birds are as numerous as the flying insects. Thousands of white breasted pintails and purple headed scaups dabble on the lake fringes. Common black scoter, colourful mallards, and green-winged teal set up raucous symphonies. Spectacled elders flash by and arctic terns circle screeching *keer keer* overhead.

Noha doesn't heed these flying creatures but stands awed, his mouth open.

He cries, "My dream and Boog's vision are realized! The Reindeer's prophecy is true!"

Before him stand the soaring mountains of the New Land!

Galvanized, he jumps from hummock to hummock, floundering exhausted into pools of plant-choked water. At the end of a second wake time, he stops by the shores of a pristine lake which stretches to his right and to his left as far as he can see. Across the blue lake and rising directly from it in sheer walls is a serrated, white cliff broken everywhere with hundred-foot-deep crevasses of shadowed green and indigo. Streams and rivulets flow into the waters at its base. He cranes backwards drinking in the beauty of the glacier, a sculptured wall of melting ice sloping to the sky, from which a cool wind sweeps to dry his salty sweat.

Noha brings the joyful news to the main camp.

Everywhere he sees admiration and relief. Even Che grins and looks at him with approval, something she doesn't often do. He is chagrined at the gratified feeling this gives him.

He asks himself, To care about my mate's opinion is surely a weakness, isn't it? Forgetting how often in the past he has sought Bara's advice.

Boog offers prayers of thanks to Manitou; he removes the sacred Reindeer bones from their pack and the people reverence them. They feast as they have not since the time of Noha's dream in the old land. The bearlike twins, Megi and Tuk, newly ripe for mating, dance themselves into a sexual frenzy and then on into exhaustion, for the maidens are blood-kin and not for them. Che's eyes never leave Noha's face. Even Jag smiles as she joins with the other females in a praise song to Mother Earth.

Che exclaims to Bara, "At last we shall find a home!"

Bara smiles, "There's a long way to go yet, Nindanis."

They set off after rest, the hunters in the vanguard travelling light, Kiconce as Ogima and Ecakik as Anikeogima in the lead. They keep a slow and steady pace. Behind come Boog accompanied by the apprentice, the Artisan, and the striplings who go only a swiftly as the shaman's stamina allows. In the rear, Che and the other females struggle through the marsh ground, loaded down as usual with hut-poles, skins, reed baskets, food, and young. Ecakik's bitch has whelped and a litter of half-grown pups scamper around the feet of the cubs old enough to walk on their own. A puppy climbs Drilla's back and sends her squealing into the water. Pu rescues her and slings her on his back, her arms and legs grasped tightly around him.

He always takes care of her, Che thinks fondly.

Che strides joyfully, her strong, short legs never failing her, Rin strapped to her chest in a moss-bag. Narima carries her Cici while one of the maidens bears Che's new girl babe, Ra. Another maiden shepherds the youngest under Bara's watchful eye. Whea has her twins but Lara and Inik help Che with the extra burdens while Jag lingers behind, stooping now and then to pull up a sodden root or to pluck the leaves from a lily plant and stuff them into the pouch tied to her hut-poles.

When the hunters come within sight of the new mountains in the third waking time, Kiconce stops and raises his arms to the sky. Behind him, the others stand respectfully silent and around them, whistling widgeons set up such a clatter and swarmed so densely that they could scarcely see the glacier-clad mountain for birds. They remain there for many hours, the more restless of them, like Noha, continually glancing back the way they have come. At last, human silhouettes appear above the waving grasses and Boog's ancient figure labours toward them, leaning heavily on the apprentice's shoulder. When he reaches them, he stands for a very long time gazing at the ice wall beyond the lake and then he gives a loud screech.

"Aaaaaaargh! Great Spirit, Father of all, Mighty Spirit of the Mountain, unknown Spirit of the New Land, we thank thee. Great totem of the Eyo we thank thee. The prophecy is fulfilled!"

Then Boog jerks and threshes to the ground, eyes starting, foam flecked with blood dribbling from his lips. The hunters watch dumbstruck at this visitation.

Later, while Boog is coming to himself, the females come chattering up to be quelled into instant silence by the hunters' glances. Even the cubs are subdued when the apprentice helps Boog to his feet and the Ancient One turns to face his people. Instead of the happiness they expect to see, there is infinite sadness on his face.

Noha bites his lip. Why must he spoil everything?

"I have visited the land of the spirits," Boog proclaims in a high, reedy voice, "and what I have witnessed there must come to pass." There is a long pause and then another voice comes from his mouth; age's frailty has disappeared from it and Boog speaks sonorously like a young hunter.

"I have seen the death of the Reindeer!"

A horrified gasp from Bara, immediately stifled. Che steps swiftly to her side. Ecakik looks confused and Kraac pales. Noha's eyes go to his nuse who has not reacted at all. What's wrong with them? What does Boog mean?

"The Mountain reached out and snatched away the Reindeer," Boog croons.

"No . . ." It was a whisper deep in Bara's throat.

Encumbered by her load, Che crowds as near as possible to her clan mother.

Boog continues.

"In the place of the Reindeer rose three even greater spirits. The first was a Brown Bear, larger even than the cave bear, who stood on his hind legs clawing the air. And there was a wolf cub which was taken and devoured by a white bear, even larger."

What white bear? Noha looks at the other hunters and sees that they are as puzzled as he. Unlike the fox or the hare or even the birds, bears don't wear white coats in winter but sleep warm and peaceful in their caves and if female, suckle newborn. This dream doesn't make sense!

Boog continues.

"I saw a battle in which the White Bear was slain and the Brown Bear was victorious and travelled across a new and desolate land where Keewatin reigns and no tree grows. Beside him ran a mighty Grey Wolf and a White Fox and they were brethren. But their comradeship lasted only for a short time and the bear went on alone into a barren land where strange animal spirits dwelled, while the fox disappeared among the high mountains and the mighty wolf walked upon the water."

The old man pauses, slumps and in his normal high-pitched voice rasps, "I have said it."

Noha frowns and scratches his head. The fox is my wisana. What does this saying mean?

He catches Che's eye. There is shock there but there is also comprehension and stifled pain. Can my ninitegamagan read this dream? Should I ask her? But I cannot discuss a shaman's prophecy with a female!

I must wait and be patient. Surely he doesn't mean . . .

There is a long silence and then the people capitulate in one shuddering breath, "Thou hast said it."

And the New Mountains gaze down upon them, unconcerned.

A subdued group sits around the council fire during that sleep time, some miles from the mountains. Boog has sequestered himself in a pole hut hastily constructed by his apprentice and he refuses to see Kiconce. Therefore, the Ogima is in charge of the proceedings at the council fire. Ecakik, as Anikeogima, squats by his side and near him sit those who are left of the elder hunters. Old Mizinawa sucks mightily on his every present pebbles. Noha and Kraac are nearby as are all the clan. There is a nebulous mantle over the company even though that day they have realized a dream.

Boog's soothsaying has upset more than Noha.

Che is filled with foreboding. I know to whom the white fox and the wolf of the seeing probably refer but Boog speaks of the Reindeer's death! I cannot accept that!

She asks herself, Who are the brown bear and the doomed wolf cub? Though in her heart she already suspects but again will not accept. Most marvellous of all, how can there be a white bear who travels the winter snows? And what about the other things the shaman said?

She sees the same questions on the faces around her; that is, on all but Bara's and Kraac's. Those two know! I cannot look into her eyes; but his? He's looking at me and he reads me. There's no need for words between us. Feeling a strange guilt, she tears her glance from Kraac's. She watches the others. They are frightened. Even my mate.

As cubs will turn to a parent in time of distress, the Eyo turn as one to their Ogima. If Kiconce shares their half-formed fears, he gives no sign but opens the council with these words, "A great blessing has come to the People of the Giant Reindeer. This day, we have looked on the New Land. *The dream is upon you*!"

This statement brings hesitant grunts of assent from all present.

"Now the people wonder," Kiconce continues. "How shall we enter this land which is forbidden us by ice, deep lakes, and pathless swamps? And mountains!"

"How indeed? It looks impossible," says crafty, cantankerous Fuum and his sycophant, Quork, nods agreement.

Che is too filled with admiration for Kiconce to be angry at Fuum and Quork. Kiconce distracts them from the shaman's predictions. What a leader he is! And the cost? She looks for Noha. He has caught this scrap thrown to the clan by Kiconce and is chewing on it. She seeks out Bara's face. It is impassive. And Kraac? He watches his nuse with adulation blazing from his dark eyes.

There is a long silence as Kiconce allows the Eyo to ponder the problem of how to pass around or through the new mountains. Finally Ecakik says slowly, "We could turn to the southland where Nerockamink dwells."

"We could. But what about the land of the dream?" Kiconce asks.

"We might find a southern path through the mountains."

Many nod agreement to this.

"What do you say?" Kiconce asks the eldest hunter, Mizinawa.

He spits pebbles into his hand and wipes his shrivelled mouth. "The winds of winter are cold on old bones," is his only comment.

A discussion follows in which all seem to agree that, if they can't find a way into the land of the mountains, they should turn to the south. All agreed, that is, but Kiconce himself who has not yet given an opinion.

Noha asks permission to speak and is granted it since he has been the first to discover the new land.

"There is no new dream to tell us which way to turn. Such a dream may come to him who is worthy," he says, looking at Kiconce.

Mizinawa asks crossly, "Must we wait for another dream?"

Big Quork says loudly, "I don't want to wait!"

"Nor do I!" says rat-faced Fuum.

"Only some will wait," Noha says then reveals his true purpose. "Of the way to the south, we know nothing." All grunt in agreement. "Of the way to the north, we know nothing except that the herds go that way." Again all grunt their agreement. "Let Ogima wait here for the Great Spirit's guidance and let chosen hunters go, some to the north and some to the south, to seek a path into the new land."

"We would have to travel near the endless lake" argues Quork.

"What about the lake monsters?" Fuum asks.

To Noha's relief, Kraac interrupts, "My Nicimec has spoken well." There are now nods from many, for, though the mature hunters have doubts about Noha, Kraac has influence among all the Eyo and is respected even by the elders.

A rueful smile quirks Kiconce's wide mouth. "And who will undertake these dangerous tasks?"

"I'll go!" Noha says before anyone else can answer.

"And I," says Kraac quietly.

"I, too." It is Laf who speaks.

Soon all the young hunters are pressing to be allowed to scout for an entrance to the new land. Finally, Kiconce and the elders decide that Noha and Kraac should travel to the north while Laf and Dinkka are chosen to go south. Kiconce says, "I'll keep Anikeogima here, as I dare not risk all my ogucen on these missions. I, myself, shall go to the shores of the glacier lake and await a spirit message."

That night, as Kiconce lies sedately by his mate, he speaks to her of many things and doesn't chide her when she weeps. Instead he takes her ample body into his arms and pleasures her and when they are replete they lie sleepless, her wide, strong hand clasped in his.

The next day, Kiconce sends off the four scouts with blessings and prayers to Manitou and, carrying his own hut poles and coverings and a meagre supply of food, and eschewing companions, he goes to the lakeshore beneath the ice wall where he constructs a small hut without hearth or other comfort and squats naked awaiting the dream spirits.

Laf tells the people, "Dinkka and I travelled far to the south, skirting the marshes and lakes and disturbing millions of birds on their nesting sites, but we found no way into the land of the mountains that the bog land had not made impassable. We were stopped at last by the mountains of a peninsula whose heights, though mostly free of ice, were surrounded at the base by mile upon mile of impenetrable marsh. We moved to the west, following the edge of the wetlands but still found no path and finally we retraced our steps."

In the meantime, while Noha and Kraac search to the north, Kiconce sits day after day in his hut, taking no food and only the merest mouthfuls of water, enough to sustain life only. Many confused visions come to him especially when his belly has shrivelled and his eyes, feverish from starvation, gaze out the hut entrance at the impassable glacier walls across the lake. But at no time is Manitou's message clear and the Giant Reindeer Spirit does not come to Kiconce.

Instead, he dreams that the ice walls break asunder with a great roar and water swallows him up.

This is not entirely a dream, for the warm sun has made inroads into the glacier, causing a strange phenomenon. The ice wall stands a hundred and fifty foot-lengths above the water and stretches below it another two hundred. However, the ice lives, grows, and moves three foot-lengths a day down the mountainside. Within it, stress patterns shift and snap with thunderous cracks and with a final explosion, massive chunks of living ice calve from the mother glacier and crash into the water below, sending wave after frigid wave rolling and shimmering to the outer edge of the lake where Kiconce crouches in his hut. The noise of the birthing can be heard miles away but for Kiconce, deep in visions, it fades soon into obscurity and fragmented dreams take its place.

Chilly waters seeping into his floorless hut bring Kiconce to himself at last. Weak from starvation, weary and disappointed because he has found no answers in his vigil, Kiconce stumbles slowly to his feet and outside. The air is very warm and the swarming insects are like a second skin to his carcass. He scrapes them weakly away from his eyes and gazes across the marsh toward the Eyo camp. Where before there were some dry islands of grass and even a few shelves of pebbled moraine, there is now only a waterlogged plain from which the grass tips protrude like a deceptive grazing ground.

Kiconce says, "I must go as best I can to the main camp and await the scouts' return."

A first he makes progress although sinking in some places up to his knees in dark green slime. Like most Eyo, he can swim if need be but always does so with reluctance. The mosquitoes torment him mercilessly and water birds fly at his head, furious at his encroachments. He has gone two laborious miles when, with breathtaking abruptness, his foot plunges into a sinkhole and he flounders face down into the water.

He flings his large head up from the mess and chokes out gobs of scum as he tries to free his eyes of soupy mud and swim at the same time. But he can't pull from the relentless mud the foot which has betrayed him and with his struggles, it sinks further and further. Finally, the mud reaches up to grab his other leg in its merciless grip. Kiconce doesn't panic. He looks about him for a rock or anything to support him and give him leverage.

There is nothing.

He sinks slowly and relentlessly into the muck. He doesn't call out for help because he knows that there is no one to hear, nor does he struggle when he knows that it is of no avail. As the brown water laps his lips, he speaks a supplication to Manitou.

"Guide this, the least of your creatures, O Manitou, and light his way . . ."

Thus courageously dies the first victim of the New Land.

When Noha and Kraac, bursting with news of their scout to the north, return to the base of the ice-clad mountains, they meet Ecakik wandering among the marshes and swamps. They see him first from a distance, a lone, mosquito shrouded figure leaping from one hummock to another, and they hear him calling. They think, at first, that it is their nuse seeking the spirit message. When they reach him and see that it is Ecakik, they greet him briefly, as is the custom, but say nothing about their mission. Nor does Ecakik immediately tell them what he has been seeking on the bogs. All are weary, so they don't travel to the Eyo camp that waking time but make fireless camp on a gravelled esker.

When they have rested and eaten dried meat from their pouches, Ecakik speaks, "I was seeking in the marshes."

Noha and Kraac nod, thinking that this must be great news indeed if Ecakik sees fit to speak of it before they meet at the council fire.

However, Kraac notices the dumb misery in his brother's red-mapped eyes and an uneasy stillness grips his chest.

"I would speak to my Nijkiwe." Ecakik's voice cracks.

"What were you seeking" Kraac asks anxiously.

"I sought the body of Ogima so that it might be buried beneath his hearthstone with due ceremony and so that his manitu might be accompanied by the light of the four fires to the spirit land. I called and called but no spirit answered me."

A crashing silence followed these words and Kraac and Noha looked at one another in shocked bewilderment, not yet willing to take in what they have heard.

Finally Kraac swallows and, with difficulty asks, "In Manitou's name, what are you saying, Nisages?"

"For many waking times I have sought for our Nuse's bones. Near the base of the ice mountain, I found his prayer hut awash in melt water but nowhere on the marshes did I find our Nuse."

"He is swallowed by the marshes?" Kraac whispers.

"I have said it."

"No!" It is a shriek.

Noha leaps to his feet, his whole body shaking, his eyes wild, great sobbing gulps tearing his throat. "Where are the Eyo hunters? Why aren't they searching? I'll search. I'll find my Nuse!" He snatches up his spear and races down the esker's sides.

Ecakik makes a move to follow but Kraac stops him. "Let him expend his grief in anger against the marshes and the imagined neglect of his fellow hunters."

"It's dangerous out there," Ecakik says.

"The fox spirit will guide him."

Quietly Kraac questions his brother.

His story is brief.

"Many waking times ago our Ninga dreamed, of what she did not say. She begged me to visit the prayer hut and seek news of her mate. I obeyed but found the hut awash and the marshes newly treacherous. Returning to camp, I took all the hunters on a long search but we were unsuccessful. Indeed, old Mizinawa almost lost his life in the bogs and was rescued just in time by Quork.

All this time, Boog was silent. And I could see that he thought our Nuse lost. Still I searched and searched. After a time, I, too, knew that our Nuse was no more."

Ecakik pauses here. Kraac studies his suffering face. There is more to hear. He steels himself.

"One sleep afterward," Ecakik continues shakily on, "Our Ninga went into the bog land never to return."

Until then Kraac has controlled his feelings but now he flinches visibly and it is with unashamed tears in his eyes and trembling voice that he says, "Then our Nuse's manitu will not wander alone in the darkness but will be accompanied by our brave Ninga." And he knows that his clan will believe that the death, even of Bara, is only the death of a female and that her manitu will better serve Kiconce than the surviving members of the clan. Even Noha and Ecakik will, in the end, believe this. But Kraac is not so certain.

"It is so," Ecakik says. "Perhaps the Fire Spirit will take pity on them and light their way?"

"It is to be wished."

"Who will tell Noha?"

"I'll do it," Kraac says.

The brothers sit in silence for a long time, gazinging out over the wetlands, watching as storm clouds of angry eider ducks rise and hover squawking over their brother's path.

Noha returns during the next waking time and they wait for him. His face is twisted into ugliness by bitterness and grief. When Kraac tells him of Bara's sacrifice, he says nothing, although the news must be like a spear ground into an already open wound.

Kraac aches with pity. Of all of us Noha was closest to our Ninga. Kraac does an unprecedented thing. He approaches Noha and puts his arm across Noha's shoulder. Better that you weep, Nicimec," he says gently.

Nevertheless, Noha cannot show this kind of weakness. He pretends not to feel Kraac's arm and finally Kraac shrugs and leaves him. In single file, the three brothers pick their way across the bogs. When they reach the Eyo camp, Boog stands on the hillside as if he has known they were coming. He is feebler than ever and leans heavily on the apprentice. His first words bring them up short.

"The Reindeer is dead," he says in his gravelly, querulous voice.

The three brothers bow their heads in submission.

Boog's glance goes to Ecakik's stolid bulk. "Anikeogima." It is a command and Ecakik's head snaps up. "Anikeogima," Boog repeats. "It is your place to call the council to give us a new leader."

"Has Boog dreamed?" Ecakik asks.

"There has been no dream. It is the custom."

"I shall call the council, O Shaman, but it *shall not* name Ogima; nobody is worthy to take my Nuse's place." There is authority and certitude in Ecakik's statement. And stubbornness, too. Kraac and Noha listen with new respect to their quiet brother. Boog says nothing but his eyes are alive with speculation.

"We shall await the will of Manitou," Ecakik declares.

"You have said it," Boog acquiesces. "The council will speak of other matters."

Noha goes to his hut where bereft Che waits for him in yearning silence.

When Che had learned of Kiconce's disappearance, she had raced immediately to Bara's hut. She found her clan mother quietly mending a tunic. Inik, Narima, and Lara were close behind Che. Bara stood and held open her muscular arms; they ran to her and she gathered them to her bosom. With arms around each other, they wept together. It was Bara who drew finally away and lovingly surveyed their swollen faces. She went to a pile of hides and selected four well chewed squares.

"Here, wipe your eyes and noses," she said. She made camomile tea and shared it with them.

After some time, she sent Lara, Inik, and Narima away but kept Che with her. She lifted a shell containing hot tea and regarded Che through its steam. She said, "My mate won't return. He has gone to the land of the spirits."

"Surely . . ." Che began.

Bara cut short her attempt at comfort. "It is done." She put down the shell and folded her hands in her lap. "My only fear is, since my ogucen can't find the body, my mate's manitu will be lost in darkness on his journey."

"We shall light the fires and sit with you for the required time."

"But we can't bury him beneath the hearthstone," said Bara, staring into the firelight.

There was no reply that Che could make to this. She thought about Kiconce, his unfailing kindness to her and the respect with which he had always treated her.

She said, "He was a good Ogima."

Bara nodded.

There was an agonized pause.

"I will soon go away," Bara said.

Che, who had been dreading just this, put her hand over her mouth to bite back a protest.

Bara looked deeply into her eyes. "My sisters will need a clan mother. You must be the one. Do not protest! You are the chosen one. I have said it."

"But . . ." The look on Bara's face silenced Che.

Bara said, "My ogucen will also need your help." Again she went on before Che could reply. "Ecakik is strong. In some ways, he is the strongest of the three. He will grieve but he will persevere. There is much of his Nuse in him. He has a good mate but neither of them is clever and they will need your friendship. Kraac will acknowledge his grief and he will suffer the most; but he, too, will take up his burden. Be to him what he needs of you but remember always your mate.

"And Noha?"

"Ah, he is the special one. He shall always need a Ninga and he shall never realize it. You must be that Ninga."

"But I want to be . . ."

"Be silent! You are his mate. You will nourish him. You will guide him secretly and always you will be by his side. Your manitu is strong. You can do these things and also you can follow the path set out for you by Mother Earth.

"I have spoken.

"Now go and await your mate."

Standing she pulled Che to her feet and kissed her on the brow. She turned her and gave her a gentle push out the hut entrance. It was the last time Che saw her.

Che looks at Noha's ravaged face and pity fills her. How can I do what Bara bid me? If I offer him comfort, he will be angry and think I consider him weak. If only he would turn to me.

But he does not. Instead, Noha draws into his quivering arms his ogucen and the new girl babe. He rocks back and forth, back and forth until the cubs sigh in contentment and sleep. Still Noha rocks on in dumb, helpless misery and Che, hiding her face in the shadows, weeps.

BOOK II

CHAPTER 13

The North Shore

A group of frightened people crouch around a fire.

For Noha and Kraac's benefit, Laf has recounted the disappointing southern scouting and everyone is now eager to learn about the land to the north and what it might hold for them.

Kraac speaks to the council. His tone is deliberate, cheerful, matter-of-fact.

"We followed the edge of the marshes to the north, always keeping the mountains to the east of us; in time, those mountains became freer of ice until only the summits were encased in white. We came at last to the edge of the Endless Lake and turned east to follow its shores as it skirted the cliffs. The heights were alive with seabirds of many kinds, many of which we had never before seen."

Che shivers. I would like to see these birds.

Kraac tells them, "We saw strange sea monsters with big dark eyes who peered at us from the water and followed us but did no harm."

Sea monsters? Che shudders, envisioning gargantuan, snake-like, evil beings.

"Were these creatures fish?" Boog interrupts with the question in all their minds.

"I don't know," Kraac replies. "If fish, they were very large and of different shape. We saw some at a distance, out of the water and resting on the shore rocks near the water's edge; they feared our approach and with strange noises, sought safety in the lake."

"They feared you?" Mizinawa asks suspiciously.

"They fled from us."

Che watches his calm face. These lake creatures don't sound very frightening. But then, I can't imagine Kraac being deterred by anything, even giant snakes.

Kraac says, "The shoreline gradually turned to the east once more and widened and the mountains receded from the shore."

"Is the land as wet as it is here?" Quork asks.

"There is water on the land but it's not so treacherous," Kraac explained as best he could; for in many cases, there were no words in their limited tongue to describe what he had seen, a cool desert of rock and sand at the edge of the endless lake and inland places of ponds and lagoons and great barrier beaches shelved in stone. "At times, dense fog enveloped the land and there were dangerous areas where large sections of grey mud came loose from their moorings and slid into the lake."

"Does anything grow in this place?" Fuum asks sarcastically.

"Oh yes! As the land widens, there are rolling dry tundra slopes rising from the gravelly beaches in plateaus and shallow escarpments to the distant mountains. On these slopes, there were reindeer moss, lichen, sedges, short grasses, and the remains of summer herbs and flowers."

Che can see that Noha is aching to interrupt but Kraac signs him to be quiet and continues, "There were dwarf willow and alder in sheltered spots as we got further inland from the beaches, and on the distant mountains, I saw multi-green patches which suggest that the tree line comes further north there than in our old land. The tundra was spongy in some places and there were grasses at the edge of countless lakes and streams though the earth above the permafrost is very thin. My nicimec and I dug holes to be certain of this."

He adds, looking at the females, "There were also many meadows of salmon berry plants on the moorland slopes," and is rewarded with nods and pleased smiles.

"It was good of him to consider our needs," Che whispers to Narima and gets only a cold glance in reply.

Mizinawa leans forward. "What animals dwell in the new land?" and Kraac finally lets Noha, who is about to explode, answer.

Noha takes a deep breath and says, "There were multitudes of cliff birds and shorebirds such as plover, sandpipers, and dunlins probing the sands for food. And we saw the empty nesting sites of many migrant birds; these downstream nests were abandoned, of course, for autumn flights south over the mountains." He tells them once more about the mysterious grey sea creatures and about lakes teeming with fish. "Best of all! I saw sign of many deer and other hoofed spoor that I could not identify. And I met among the rocks a grey fox who smiled at me!" He pauses, but for once the clan is not interested in Noha's foxes.

He goes quickly on, "The moorlands were full of burrows of lemming and ground squirrel and I flushed ptarmigan . . ."

"Well did you or did you not find a way through the mountains?" old Mizinawa interrupts belligerently.

"We didn't go so far, fearing that we would leave our journey too late and that the Eyo would be caught in the bog land when Pepoon comes. But do not fear, the mountains there are free of ice and the land often wet but not bog-like. Also, the shapes of the mountains told us that paths must exist through them and rivers flow from them to the endless lake just like they did in the old land!"

Che stills. Noha is so enthralled with his tale that the sorrow which has shrouded him since his parents' deaths has lifted. He's truly enamoured of this new land. And he shall get his way. He always does. But this time it's Kraac's wish, too. I wonder what the new land will hold for me.

Fuum is not yet convinced. "It seems that this new land is harsh. Where are the mighty herds of reindeer and the grasslands we have come to treasure?"

"Yes. Where are they?" Quork grumbles, always quick to back up his friend.

"We saw none," Noha admits, "though here is much sign of deer."

"Would it not then be wise to return to the land where the reindeer and mammoth followed their trails with the seasons?" Mizinawa asks.

"I said that there are such trails into the mountains!" Noha turns to confront him. "Awaskesh will return to the north shore at the time of Nerockamink, just as he did in the old land!"

Mizinawa's furrowed face hardens and he stares balefully at Noha.

Che fidgets. Take care, my Noha.

"The time of darkness will be soon upon us," tall Laf puts in reasonably. "If we go to the north, wouldn't the time of darkness stay longer with us, since it is Keewatin's land?"

He asked the question of Noha, but it is Kraac who, seeing that Noha is about to really lose his temper, replies, "It is so. Shouldn't we begin our trek before this happens?"

However, Noha can hold himself in no longer. He shouts, "We will find a path through the mountains! We will go south into the land of the dream! *My dream*!"

Che, like some of the others, feels her fears dissolve at these courageous words. Noha sounds different. He speaks like a determined leader not just like someone who follows without thinking. She sees Boog nod sagely his old head. Mizinawa has been watching the shaman, too, and he shrugs and begins putting pebbles one by one between his yellowed teeth, a sign that he has had his say.

"Will the wise shaman speak?" Kraac requests.

Boog complies, saying nothing of his own visions. "The dream of ogima's ogucen said that the Eyo would live in the land of the new mountains. Ogima now wanders in the darkness of the spirit world and no new Ogima speaks to us. But Ogima's word is yet with us. We must go to the land of the new mountains."

"You have said it," Kraac intones, obviously pleased.

The phrase of compliance is repeated on all sides even by those, like Fuum, Quork, Mizinawa, and Laf who have raised objections to the scheme, because Boog's power and Noha's dream still held sway over them.

Noha is delighted and quickly draws aside the younger hunters to fill their ears with wondrous tales. Dinkka, Fuum, Quork, and the twins follow readily but Che notices that Laf doesn't go along but stays to talk with Kraac and Ecakik.

She tells herself. Maybe we'll find a true home in this new land. What choice do I have anyway? I won't think about it!

"It is your destiny. And I go with you," says a voice in her manitu.

Che starts. Who speaks to me? Is it you, Bara? But the voice was not Bara's. Could it be my Ninga? But the voice had been her own . . . yet not her own.

She shakes her head and walks off to prepare food for Noha.

It takes the Eyo many waking times to prepare for the journey. Ecakik, as Anikeogima, gives the orders. Four hunting parties are sent southwest under the leadership of Noha, Kraac, and two elders. Many reindeer are killed, slaughtered, dried over fires or covered with boiled fat and then stowed in scraped skins. The striplings snare easily the many water birds who have remained in the land of the Spirit Bridge for the winter, skin them and give them to the maidens to dry. A hunting party led by Fuum comes upon an old mammoth mired in the bogs near the ice mountains and dispatches him. Che works to near exhaustion and finds little time to mourn her beloved Bara, which is a mercy in itself.

One day, Inik says anxiously, "Narima, as eldest daughter, tries to guide the younger females and to care for the elder, but she is no leader. They resent her."

Che refuses to reply. She often thinks of Bara's last instructions to her but has decided that, as youngest, she cannot interfere. So she lends support to everyone as unobtrusively as she can. Inik helps the artisan to fashion fertility figures for Lara and others who don't already have them, and to carve fish hooks and needles. The maidens run about to everyone and end by helping no one very much.

Even shy Lara says to Che, "I sorely miss our clan mother's direction."

Young Pu assists with the carving and guards Drilla who is a thin, big eyed cub with four summers, a serious expression and timid ways. She idolizes Pu.

Jag is busy with her herbs and potions.

"Jag seems almost happy," Che says to Inik.

Once, while seeking a stolen moment's respite, Che edges her way from camp and walks towards a distant crescent shaped lake. As she walks, she stretches her aching spine and tries to rub away the pain in her arms and hands. Autumn is warm and friendly, the earth is dry along this path and Paternal Sun has driven away the mosquitoes. Lifting her face to the sun's golden warmth, Che revels in the soft kiss of his fingers. So enthralled is she that she doesn't see a figure seated at the lakeshore. Though her mackisined feet make no sound on the grass, the hunter stands and whirls to confront her. With dismay, she realizes that it is Kraac.

She is still uncomfortable with this silent one who hasn't spoken directly to her since the long ago night on the icy plain. Her instinct is to turn and flee those dark eyes. But mating with Noha has taught her that hunters, though seemingly forbidding, are in many things as frail as she. So she stands her ground.

Nevertheless, she is surprised when Kraac speaks to her. "Where are you going, Nimi?" he asks in a pleasant enough tone.

"I seek solace from my weariness," Che replies.

"You are weary?" Kraac asks teasingly.

Che is not in a receptive mood for teasing. She longs to rail at him, to number her tasks and to challenge his right to sit idle by the lake while she and her nimi slave. She says nothing, simply stands as tall as she can and stares angrily out over the azure-grey waters.

"Perhaps you wished to clean yourself in the lake?" he teases. A hunter never speaks of such things to any female but his own mate.

Che's face flames but she divines his innocent mischief and speaks just as boldly in return, "I had thought of it and still intend to enter the lake."

This is challenge indeed and Kraac realizes that he has gone too far and his face flushes. He bristles. He mutters, "This female has no shame!"

"And if I remain?" he asks testily.

The suggestion that he might even consider staying there to watch her in her nakedness would have put any other female to flight. But not Che.

"That is your choice," she says. And bending, she calmly removes first one mackisin and then the other. She reaches up to undo the thongs that hold her tunic. There is a sudden rustling in the grass, and when Che has dropped her tunic, she glances up to see empty the spot where Kraac had stood. Turning, she sees him running like a startled buck back to the camp.

"So the tall, cool one can be routed after all?" she giggles and laughing, leaps across the grass to land with a resounding splash in the lake.

She worries a little that Kraac will report her wickedness to Narima if not Noha and that she will suffer some punishment. However, she finds that Narima ignores her and Noha, who has regained most of his good cheer though he still has not spoken to her about Bara or Kiconce, is content enough. No mention is ever made of the incident.

Kraac didn't tell, she realizes and feels suddenly ashamed of her behaviour. For there had been no need to embarrass Kraac who had done her no harm and to whom she owed her life. She begins to have even greater respect for him and seeks to do him some small service. Kraac avoids her and seems always to have some other occupation to attend to when she approaches Narima's hut.

I guess he doesn't like me. Che feels a nagging hurt at the thought.

CHAPTER 14

The New Land

It is late in light time before the Eyo are ready to leave the Old Land. Most of the marsh birds have flown off to winter feeding grounds. One night brings the first frost and ice forms thin, transparent floating sheets on the ponds. Only flocks of small birds now fly about the Spirit Bridge and far overhead, garlands of the last summer geese wing their way to the south, honking and calling as if to tempt the Eyo to follow. Che watches them go with lonesome eyes. But the Eyo, fifty-eight persons, hunters, females, and young, and a dozen dogs, turn stolidly to the north.

Che consoles herself and the other females. "Soon we shall be in our new home!" she says.

After some day's march, they arrive timorously at the endless lake's beaches which rise in shelved stages, visibly marking each part of the shoreline where Ice had rested in the past. The endless lake stretches chilly, slate-grey fingers towards them, its surface empty except for scattered shore birds who retreat at their approach along the sand and gravel bars, leaving three-toed tracks behind. The sun is getting closer and closer to the horizon at the time of rest and soon the days and nights are of equal length.

Che finds this new landscape bare and bleak and, as the last areas of shimmering white light fade from the grey waves, she quickly lights with her flint some dried moss, which she has wisely carried with her, and huddles by it, her cubs nearby.

She prays silently to her familiar spirits. *During the night, may no Mishikinebig, Sea Monster, rise from the waves and devour the camp.* And though she hears no answering inner voice, the sea monsters do not come to eat her cubs.

When the Eyo come finally to the weathered, rocky cliffs and the north shore's scree slopes, the noisy seabird colonies overwhelm Che. She is particularly intrigued by the little white fulmar chicks with black beaks and stockings. The chicks have begun to leave their ledge nests to join their petrel parents in a winter spent upon the sea. The parents, consummate gliders, soar on grey-white wings above the water, stopping only to bob for small fish and crustaceans, while their chubby chicks sit in thousands on the rock ledges, living on their own fat until they are slim enough to skim like cubs on snow slides into the sea. There they will continue to starve until able to propel themselves into the sky. The stink from the ledges is almost tangible.

Che grabs Inik's arm and cries, "See the little chicks!"

"Just like fat babes!" says Inik as they stand side by side to watch.

Che doesn't like the glaucous gulls, with whom she is already familiar as villains who slaughter birds on the wing and rob nests. Many of them, soft white in colour with fog grey scarves across their wings, now strut along the shore. Others soar arrogantly above the waves, molding their wide wings to the winds.

She sees that another cliff dweller, the murres, interest Pu. They crowd every shelf like elegant, black and white tenpins forever coming and going as if they could not make up their minds where they wanted to be. Their racket deafens and Pu and Drilla laugh and put their hands over their ears as they and the other cubs file along the rocks under the sheer cliffs.

"See, Che!" Pu cries, pointing upwards, so excited that he forgets custom and calls her by name.

Some young murres have decided that it is time to go to sea and have jumped from their rocky ledges, wings frantically flapping. The adults call to them, encouraging them in their perilous maiden flight. The birds seem to have no real fear of the clan below on the shore, but give them wide berth in their immediate area. Pu squeals with delight as one fat fledgling, caught on an air current, lands short of the water near him. He picks it up and places it carefully on a wave while the parents scold and dive at him from above.

Che smiles. He is gentle as well as brave, like his nuse. He will be a fine hunter. She pushes away the familiar, ridiculous, inexplicable anxiety which engulfs her at the thought.

The murres share their cliffs with puffins. They have large, hooked bills that are striped with red, orange, and black. Che thinks them beautiful and stops to watch as they dive headlong into the blue-black water and continue to fly, small wings working frantically underwater. Finding a dead one among the rocks, she carefully cuts away the beak and places it in a small deerskin bag.

"I hope that you will consent to be one of my guardian spirits," she whispers, "for you are very pleasing."

In time, Che will discover that the new land houses many other birds to fill her eyes and her larder but she is never again to be as dumbfounded as she is in the time she spends passing the raucous cliff colonies.

However, she soon forgets cliff birds when Fuum yells, "A monster is watching us from the endless lake!"

Che whirls, spots the creature. "Why it's not a monster at all! It is an attractive little animal," she says to Inik.

The creature, having never seen people, is intensely inquisitive about this band of upright strangers who move along the shoreline. He follows them for a long time and then strikes out through the grey waves, easily outdistancing them, and wiggles ashore on a rock escarpment. There he rests peacefully and finally falls asleep. He is rather upset, therefore, when he awakes to find himself surrounded by a group of tall hunters, timorous females and cubs. Feeling that flight is perhaps the wisest course, the seal begins to scuffle along on his stiff flippers toward the shore only to find that his path is blocked by a pair of legs and feet clad in reindeer skin. He lunges to the right and then to the left but, because he is chubby and slow on land, his way is easily blocked.

"Don't be afraid," Noha says.

He is enchanted with this creature with its smooth, grey fur hide, distinctively mapped with irregular white circles. And unlike some of the clan, Noha doesn't fear the seal, so he reaches down to touch the animal and is immediately and bravely bitten on the hand. Laughing and sucking the blood from his fingers, he kneels and gets a firm grip around the young seal's fat belly and lifts it with some difficulty into his arms. At first, the animal struggles and almost wiggles away but it is not long before it relaxes in Noha's grip and looks plaintively up at him from big, limpid eyes, making an odd belching sound. Then Noha is amazed to see tears begin to seep from the strangely cub-like eyes.

"I have disturbed the manitu of the creature; this is surely a spirit-sent animal."

He puts the seal down at once upon the rocks, expecting it to lay aside its animal clothing and step forth a spirit-cub. However the little animal does no such thing.

"Make a path," Noha orders, and even Boog obeys him as the clan stand back, leaving a corridor to the water. Boog is watching Noha, not the seal.

The animal wriggles frantically down the path and plunges into the cold waves. However, he doesn't disappear. Instead, he follows the Eyo as they continue their trek along the rocky shore, bobbing up every now and then to regard them curiously. He and others like him dog the clan's path for several lights and are looked upon as a good omen, especially by Noha and Ecakik.

Ecakik is becoming as enamoured as his brothers of the north shore. He says to Kraac, "This sea creature will make easy prey and the females and cubs could catch his kind on the shore and take their coats for clothing and their flesh for food."

"I doubt that they will be so easy to catch when they know us better," Kraac laughs.

"This is true, but surely there are other ways."

It is near the time of darkness when they reach the area where they will make winter camp. It is too late that year to find a way through the mountains, so they plan to go well inland on the coast and there build their huts. They turn toward the mountains.

Despite her interest in the birds and the seals, Che regards with some chagrin this new, stark home to which her mate has led them. She sees a broad belt of desolate, treeless tundra which, though still showing the season's warm golds and vermilions, is already swept by the infrequent, frigid rains and fogs of autumn. Near the shore, thin ice has formed and the tundra itself has a patterned appearance probably formed by past yearly freezings and thawings. Mother Earth's flesh has shrunk in the dry winter cold making long, polygon cracks along weak ridges; then the openings have filled with ice which in summer melts and expands to be pressured into new ridges.

This land could be unfriendly.

The days are short now and colder and the Eyo come across large mounds of almost two hundred foot-lengths height with cores of perpetual ice. The hunters decide that these have been forced up by constant movement and churning of the land.

Boog says, "I name them *Pingo*."

As the Eyo come closer to the mountains, the land, as Kraac promised, changes from barren, ahumic desert to rising moorlands of peaty heaths, sedges, grasses, and lichens. There are thin growths of foot-high willows with branches no thicker than thumbs.

"These will provide some winter fuel," Che says to Inik.

She can now see in the distance on the mountainside dark green areas of scattered thin pine and spruce forests.

I forgot that Kraac mentioned these, she thinks and begins to cheer up because she loves woodlands more than anything. Her former clan, the Omeeseh, used to yearly wander to the western woods in the old land.

On the moorlands and herb slopes, the ground is dry and well drained and there is a good supply of reindeer mosses.

Che calls to the other females, "Let's chop some of this moss and take it along."

They fall to eagerly and Che is surprised how easy it was to give the order and realizes, too, that she had unconsciously expected it to be obeyed. Even Narima and Jag have done her bidding, though somewhat sulkily on Narima's part.

Inik is nearby as she works and Che asks in a low voice so that the others might not hear, "What do you think of this land, Nimi?"

Inik purses her lips. "I do not know my heart yet," she declares. "There are times when the endless lake fills me with foreboding; I don't know why. And the land also. But our hunters are well enough pleased. Ecakik cannot see enough of the new land."

"That is true," Che agrees. "But I am also troubled."

"Tell me," Inik says with her usual kindness.

"I cannot find the words. It's just that there is an emptiness in the land."

"Emptiness?"

"I don't mean that no spirits dwell here. But they are strange manitu who don't know our kind. Perhaps there are no peoples in this land. Have you seen how the animals come willingly to the slaughter? And remember how the small sea monster wept in my mate's arms."

"I remember well," Inik says but adds practically, "Do our troubles matter? Our hunters and the shaman are eager to dwell here. We must hide our thoughts and go with the Eyo in obedience."

"Yes . . . But . . ." Che's glance rises in strange confusion to the distant mountains with their green, patched mantle. She wishes that Bara were alive so that she might unburden her spirit on that wise one.

Nevertheless, she has to admit that she sees everywhere the tracks of hoofed creatures. On the fell-field, the driest part of the moorland, are heath and rocks, sedges and patches of grass and rushes; gravelly soil makes homes for colonies of arctic hare, lemmings, and sisiks who chatter stridently at them for their invasion before scampering away.

Even Che laughs to see the gallant anger of the little creatures who scold her as she digs the hole for her pit-hut.

"That's it," she says to them. "Do not let anyone bully you?"

Noha, who is in a generous mood, coerces some striplings into digging food-pits nearby with their stone axes. He even helps them for a while until distracted by a passing fox, already white for the coming winter. Che stores the remains of her dried meat, roots, and herbs in the pit while Noha watches the stowing, in Boog's hut, of the sacred Reindeer relics along with the records, painted on skins, of the Eyo's history.

Che visits Inik. Her friend has done a good job on her hut, using many reindeer skins. Since the ground above the permafrost is only five foot-lengths deep here, Inik has lined the floor of the hut with bundles of dead grasses which she had carried with her. Pu helped her with the construction and now watches with equal pride when she puts the finishing touches to their new home by sticking her stone fertility statues into a dirt mound at the head of the sleeping platform.

"Your *Ninikokomesin,* Grandmother, fashioned this statue for me," she tells him.

Inik has confided in Che that Pu has never asked her about Bara's and Kiconce's deaths, so she tries to mention them as often as possible, hoping that he will one day unburden himself. She allows him to bring a flaming brand from the Artisan's fire to light theirs, and the hut is snug against the cold wind that sweeps headlong up from the endless lake.

The boy then goes to see if he can watch Drilla for Narima.

Che and Inik squat contentedly beside the fire, punching holes with bone awls into cured and cut reindeer hides intended for extra winter leggings for Pu and Che's babes.

"Let's try a new technique," Che suggests.

"How so?"

"We could sew the skins together to fashion a second pair of leggings, fur side inward next to the wearer's skin. This would give double warmth."

"What a wonderful notion! Combined with moss-packed foot coverings and long tunics with hood and mittens, they will protect Pu, Rin, and Ra from the cold night."

"And we could make similar outfits for ourselves and our mates."

Che has already begged shell, bone, and red ochre paints from the apprentice and the Artisan to decorate the garments during the long winter night. The two friends work companionably.

"Our clan mother would have approved of these," Inik says.

"She would. We are coping well with this new land. Perhaps we shall be content here after all," Che smiles.

They hear a noise in the tunnel which leads in a slant from the hut floor to the ground above and look up to see Pu enter. Che is surprised, as she had not expected him back so soon.

"Are you hungry, Ogucen?" Inik asks, offering strips of dried hare flesh.

He refuses the food and squats near her and stares into the fire.

For a long time Inik says nothing but finally she asks, "Is my ogucen troubled?"

Pu nods but doesn't look at her, trying perhaps to hide cubish tears.

"What has saddened you?" Inik persists.

"I have lost my medicine," Pu says, putting his hands to his tunic neck and parting it so that she can see that no amulet bag hangs against his chest.

A spasm of fear churns Che's stomach but Inik smiles gently and says, "Have you searched well about the camp?"

"Yes, Ninga."

"Then you must have lost it on the trail and there is no use looking further. You shall have another. I myself will ask the shaman."

However, Che can see that Pu is not greatly comforted by this promise.

"It contained the fox teeth that the shaman gave me and also my ptarmigan medicine. Evil will come of it." Pu starts to cry quietly, with chin down on his chest so they won't notice.

They have no consolation to give him; for had not a fox, white out of season, visited his birthing hut; and had not Boog himself feared this omen? Nevertheless, Inik makes her tone matter-of-fact and scolds him. "I think that the daughter of my Nimises will be lost on the moors because Pu is not there to guard her. I am ashamed."

Pu stops crying. He immediately leaves the hut to go in search of Drilla. However, he doesn't apologize to his ninga. Even a male of seven summers does not apologize to a female.

The hunters have dispersed across the tundra in search of prey to augment the dried reindeer meat supplies. The air has turned suddenly cold and the time of light is very short and ice and powdered snow lie upon the land. The hunters don't follow the trails of the awaskesh, knowing that they will now be far south among the forests' sheltering trees, nor do they venture into the looming mountains which are already showing signs of winter whiteness. Instead, they concentrate on the far off beaches where seals have begun to gather in great numbers in preparation for pup birthing. Besides the little ringed seal, Ecakik has found a much larger seal with a grey-brown, sleek fur hide and bushy moustache. At first, he kills both types of seal easily but it is not long before they learned to fear him and scarper into the icy water to stare boldly at the hunter who stands helplessly on the shore.

"I would follow you if I could! He shouts. Ecakik, unlike most of the Eyo, can't swim.

Though seal flesh proves unpalatable, the Eyo will have to force themselves to consume it when their stores run out and the flesh oil can be used to light their huts.

Ecakik tells Inik. "The ringed seals hide is very soft and ideal for clothing while that of the bearded one would make good tough thongs and ropes."

Hunting the seals is becoming more difficult with each passing day. Laf, who has fallen into the habit of accompanying Ecakik, says to him, "I think that the holes in the thickest shore ice are breathing-holes for the seals."

"Why are there more holes than seals, then?" Ecakik asks.

"I have noticed that when it snows the breathing holes are difficult to find and each seal has many holes for his use."

Now Ecakik is lacking in imagination but when a thing is pointed out to him, he is quick to act. He tries running to a breathing hole when he sees a seal resting there but soon learns that the seals have excellent hearing and can discern his crunching steps not only on the ice surface but from beneath it.

It is Laf who suggests, "Let's search out some lightly covered holes with the help of your dog and build a snow windbreak and squat behind it to spy on the breathing hole."

Laf is spending more and more time with Ecakik rather than Noha. Since the rhino hunt, he finds less joy in the chase and often thinks his former companion's zeal tiresome. He leaves his old place for Dinkka, who he knows is anxious to fill it, and joins his Anikeogima in his interest in the seals. Noha hates killing seals, perhaps because he feels them to be somewhat of a personal totem.

So Ecakik and Laf build a snow-break and hide there together. The seal's approach is noiseless and swift and they miss many tries at catching him. It will take a patient and alert hunter to become aware of the seal and drive a barbed spear into the hole speedily enough to kill him. But Laf and Ecacik are tenacious and they worked well together. Laf gets the first seal and he and Ecakik are so pleased that they do a dance around it, hooting and hollering like striplings.

Inik and Che, who were walking along the beach, watch them indulgently. "I am glad to see Laf happy,"

Inik says fondly. "If only he hadn't chosen Jag. She will never make him laugh as often as he used to."

Meanwhile, Noha convinces a group of hunters including Dinkka, Fuum, and Quork to explore further to the east along the shore country. Consequently, it is he and his companions who discover the sea unicorn.

"See? A fish with a horn!" Noha yells. "This constant discovering of new creatures is much to my taste."

The dead one-horn is beached. It is twelve foot-lengths long and has a beautiful spiral ivory tusk protruding from the left side of its head and tapering to a length of two arms. The hide is smooth and slate blue in colour and its underside is white with grey mottling, while its top is black with greyish white and black markings. Upon butchering the animal, they find that the horn is of very good ivory under a scum of green algae, but that the blubber, though edible, has a bad taste. Even worse than seal meat.

"It's useless after all," says Fuum crankily.

Noha quells him with a glare.

They later see schools of one-horns swimming in the open water, their long horns jutting from the waves in cadence while gobs of silver spray twinkle around them before they disappear again in graceful dives. The hunters are never again, however, able to get close to a narwhal or any of the whales they sight, as beaching of the animals is rare and the hunters have no method of travelling over the water. Noha watches enthralled one day early in winter while a distant pack of killer whales hunts narwhal, ramming and stunning them, but he has to be content with the possession of his one narwhal horn which he prizes greatly and brings out on ceremonial occasions.

"No one else has such a horn," he says smugly to Che.

He discovers walrus, huge, noisy, ugly, tusked creatures with wrinkled jowls and mammoth-like skin and blood veined eyes. The creatures move in small groups and, unlike seals, are belligerent. Sometimes, they congregate in large packs on the ice but usually they lumber from land to open water with the speed of a running man at even the most distant approach. They dive and come to the surface to bellow and clack furiously at the hunters. Noha realizes that he will never successfully hunt these animals either though he would have liked to have killed at least one just to prove himself capable of it.

"If only I could swim in the icy water like the lake creatures," he says absently to Che, "Or find some way to float upon it like the seabirds."

Che raises her eyebrows. My Napima, you will never figure out a way of going on the water. Your particular genius is not of the creative kind. It is an instinctive wonderment and love of exploration and discovery, an urge stronger in you than in any other hunter. Perhaps the one who shares it most is the stripling, Dinkka, whom you keep more and more by your side.

Of course, she says none of this aloud.

It is Kraac, as usual wandering alone, who discovers the mammoth herds far inland near the mountains.

It is during the time of darkness, when the noon sun travels along the horizon, creating a sculptured landscape of indigo and gold tinted snow, against which Kraac in his furred winter garb is silhouetted like some strange, upright, skinny bear. These are not old, lost elephants but a group of fiery tempered young, whose lead bull charges repeatedly from the protective circle, churning up storms of snow and ice; a huge, black shadow against the pale light of the sky.

Kraac speeds immediately for the hunters.

Noha is overjoyed and Kraac cannot help smiling at the way he and Dinkka carry on.

He tells Ecakik, "They are even worse than you and Laf with the seals."

Nevertheless, though Kraac controls his own delight, he is well in the foreground as they hunt the mammoth with single minded determination, bringing home to Narima enormous chunks of meat and tusks until even he is driven into his underground hut by Keewatin and Pepoon's icy ravages.

Narima hates winter and spends a great deal of time complaining to Kraac that she cannot go outside when she wishes. He remembers the winter when Che ventured on the tundra, and how he rescued her.

He frowns. Somehow I don't think Narima would do such a thing and I ought to be grateful for this; but sometimes I wish she were a little more venturesome and voiced her miseries a little less. Kraac's mouth twitches and his black eyes spark with amusement. What a game little hen Noha's mate is, how sturdy and dependable yet independent, as are none of the other females, except dead Bara and perhaps Jag. I wish . . .

Despite the cold, he begins once more to make individual frigid forays upon the tundra out of both curiosity and boredom.

In the end, the mammoth herd move off into the mountains and the long winter's night settles upon the snowy plains; and Waté dances among gorgeous rainbows in the dark skies; and the perpetual wind moans and shrieks above the huts.

As for Noha, he turns once more to Che's body for pleasure, a thing he has not done in many sleep times, having been too exhausted by his adventures in the New Lands. Che is grateful for this because, no matter what their problems, on the sleeping platform they writhe in unison.

She decides, If it is not enough, I know no other way.

After her first misgivings Che, too, allows herself to become enchanted with the New Land. Before Pepoon drives her into her pit hut, she spends much time exploring the seashore, watching the seals and the birds. She looks, too, to the mountains, wondering what lies beyond them.

I wonder if there are really large forests.

One sleep time when Noha has filled her with his sap and lies content on his back on the sleep platform, and Rin and Ra are bundled like two fox pups at her feet, Che dares utter her feelings.

"I would speak with you, Napima," she says softly.

"I am listening," Noha replies, yawning.

"What do you think of this land?"

Noha is nonplussed. A hunter never asks another to express his idle thoughts or feelings, a female seldom. Nevertheless, he is surfeit with pleasure and full of tenderness toward his mate, so he does not chastise her but says instead, "It is well enough."

When Che waits silently as if expecting more, he adds, "There is much food here. We will live."

There is a longer silence and then Che makes bold to say, "My heart is full of the wonders of this place and I am not afraid of the darkness." She wants to add, *because you are near,* but does not dare because Noha would think this sentimental foolishness.

"Take care, Ninitegemagan, or the spirits of darkness will hear you and send evil upon us!" Noha says impatiently.

"I meant no harm," Che replies. And you are even more taken with the new land than I!

Hoping to grow closer to him by sharing his enthusiasm, she plunges recklessly on, "When Nerockamink comes, shall we stay here or travel over the distant mountains to see new wonders, Napima?"

Noha bolts upright, an edge of outrage in his tone. "Why do you ask so many questions? It is not for you to scout the distant lands and taste its wonders. I and my brother hunters shall do this thing if it is to be done."

Che bites her lip and recoils, hurt as much by his tone as by the words which she knows to be true. *Why must he regard my heart's wonder as a challenge to his authority and his place in the clan?*

Bara's last words came unbidden to her. "*Always he will need a Ninga.*"

Che says grudgingly, "Forgive me, Napima."

She speaks the ritual words but in her heart, helpless rebellion finds its first roots.

CHAPTER 15

Nanook

Another nomadic hunter roams the tundra.

He is Nanook! Monarch of the Northlands.

As fearlessly confident as the Eyo and easily as cunning, he is infinitely more majestic. The only creatures willing to approach him are mammoths, killer whales, and walruses. The mammoths ignore him as long as he keeps his distance, which he does, having no wish to deal with their long tusks. Killer whales attack him only when provoked and walrus attacks are also defensive and usually take place in water where the bear, though a good swimmer who sometimes covers distances of twenty to thirty miles in one stretch, nevertheless is slow in manoeuvring. He twists and turns ponderously, needing most of his stamina just to keep his immense body afloat.

When the Eyo first set foot on the North Shore, mighty Nanook and his brethren range over the vast area with impunity.

The summer before the arrival of the Eyo, Nanook is as usual confined to the land in his never ending search for sustenance. In this season, he will eat anything, whether it be rodents, berries, eggs, birds, moss, grass, even carrion. He has made a good meal weeks before of a whale carcass that had washed up on the pebbly beach. Now he is suffering painful hunger pangs and is grateful to come upon a pinkish red salmon berry field. He squats on his haunches and devours the succulent berries, a deceptively docile looking giant.

By the summer's height, he is starving.

Nanook meanders with a languid, bow-legged shamble along a gravelled esker, his body thin and appearing taller. Finally he stops, picks out a likely spot and shovels an excavation with his long-clawed paws. Here he will nod away the days, not hibernating, not even really sleeping, just conserving his fat stores until autumn.

He mated in March, wandering briefly with the female and then going on his solitary way as he will have no hand in the cub raising, and indeed will be unwelcome if he were to approach his mate now. She, a smaller bear weighing only eight hundred pounds, has also had a lean summer and is relieved in autumn when her instincts tell her that it is time to rest. She is lucky enough to come upon a musk ox who is old and dying and has been left behind by the herd. She kills him easily and devours him, grey hide and all. Her hunger satiated, she excavates a rocky shelter about ten feet by four feet for her lair. Here she will allow the snow to build over her a mounded cave and she will rest, her body temperature only slightly below normal.

She will awaken at the slightest disturbance.

In January, the female gives birth to two tiny, naked cubs. They are blind and deaf and they snuggle against her white fur completely dependent upon her for warmth and the nourishment of her milk. She is an affectionate, sometimes timid bear and she curls softly around the two cubs, making sure that their vulnerable bodies are exposed no more than necessary to the cold air.

In six weeks, the cubs are furred balls and moving about the lair in the shadowy blue-white light that filters through the snow. When Nerockamink blesses the land, they break out after their mother into the air. Her first excursions are short, for her bones are stiff after the long confinement and she also is on the lookout for Nanook, who will not hesitate to eat his young. Nevertheless, the three are soon wandering in search of food. She requires sustenance to make milk for her young and besides, they need training. There are many seals along the shore ice and fish are abundant.

The largest cub is male, a particularly boisterous and self-willed cub who loves to play and toboggan on his rump among the shore ice floes. His nimi is shy and retiring and once tries to hide her now considerable bulk behind a small stone, paw lifted to conceal her very black nose which stands out like a beacon against the white snow; this when a cross old bull walrus chases her curious nisages, and he runs, rump tucked under him, and leaves his nimi to her fate. Their mother lumbers to the rescue and the old walrus retreats into the water, preferring not to face alone a polar bear on the surface, especially a female with young.

Nanook, too, has passed a long, difficult winter, denning in time of blizzard and eating when he could. He lay for days beside ice breathing holes and scooped up, with a left pawed swipe, the startled seals who ventured there. He was sometimes accompanied on his treks across the ice by a dog-like shadow. This was Noha's mentor, Assinbo, Fox, who in hungry times followed Nanook to feed on the scraps left behind after a feast. Nanook ignored the fox, knowing that the wily animal would be quick to retreat out of range if he should begin to move in its direction.

Sometimes Nanook caught unwary seals by stealthily stalking them on the surface and catching them before they could dive into a blow-hole. On one occasion, he gorged when three seals, basking around a single hole, were simultaneously warned of his approach and all three dived for the hole at once, becoming an effective plug of seal bodies, ends frantically struggling. Nanook snatched them singly, stunned them, and then hugged them to his chest and bit off their heads.

Nanook has a favourite trick. He travels along the shore ice watching for grey ringed seals asleep in the distance. He then slips into the water, dog paddling quickly along, his legs trailing, his profile low. When he comes within a certain distance of the seals, he dives to come up beside the startled prey, swooshing out of the water with one swift lunge. Very few seals survive his attacks.

His belly full, Nanook decides to make a temporary den and rest.

It is fated that, during this particular spring, when the snow is still on the ground and the pale sun low in the sky during waking hours, mankind shall first encounter the Great White Bear.

Pu treks to the shore with the females on a sealing expedition, while the hunters and striplings travel to the mountains to intercept the hoped for deer migration. Boog, who is feeble and suffering from twisted and swollen bones, stays behind in the camp with the apprentice, but Artisan and the cubs, even infants, go to the shore with the females. Seal catching is not as easily done as they hoped, so they set up a temporary ice-fishing camp on a still frozen river that flows into the endless lake. Pu and the other males of his age are allowed to try their luck at felling with bolas early rising sisiks.

There is still much snow on the ground and the air is cold while shore ice yet stretches solidly out into the Endless Lake. In the sparse light, the snow is shadowed sapphire topped by a glistening transparency of treacherous ice crust. Pu, hoping he will fell and slay a sea creature, wanders away from the others and moves along the ice with his short spear ready in his hand. His mouth falls open in sheer astonishment when he comes upon the tracks. They are the spoor of some big animal, so immense that Pu could squat in one of the tracks and not overflow its edges. He should return to camp and reported this discovery to his Ninga. He might even be sent as a runner to the mountains to summon the hunters. However, he can't resist following the tracks for just a little way.

After all, he is the hunter of ptarmigan.

He finds that there is not one set of tracks but four. Two are smaller than the first set but of the same kind and probably of young. The fourth is Assinbo's. A fox's spoor overlaps the big creature's.

Pu smiles. His uncle's friend must be following the giant.

The little way that Pu has intended to stray becomes longer and longer and finally he comes cautiously over a rise to see a white fox sitting like a pretty dog on a snow mound and looking back the way Pu has come. Assinbo seems to be waiting. When he sees Pu, he gives three short yowls and then is quiet.

At the fox's first warning, a cold premonition grips Pu's middle, for he has never seen a winter fox without regretting the loss of his medicine bag. However, he knows very well that the fox would do him no harm, even though this one is acting strangely.

As Pu continues to move forward, the fox again yips plaintively.

Pu bites his lip. If only he could interpret the fox's speech like his Uncle. But he cannot understand the fox's warning. As he comes closer, the fox turns and disappears over the rise angling off to the east. When Pu reaches the spot, he sees that the giant tracks and that of the fox have separated.

Pu says, "Almost as if Assinbo wants me to follow him! Then I would have to abandon the big tracks. I must be careful."

Pu approaches the summit of the next rise on his stomach and peers over it. Below, Nanook's mate is teaching her cubs how to hunt seal. As Pu watches, dumbfounded, she smells out a ringed seal's lair under a snowdrift. Not far from her, the cubs chase each other among the ice mounds, sliding about, falling and slithering on their bellies down slippery slopes. Pu watches fascinated, wanting to laugh aloud at their antics. He has never before seen a live bear but has sat enthralled on many long winter's nights listening to tales about them.

Most amazing! These bears don't fit the description of the cave bear. They are much larger and wear majestic robes of white!

Pu is gazing at them, scarcely able to breath from excitement, when the beautiful female bear suddenly lunges into a snow bank, sending chunks of ice flying in every directtion. She scoops out an ill-fated seal and crushes it with a mighty hug. She then devours it and the seal pups who are in the den.

Pu gulps. What could such a bear do to a mere stripling like himself?

He decides that he must be more cautious and wiggles backwards down the slope until he is out of the bears' sight. He runs like one possessed of matchee manitou to the fishing camp. The first female he meets is Narima and he blurts his tale about the white bears.

Narima laughs derisively. "Has the snow affected your vision?"

Pu haughtily stands his ground and insists, "I saw clearly a giant white bear with two white cubs. They hunted seals."

The laughter on Narima's face fades. She knows that no adult Eyo would tell such a lie. It would be a stupid and unthinkable thing to do. However cubs sometimes tell exaggerated stories in order to get attention or praise. Lara and some other females approach to listen. They all know that Pu is inordinately mature for his age, and honest, so it isn't long before they are whispering among themselves about this awesome news. If the tale is true, a bear with a white coat is surely a great omen.

Lara remembers Boog's prophecy and runs for Inik and Che.

They listen attentively to Pu's tale.

"The hunters must be told," Che says.

"You have said it," Inik agrees.

"First we must seek Boog's advice!" Jag, who seldom speaks, cries.

Lara voices a lingering doubt. "How can we do this? There is no runner to send to the hunters and even Boog is far away across the snowy tundra."

"I'll go," Pu announces hopefully.

They all turn to stare at the boy. It is Che who says, "You are very brave and will always be remembered as the boy who discovered the white bear. But as yet you are too young to be sent out alone across the tundra." Che is always to remember this decision of hers, the first that she made with the confidence of a clan mother. It is, indeed, as sensible decision. But the results . . . ?

"I'm not scared!" Pu insists angrily.

"Your Anikeogima would be angry," Che tells him in a quiet, final tone.

Pu bites back a retort and blinks away tears of frustration. He turns on his heel and strides to the riverbank where he stands looking out over the ice as if counting the fishing holes. His back is stiff with disappointment.

"He is so like Noha," Che mutters.

The females shrug and resume the work which Pu interrupted. That is, all but two do so. Inik and Che stand together watching the boy. Che finally approaches him and lightly touches his arm. He whirls.

"We have many fish. In one sleep time we shall all return to the camp where the shaman rests. He will advise us," Che says.

There is nothing Pu can do but agree. "You have said it." But they both know that he will never again be allowed to follow the white bear.

Smiling reassuringly, Che strides across the ice to fish, trailed reluctantly by a worried Inik. Seeing that Pu is no longer so angry, the other cubs and the maidens gather round him to ask questions and fairly dance with excitement at his answers. Pu enjoys the attention but it is not long before he feels a small tug at his leggings and, looking down, sees Drilla. She doesn't speak but points toward the artisan's hut.

Pu realizes that Artisan will understand and appreciate his discovery as no female can, so he allows the little female to pull him in the hut's direction. The Artisan is getting on in winters and has been snoozing but he quickly wakes and listens with courtesy to Pu's words, questioning him minutely and congratulating him on his important discovery.

He doesn't doubt Pu's word.

"Do you think that the Great White Bear will speak to me as the Giant Reindeer spoke to my Uncle?" Pu asks wistfully.

"I do not know. Manitou must decide and in this thing we should await the counsel of the shaman and your nuse."

Pu knows that this is true, but as he lies in the skin hut at sleep time listening to his ninga's quiet breathing, his eyes will not close and his mind seethes with brave imaginings.

It is a frosty day when the hunters set out to search for the returning reindeer. They have already decided that no scouts will be sent ahead but that they will split into ten pairs, each pair fanning in a different direction across the tundra and travelling toward the mountains.

Ecakik says, "If we can find the passes used by the deer, we shall know which path to take to the south. In fourteen sleeps, we shall gather at a chosen spot and take counsel."

Noha pairs with Dinkka and brings along one of the newly trained hunting dogs. It is a yellow bitch from a litter of Ecakik's companion. Dinkka is a good comrade, younger than Noha by four summers but already adept at hunting techniques and full of curiosity.

Noha is feeling paternal. He murmurs, "Some day, Pu will be very much like this young hunter. I hope that Rin will follow in both their footsteps."

He is unusually patient with Dinkka's questions and grunts swift approval when the stripling discovers the strange tracks of a group of hoofed animals going east across a snowfield. There are six of the beasts and two young by the sign, and here and there they have stopped on a southward facing slope to paw away the shallow snow to get at low lying willows and saxifrage plants. The sign is only a few hours old, as far as Noha can tell.

He says, "Instead of going on toward the mountain, we'll follow this spoor for a time."

And so they do for many miles. The going is not too difficult when they skirt the snowfields, although the animals they trail have ploughed right across them. Noha and Dinkka move along gravelled ridges and pick up the spoor on the far side. Although it is still fairly cold, the hunters soon take off their outer tunics and tie them to their waists as the steady pace which Noha sets keeps them warm. They each carry two spears, a bola, and their stone knives.

They trek some few miles before spotting the musk oxen. The unfamiliar silhouettes are moving in single file along a snowy ridge, two calves near the center of the line and the largest animal, probably a bull, in the lead. As the oxen are walking into the wind, they do not scent the hunters who slowly crouch behind them to observe these wonderful new animals who have such a stately manner with heads lowered and long, shaggy brown hair streaming back in the icy blast.

"I have heard of such but never seen them," Noha says. "I wonder if these are the bison of my dream."

Both hunters are exceedingly pleased by their find. Noha says, "Here are beasts worthy of our skill and who, by their size, will give even more meat than Awaskesh's brethren, to say nothing of those fine, long-haired hides. However, I don't think we should attack but should follow them and observe every detail of their behaviour so as to give a good report to the council."

"You have said it," Dinkka agrees.

So they move out across the plain, keeping upwind of the musk oxen and carefully out of sight. All this time, they kept the bitch muzzled and on a leather thong. She would harry the herd if she were left unchecked, for she is still not completely trained.

They have been tracking for twelve hours when one of the female oxen and a calf slow and fall behind the herd. Noha is surprised to see the others stop to wait for her and he feels kinship toward these big, slow moving animals who shamble along in so stately a manner despite their ungainly appearance, who race with surefooted speed up the trickiest slopes and yet obviously care for the safety of each member of their herd just as the Eyo care for the least of the clan.

He decides, "Let us approach more closely and see the animals' reactions."

Dinkka nods.

They wait until the oxen have abandoned the ridge before running at top speed, hoping to catch them munching on saxifrage and willow in the shallow valley beyond. Upon coming to the ridge, they hunker down and peer over the top. Sure enough, the oxen are gathered in a loose group only fifty yards away.

Noha whispers, "I'll let the bitch loose."

She, delighted at her freedom, immediately runs barking and careening over the ridge toward the musk oxen. The moment they see her, the oxen bunched in a circle like mammoths, heads out, calves in the middle, the lead bull in front pawing the ground and rubbing his massive head against his foreleg, a signal of impending attack. As the yellow bitch runs up yipping, the lead bull charges with tremendous speed toward her. He snorts, head lowered, two wicked looking, outwardly curved horns ready to gore. At first the bitch stands her ground but then, young and inexperienced, she turns tail and speeds terrified back to Noha and Dinkka. The hunters then show themselves, and the bull, facing this new and completely unfamiliar threat, returns to the circle and takes his place once more among his herd.

Noha and Dinkka can see, since they are now much closer, that these are truly wonderful animals, humped and bovine but majestic. Their long, dark hair hangs almost to the ground over dirty white stockings; suspended from it, are long skeins of silky, winter wool ready to be rubbed off against some rock. Shield-like, yellowish, horny growths curved up at the ends into lethal hooks, stretch across the bulls' foreheads.

Noha whispers, "One of these beasts will give as much meat as three reindeer and my mate could make good use of the pelts and horns. How my Ninga and Nuse would have valued such as these!"

At length, the oxen decide that they are not going to be immediately attacked, and they moved apart, wheel and scrape the ground before suddenly turning to flee at a speed that surprises the hunters. However this time the animals move too unexpectedly and the calf who had held up the herd once before is left behind, bawling like an abandoned infant. The rest of the herd, perhaps hearing him above the racket of their flight or sensing his absence by some inner instinct, stop and formed again their circle.

"Take hold of the bitch," Noha cautions Dinkka.

He moves swiftly to where the calf stands on unsteady legs. It is a handsome little brute with thick, dark brown coat, white fat legs, and big innocent eyes. It is male and, as Noha creeps close, the head goes down and the calf wobbles toward him, trying bravely to butt his thighs.

Noha laughs, warding off its little head and picking it up like he had the seal. The calf immediately stills.

"Do not be afraid my brave little nidjkiwe," Noha whispers and approaches the herd carrying the baby musk ox, while behind him, Dinkka, ready for any eventually, grips his spear.

Noha makes two strides and then stops to wait for a time. He repeats this pattern until he has come to within twenty foot lengths of the herd and then puts down the calf. The animal bleats piteously as soon as his feet touch the snow. Noha backs away and slowly returns to join Dinkka, who is grinning widely. After some time, the bull leads the herd toward the bawling calf, who immediately runs to its ninga to stand safely beneath her belly and to peer out through the curtain of her long guard hairs. The herd encloses them and move off, the bull keeping an eye on the hunters.

"Shall we kill" Dinkka asks.

"I do not wish to," Noha says.

Dinkka is ever practical and more sure of his status with Noha and he does not now hesitate to voice his thoughts. "You have said it. However, we must test these animals."

"There will be more to see," Noha promises him, for some emotion that he does not fully understand inspires him to let this first herd go unmolested.

They agree to wait and are rewarded that very day by coming upon a lone bull, driven out by the lead bull. It is not they who will test him for the old one is being stalked by Mahingan.

Noha smiles.

Mahingan, I do not begrudge you the sick and weak animals that you winnow from the awaskesh herds. You have your place among the meat hunters and you are a cunning adversary who seldom approaches man. In fact, you did not eat my Ninitegamagan when you had the chance.

He remembers once watching delighted with Ecakik as two wolves, a white male and a grey she wolf, played a game of *chase me.*

You are much more dignified and handsome than our dogs and are you not also my Nisages's Wisana?

He says to Dinkka, "We shall not interfere."

This particular wolf is a large male with pale grey undersides and a darker grey saddle across his back. The darker colour is repeated on his haunches and again in a mask-like covering around his intelligent eyes. He has come upon the old bull while curiously following the scent of the two hunters. He is hungry.

However, the meal is not to be easily obtained. The old bull is still a formidable adversary, horns fairly sharp and spirit undimmed. At the wolf's approach, he turns and rubs his face against his foreleg. The wolf pauses while the bull turns his rear to a gravelled bank and stands facing his enemy. The wolf charges. He directs his fangs toward the head of the ox who sweeps his dangerous horns in ferocious arcs, trying to hook his attacker. The wolf dances aside just in time and prances in front of the ox like a teasing cub. The contest continues with the wolf attacking tirelessly and relentlessly and the old ox trying to parry the onslaught with his horns.

Finally, the inevitable happens and the wolf draws first blood with a vicious tearing away of the ox's right eye and part of his face. The old bull perseveres until blood loss brings him to his knees. A quick, tearing gash to the throat and Mahingan has won the contest. It is only a matter of seconds before he is ripping away the tongue.

Now he looks back at the hunters, letting them know that he does not fear them and that they are not to share in the kill just yet.

Noha understands. "You see why Ecakik holds wolves in such admiration" he says.

Dinkka has been moved more by the musk ox's struggle. "It seems hard that the old one had to die like that," He says quietly.

"It is the way of things," Noha replies, not without sympathy. He is remembering the day when he killed the mammoth.

"I am glad that the Eyo care for their old," Dinkka says.

"I, too." Noha feels suddenly close to this stripling who is almost a hunter grown.

Having seen enough, they returned to the meeting place and find the excited hunters full of tales about the forerunners of Awaskesh's herds. They claim that these new beasts are different from the reindeer of the old land and the grassy plain but that their habits are the same and that they haven't yet learned to fear man.

Kraac says, "They came down through one particular mountain pass as if following a yearly migration route."

Noha, jealous at not having been the first to spot the deer, says little but immediately forgets the musk oxen in his eagerness to test himself against the new deer. He allows Dinkka to tell the stories of the musk ox calf and the old bull. As it turns out, other hunters have also seen small herds of musk oxen but none have made a kill or seen such a sight as the wolf's attack. After the hunters have taken counsel, they are ready to begin the hunt on the morning when Boog's apprentice limps into their camp with a tragic tale.

CHAPTER 16

Pu and Drilla

Pu creeps from beneath the hare blanket, throws on a second reindeer skin tunic with a hood and taking his spear, goes out to relieve himself in a spot some distance from the huts. When he is finished, he strides over the frozen tundra in the direction of the endless Lake, not thinking to disobey, not really thinking at all.

The night is softly beautiful and Sun is already coming over the horizon, a harbinger of spring. In fact, Pu is so pleased and preoccupied that he doesn't see or hear the tiny person who steals from another hut and follows him.

Drilla is robed in a blanket of white hare skins and she blends into the snowy landscape, except for her small, brown moon face and a fringe of black hair drooping across her wide forehead. Without a word, she trots after her adored cousin, the great hunter of ptarmigan.

Pu has walked almost two miles when he hears the scream behind him.

He is travelling along a gravelled esker's crest, keeping a steady pace now on this dry place where Wind has prevented the snow from gathering. He whirls and sees a tiny, white form some distance back, almost invisible against the morning sky. He knows at once that it is Drilla. The cub turns and starts to run towards him. A huge White Bear, more majestic and terrifying than the others Pu had seen, lumbers over the top of the esker.

Pu feels no fear only a strange, exultant fury.

Nanook, belly half-full of seal meat, had been dozing in his gravel pit, trying to arouse himself to break through the thinning snow roof of this temporary shelter when Pu passed. The great bear sniffed the air curiously. A new, strange scent. His black eyes lazily opened, but he did not yet move. When shortly afterwards he detected another of the strange creatures' approach, he growled irascibly and with a mighty heave and a bellow, bounded out of his cave, sending ice sheets flying in every direction.

It was this horrifying sight that Drilla saw before she screamed.

Nanook shakes himself free of snow and ice slabs and stands swaying sleepily on legs like pine trunks. He shambles up the slope toward the girl, curious about this white thing who is not a bear cub but is also not a fox or a hare. The cub stands frozen as the mountain of white fur approaches; her black eyes roll back and she slumps to the ground. The bear grunts sleepily at this unusual behaviour and approaches to sniff the tiny form.

A feeble cry of rage from his rear swings the great head in Pu's direction. Nanook sees another strange animal, a bigger one but not very big, and grey this time. The thing is daring to charge him, caterwauling and waving a skinny, little tusk in front of it. This behaviour annoys Nanook and he growls warningly and follows the growl with a feline-like hiss, blowing out his upper lip. Still the creature barrels toward him across the esker, uttering its hostile mewings. Nanook, angry at such effrontery, shambles purposefully toward the troublemaker.

He kills Pu with one careless swipe of his huge left paw and the shattered body flies against the stony bank and lies there broken.

Nanook ignores both Pu's body and the unconscious Drilla and charges across the tundra towards the endless lake, fully awake now and hungry for seal. In the distance, a white fox sends a mournful howl into the lowering sky.

This is the terrible news that the apprentice brings to the Eyo hunters.

They sympathize with their Anikeogima's agony at the loss of such a promising ogucen; however, their sympathy is overshadowed by the fantastic claim that a white bear had slain the cub.

Noha immediately recalls Boog's prediction that a white bear would kill the wolf cub, and he hears Quork say enviously to Fuum, "The shaman said that a brown bear would kill the white bear. Anikeogima must be the brown bear of the prophecy!"

"What does it matter?" replies Fuum crankily.

"Of course it matters! Wouldn't you like to be the one to kill a white bear?"

"I don't put myself forward."

"And I do?"

"Since you took a mate, you have little time for putting yourself forward . . . or for companions," whines Fuum.

"Whea is a good mate who has given me twin sons," snaps Quork. "And what about you? At least I don't prefer the company of striplings to my mate's."

At the stricken look on Fuum's face, Quork falters.

"Anyway," he says, "we should be thinking of our Anikeogima now. Let us not quarrel."

Fuum nods and they both turn to watch Ecakik. Noha's gaze follows theirs.

Ecakik's face is a stiff mask of scarcely concealed anguish. No one questions his decision to return to the main camp with Boog's apprentice.

"I shall go with you," Kraac offers. "Pu gave his life to save Drilla . . . whom the apprentice had said was recovering from her terrifying encounter with the white bear . . . "I would like to sit with you and your mate over Pu's funeral fire."

"Noha declares, "I, too, shall return."

Kraac glances quizzically at him, annoyance barely concealed. "There is no need for you to go."

"But I could help!" Noha protests, wanting the chance to see the white bear.

"You could also help here on the hunt," Kraac reminds him coldly.

A calculating gleam lights Noha's hazel coloured eyes. "Who shall head the hunt in your absence?" He boldly asked Ecakik, ignoring Kraac.

Before the distraught Ecakik can answer, Kraac steps between him and Noha, his back firmly toward the latter. He suggests that one of the elder hunters whom Kiconce had trusted should lead the hunt. And so it is decided.

Noha watches his brothers and the apprentice lope homeward across the plain with thoughts whirling in his skull.

To the demons with Kraac! I just wanted to avenge the death of Pu though he was only a cub and therefore not as valuable to the clan as a hunter. I wanted to go! Kraac treats me like a stripling! I will bear it no longer!

A hand touches his forearm. He begins to shake it off and realizes it is Dinkka.

"Come Nisages," Dinkka says. "We have great need of you in the chase. Come lest Awaskesh escape our slow feet."

Noha's eyes clear. Always susceptible to flattery especially when honestly meant, he smiles. "You have reason, Nicimec," he says, for the first time giving Dinkka the title of *Younger Brother*.

Dinkka grins.

Together, they turn to face the mountains.

Noha's last thought as he begins to run is, *Kraac has a lesson to learn.*

CHAPTER 17

The Unwelcome Hunter

Che knows that Inik wants to die.

That dawning, when Drilla regained consciousness, she tried in vain to arouse Pu. Finally, she struggled back to camp following her own tracks on the snow patches. The two cubs had been missed, of course, and Artisan and the apprentice had led a group of young striplings in search of them. Artisan found Drilla crawling dazedly up a steep esker and carried her home to Narima.

The terrified cub is unable to speak at first but it is easy to retrace her path. Stricken Artisan discovers Pu's shattered body and sees the gigantic bear's spoor. He kneels for a long time, clutching the little hunter to his chest, and then he carries Pu home and places him in his ninga's arms.

Inik is quiet and self-effacing in her agony. With Che and Narima's help, she dresses her son in a soft new tunic and leggings that she had just sewn for him and they bury him beneath her hearthstone, his little broken spear by his side. There is no scarcity of volunteers to tend the four-day fire which will light Pu's way to the spirit land, but Inik prefers to sit alone by the flames and give way to the anguish she hides so well when others are near. For a time, she does not allow even Che or Artisan to sit watch with her.

Che is fighting her own battle and her heart aches for her friend; however, she respects Inik too much to go against her wishes.

"I am frightened for her," she tells Artisan.

The old artist and Che go to Inik on the third night. At first, Artisan doesn't break into her silence but squats nearby, scraping at a piece of ivory horn. He watches Inik feed willow sticks into the fire and when darkness is deepest, he speaks.

"I would tell a tale to you, *Katcidjininimi*, Little Sister."

Inik doesn't reply and he regards her with understanding compassion, saying after some time has passed, "It is a tale that your Ogucen loved to hear."

Inik looks into his aging face. "Tell your tale," she says.

Che sighs.

Artisan folds his long bony hands across his stomach.

"Maywisher, Long Time Ago, the son of a great ogima took a mate. They were happy until the female gave birth and the male cub, newly come from her body, died. The son of the ogima mourned him for two days and on the third day, he buried him beneath his hearthstone. However, he was not willing to let his son's manitu go to the Land of the Spirits and,

instead of building a new hut, he slept every night beside the grave."

Smoke curls from the fire, wreaths the three bent heads. Artisan pauses and peers at Inik who seems to be listening. He continues.

The people brought the hunter food but he would not eat it. At last, his ninga begged him to eat and he ate but he did not leave the grave during sleep times. Finally, Pepoon came and Keewatin drove the hunter to his ninga's fire, and he slept there."

Che hopes that Inik's continued stillness shows that she is heeding his words.

Artisan continues.

"When spring came, the ogima's son visited the grave once more and there he saw a small male cub gathering red fireweed and taking it down into the grave. He watched. At times, the spirit cub gathered other things and took them into the grave. Knowing that this was his ogucen's manitu, the man decided to trap the spirit cub. He fashioned four tiny spear points, like small stone leaves, and he cut and stripped four shafts which he stained crimson and fastened to the spear points with reindeer gut. When his ninga and his mate saw him working, they rejoiced, for they thought that his mourning was complete. Three sleeping times passed and the man visited the grave once more with one of the spears wrapped in soft doe skin. Once more the spirit cub appeared. It was older now, about the size of eight summers. When the spirit cub re-entered the

grave, the hunter put a spear on the grave and hid himself."

Che thinks she sees Inik tense, possibly remembering Pu's little spear.

Artisan mumbles slowly on, *"When the spirit cub emerged and saw the spear, he was afraid at first but, gathering courage, took up the spear and, laughing, returned with it to the grave. Three times more, the hunter left spears and each time the boy came to retrieve them. One night, the hunter fashioned six more spears and as before, the boy-spirit took them happily.*

"At length, the hunter told his ninga and his mate and the shaman about the spirit cub. It was decided that they would capture him. Each day, spears were left on the grave and near it and then further away until the spirit cub would venture very far from the grave to retrieve the red spears."

Inik is now leaning forward.

"Daily the spear trail became longer and longer until one day it ended at last at the house of the shaman who sat within in a trance. On that day, the shaman captured the spirit cub who, with terrified cries, shrivelled to almost nothing in his grasp."

Inik's hand goes to her mouth.

"For three days and four nights, the shaman sang, danced, and shook his rattles over the spirit cub, trying to breathe life into his body; however, when

the cub awoke at last he was a wraith who did not truly live."

Inik opens her lips to speak but Artisan lifts a hand to forestall her.

Che squirms. This old male had better be careful.

"Now it happened that, in another village, there was a very wise shaman, a female. The shaman who had captured the spirit cub went to her for counsel, telling her that ogima's son wished the boy to have full life and not the half-life of a spirit cub.

"She told him to take the spirit cub and his cousin of the same age and go on the mountain and there set fire to a spruce tree so that the hot gum would fall on their bodies. They should then wash their bodies in the great waterfall on the mountain.

"All this they did. The spirit cub became a true cub and grew to manhood along with his cousin."

Artisan stops speaking and Inik stares at him, confused.

Che holds her breath. At least the old man has Inik's attention.

"Must I watch for the spirit of my Ogucen and bathe him in the gum from a spruce tree and water?" Inik asks dazedly.

Che bites her lips until she tastes salty blood. There is false hope in Inik's eyes. What does the old fool think he is doing?

The Artisan shakes his head in sympathy probably loathe to extinguish the spark of hope but wishing to kindle with it a different blaze.

"No, my Nimi," he says softly.

"What then? What does this tale mean? It will not bring back my Ogucen!" Inik's voice is rising, verging on hysteria.

Che's fingernails bite into her palms. Now is the moment, when Inik is fighting back, when she is no longer the acquiescent sufferer!

Artisan holds up a wrinkled hand toward Che as if to silence her but he keeps his eyes firmly on Inik. "Don't you understand that although you cannot see your cub, though you cannot hold him in your arms; don't you see that what gives life to the spruce tree and to the water and to the fire and to the animals and to the rocks and to all that we know, gives life also to a cub? All life is one. There is no death. Pu has simply gone on a journey to another place! A good place! Pu is not dead! From the beginning, he was. And he shall always be."

"But what about the place of darkness?" Inik quails. "Why must I light my Ogucen's way with fire?"

"Ah, that is the question. I am afraid that, for all there must be a time of darkness. Perhaps your fire will help him on his journey. And the one who came before him and the one who comes after shall guide him."

Che frowns, puzzled. *The one who comes after him?*

Confusion still fills Inik's eyes but there is a beginning of something else. "I am not clever, she says. I do not fully understand."

Artisan leans over and takes her small, work scarred hands in his. He grasps them tightly as if to hold her back from an abyss out of which there is no climbing.

He says, "It is enough to know."

Inik asks no more questions and is comforted.

Che scrambles out of the hut.

It's not enough for me!

When Ecakik arrives the next day, Inik greets him calmly. While in the company of others, she does not try to console her mate because such a display would be unseemly. Instead, she gently tends his immediate needs.

Drilla seems to shake off her numbness at the sight of Kraac and runs to him. He lifts her and holds her safe against his chest while Narima anxiously watches from the hut entrance. Kraac's hold on Drilla tightens as if this cub, who had almost been lost, would be doubly precious to him now.

As for broken hearted Che, she had hoped in vain that Noha would be the one to come with Ecakik.

I need him! She sighs inwardly.

Fury not sorrow had swollen her heart when she heard about Pu's death. Pu who was to her a second son. He was so young! So promising! She wanted to scream, "Why? Why?" Into the ears of Manitou.

"There's nothing I can do!" she wails. If such as Pu must die, why can't I at least find revenge through my hunter's arm? I would slay the white beast with my own hands! Would that I could! If only I had let Pu run for the hunters as he wanted! But I had to put myself forward and forbid it. I am no clan mother. I am a vain fool!

No answer comes to her. No voice speaks to her. Pu is dead and there seems nothing she can do about it.

All those who had talked with Pu about the White Bear are questioned again and Drilla adds what she can. When Ecakik and Kraac have rested, they spend long hours in Boog's hut where the fragile old shaman treats them with courteous ceremony, his way of showing sympathy. Artisan is also allowed to join in counsel because he had loved Pu and his good sense is valued even by Boog, especially since Kiconce died.

Ecakik asks, "Was the bear who killed Pu, *Wabimakwa*, the White Bear of your prophecy?"

Boog admits reluctantly that it might be so.

"Is he a relative of *Makwa*, the Cave Bear?"

"Manitou has not spoken to me of this," Boog replies.

For once Ecakik loses patience. "Well, is it permitted to kill him? Speak!"

The shaman's eyes narrow but he doesn't remonstrate. He says only, "It is permitted to try."

The apprentice, exhausted from his journey to fetch Ecakik and Kraac, snores in a dark corner of the hut, so Che and Jag serve the hunters. Kraac and Ecakik discuss the coming hunt for Wabimakwa, seeking to devise new methods of killing him and begging the shaman to call down from the spirit world the acquiescence and forgiveness of the White One's powerful manitu. They have completely forgotten the females' presence and start when Che, scared but determined, interrupts.

"I beg, O shaman, permission to speak."

Kraac's dark eyes flash with controlled anger. Ecakik merely looks astonished. Boog's face is impassive but Jag watches Che with narrowed eyes full of venom.

Artisan says respectfully, "O shaman, I remind you that Mother Earth sometimes speaks through her daughters' mouths. Let us listen to what the mate of Kiconce's ogucen wishes to say."

There is no reading the expression in Boog's eyes but he orders hoarsely, "Speak, female."

Jag makes a clicking sound of disapproval. Ecakik merely shrugs. It is Kraac who seems most put out.

Che takes a deep, tremulous breath.

Help me, Bara.

She declares, "I honoured the hunter of ptarmigan as if he had come from my body instead of my friend's. I wish to help avenge his death."

Amusement twitches Kraac's lips and his eyes soften. "And how will such as you accomplish this?" he asks.

Che stills. *You shall not frighten me, Cold One."*

Che blurts, "I cannot, of course, slay Wabimakwa." The males simply stare at her and Jag ostentatiously turns her back. Che stumbles on, "But perhaps I can be of some help to his hunters?"

"Help?" Ecakik asks, not unkindly.

Che's heart quivers. He didn't say *No*! Now if only she can convince Kraac. Not daring to look at either Kraac or the shaman, Che concentrates on Ecakik's open face.

"I could carry your food and water and extra hides and spears. I could tend the fire while you rest. This hunt is certain to be difficult and will need all your strength, and there are no grown striplings here to help. I could make it easier for you."

"This is folly," Kraac begins.

"Wait," Artisan interrupts. "She talks sense. Never before have you hunted Wabimakwa. Who knows what adventures and terrors await you? You will need all your stamina and cunning for the hunt. Perhaps the female could help."

"She'll fall behind," Kraac objects again.

"I shall not," Che insists, meeting those black eyes without faltering.

"If you do fall behind," Ecakik interjects worriedly, "we could not stop to bring you safely to the clan."

Kraac says, obviously hoping to frighten her. "We would leave you a victim to the tundra animals. You would die."

"I shall not die."

Jag, who is quick to pick up nuances, recognizes the subtle change in the hunters' attitude. They are looking directly at Che now, taking her seriously. Jag, who is cunning, tries to mend her mistake. "One of you hunters might be hurt and need help."

Che turns to look at her, surprised to get support from that quarter.

"I suppose you also want to come on the hunt!" Kraac snarls, exasperated.

Jag shrugs. "I would simply give her some of my herbs and remedies. Perhaps you will have sore need of them."

"She speaks the truth." Artisan says.

Kraac throws up his hands. "What do you say, O Shaman?"

Boog has been watching Kraac with interest. A hint of irony tinges Boog's tone as he replies, "Take her. If you need her, use her." Kraac's handsome face flushes and he looks angrier than ever. Boog adds, "If she falls behind, leave her. Above all, Wabimakwa must die. The Brown Bear must kill him! So sayeth the vision!"

When the hunters have gone, Che approaches Jag. "Thank you for helping me," she says warmly. Jag stares at her with icy eyes. Che retreats. Whatever Jag's motive was, it certainly was not friendship for her.

Word of Che's coming escapade spreads quickly through the camp. Many females disapprove. The foremost among them come to confront Che as she gathers supplies for the journey. Inik emerges from her hut and follows them.

Narima says nastily to Che, "Your actions are unseemly and wrong!"

Big Whea declares, "You should be punished!"

Lara's lovely eyes are full of compassion for Che but she is too timid to speak up in her defence.

Strangely enough, Inik shuts all their mouths by declaring, "When Che goes, I shall care for her cubs. She is braver than all of us, and if she dies, which could very well happen, I shall guard her little ones forever!"

Che is fighting back tears when she runs to Inik and throws her arms around her. It is not merely guilt; it is not merely a need to prove her worth to Kraac; it is not even a selfish desire to accompany hunters on an adventure that drives her. Even Che, herself, doesn't fully understand her burning need to go on this hunt. She simply knows that she must go.

CHAPTER 18

Sweet Conquest

Che follows the hunters, as unobtrusive as a shadow.

They track Wabimakwa from the spot where Pu's body was found. For fourteen sleeps, they trail him, using two dogs. The pace is slow so Che has no difficulty in keeping up and she is certain that the hunters enjoy the fire she readies for them at rest time and the good hot food that warms their bellies. Ecakik, having accepted her presence, is pleasant with her. Kraac simply ignores her.

As is his custom, Nanook has ranged far along the shore ice, feasting on seals and fattening for the summer ahead. Kraac and Ecakik come upon him at last as he shambles on the ice near some coastal rocks. After roping and muzzling their dogs, they wriggle on their bellies to within two hundred strides of the white bear, making certain that they are upwind of him and well hidden among the ash grey rocks.

Both hunters are struck dumb at the animal's majesty.

Ecakik whispers to Kraac, "To die at the hand of such a creature was a death of great honour. A powerful manitu must dwell in such a bear. I am glad that Pu was buried with his broken spear by his side."

They follow the bear for days, using all their skills to remain beyond his awareness but close enough to observe his habits. Che, just as curious as they, is careful to stay always in the far distance, a small companion to Ecakik and Kraac, just as the white fox is to Nanook.

Ecakik notices that Wabimakwa is more vulnerable in water. One night at the fire he says wistfully, "I cannot swim but I wish the new land contained large trees so I might fell one and drag it to the water and float on it and do battle with the white bear. I used to catch lots of small animals that way, in the old land. Two hunters alone and on foot cannot bring down Wabimakwa."

Che, imagining Ecakik perched on a floating tree and trying to wrestle Wabimakwa, stifles a giggle.

"I have an idea," Kraac says.

"Speak," Ecakik says hopefully.

"I would use a snare."

"A snare for such as he? Surely he's not a hare."

Kraac explains his plan.

They set their snare between two huge black boulders deposited on the beach by an ancient glacier. They place the bait, a fresh seal carcass, so that it can only be approached from one direction between rows of pointed sticks pounded into the ground. Between the sticks, they conceal under spongy moss a snare made from the strongest ropes they can fashion. They don't expect the ropes to hold the bear but only to distract him.

When they have completed the trap, they show themselves on a nearby slope and it is not long before Nanook smells their strange odour on the wind and lumbers to investigate, not intending to attack because his belly is full. He wonders what these skinny, strange, upright creatures are, having seen only their young. When he notices the seal carcass between the boulders; he hesitates and then decides that a free meal is worth investigation and marches purposefully into the snare.

He is so busy with the food that he doesn't notice the deerhide rope on his leg until it begins to tighten with his movements. He bellows and throws himself so strongly backward that he flips completely over. The two guant hunting dogs, fangs bared, swoop across the plain to harass him. Nanook immediately crouches low, white back humped, gargantuan head near the ground, curved claws gripping the earth, a manic growl coming from his throat.

The dogs, though staunch, have never before faced a polar bear and they stop at a safe distance, snarling and yelping. For some reason, Nanook doesn't charge, and it isn't the snare that holds him because he has already snapped the rope. Perhaps he is confused by these creatures who look like wolves but are not wolves though they smell like animals. He is certain, too, that he has nothing to fear from the stupid, yapping non-wolves or their fragile friends who walk in a rearing position. Nanook makes a contemptuous feint at the dogs, who immediately retreat, turns and ambles away. The dogs are about to resume their attack when the hunters whistle them back.

"It will take many dogs and many hunters to kill such a bear," Ecakik reiterates.

"Perhaps," Kraac answers.

They make a fireless camp near the ice that sleep time, trusting to their dogs to warn them if Wabimakwa should reappear. All through the night, they discuss various ways and means of killing the bear. Methods used with reindeer and mammoth will not work on such a creature, and the ground below the surface is too solidly frozen to dig a pit-trap like they had for the rhino.

Ecakik repeats, "Spearing in water would be the best way if we knew how to float on it like ducks and geese."

Che had been a distant spectator at the snaring. She, too, is elated and bursting with excitement though she has the wisdom to simply fill the hunter's needs before they know they have them and to be grateful to be allowed to listen. However, when her work is done, she lies long awake, thinking.

Kraac notices her self-control and she overhears him admit to Ecakik, "Perhaps it was not a bad notion to bring along the female."

Pleasure wells in Che and then she is angry with herself for caring what Kraac thinks.

To learn Wabimakwa's ways, they follow the bear long into the time of Nerockamink, stopping only to hunt for meat. Always Che keeps pace with the hunters, never complaining and continuing to remain in the background when not needed. However, should Kraac or Ecakik want food, he finds it always near his hand. She carries their wet footgear next to her skin to thaw and warm them. She builds small, smokeless fires over which she brews strength-giving herbal drinks. She totes their trappings and takes her turn at watch during sleep time.

Although it is not difficult for the humans to supply their needs Nanook is having a tougher time. The ice has melted, the seals and walruses have departed, and Nanook is confined to land and river forage. Bearberries, lemmings, and salmon make light eating. He becomes thin and tired. The trackers he ignores. He knows very well that they follow him but he has become used to their presence and regards them somewhat as he does the fox who eats the remains of his meals in winter. He has not yet begun to regard men as food.

Ecakik finds the whale carcass on the beach. Both hunters are flabbergasted at the size of the fish, as they think it, for it is bigger even than the one-horn Noha found. The skin proves extremely tough and the meat unpalatable and putrid but the dogs tear voraciously at the carcass. The rotting flesh falls away in chunks and before long a rib is bared, then two.

"Such a smell!" Che complains to herself.

She stares and stares at the ribs. She rubs her forehead and mumbles, "If I were to cut away the meat and wrap the ribcage in skins, perhaps I could float within it on the water like the giant fish. The clan would be impressed by such a deed. I could collect some bones but how could I carry them?"

The notion plagues her for hours and at last, she breaks her promise to herself not to bother the hunters and goes to Ecakik, not only because he talks so much about wanting to float on the water but because she fears Kraac's contempt. He might just get angry. She sighs. How can he be so skilful a hunter who has the respect of everyone in the clan and still be so unfriendly? Guilt stabs. I am not being fair. After all, he saved my life. And I have to admit that he is comely, so tall and austere with those flashing, ardent eyes that spear me with their glance.

Nevertheless, she knows that the patient Ecakik, who is always amazed at inventiveness in others, will bend willing ears to her suggestion.

Of course, Ecakik immediately goes to Kraac with her idea and the latter is annoyed.

Kraac's hands clench. "I don't like it. Our Nicimec's mate once more puts herself forward in unseemly fashion."

Ecakik's face stiffens. "You are too hard on her! Besides, I think she is smart and I like her. I will do the thing she suggests. For now, I shall collect some of the whale bones."

"Do what you want."

Beneath his anger, however, Kraac can't subdue admiration for the female's ingenuity and he makes an effort to be completely honest with himself. She is not only clever but has also been brave and circumspect on the hunt. Could I be jealous because she went to Ecakik and not to me with her thoughts? After all, she owes me her life. He remembers Noha's reaction on finding them in each other's arms. He remembers the feel of her small body against his. He jumps up.

"I will not wait for you to gather bones," he announces to his brother, ignoring Che. "I shall find Wabimakwa's tracks. Have you forgotten, Nidjkiwe, that we lost his spoor before we slept?"

"I do not forget," Ecakik says stubbornly. "Allow me one sleep for this new task. Then I shall follow."

"As you wish but keep the female with you," Kraac says offhandedly. "I don't want her."

"I had intended as much," Ecakik said evenly. "She is a help and a comfort."

Kraac whistles his reluctant dog away from the whale carcass and sets off. He is unaware that the reason they had lost Nanook's trail was because the bear had employed a favourite trick and made a big circle to come up behind and upwind to surprise his trackers; he, too, has smelled the whale carcass and he is very hungry. Thus it is that Kraac's dog growls too late as his master passes a moss covered ice pingo. From behind it, a great, hairy white paw slashes downward, tears away part of Kraac's scalp and hair, rakes his cheek, gouges his left shoulder.

Even though the blow is glancing, the very strength of it knocks Kraac through the air to slam down, stunned but not unconscious. His dog yowls and leaps for the bear's throat only to be crushed against the mighty chest, its bones snapping as it dies. His sacrifice has given Kraac the time he needs. He struggles to his feet, sees that the squatting bear is intent upon devouring the dog and, with a lunge and a master hunter's accuracy and strength of hand and arm, thrusts his spear directly through Nanook's black eye and into his brain. The spirits, this day, are on the side of man. Before he faints, Kraac hopes that Wabimakwa is dead.

Che and Ecakik select and gather whale bones for one sleep time.

They work well together, laughing and grimacing at the unpleasantness of the task and discussing possible ways of making the future watercraft. When they have finished and washed in the endless lake, they pile the bones, quickly pick up their things and hurry off along Kraac's trail. Ecakik's dog finds the injured hunter and at the sound of the animal's howls, Che rushes to the place where Kraac lies. She stifles a horrified scream and falls to her knees beside him.

Ecakik charges up.

Che shouts, "He lives! He lives!"

They carry him to the shore of the Endless Lake, bathe his terrible wounds and cover those on the side of his head and his left cheek with moss and some of Jag's spider webs from a pouch Che carries on her belt. With a clean sliver of pierced whalebone and strips of washed intestine, Che gently sews together the gash on Kraac's shoulder, after sprinkling in it some of Jag's ground roots. She lights a fire inland and directs Ecakik to carry Kraac to it. Ecakik, suddenly awkward and helpless, follows her instructions and then orders his dog to guard them.

"I shall tend to the white bear," he says.

Returning to Wabimakwa, Ecakik guts him so that his meat will not spoil, skins and butchers the carcass, leaving the head attached to the intact body hide, and digs a pit in which he caches the hide and the meat just above permafrost. When he has stayed away as long as he decently can, he returns to them. Kraac had lapsed into deep unconsciousness and fever.

"I have lost Pu and my parents. Don't let me lose my Nicimec, too!" he sobs openly.

Che bites back angry words. Why can't the big fool help instead of wailing?

As if reading her thoughts, Ecakik makes an effort, poking at the fires, picking things up and putting them down, getting in Che's way. He soon finds that watching Kraac's sufferings is more than he can bear. He again occupies himself with dragging the whale bones to the campsite. He constructs with them a bone hut around Kraac's pallet and over it he drapes the soiled skin of Wabimakwa which he has dug up.

He says, "It will be strong medicine."

One morning, Che takes pity on him and says, "I need fresh meat to make broth for our Nikjkiwe should he awake. Will you get some for me?"

Ecakik leaps up as if scalded and Che watches him go with tender compassion tightening her throat. Besides, his absence will leave her in peace to fight for Kraac's life.

Kraac passes quickly from fever to delirium and Che realizes that she could well lose him. She grits her pointy teeth.

"I shall not let you die! You shall not die!"

She cleans the wounds daily with sea water and gathers fresh moss to pack them. She strips away his coverings and bathes his burning body when fever is upon him, and when he shakes with chills and calls out in his raving for help, she slips off her tunic, crawls beneath the skins that cover him and warms him with her body.

She cuts away the proud flesh from his wounds when they look like they might putrefy, binds and packs the wounds again, tying his threshing hands and legs to stakes before she begins and whispering encouragement while she performs the cruel task.

When he gets a hand loose and its wild swing sends her crashing backwards, she rights herself and whispers, "Yes, fight, Nijkiwe. Dear, dear Kraac. Such a special one as you must live!"

When Kraac comes at last from the land of the spirit-tortured, Ecakik is away from the hut. It is Che's happy smile he sees first. He tries to smile in return.

"Did I kill Wabimakwa?" he croaks.

Tenderness for him makes her hands shake as she quickly holds a shell of water to his lips and when he has drunk, she tells him, "With one thrust of your spear, you pierced through Wabimackwa's eye and even unto his knowing place. Legends will tell of your mighty deed."

As he becomes aware of his wounds, Kraac stifles an agonized moan and whispers, "Who has healed me? My body is much torn."

"Your Nisages and your nimi have tended you."

"How long have I wandered in the land of dreams?"

"Twenty sleeps," she says. "But you must speak no more. You must rest. Time enough for questions when you are fully healed."

"I fear sleep," he whispers like a vulnerable cub. "It holds many bad dreams."

Embarrassed for him but pleased that he should confide in her, she says the only thing she can think of, "Surely not all of your dreams were so terrible."

"Not all," he says, the old teasing gleam in his black eyes. "I remember cool hands on my brow and a silken body warming me."

Che lowers her eyelids. "Sleep now, Nijkiwe," she begs.

Hours later Ecakik finds her still kneeling beside his brother. She is holding Kraac's hand. "He spoke," she says quietly. "He will live."

Ecakik races from the hut and moments later, she hears his joyful shout from beyond a nearby knoll.

Kraac improves quickly. He will always have a hairless patch on the left side of his scalp and a deep scar on his cheek. His shoulder is still swollen, crazily red-ridged and painful, but he can move it if necessary and it promises to be useful again. Luckily it is his left shoulder. When he is near full recovery, Ecakik tells them that he must travel back to the Eyo camp, leaving the dog to protect them.

"I have made certain that there are no more bears in this place. I shall bring back females to carry the whalebones and the meat and Wabimakwa's hide. Meanwhile, you must rest here, Nidjkiwe. Our Nimi will remain with you."

Che stiffens. She doesn't want to stay alone with Kraac because she fears the intimacy that has inevitably grown between them during his long convalescence. And she still feels uncomfortable with this man who, unlike Noha, seems always to know what she is thinking. Furthermore, he now not only listens to her talk but encourages her to speak of her inner thoughts and about the wonders she feels are still to be discovered in the new land. Truly he speaks with her as if she were a brother hunter and doesn't hide his gratitude . . . nor the hunger that is slowly growing in him.

There is no choice. Ecakik, having made his decision, is quickly gone.

Che, famished for communication with one of her own capacity, ignores the knawings of guilt and decides; I shall talk with this hunter as I have never been allowed to talk with my mate.

They speak of many things, of Noha's and Boog's dreams, of the New Land's strange animals, of Pu, of death, of the clan ways. Che even finds the strength to tell him about how she once stole her brother's spear and hunted. How he laughs when she tells him that tale! And it is not derisive laughter but sensitive and sweet. She finds herself talking about Bara and of the role Bara bade her take. She even admits that she often wishes she was a hunter.

"I am glad that you are not a hunter," he says in the old bantering way.

"But you males have such freedom while we females . . ." she pauses, thinking she has overstepped. "It's just that I have no one to talk to about the things that enter my head." She stops herself again. She will *not* complain about Noha.

"It's strange. I have never considered that females had such thoughts," says Kraac. "However, with you it does not surprise me." He stares long and hard at her until she flushes and leaves him on some excuse.

What she feared happens. When she carries food to him Kraac allows his fingers to linger on hers and follows with yearning eyes her movements in the small hut. The result of this on her is dizzying. She finds it difficult to breathe and blood drums in her tightened throat. She pretends not to react and prays to Mother Earth for the strength not to shiver with desire at his touch. Sleep time is almost unbearable; she lies rigid near him, knowing that he too is awake and pretending to sleep.

Kraac holds back as long as he can. It isn't until some time after Ecakik's departure that he comes to her where she lies on her sleep platform and taking her face between his hands, looks full into her amber hued eyes. She gazes back, seeing not the terrible wounds but the finely sculptured head, the black eyes, the mouth.

"What shall we do, little Nimi?" he asks and there is anguish in his words. "Do you feel also this unquenchable fire in your loins? My body cries out for you in pain worse than what I suffered with my wounds. Never before have I felt like this." He pauses, obviously trying to get a grip on his emotions. He says, "It is for you to say."

Che is imagining his lips against her breasts, his hands kneading her belly. Longing tightens her throat and her mound throbs and swells, but she gasps, "It cannot be, Nidjkiwe. What about our mates? Would you give them such return for their faith?"

There is no deception in Kraac. "Never will I put aside my mate, little Nimi. You must know this above all."

"I know it. But do you think I could leave my Napima and the cubs of my flesh and come to you?"

"If you wished it, it would be so. But I do not ask it."

"What do you ask?" The words are out before she can stop them.

"I ask that this time shall be ours. We are far from the huts of our clan. None shall know of our union unless you wish it. But I won't force you."

Still she hesitates.

He says, "I have dreamed and in my dream, the spirits told me that they look with understanding upon us. We do no evil. We are born of different clans but are the same in our manitu. Our bodies were made to fit one the other. Our knowing places are equal."

His voice catches, "I want you so. Little One?"

She thinks of Noha. But her very silence betrays her.

And she doesn't protest as he gently removes her tunic and nuzzles her breasts bringing her nipples upright with his tongue. Her thighs opened as if of their own volition to his seeking hands and mouth and when his desire outdistances his control as she begins to moan and thresh under his magic, she screams with pleasure as he spears her to the earth and rides her to delight. And after the first wild union, they lie for days exploring each other's bodies and minds. He devises infinite ways of giving her pleasure, teaching her subtle nuances of sensation and abandoning himself when she, in turn, stimulates and torments his body into cataclysms.

And when they are exhausted, she brews herb tea and prepares food and they eat and drink and talk and talk and talk before once more plunging into passion. Che has never before been so happy and she knows without being told that the same is true for Kraac.

Beyond the haven they have created in the whalebone hut, the world continues as before. The news of Wabimakwa's death strikes awe into the hearts of the females in the Eyo camp. They hurry with Ecakik toward the bone hut, Narima in the lead. There they find Kraac almost recovered. His relieved mate throws herself upon him. He holds her tightly, looking over her dark head at Che. There is infinite pain in his black eyes.

Che manages a querulous smile before she turns away.

She is glad that Inik stayed behind with the cubs because she never could have hidden her guilt from her friend. As it was, she avoids Narima as much as she can and chooses Lara as her workmate while helping Ecakik to bring the bear meat and skin and some of the whalebones to the camp where Boog awaits the return of the Killer of Wabimakwa. There the trophies are secured until the arrival of the reindeer hunters and the celebration feast.

As for Kraac, he looks not on Che but on Narima, and when he meets Che accidentally, he treats her as he promised, as the respected nimi she has always been. Che knows that she should be grateful for his forbearance; however, she feels the emptiness of betrayal in her heart. And she awaits with trembling her mate's return.

Surely he'll know!

CHAPTER 19

Disillusion

While Che and Kraac lie entwined in the bone hut, Noha at last encounters his beloved deer. The caribou are noisy animals and bigger than the reindeer of the old land.

Noha says to Dinkka, "These animals will provide the Eyo with much more than meat and tunics. My mate will make summer hut coverings and daggers and chisels for me. She'll be pleased." He doesn't notice Dinkka's quizzical look.

This particular herd migrates yearly from the taiga of the mountains' interior valleys and river plateaus, where they feed on tree branches, moss, and grass and on through a mountain pass to the shore of the Endless Lake. As they make their vociferate way along the mountain ridges and the frozen river in the valley, their foot joints clack and the air reverberates with snuffling, snorting, and asthmatic wheezing.

When Noha and his fellow hunters had first set out from the camp, the caribou were already in the mountain pass and the main herd was spread over the glacier-formed valley where they followed the river, wandering among the stunted trees that marked its banks or moving placidly upstream into the high pass until they reached the river's source. On either side rose a mosaic of purple-blue against white crowned by distant snowy peaks, while the lower mountain slopes were clothed with thin forests of spruce, birch, willow and alder.

On the rock strewn upper slopes, the cows gathered in groups of ten or less. When the time came to drop her calf, each cow drifted to a secluded spot where she lay in labour, struggled finally to her feet and expelled a single calf on the bare rock. In a short time, the calf stood on its thin legs to nurse.

Most of the calves had coats of warm, sienna brown with white undersides, velvety black noses and long lashed eyes. A few were light in colour. As delicate as they seemed, in two or three sleeps, they were able to outdistance a running man. That year, no late frost or freezing rain decimated the herd so the calf crop was large.

When the fuzzy catkins were just beginning to appear on the dwarf willows and the weather warmed, the stately cows, with their offspring prancing about them, left the rocky highlands to join the herd in the pass. From there, they wandered slowly northward following paths worn deep by passing generations. Their restlessness assuaged now that the calving was safely completed, Nerockamink found them munching on algar moss, lichens, grass, sedges, and herbs on the northern plateaus' and escarpments' treeless tundra.

Wolves followed, feasting on the young and the slow but presenting no danger to the herd as a whole; however, this particular spring the caribou were to find a new enemy on the tundra, a two legged creature who could run like a deer, who carried a sharp killing stick and who would hunt them at river crossings and narrows and from stone ambushes on the tundra.

Dinkka sights the first of the herd filtering from the mountain valley. Runners are sent out and the hunters gather. As they form their hunting teams, Noha is surprised when Quork offers to hunt with him, Dinkka, and the twins.

"What about Fuum?" Megi, the biggest twin, asks stupidly.

"He will probably run with the striplings," a sullen Quork replies.

Little Fuum overheards and stepping forward, looks Noha directly in the eyes and says, "The elder hunters will need the striplings. I go with you, too, if you will have me."

Noha sees Dinkka watching him, obviously curious to hear his reply. He frowns. What has gotten into the manitu of these hunters? "Of course I shall have you. You are one of the clan's best hunters."

Everyone looks pleased but Noha has neither the time nor inclination to think about the subtle relationships among hunters; he is curious about the sheltered valley and the river that meanders along its floor.

He says to Dinkka, "This is certain to be a passageway to the south. We need only follow the herd in autumn and the new land will be ours. I shall raise the notion in council and all must agree!"

For some reason, Dinkka makes no comment.

As for the caribou, they are everything Noha dreamed. At first, they are ridiculously easy to kill, having never seen man. One needed only to approach a group slowly and then turn and walk away. The caribou would follow like lambs directly into ambush among the rocks. This is somehow disappointing but after a time, the animals learn to fear man and once more Noha is flying across the tundra, his lightly shod feet scarcely touching the ground. They hunt for many waking times, slaughtering their own kills because their females are far off in the fishing camps.

In late spring, a stripling is sent back to summon the females to carry meat and hides from the slaughtering areas. To Noha's amazement, word comes from Boog himself that they must break off the hunt for the time being, cache their meat, and return to the river camp for a great council.

Che waits circumspectly until after their reunion and their first coupling to tell Noha about her part in the hunt for the Great White Bear.

"You went on the hunt!" he cries, incredulous.

"I went."

"Who allowed this thing?"

"I had the permission of your Nijkiwe and the Shaman."

Noha fumes. She went on the most important hunt, a hunt which will be legend in times to come. And I was told to stay behind! By Kraac!

"I am shamed!" he shouts. "You have disgraced your mate and betrayed your cubs!"

"No! There was need of me. Look at your Nisages. I healed him!"

Noha strides out of the hut and goes in search of Kraac, determined to quarrel with him. He finds him in conversation with the caribou hunters.

"Greetings, Nicimec," Kraac says carefully when Noha marches up to the group.

Seeing his brother's livid scars, Noha hesitates momentarily but envy knawing at his bowels, says sarcastically, "Greetings, Nisages. I hear strange tales about your adventures. We must speak of this."

"So we shall," Kraac smiles nervously but amiably.

Noha barges on. "My mate tells me you have taken her on the hunt."

Kraac's smile fades.

"Why did you! It is unseemly and I am shamed."

"Shamed? Why?" Kraac flounders.

Delighted at Kraac's unusual discomfiture, Noha says, "Females do not hunt!"

Kraac draws a deep breath. "May females not follow the hunter, feed him, tend his fire and his wounds?"

"Perhaps," Noha concedes. "But the hunter whom they follow should be their sworn mate."

Noha is surprised to see his usually impermeable brother pale. His glance drifts to the gouged shoulder and guilt again runs through him. The others are listening to this escalating argument with downcast eyes and, led by Laf, one by one they drift away until Noha and Kraac stand alone.

Kraac rallies quickly. "Take care, Nicimec," he warns coldly. "You should be proud of your mate. She saved my life."

There is no reply Noha can make to this.

Che stands helplessly in her hut entrance watching the brothers, knowing by the set of Noha's shoulders that his anger has not abated.

Surely Kraac will defend me. Surely . . .

Noha swings on his heel and stomps back to face her. "You weren't wanted on the hunt."

"Does your Nisages say this?" Che asks, stricken.

"Yes."

What Kraac had said was that he had at first disapproved of her coming but that Artisan's pleas had swayed him and that her exemplary conduct on the hunt had changed his mind.

"Then it is so. I was not wanted." Che's neck bent, tears brimmed.

Kraac. I trusted you. To you I bared my manitu. I felt for you . . . yes, I felt for you the feeling for which there is no word . . . And you betrayed me!

She says abjectly, "I ask forgiveness, Napima. Never again shall I go on a hunt!"

"I forgive you," Noha says, but she knows that he does not and her own guilt forbids her to judge his harshness. Little does her blind Napima know how much he has to forgive.

The following sleep time finds Che lying alone on her sleeping platform. She is split in two. She had thought, having given herself so completely to Kraac that Noha would no longer have the power to stir her. But she is wrong. During his plundering of her body on his return from the hunt, she responded to him as always. True he hadn't thought of her pleasure and she had not reached an apex, but the old desire had still been there. Since then he has ignored her and seems even to avoid touching her.

Am I merely a rutting rodent that I can be aroused by any hunter?

She remembers the long intimate hours with Kraac, the exquisite sensations, the depth of their mutual understanding. She looks over at her mate. Pretending fatigue or indifference, Noha lies with his back turned to her and stares into the fire.

Is he just angry about the hunt or does he sense . . . ? She is suddenly afraid. What if he never changes? What will happen to me?

Doubly bereft, since she feels deserving of Noha's rejection, Che doesn't complain. She longs to ask of Kraac, "Why did you betray me? Why is it always like this?"

And Kraac, seeing her unhappiness from a distance, agonizes.

Noha must have punished her for going on the hunt. He doesn't deserve her! If she came to me, I would take her in. I need her so.

Having tasted magic, he now feels only animal comfort in coupling with Narima and sadly realizes it was all he had ever felt with her. Even Little Drilla and Cici are not enough to fill his heart; nevertheless, he remembers his vow of silence and he doesn't approach Che nor does he challenge Noha's anger which will soon dissipate.

Noha soon forgets the pain he causes.

And what about the pain I cause . . . ?

CHAPTER 20

Three Fires

All the clan attend the great council from ancient Boog to the smallest infant cradled in a skin on his ninga's back. The smells of Nerockamink lie gently upon the wind.

Since the caribou hunters are first called upon to speak, the eldest, Mizinawa, says, "These new deer are numerous and bigger than the reindeer we formerly hunted, but they have similar habits. Their arrival on the tundra means that the Eyo will never want for anything in this new land!"

Ecakick's sudden appearance silences delighted laughter. Over his head, he has draped Wabimakwa's arrogant skull, and the heavy, white pelt trails on the ground. He has fitted his hands inside the paws and it takes all of his strength to flail the air with their vicious spikes. In the fire's dim light, the huge bear comes alive again as Ecakik shambles and charges about in ritual. The cubs squeal. Che, remembering what Wabimakwa did to Kraac, shrinks involuntarily against Inik. However the latter shows no sign of the terror she must feel upon confronting this effigy of the animal who had killed Pu.

Kraac strides into the circle. He is naked and the deep grooves in his scalp and shoulder gleam purple in the firelight. He carries a single spear. He stands tall, slim and fearless facing the bear. Kraac advances and, his dark skin glistening with sweat, stalks his prey around the circle.

Che stares. She watched muscles play in his long legs; his buttocks tighten as he moves. Seeing his member stand slightly erect, she feels her own loins contract painfully. She bites her lip.

I must forget!

Again and again Wabimakwa charges until finally he sends Kraac sprawling with a heavy blow to the head. Into the arena leaps a cub who represents Kraac's dog. He wears a wolf pelt. He springs upon the bear, is seized and cast aside to lie still upon the ground. Che feels Inik tremble against her. She puts a consoling hand on her forearm.

Kraac rises and with a mighty spear-thrust, pierces the eye and brain of Wabimakwa.

Wild singing and shouting. Noha and the other hunters leap to they feet, prancing and yelling as if moon mad. Even Che and Inik smile tremulously and join in the females' more sedate dance, taking care to keep their mackisins' soles always in contact with Mother Earth. After a time, Ecakik emerges from the bearskin and impales the big bear head on a pole which he sticks into the ground. When this is done, Boog clothed in a hairless hide painted with strange signs and symbols of which only he knows the meaning and origins, comes forward. Red and black hide ribbands hang from his fingers. He attaches them to the bear's head, chanting all the while in a reedy voice and shuffling his feet in ritual dance.

"We are the people of *Awaskesh*," he sings. "O *Wabimakwa*, long have we honoured your cousin, *Makwa*, Cave Bear. Do not be angry with us but join with us in this feast where for the first time we shall eat of your flesh. Your bones shall be honoured among us forever and we shall emulate your courage. Allow your manitu to enter into our hearts."

He paints black strips on the bear's face and returns to his place in the circle. Quickly Che and the other females place a long, woven hide on the ground and, on it they spread strips of cooked and raw bear meat. A general rush and the feasting begins.

Kraac had been right about Noha. Che sees how his naturally gregarious nature has surfaced once more and he cannot take his eyes from Kraac, so great now is his admiration. His former anger has evaporated.

She grumbles, "Why can't he be like that with me?"

Noha is not the only one who reveres Kraac. When the feasting is done and the females and cubs had retired into the shadows, Mizinawa spits out his pebbles, stands and commands silence.

"I would speak!" he says. All await his words.

"Many sleeps have the Eyo been without an Ogima."

"You have said it," murmur the hunters.

"It is time that we looked about us and chose from among the hunters a new leader."

There are assenting grunts from all sides.

Che straightens. What is this?

"What does the Shaman say?" Mizinawa asks diffidently.

"You have spoken," Boog mumbles, continuing to chew on a piece of raw bear meat. Whom do you put forward?"

"I speak for the Killer of Wabimakwa. He shall be Ogima!"

Kraac starts. Che feels a stab of pride for him. Noha's head whips round to stare at Mizinawa.

"*Éhé!*" is the immediate and positive response from many throats, but Che realizes not from all, and not from Noha's.

Mizinawa's face reddens as he notes that some of the younger males have abstained from shouting their *éhés*, and that even some of the elder hunters are silent. Boog himself continues to stare into the fire as if ignoring the whole proceeding.

Mizinawa says reluctantly, "Who would speak?"

"I shall speak." It is Dinkka who strides boldly forward and a surprised gasp rises from the gathering at the temerity of the young hunter who a few months before had been but a stripling. However, Dinkka, though reserved, never hesitates to express himself when he thinks it important.

"Great is the killer of the white bear!" he says. "I honour his deed and am humble before him."

Old heads nod wisely.

Dinkka does not stop there. "I am young and my voice is as a sigh in the wind to the wise ones' ears. But even such as I are heard by the great council."

"You have said it," many agree.

"I put forward for Ogima the name of the friend of Assinbo, the third Ogucen of Kiconce."

Noha? Che feels suddenly numb.

Noha's mouth falls open and he grunts as if all the air has been sucked from his lungs. He seems even more amazed when, from around him comes the sound of other young voices shouting, "Éhé! Éhé!" He humbly bows his head.

In the shadows, Che's eyes shine amber. This will make him so happy! Then with a pang, What about Kraac?

Everywhere the people are muttering, looking at each other and from Noha to Kraac. They scarcely notice when Laf stands and steps into the circle of firelight.

"I would speak," he says.

Confused silence follows this new announcement.

"The killing of the white bear was a great deed," Laf says and pauses. "Always has my manitu been one with the friend of Assinbo. He is as my right arm. But there is one among us who is also brave and a mighty hunter and has led us in patience and strength. I put forward the name of Anikeogima!"

Che and Inik stare at each other.

"Éhé! Éhé!" Different spears wave in assent.

Noha must know the truth of Laf's words, but chagrin twists his face when he realizes that the companion of his youth has chosen Ecakik over him.

Che's frantic glance darts from his worried face to Kraac's still countenance.

Laf looks to Boog. "What say you, Shaman?"

"Spears must be shown," Boog says and gestures to Mizinawa.

The old hunter rises to his feet and calls in turn the names of Kraac, Noha, and Ecakik, the only time, other than at their naming feasts, when their actual names will be uttered aloud in council. For each name, a number of hunters stand, raising their spears at arms length above their heads. The old hunters and a few young males like Laf vote for Ecakik. The youngest among them, Dinkka and the twins, Tuk and Megi, cast their lot with Noha as do Artisan, Fuum and Quork; while Kraac claims the loyalty of four young males and two elders, one of whom is Mizinawa. The three nominees squat and stared fixedly at the ground during the spear showing.

Consternation seizes the people. A decision must be made and they are evenly divided.

Boog speaks. "I would hear the words of the three chosen ones. I would hear them answer a question." The three look up expectantly.

"Where is the land of the Eyo?" Boog asks and points a bony finger at Kraac.

Kraac stands slowly, not at all intimidated. As usual, he thinks quietly before answering and then says, "This is a land of many things. The deer have returned. Food aplenty have we here and protection from the darkness and the cold. This is the land of the Eyo."

The finger points next to Ecakik who answers, "Along the shores of the Endless Lake, we have found many creatures. I wish to know what further wonders lie along the shores to the east. Perhaps there we will find the land of the Eyo?"

Noha is last to answer the question.

Che holds her breath.

He says, "This is a good land and blessed by the spirits of many animals. To the east lie perhaps new wonders on the shores of the Endless lake, but my heart speaks to me and I would follow the caribou and journey through the high mountains to the unknown southern country to search for the *Valley of the Dream*."

Boog allows to stretch out a long, thoughtful silence in which each hunter might weigh the words of Kraac, Ecakik, and Noha and make his personal choice. Finally, Boog takes each of the chosen by the arm and leads them to the fire's corners.

He hisses, "From this day, there shall be *three* fires! All of those who would follow the bear killer, join him now!"

Six go to stand near Kraac.

Che moans and clutches at Inik's arm. Her friend starts and suddenly realizes what Che has already seen, what this choosing would mean to them. She doesn't guess what other special sorrow it holds for Che.

"Those who would follow Anikeogima!" Boog cries. Again six hunters including Laf, move to join Ecakik.

"Those who would follow the friend of Assinbo!" The remaining six males go to stand beside Noha: Artisan, Dinkka, Fuum, Quork, and the twins, Tak and Megi.

"THE PROPHECY IS FULFILLED!" Boog shouts in a cracking voice. "NO LONGER SHALL THE BROWN BEAR, THE WOLF, AND THE FOX RUN TOGETHER."

The brothers look with sudden anguish at one another. Even Noha, his bright eyes filled with pride at this dream suddenly come true, shows no desire to be parted forever from his brothers. Kraac is calm but Ecakik's wide face is wretched with sadness.

Che puts her hands to the sides of her head. How can they, who are the complements of one another, survive on their own? She and Inik look into each other's eyes.

However, Boog gives no one time to protest. He goes to Kraac. "I name thee OGIMA OF THE BEAR CLAN," he pronounces. "Guard your people here in the land of *Keewatin*." Kraac seems about to speak but a menacing look from Boog silences him.

The shaman then moves to Ecakik. "I name thee OGIMA OF THE WOLF CLAN," he says. "Take thy spear," putting his hand on the long spear that Ecakik holds, "and with it, find sustenance for thy people along the shores of the Endless Lake." Ecakik bows his head in submission.

Boog comes last to Noha. He places his gnarled hand on his shoulder. "I name thee OGIMA OF THE FOX CLAN," he says and Noha quivers. "Go ye beyond the mountains for your destiny lies there. Listen to the counsel of the eldest among you," he points his long finger at Artisan. *"Find your new country, but never forget that you are of the blood of THE REINDEER!"*

Noha is too overcome to answer so he nods.

Now that the dreadful decisions are made, the ever practical Dinkka once more asks permission to speak and is granted it.

"The people will follow three separate paths, O shaman. Upon which path shall the sacred feet of the shaman walk, and what is to become of those bereft of his counsel?"

"I, too, have a path to follow," Boog says quietly. "It is an old path, familiar and homely to me. I shall rejoice in it. This time I shall not return."

Dismayed moans came from the males and cries of fear from some of the females. Che is swaying back and forth in agitation.

Boog smiles toothlessly, something that few but the apprentice have ever before seen him do, and he tries to comfort his people.

"There are those among you who know many of my crafts. The *mashkikike,* herb woman, Jag, goes with the people of the Long Spear," gesturing toward Ecakik's group. Ecakik's hand tightens on his spear which is indeed much longer than most. Boog continues, "Already Artisan has cast his lot among the young. He will teach the People of the Fox. As for the people of the Bear who remain in the land of Keewatin, let my faithful servant accompany them.

The apprentice jerks as if he has suffered a blow, but he does not speak.

Boog turns to him. "Take with thee, Nijkiwe, the sacred records and the bones of the Giant Reindeer and guard them for all time, keeping them secret and adding to the writings and passing them on to the worthy."

"It shall be so," the apprentice says. Tears seep down his cheeks.

"Take also the herbs and the medicines and the paints. Divide them among the three clans so none shall want and wherever necessary, teach them how to make and gather such things."

"It shall be so, O Shaman."

"Finally take this." He removes the painted blanket from his scrawny shoulders and drapes it across the boy's bare back. "Wear it as a mark of the *Midewiwin,* Brotherhood of the Medicine Men, for you now are of the *Medé*." He turns and walks away.

With this, all disperse to their huts, there to whisper among themselves and wonder at the great and terrible happenings. Che does not go to her hut. Instead she wanders along the fishing lake's shore. Seeing this, Kraac strides openly after her. Noha, surrounded by his new followers and distracted with joy, sees nothing of this. Narima sees and for once holds the knowledge silent in her heart.

Kraac comes up behind Che. He doesn't touch her. Instead, his words leap the space between them like a caress. "You are sad, Little One?"

She doesn't turn to him but keeps her back stiff, her face averted. "My mate does not want me," she says. "And you, whom I trusted, have betrayed me."

"I did not betray you," Kraac protests.

Che is torn. Surely he would not lie to her. But would Noha have lied? Or did he, in his pain, say the first cruel thing that came to his mind and then let resentment hold him back from pleasuring her?

What does it matter now?

"We shall soon part forever," she says.

"Yes."

What did she hear in his voice? Was it the feeling for which there is no word? At last? And too late?

"I know great misery. I am alone." It is wrenched from her.

"No! I will not have it!" Kraac snarls. "If Noha does not come to your sleeping place, he is a fool and he does wrong. I shall request of the shaman that you be allowed to come to me as second mate." He does not hide the hope in his voice.

For a moment, Che lets herself enjoy the prospect of living with such a man. But then she says, "And Narima? And my cubs?" And her heart adds, *And Noha*?

Kraac's face falls. "My Nicimec will never let go his male cub."

There was a long, painful pause. Che longs to throw herself into his arms, to feel once more the safety and pleasure of his touch. She longs to beg him to run off into the mountains with her, leaving all behind. Nevertheless, she knows that she would never live in peace with herself if she were to suggest such a thing.

She says, "Nor will I leave my own. But I thank you for wanting me."

"Who would not want such as you?" Kraac's voice shakes.

"You have spoken?" he asks forlornly.

"I have spoken."

Kraac moves as if to turn away but then swings once more to her. "My Nicimec is right, Little One. It is not the place of a female to go on the hunt."

Che's face kindles with sudden fury and pain shafts across her chest and down her arms. And he can't, in the end, leave her like that, hating him.

He smiles. "But you are not as other females, are you? You are too brave. You won't listen to me, will you, if I beg you to remain always safe in your hut? Therefore I commend you to the care of Mother Earth. You are my Che whom I thank for my life. I name you a name."

"A name?"

"A name. Now and forever in my heart you shall dwell and you shall be LITTLE HUNTER."

He turns.

He walks away.

Che wanders long on the shore and she looks honestly into her manitu and there she sees the faces of Noha and Kraac and knows that she must choose now and forever between them. When she returns at last to her hut, she finds a repentant Noha waiting naked on the sleeping platform. She goes to him and kneels. As he slips from her body her tunic, and his hands grip her breasts and his shaft presses itself hard against her private place, she fights at first the response that leaps in her. However, in the end, seduced and repelled at the same time by his assuredness, his certainty that she will gladly open her body to him, she succumbs, and as her lust rises to meet his, she suddenly pushes him backwards and mounts him. She pulls him violently into her, thrusting her body again and again on his shaft.

At first he is so shocked that his erection falters, but he is soon so aroused by her violation that his manhood leaps again to life, his hips raise to meet her and as she rides him, he cries her name as he pumps into her the sap of life.

Afterwards Noha is embarrassed but delighted, too. He caresses her and laughs softly at her, calling her his *bold little vixen*. He does not say that he regrets his recent treatment of her nor does he share with her his feelings about being named Ogima of the Fox Clan.

Hours later, when all sleep and half darkness and cold envelop the land, the manitu of Boog leaves his body for a final journey to the land of the Spirits. His old, shrivelled bones rattle as if in a spell of prophecy, and then he is still forever. Beside him squats his faithful servant, the apprentice, who composes the knobbly limbs and sprinkles herbs on the wrinkled flesh. He hunkers down by the hearth. This last night he will spend alone with his master.

BOOK III

CHAPTER 21

The People of the Fox

Che stares into the distance where the New Mountains loom. "What does it mean? Where are we going? Why? Why?" Her muttered words hang in the air.

Narima doesn't care. She knows or suspects . . . But Inik? My dear, dear Nimi. She will be so lonely among the elders and there is small comfort in Jag. I shall not, I must not think about it. There is a little time yet.

She goes to sit with her friend.

The day comes late in the time of *Nerockamink*, when the People of the Fox are ready to leave. They gather near the Eyo camp's edge. All they own goes with them. Each hunter carries several newly-fashioned spears, his stone knife, a bola, and a medicine bag tied at his waist. The females strap to their backs bundles of hides with attached sacks of dried food, herbs and a few personal possessions such as skinning knives, shells or earth mother figurines. Three maidens have been allotted to Noha's clan. One called Berick, a plump, good-humoured, fair-skinned maiden, has charge of big Whea's lively twins.

"Hold my hands," Berick admonishes them. "Or I shall tell your ninga."

Behind her, Tina, a small, dark, shrewd, homely maiden, totes a bag lined with moss where Che's son, Rin, nestles. Che, having hefted her usual heavy pack . . . to which Noha has added the one-horn . . . and wishing her hands as free as possible, entrusts baby Ra to the third maiden, Naic, who is pretty, vapid and sad to leave her blood ninga, but reliable.

"These maidens will need a lot of training, especially that ugly little Tina!" Che mutters testily.

Whea and Lara, similarly burdened, stand near her, and Artisan leads two month-old pups, a bitch and a male which he plans to breed as hunting and carrier dogs. Even he totes many bundles containing bone knives and chisels, choice quartz rocks and things the apprentice gave him. If he feels bereft at leaving the cub of his blood, he shows no sign of it.

The goodbyes are brief. Che bade Inik a tearful farewell the night before and she now stands stoically behind her mate. Her gaze, when it falls on Kraac, is resigned. She holds her burdened shoulders straight and her head high.

Thus the People of the Fox set off toward the distant mountains, a band of seven males; three chosen females, three maidens, four young, and two dogs. It is a pitifully small band and with the exception of Artisan, a young one. Dinkka runs ahead as scout and behind him, Noha, a new stateliness in his step, marches at the head of his people. They set their gaze upon the mountains and their feet upon the caribou's spoor as they go in search of the New Land beyond the mountains.

The remainder of that summer, his twenty-first, is the most carefree and happy of Noha's life. The responsibility of his new position lies lightly on his shoulders because there is plenty of caribou meat for the taking and the females fill skins with bearberries and roots to give variety to the clan's diet.

He sits smiling benignly on a knoll from which he can see Che busily instructing one of the maidens in some female thing. His Che has suddenly blossomed into maturity and the others, even Whea who is older, look to her for guidance as Che once had looked to Bara. Che walks proudly, shoulders thrown back, and keeps a dutiful and busy eye on the doings of her nimi and the four cubs.

Feeling generously paternal, he leaves the knoll and calls to Che to join him. "I want you to teach the maidens a good mate's skills just in case we some day meet another clan beyond the mountains."

Che doesn't point out that she had already started to do this. "Yes, Napima," she says absently.

Che's real focus now is not Noha but Rin who has grown into a sturdy two-year-old, small like his nuse and ninga but already nimble footed. Che sees uniqueness in him which she is determined to nourish.

Noha shall not turn him into another Dinkka, she vows. She cannot understand why Dinkka, who is so skilled and clever, seems to worship Noha.

Che's girl babe, Ra, is an enigmatic cub who looks at the world from clear black eyes. She's like Kraac, Che thought, and quickly pushes the notion from her knowing place.

Che is lonely. Inik's going has left a bleeding hole in her existence, to say nothing of Kraac of whom she refuses even to think. She finds friends of a sort in Whea and gentle Lara. She studies them carefully knowing there will be many occasions when she will have to rely upon them. Whea towers over Che. Despite her size, however, she is no challenge to Che's wit if she is sometimes to her patience. She is a willing worker if handled well and she adores her big mate, Quork, with whom she fights incessantly, and her twins, Lee and Eci, who can do no wrong.

Che mumbles, "I can handle Whea, but she has a tendency to look down on Lara and to bully the maidens, though she walks carefully around me. And well she might!"

Lara has always submitted to Che. Unfortunately, she has not yet given cranky, little Fuum a babe though they had been mated for some time and she is the least happy of the females and glad of Che's kindness. As for the maidens, they seem obedient so far and cause no trouble. Nevertheless, Che often thanks Mother Earth for sending with them Artisan.

The old man seems quite content to have as his companions such young people. He spends all his spare time with Rin and Whea's twins, leaving the females to go about their tasks in peace with only Ra to nurse. The two male cubs will certainly need his guidance. She hopes Inik will not miss him too much.

Noha chooses for their first camp a site on an outer mountain's bare slopes.

Che overhears him say to Dinkka, "It reminds me of our home in the old land."

Inspired by his new patriarchal feelings, he leads the hunters on a foraging trip up a valley to cut spruce hut poles. On his return, he grandly presents them to Che.

"Thank you, Napima," she says, nonplussed. Noha does not usually do such tasks.

She calls to her nimi, "Set your huts here!" It is a good spot. Nearby, a narrow river, fed by the glacier far above and teeming with spawning fish, tumbles down the slope.

When it is time to dig food pits, Che decides that it is also time to establish her authority. She motions Dinkka to her. "You, Tuk, and Megi will help the maidens, and please get Quork and Fuum digging for their mates."

Dinkka suppresses a grin and says, "Yes, Ninga."

Brat! Che has a difficult time keeping her own lips in a straight line.

It is not long, however, before Noha appropriates her male helpers for a caribou hunt, and before many sleeps have passed, the clan has abundant stores to last the winter.

Noha orders, "Put only dried meat in the pits, because with the autumn, we shall move far ahead into the mountains and await the time of *Nerockamink*."

Che does not see any reason to move camp this year but, if she has learned anything about Noha, it is that she will get nowhere be disagreeing openly with him. So she bites her tongue.

The time may come when I shall have to speak out, she thinks unhappily.

Autumn finds them high in the mountain range at the very source of a southward flowing river. The river itself has begun to freeze and snow skeins the mountains that tower on either side of the valley.

During their passage, Che, who has never before traveled in mountains, sees her first sheep. "Rin, see how fine they are with their curved horns!" she calls to her son. The little male gazes round-eyed.

Noha says, "My Nuse used to bring down such big-horns with consummate skill,"

Che doesn't hear. She is remembering the Mahantanis and the days when Hun courted Fina. She hopes her nimises is happy in the land of the spirits.

The sheep pick their way along inaccessible heights, their cloven hooves moving surely along the narrowest paths. This frustrates Noha, but Che is glad he can't kill the graceful creatures. There are plenty of hare to add to the larder. Moreover, there is an even more beautiful animal on whom the hunters can prey. It is the bob-tailed lynx. He prowls the open slopes, his luxurious pale brown fur, beard, and tufted ears attractive against the snow. Dinkka, Tuk, and Megi delight in pursuing the lynx over the rocky hillsides. They take pelts which will make enviable winter blankets.

Having no mates, the twins approach the three maidens. "Would you make coverings for us?" nearsighted Tuk asks, squinting shyly. He is big, well muscled and almost as beautiful as Lara, in a rougher way. As is his brother Megi.

Pretty Berick giggles and little Naic blushes, but homely Tina says, "And what will you do for us?"

Berick snorts.

"We'll kill for you, too," Tuk replies, his face crimson.

Tina agrees for all.

Che watches this exchange worriedly. Though she has tutored them, she is beginning to feel uneasy about the maidens' demeanour. They lack humility. Especially Tina.

How am I going to handle this? Where shall we find mates for our young? This going off into new lands could lead to trouble. Come *Nerockamink*, their sap will rise. I shall just have to watch them with the eyes of *Omeeseh*. Poor things. But then, remembering her stolen days with Kraac in the bone hut, she decides not to be too strict.

One day that winter, Che huddles in her hut with Lara and Whea. They are trying to push with stiff fingers their bone needles into caribou hide. The maidens are in their own hut and the hunters who never tire of describing their prowess have gathered to brag in Quork's hut. Whea's little twins sleep on a pile of skins while Rin toddles and Ra crawls from one female to the other, having to be saved periodically from falling into the fire.

"I hate this cold! Whea breathes on her thick fingers.

"It is hard," Che agrees, "but let's be grateful to Manitou that our food pits are full and that dwarf willows grow in abundance near our camp, and that there are spruce groves and even tall willows in the pass. We shall not go short of firewood."

Che, who is as uncomfortable as anyone, thinks wryly, Bara would be proud of me for that motherly little speech.

Whea squeals, "There! I have pierced myself again! It's too dark in here and I can't breathe in this smoke!"

She's right," Lara agrees. "My eyes burn until I rub them and then I do that, they burn more strongly."

Che frowns. If Lara is complaining, I had better do something before we all go blind. But what?

Outside, *Keewatin* screeches and howls, rattling the little pit-hut as if he might rip it up and toss it over the mountain. "Perhaps if we piled more snow over our huts, they would be warm enough to allow us to cut a hole in the roof," Che suggests.

"What good would that do?" Whea snarls.

"The smoke will rise and seep out of the hole, and light will get in," Lara explains.

Che hides a smile behind her hand. That Lara is quick enough when she dares to be.

"I didn't ask you!" Whea snaps at Lara.

Che sighs. Oh for the patience of Bara and the good humour of Inik! How I miss them!

She says, "With the first thaw, let's go out and do it."

And so they do. They cut a hole in the roof, devising over the hole a second tiny roof to keep snow out but allow smoke to escape. They wade in wet snow up to their thighs, packing with hare skin mittens great handfuls of snow until the hut has swollen to twice its size. They move on to Lara's and Whea's huts, the huts of the single males, the maidens' and finally Artisan's.

"Foolish females, playing in the snow," says Noha as he and the other hunters make ready to stalk a lynx who had left paw prints near the camp. However, Artisan praises the females and in the end, Noha notices the improvement in the huts' air, though he doesn't think to comment on it to Che.

One waking time, Artisan sits musing and staring into the fire. Rin has come to visit and listen wide eyed to the old man's stories, although he cannot yet have understood very much of their import. However, the cub has finally fallen asleep near the fire and lies there covered by one of Artisan's hare blankets.

"How like and yet unlike Pu he is," murmurs the old man fondly who often holds conversations with himself when alone. "Noha will try to make a master hunter of this one. But my manitu tells me that there is more to this cub than a chaser of caribou. His spirit will speak to many creatures as it now speaks to mine even though he has yet few words."

He idly picks up a skinned, smooth hut pole left over from the building of his pit hut. He runs his hands along it, enjoying the feel of the wood. He is remembering the Great White Bear who killed Pu. "How easy it would be for Wabimakwa to travel with his big, flat paws across the snow outside." Artisan's hands stop caressing and he stares unseeing into the yellow flames for some minutes. Putting down the pole, he goes to a corner and gets out a sharp stone axe and a stone awl. With the axe, he cuts the pole to a length of four strides. It is a particularly supple spruce branch, so it bends easily. He brings the two ends together to form a rounded egg shape and ties them securely with a piece of wet caribou sinew.

"Yes, this might do. But how shall I fill the center? Che and Lara are good at things like this. I shall consult them."

He crawls out of the hut and struggles through the snow to Lara's hut. Luckily Che is there, too. And Whea. They listen to his problem.

"What about something like this?" asks Che, holding up a woven grass mat."

"It would not be strong enough for my purpose," Artisan says.

"Well, then, use caribou thongs instead of grass."

"I have plenty of extra," Lara offers.

"Of course. Thank you, Nimi!" With a gap-toothed grin, he is off.

With a bone awl, he makes two holes on either side of his spruce frame and then, cutting two more pieces of hut-pole, he fits crossbars into the frame and fastens them tightly. Next, he laboriously bores tiny holes at intervals around the perimeter of the frame. Lastly, he assembles Lara's caribou sinews and ties their ends through the holes he has made. Using Che's method of making grass mats and hare blankets, he weaves a thick sinew mesh until the wood oval is completely filled.

I'll have to make it even stronger," he says aloud.

Rin wakes and comes to watch.

"See," says Artisan. "The space between these crossbars must be woven a second time until it is thick enough to hold a hunter's weight."

When he has done this, he inserts a thong just behind the first crossbar, where he has left an open space the size of his toes. Behind that he uses a wide piece of hide securely fastened to the cross stitches and big enough to hold the ball of a hunter's foot swathed in winter foot coverings. To this he attaches two long, strong hide strips which will be tied behind the hunter's heel. He experiments a long time with his thongs until he finds a placement that holds his foot most securely.

When he shows his handiwork to the females, Che asks courteously, "Will the thongs not stretch when they are wet?"

Artisan laughs. "Yes, I thought of that and made the place where the hunter stands very thick. The crossbars will help, too."

"Perhaps at sap time we could cover the thongs with melted tree sap to make them very strong and waterproof." It is Whea who speaks.

Everyone looks at her with new respect. They will devise something and experiment too with the wooden part of the bear paws to find a tree that can give them the strongest and yet most supple of woods."

"We shall be like bears on the snow!" Lara squeals and everyone laughs.

With a pleased grunt Artisan removes the contraption from his foot and returning to his hut sets to work to fashion another. Rin watches fascinated. When the set is complete, Artisan picks up the cub and crawls outside. He plunks Rin down on a pile of snow while he retrieves and straps his invention to his feet and then lifting the wide-eye cub, walks like Wabimakwa across the snow, sinking only a few inches.

When Noha and his hunters return the whole camp is soon in an uproar. Noha is delighted with this new thing and quick to see its advantages now that someone else has created it.

"Why did no one make these things before?" he asks ingenuously.

Artisan simply smiles modestly.

There is a scramble for unused poles and Quork is soon in trouble with Whea for pulling one from the hut structure itself.

"Hut poles are female property!" Whea yells.

"But I need the pole. I want to make some bear mackisins."

Whea, who is bad tempered and judgmental but not actually ungenerous, says, "Next time ask." And proceeds to search out some caribou sinews for him.

He and Fuum, with whom he is once more on their old friendly terms, hurry to Artisan's hut. The maidens have given Tuk and Megi poles, and Dinkka gets some from Che. The six hunters squeeze into the hut and work, with varying degrees of clumsiness, to fashion bear-paw mackisins for themselves. Pole ends are thrust in every direction, jabbing stomachs and whacking heads and shins.

Fuum snarls at Megi, "Will you be careful, you big stupid head!"

"Now, now," soothes Artisan. "There is room for all."

He later says to Lara, "Thank Manitou that the Fox clan has Che among its members. She has more pictures in her knowing place than a dozen of our much lauded hunters. Myself excluded, of course." He grins his toothless old grin.

Once Noha, Dinkka, Fuum, and Quork have the method explained to them, they make their bear-paws quickly but poor Megi and Tuk have some trouble. Megi's poles are too brittle and crack when he tries to bend them into a circle and nearsighted Tuk cannot manage to stick a piece of sinew's end into the holes which Artisan has generously bored for him in his paw frame. The hunters forget to eat, so great is their industry, and the females, who have been excluded from the undertaking, lie alone on their sleeping platforms that night.

By the time Paternal Sun had shed the dim, blue light of winter's day upon the snow, all six hunters are lined up for a race. They don't realize that the circular shapes of the snowshoes will make it impossible for them to hold their legs as closely as they ordinarily would, and that even walking on snow mackisins will be a frustrating procedure until they master the peculiar gait necessary.

Noha is beaming like a boy cub and Che is smiling fondly.

The race starts off rather well with a signal from Artisan and encouragement from the females, who have been ordered from their warm huts and stand shivering to witness the great event. In fact, all the hunters succeeded in going only a few paces before becoming entangled in the wonderful bear paws and falling headlong into snowdrifts, arms and leg sticking out at strange angles and furious cries muffled by mouthfuls of snow searing the air.

Che hides her lips behind her mittens while Rin and Whea's twins howl with laughter. Noha climbs awkwardly to his feet and glares at his two-winters-old ogucen and his suspiciously quivering mate until they look back at him with faces innocent of mirth. He turns and falls flat on his face in the snow. Artisan can no longer control himself and breaks into shouts of merriment, dancing around and slapping his thighs. The corners of Noha's mouth begin to twitch, still, and then curve upwards. He looks at his snow covered fellow hunters and they at him and before long, everyone, females and young included, is rolling about in the snow, shouting and laughing like cubs. Noha grabs Che and slings her into a drift where he washes her face with snow and pretends to bite her red nose. Artisan stands aside watching them and wishing they could always remain just as they are at this moment.

By the time *Nerockamink* comes, every one of the hunters can run down a hare on his bear paw mackisins, and the females have fashioned pairs for themselves and use them for ice-fishing excursions on the frozen river. Theirs are made in a long, lozenge shape which works better on open ground. Even Rin and Whea's twins have tiny bear paws and strut about on them, pretending to be the great White Bear.

With spring comes the northward movement of the caribou and disagreement within the clan.

Noha calls a council at which Quork expresses the wishes of most. "Let us follow the caribou back to the northern slopes for a time," he says, scratching at his unruly hair which is kept under limited control by a faded crimson painted hide strip tied around his head. Physically, he is a lot like Ecakik, but there the resemblance ends because of his tendency to be argumentative and to talk in a loud voice. Neither he nor Whea ever win their splendid quarrels.

Che watches him. He and Fuum are as unlike as can be. Fuum is scrawny and rodent faced, with fine, black hair hacked short and with deformed, arthritic limbs. How he convinced Lara to be his mate still amazes Che.

This unlikely pair, Quork and Fuum, are again inseparable companions, as are the twins, Tuk and Megi, who are fast on their feet if not intelligent. They would have been identical twins if it had not been for Megi's slight advantage in height and Tuk's large round brown eyes, a feature which doesn't improve his poor eyesight. In compensation for this weakness, Tuk has developed an unusually keen sense of smell and is invaluable in the hunt where he and Megi run together. This leaves Dinkka with Noha.

Che can see that Noha is disgruntled by Quork's suggestion that they return to the north. He doesn't like disagreement from his hunters.

"There are lots of caribou here in the pass, aren't there?" Noha asks quietly enough.

Quork nods grudgingly.

"Can't we take enough meat and hides for our needs?"

"I would like to see the Eyo once more!" Quork says stubbornly.

"But if we return to the tundra now, we won't have time this year to go beyond the mountains."

Fuum interrupts in his reedy voice. "Don't you remember how difficult it was to travel south along the mountain ridges and the rocky valleys. We aren't sheep!"

Che squirms. This will set Noha off! He'll never listen. Will he remember that these hunters have shown spears for him when he first suggested going beyond the mountains?

Noha surprises her.

"When did Fuum ever run from a difficult task?" he says.

Che is pleased at this clever reply and realizes that Noha's real strength is that he actually means what he says.

They argue for some time, with Tuk and Megi adding nothing to the discussion but vacillating according to who is speaking. Dinkka remains silent.

Noha's goals are Dinkka's goals. Che feels no jealousy. She likes the reliable Dinkka with his quiet sense of humour.

At last, Noha remembers Boog's advice at the great council and turns to Artisan for mediation.

"Well," says Artisan reasonably, "If we go to the tundra during the time of perpetual light, we shall take many caribou and perhaps join with the other Eyo clans in the hunt. But the People of the Fox cannot go to the other side of the mountains this year. Why not compromise, hunt for a time on the tundra and before the dark night comes upon us, return to the mountains at the time of rutting? Establish no camp but follow the old caribou trails to the south, arriving beyond the mountains before the time of darkness."

"What if the snow should catch us still in the mountains?" Fuum asks sulkily.

"We have our snow paws," Artisan says archly.

Even Fuum smiles. "Yes, the Eyo will be surprised to see our snow paws, won't they?"

Noha laughs with relief and says later to Che, "If we follow Artisan's wise words, all of my people will be happy.

Che wishes she dare say, "There is more to happiness than that, Napima."

Therefore, at the time of tree buds, a joyful reunion takes place on the northern slopes between the people of the Fox and Kraac's clan. Once more the Bear and the Fox run together.

Che is pleased to see the other females, even if their clan mother is Narima who is cool to her, but she avoids Kraac as long as she can because she still fears his power over her. True, he doesn't seek her out but she sees him often around the council fire, and his dark glance burns her.

As for Noha, he has completely forgotten his former anger with his Nisages and monopolizes Kraac's attention, prattling on about his clan's many adventures and scarcely allowing Kraac to relate his own experiences. Everyone admires the Fox Clan's snow paws and the Bear Clan females asked eagerly to be taught to make them. Che makes a point of personally teaching Narima, as much to reassure herself as Kraac's mate.

When the inevitable happens and she finds herself alone with Kraac, she is able to accept his greeting, "Hello, Little Hunter," with a smile of loving friendship and no more.

She is amazed at herself. My hunger for him is gone! Dazed she realizes. It's as if madness seized me as it once seized the one whose name must never be spoken even in one's thoughts. And the madness has died, though Kraac will always be dear to me. Thank my familiar spirits that Noha never guessed our transgression!

But what about me? Did I deceive myself? Am I naturally disloyal? Surely not! I do care about Kraac. I am his *Little Hunter*. And if we were to explore one another's minds and bodies once again, it would be just as full of pleasure as before.

But I do not NEED him.

Then what do I need? Why do I still suffer this hopeless yearning, which the sights and scents of spring make even stronger.

Che ponders long and she prays to Mother Earth but no answering voice comes to her heart.

She misses Inik sorely. Ecakik's people must have traveled far to the east and didn't return. The remaining two clans spend the greater part of the caribou hunting season together and in early autumn, they part knowing they will never meet again, for Noha has declared that his people will never more cross the mountains to the north shore and Kraac and his dark skinned, dark eyed companions are committed to living in the land of Keewatin. It is a subdued Fox Clan who climb once more to the river's source and follow its course through the pass.

From the tundra, a lone hunter watches them go, wondering if he will ever meet again a female like Che.

"Go safely, Little Hunter," Kraac says to the wind. "And remember me."

CHAPTER 22

A Piece of Sun

As the season progresses and the river begins to freeze, Noha marvels at this new country where green-black spruce forests become thicker day by day and above them stretches the bare and splendidly rolling alpine tundra of the mountain slopes. The clan have plenty of food in their packs, so they concentrate on covering as much ground as they can, using the caribou trails. By early winter, they have reached a snow-mantled plateau where the river joins with another mountain stream and flows to the west. They set up winter camp on the plateau's edge, spending the dark months in the usual pursuits of hide tailoring, weapons making, tool making, and storytelling. On good days, they hunt the forests that surround the plateau.

One day, Noha and Dinkka come upon a large deer the like of which they have never before seen.

"See how he travels alone," Noha whispers.

"Such weapons!" Dinkka points to the animal's majestic, spreading antlers.

"He's much taller at the shoulder than I," Noha marvels.

"Heavy as a bear. Shall we name him?"

"Not yet."

Perhaps because of his great size, the animal is at a disadvantage in the deep woodland snow, and the People of the Fox become adept at running him down on bear paw mackisins. The meat is delicious, although not as fat and tender as it would prove in summer. Che is pleased with the quality and strength of the new hides and Noha is gratified. Artisan names the new deer *Moose*.

Nevertheless, Noha is not yet satisfied. He stands on the plain at sleep time and looks up at the lovely, luminous lights of frosty blue and emerald that dance and arch and crisscross the black sky vault.

"Help me, O Spirit of the *Waté,* to guard my people well and to lead them to the new land," he says. He is now even more certain that his fate is to search always for this faraway place which would become the permanent home of his people.

He sighs. I wish my clan would hold willingly to the same resolve but it doesn't really matter what they think. I am Ogima.

As for Che, she is content for the time to live her life in seemly fashion, keeping to herself the thoughts she used to confide to Bara and Inik and presenting to her Nimi a clan mother's calm visage. She finds release in watching her ogucen grow and in fostering his intense interest in the forest's sights and sounds.

Before the snow became too deep, she had taken him and Ra for walks among the trees, the girl's hand as soft and delicate in hers as a moth's wing. Rin, already at home in his surroundings, ran ahead on his little bear mackisins.

"Don't go far away," she called, thinking of Pu.

Rin grinned and cried, "I am not afraid!" And he was not. He walked in the forest animals' habitat as one who belonged there.

Che came upon an opening in the trees to find him standing with his arm about a fawn's neck. The dainty animal leaned against him as a dog against his master. Ra laughed and stumbled forward. Immediately the fawn took flight while in the nearby trees, a doe called anxiously.

Rin's face flushed. "Why did you allow her to chase away the fawn?" he accused his ninga.

"Ra is but a babe. She, too, would like to fondle the pretty animal."

"But the animals talk to me. They fear the rest of you!"

"Our mentor, *Assinbo*, speaks to your Nuse," Che said mildly.

"But not to Ra," Rin replied, a stubborn light in his eyes reminiscent of his nuse.

Che bit her lip. *No. He shall not be allowed to think himself the center of his own world*!

But she had learned to go carefully. "Nevertheless," she said. "Your *Katcidjininimi* . . ." referring to Ra, "may love animals just as you do, may she not?"

The dark hazel eyes, so much like Noha's, cleared, are mollified.

He understands. O this is a special one!

"You have reason, Ninga," Rin said. "Come little Nimi." He grabbed Ra's hand. "I shall show you a den where a vixen guards her kits!"

Che smiled happily and let them get a bit ahead into the thick trees before she followed, though she was worried about their safety. There were times when one must not interfere in the lives of one's cubs.

For the most part, Che was satisfied. Noha's new authority and his self confidence gave her pride and she was determined to perform her own role well. Her reward was to bask in the females' approbation. All strange yearnings and spirit longings were best dismissed.

Or so she thought.

When *Nerockamink* comes once more, the thawing plateau where the Eyo camp presents a different face, a more alien face. The caribou have left for their calving grounds in the north. Noha calls a council and all finally agree that they will not as yet go south but will investigate the mountains to the east. They break camp and, carrying such dried food as remains to them, they set off through the mountains once more to see what lies beyond. Before they leave it, the plateau has become a place of burgeoning drowned muskeg and rolling, virescent marshes. Already water birds are beginning to arrive from the south, and the air is warm. They are to learn that the inner plains, though desperately cold in winter can be uncomfortably hot in summer.

As there are no caribou trails leading east, they follow the streams and ravines, and the going is difficult. At times, the hunters have to help the females with their burdens. Lara wisely carries fire with her in a large seashell lined with clay and filled with powdery rotten wood so that they might have hot food at rest time.

It is in the mountains that Che finds a treasure and that she meets a grizzly bear.

Che is well ahead of the other females and far behind the hunters who have as usual outstripped them. Her pack is heavy and the tumpline bites into her forehead despite the hare fur she has put there to cushion the thong. The air is hot and she is thirsty, her discomfort multiplied a thousand fold by a dense cloud of black flies which descended upon her when she first entered the ravine.

It is a narrow alley which splits two moss covered areas of mountain tundra. Che has chosen the seemingly more difficult path because she has learned from sad experience that the tundra's spring moss, with its tempting golden carpet of arctic poppies, can be treacherously slippery and that she can make better time by following the drier ravine. Apparently, another creature has a similar idea. As Che rounds a particularly sharp bend, she sees before her an animal so gigantic that he seems to fill the ravine from bank to bank. It is a Grizzly.

The bear, who had such breeze as there was to his back, is just as surprised as Che, and he stops in midstride, his big right forepaw off the ground. She freezes, a lump of mindless terror. The bruin has just wakened from his long winter's sleep and he is still groggy and a little drunk but he is also voraciously hungry, and this animal before him, though small and scrawny, might be food for even a hungry giant such as he.

They stand staring into each other's amber coloured eyes. After some time, Che lets out a deep, shuddering breath and speaks to the bear.

"Makwa, I am of the Reindeer tribe," she says, "of the clan of Assinbo. My people have long reverenced you." This is not entirely true, as Che had mated into the clan, but she prays that the bear's manitu will overlook this prevarication.

The bear sways ominously but doesn't rise to his hind legs or attack.

Che gulps. "I am only a female, Honoured One, with little meat on my bones, meat which is no doubt ill tasting. But I have here in my pack much that is good." Slowly she begins to inch her hands up to her tumpline, never taking her eyes from the bear's.

The bear quivers.

"Do not be angry, Makwa," Che pleads in a soothing monotone as she works the heavy pack to the ground. With infinite care, she undoes the thongs and begins to place the dried meat and berries on the dirt. For the first time, the bear's eyes leave hers and center on the food. His muzzle twitches.

Che backs slowly, warily away, keeping her head averted now, a sign of submission, though she watches from the corner of her eye. The bear moves forward, lowers his head and nuzzles the dried meat. It takes minutes of agonized, slow creeping for Che to back around the bend in the ravine. She turns and flees, tears streaming down her face and great hiccoughing sighs wrenched from her throat.

She runs for a short time when she sees her nimi coming toward her. They look up at her in surprise as she swoops down upon them, and it takes a few seconds for them to react to her snarled orders.

"Up! Up on the tundra! Makwa is upon us!"

She snatches Rin and Ra from the hand and back of Tina and scrambles up the ravine's side. The twins start to howl as Whea throws herself and them against the ravine's banks. Lara is slower than any of them because she will not abandon her pack or the fire-shell. She, Berick, and Naic have just reached the tundra and are slithering away from the ravine's lip on their hands and knees when the grizzly ambles along beneath them. Hands are clapped over whimpering baby mouths, but the bruin is well aware of the terrified humans and could, with small effort, heave himself after them and slaughter every one of them with a few well aimed swipes. Instead, he crankily shakes himself, grumbles deep in his throat, and goes on his way.

When they catch up with the hunters, they quickly build their fire to cook some tundra rodents Quork has killed that afternoon. It is not until after all have eaten that Che approaches Noha.

"I have done wrong, Napima," she says. She is truly contrite because the food the bear ate was a great loss.

Noha glances up from the fishhook he is carving. Che has done nothing to displease him for some time and she can see he is angry that she can still dare to do wrong. His hazel gaze flashes.

"Speak!" he orders.

"I have fed our pemmican to a bear."

Fear leaps into his yes. "How did this happen?"

By the time Che has finished telling him, his hands are shaking at the thought of what might have happened to her and to his cubs. But he doesn't reach out to comfort her.

"You have done no wrong," he assures her and, after a pause, adds awkwardly. "You are truly a worthy member of the Assinbo."

Che gapes. Che can't believe her ears!

Somehow she thanks him, trying to hide the pleased smile that wreathes her face. Turning from him she walks into a spruce grove, lest the rest of the females notice her salmonberry red cheeks. She goes to a stream and kneels to cool her face in its icy waters. As she whisks away the water from her eyelashes, something on the pebbled bed of the stream catches her eye. It twinkles like a star. Plunging her hand into the stream, she picks up a golden stone and dries it against her tunic. It is only about the size of Ra's little fist but it is lovely.

Surely a piece of the Father Sun has fallen from the sky and been cooled in this stream.

Immediately she runs back to camp and once more approaches Noha. "This stone will make a magic spear point."

Noha is interested at first, looking at the bright stone from every direction and tapping it with his stone hammer. Finally, he scratches it with a bone awl. The enthusiasm melts; however, he speaks haltingly, obviously not wishing to insult her by returning her gift as worthless. And for once, Noha says the wise thing.

"The sun spirit does not wish me to use this stone for killing. He made it too soft and beautiful.

He led you to it because you are also soft and beautiful."

She is certain he didn't mean the compliment but she doesn't care. He said it.

Noha smiles. There is tenderness in it. He must have seen the pleasure in her eyes. "Will you safeguard the stone for me, Ninitegamagan?"

Che can only nod breathlessly. She remembers the long ago day on a beach when Noha had asked her to be his mate and how happy she had been. And how hopeful. Perhaps . . . ?

Artisan bores a tiny hole through the nugget and through it pushes a soft chewed thong.

Che tells herself, It's not Noha's fault that other things are more important to him than I. After all, he is no different from the other hunters.

Che wears the pendant of gold against her breast always. It will prove a comfort in the terrible journey to come.

CHAPTER 23

The Eastern Mountains

Noha said, "See, my people! It is a fine valley!"

They came unexpectedly from the mountains to a sweeping marsh basin's rim. There a great river widened into an intricate maze of sloughs, lakes, islets, and quicksand bars. Log strewn mud banks formed wide, shifting channels. Over it all a fierce, sap scented wind blew.

Éhé," said the clan.

"See the trees! Megi cried.

"So many mountains all around!" Tuk said.

"Beyond the flats lay lush green spruce forests and beyond them, tundra and muskeg reached to foothills. Distant mountains surrounded the flats. Those to the south had flowing glaciers, but the ice had stopped short of the southern highlands. An interior oasis stretched far to the west. The river had many moods, and not far from where the Fox Clan emerged from the pass, it regained its strength after a rest on the flats and rushed recklessly between poplar covered ridges and stony crests. There, in a ramparted canyon, trees peered over cliffs to rapids below.

"So different!" said Che. "And so beautiful. What a home it will make!"

"I suppose so," the maiden, Tina, said half heartedly.

Che's attention was on Rin whose eyes rounded in awe and something like recognition. The others were chattering and pointing out one wonder after another. Noha was everywhere and everything.

OGIMA! The word sang on his clan's lips. Che felt pride surge in her. Her loins swelled and she wished it were night so she could ride Noha's shaft as she once had dared.

Thus the people of the mountains and the tundra willingly became the people of the river and the forest. And though Pepoon smote them that winter, they endured. In spring, Noha watched exultant as the river ice cracked thunderously, and the cubs ran screaming to their ninga, and even Dinkka shrank into himself. Noha shrieked gleefully as the big ice chunks ground against each other before breaking away to rush to the western sea.

"We must make offering to the manitu of the river; He is powerful indeed," Noha told his clan.

That spring, Artisan and Fuum devise snares in the forest for porcupines, snowshoe rabbits and compact, immensely ferocious wolverines with bear faces who could crunch the bones of prey that even wolves reject. Deadfalls give the clan woodland caribou, moose, and even bear. For, although Wabimakwa doesn't come this far south, and the cave bear doesn't dwell here, and no more grizzlies have been seen, there are black bears and mild-tempered brown bears who feed on roots, leaves, grass, rodents, insects, and eggs.

Noha loves to watch the bears fishing. They are consummate fishermen and swipe by the hundreds spawning salmon from the streams. Noha also establishes footpaths through the forest and becomes expert at running down local woods deer among the trees.

He's happy, Che smiles. I am so glad the forest speaks to him like the tundra did! She loves the forest.

In summer, myriad geese and ducks nest on the flats. Greyish blue cranes lift majestically from the water, and fox, moose, and bear tracks appear on the grassy edges of small rivers. Che particularly likes to watch the birds.

She often says, "To fly must be the ultimate pleasure!"

There are even mammoths in the wooded valley and, though there is no need for their meat, Noha, Dinkka, and the others find opportunity to drive some of them into the bird-flats and kill them as they wallow and bellow in the mud. Here, too, Megi and Tuk find a small, isolated herd of bison. They are huge, straight horned animals who stampede when frightened and who have keen senses of smell and bad vision, which appeals to the twins who share these qualities.

Noha tells them, "You may kill a few but be careful as I have seen only one herd in the valley."

Che overhears him say to Dinkka privately, "These cannot be the immense herds foretold in the dream."

And her heart stills. Surely he will be satisfied with this abundance. She pushes the worry aside.

Whea and the maidens also seem content enough in their new home and perhaps the only unhappy person in the clan is Lara. Che sees this and gets her alone. They rest among the berry fields, the smell of crushed fruit tangy and sweet in their nostrils.

Che bites her lip. There is only one way of doing this. I must ask her directly.

"Nimi," she says, "I fear you aren't happy. Don't you like the forest and the river?"

"They are well enough."

"Yet you are sad."

"It's not what you think."

Che represses a sigh. You know very well what I think, but I suppose I must ask and there's no kindly way to do it. She takes Lara's berry-stained hand in hers. "Is it because you are barren?" Lara begins to weep and, Che, worried that she has spoken too openly, begs, "Forgive me, Nimi. I meant only to help."

"I know," Lara whispers, snuffling and wiping her face.

Che locks her fingers together. Lara is afraid Fuum will cast her off. If he contemplates it, he shall have to deal with me first, no matter what Noha says.

She says, "You shall not be put aside. I'll not allow it."

"I don't fear that. There is no one to take my place, and who would cook and mend for my mate?"

"Then what is it?" Che prompts. "There's no one to steal your sleeping platform and such a beautiful female as you must be pierced nightly by Fuum's shaft."

Che almost upsets her basket of berries when Lara says, "He comes seldom if at all to me," and hangs her head.

"What? How long has this been going on? Why didn't you speak? I shall complain of this to Ogima."

"No! I beg you, Nimi! Say nothing to your mate. I am content."

Casting about her as if to prove how happy she truly is, Lara draws from a pouch a curious knife. "See what Artisan has made for me. I have never owned such a fine blade."

And you don't want to talk about Fuum. Che decides to let the matter drop for the time being and takes the thin implement. Artisan makes micro blades by chipping out needle-like slivers from antlers. He uses these slivers as engraving tools. He makes similar blades of bone, which he inserts into spearheads so that they protrude at either side making a more jagged and lethal weapon. The tool that Lara holds had been fashioned from a beaver tooth.

"There's no end to Artisan's ingenuity, is there?" Che says.

Che actually hates the killing of the brave, family oriented beaver. She prizes the pelts of otter, mink, marten, and ermine, but she will not wear a beaver pelt. It is, nevertheless, her duty to break through their lodge roofs after diving to block the entrances, and club the beaver as they defend their kits.

"At least we let the kits go free," she would say to her nimi.

A hunter who felt like this could have, with honour, declare the beaver his totem and declined to kill it, but even Che dares not refuse to do her appointed tasks. And there are many tasks.

Strangely enough, even though she loves birds, she doesn't mind killing them when there is good reason for it. On the sandbars and nesting places there are whistling swans, mallard, widgeon, pintail, and many others such as loons, geese, plovers, and even tiny stints. Che enjoys teaching the maidens to swim along the estuaries with goose feathers covering their dark hair and to dive beneath unsuspecting water birds, grab their feet and drag them down.

Little Tina, who hates the water, says, "I prefer to rob nests, make holes in the eggs and suck out the goodness."

"Nevertheless, you'll do as you must, not as you prefer!" Che scolds and doesn't notice resentful looks from the usually cooperative Naic and Berick.

Industrious Whea builds weirs across the narrow places in the side streams to trap spawning salmon and she doesn't hesitate to vie with the bears in scooping up the giant fish with her caribou-sinew net.

Quork says once to everyone's amusement, "Not even the bears win arguments with Whea."

That winter they all cut holes in the lake ice and catch big lake trout and whitefish on lines of spruce root with bright stones or pieces of animal gut for bait. Even the cubs help.

The following summer, Che says to Lara, "How Rin and Ra love to pick blueberries."

She looks over to where they sit. They are strong and brown. Their hair and eyes shine. Whea's twins, Lee and Eci, who are now sturdy five summers old trouble makers, have a new baby brother to play with, and they are watching him now to prevent him from crawling away among the lichen covered rocks of the mountain slope. Rin abandons his berries and joins the females.

"He resembles Noha even more now," Lara says.

"I suppose he does look like him."

Che's relationship with Noha has settled into a thing of habit and sometimes of soaring lust. She searches no longer in her mate for signs of the feeling for which there is no word. Instead she turns her energies to the clan's good, and without realizing it, is becoming a formidable leader in her own right. But sometimes, at sleep time, Che leaves her hut and goes to sit on the riverbank, her chin on her knees and a faraway longing in her eyes. Then she allows herself to remember the days in the whalebone hut.

It is not really Kraac I want, she admits. What? What is it?

I like it here. In fact, often I am happy, especially when teaching the cubs or the maidens. This is a good place.

"It's not your belonging place but it is a place where you were meant to go," says the voice in her manitu.

Che's contentment is once more to be snatched away.

In the summer of the second year in the valley, Noha is hunting alone in the woods. He is trotting along a narrow path, spear in hand, when he sees ahead of him a small, dog-like red fox, cousin to his mentor. Noha has forbidden his people to molest these creatures, so this one has no fear of him. It looks across its shoulder along its russet coat and turns to sit on the path its light chest hair smooth, its fine brush wound around its feet. It barks a greeting to Noha who stops to speak to it.

"Greeting, *Outgamy*, Red Fox," he says.

The fox gazes at him from bottomless oval pupils in glistening dark eyes.

Noha speaks at length to the animal and that night at the cook fire, he tells his people, "Today, I have spoken with my brother, Outagamy."

"What did he say, Ogima?" Dinkka immediately inquires.

"He told me of many things," Noha replies, a far-off look in his eyes. "We spoke about distant rivers and mountains, lands of strange growths and even stranger animal spirits. We spoke of the Valley of the Dream. Noha pauses, breathing shallowly.

"But surely, this is the valley of the dream!" Dinkka urges.

"Not so."

The people stare at him. Che feels the muscles of her midriff tighten.

Noha says, "I thought so, too. I had forgotten the Reindeer Spirit's words. Though this is a good place, it is not the true valley. We shall not remain here."

Che clenches her fists. No! We have made a home here!

However, she has learned control and she quickly bends her head so that none can read her face, and bites back the words thinking, I'll have to consider carefully this obsession of Noha's. Is he just an aimless wanderer or is there truly a destiny for him to follow? Is he the chosen one of the Eyo?

Quork and Fuum are also upset.

"I do not understand why you want to leave this valley. It's a fine place," Fuum says. Big Quork nods vigorously.

Che sees anger play across Noha's face but he has matured. And he knows that he hasn't yet enough power to order their compliance, she thinks nastily.

Noha says reasonably enough, "Surely it would do no harm for Dinkka and I to scout the river that flows to the northeast and into the basin. We would see what lies beyond the distant mountains and bring the news to you. Then we could discuss it."

"I see no objection to that," Artisan interjects.

Che shrugs dismally. Artisan either shares Noha's goals or has some other reason. They are very different in character, but he often backs Noha's notions. Hadn't he shown spear for him at the clan parting?

Since Quork and Fuum have no further objections, Noha and Dinkka will set out the next day. Che sees the delighted anticipation of exploration on her mate's face and cannot help but feel some empathy. She sees Dinkka watching her.

That one suspects what is in my heart. He is far more sensitive than Noha realizes.

CHAPTER 24

The Stonefish

Noha and Dinkka have been gone many sleeps when an amazing thing happens at the Fox camp. Megi and Tuk have trekked into the northern mountains to hunt bear, Noha having generously lifted the old restriction of only an ogima hunting bear. For this purpose, they have followed the eastern fork of a grey rippled tributary river.

They set up camp on a granite cliff over the river and are preparing themselves for sleep when Megi lifts his handsome head to stare into the brush. He sees movement there, a big, brown shape which could be a bear.

He touches Tuk's arm in silent signal. Tuk sniffs the air, looking puzzled, and both hunters heft their spears. Moving in opposite directions, they circle the beast.

They have a dog with them, but it is well trained to make no sound until the time comes for actual attack. When they are in advantageous positions, the bear is standing on his hind legs, peering forward through the brush at their campfire. Tuk signals the dog and with a bloodcurdling howl, it launches itself at the bear and fastens itself to its hide. To their amazement, instead of a furious bruin's roar, they hear the angry snarl of a man! For once, Tuk thinks quickly and calls off the dog.

The man is big and ugly and hairy faced, with rheumy eyes peering from narrowly slit lids. Despite the heat, he is robed from head to foot in filthy brown bearskins. Not only are his clothing and weapons different but they are larger and more cumbersome than the Eyo's. Most amazingly he is not a member of any tribe they know. He is a stranger.

Megi collects his wits. "Greetings, Nijkiwe."

The stranger answers in a guttural tongue they do not understand. He doesn't seem injured by the dog's attack or even very surprised to see them. Using signs, they invite him to join them at their campfire, and he ambles along in a friendly enough fashion. Neither notice the quick appraising glance he gives their possessions. It would be unseemly to question him, so they tell him instead who they are, where their main campsite is situated, and how they reached the valley. All of this is done with signs, grunts, and marks upon the ground.

He, in turn, tells them that he is the Ogima of the *Howwaydosey,* Stonefish Clan. His people, too, have travelled across the spirit bridge and along the northern shores where he saw the remains of the Eyo camps but met no man.

Megi finally signs boldly, "Where are your people?"

The Howwaydosey's sleepy eyes shift. He draws a map in the dirt. They are apparently camped not far to the north on the river shore.

He leads them to his camp, where they are greeted with enthusiasm, stuffed with bear meat and made much of. It is a small clan of only twenty people, but the most wonderful circumstance is that among them, there are no less than seven maidens! And such maidens! They have no shame. They examine with laughing eyes the Asssinbo hunters' muscular bodies. They giggle deliciously behind their fingers while Megi and Tuk blush. One audacious girl approaches Megi and runs a cool hand across his buttocks.

With such a bonanza as this available, Megi soon convinces the Stonefish to journey to the Fox camp on the flats by making them understand that there are three maidens in the Assinbo clan. The younger Stonefish hunters' ugly heads bob at this news, and they leer knowingly at one another.

Quork and Fuum fairly dance with glee when the Stonefish march behind the twins into their camp. Artisan stands quietly back to examine these newcomers, and the Assinbo females cluster in an excited group. All that is but Che. Her initial response had been joy, too, but it doesn't take her and Artisan long to see how unseemly are the Stonefish. The hunters eye the Fox maidens lasciviously and even stare with calculation at Lara, Whea, and Che. They walk into huts and pick up weapons and tools to judge their heft, all of this without invitation. Even their females, though a little more reticent, finger the Fox females' tunics and poke curious fingers into their baskets. Che sees a Stonefish hunter knock down another who said something which Che doesn't understand.

"Imagine! Striking one of his clan!" she mutters to Whea.

Nevertheless, when Che whispers to Artisan, "What shall I do with these newcomers?" he says simply, "Feed them."

She gathers her nimi. "Prepare a feast," she orders resolving to keep a close eye on her maidens; however, she is soon so busy satisfying her guests' voracious appetites that her vigilance wanes and she looks up from gathering used bark plates and shell and horn cups to see Naic, the prettiest and most pliable of her maidens, disappearing into the trees with a Stonefish hunter. A quick look around shows her that Berick and Tina are likewise gone. Fuum and Quork are busy exchanging hunting stories with the Stonefish but she sees that Artisan has seen Naic's departure. He makes no move to interfere.

What's wrong with him? Well, if our males will do nothing, I will? She strides furiously after Naic.

"I'll show these beasts that my maidens are not theirs for the taking!" she snarls as she peers into the gloom under the trees.

Che wanders and stumbles about for some time in the twilight before she finds them. And then she gazes in shock when, rounding a bend in a game trail, she comes upon Naic. The girl is kneeling and in front of her, a Stonefish hunter sways in pleasure as she licks and sucks his shaft. But this is not what makes Che gag and grab her mouth; for another hunter, grinning in glee, at the same time ruts from behind on Naic like a dog on a bitch.

Thinking this a rape, Che grabs the skinning knife tucked in her waistband and hurls herself into the clearing, screaming threats as she comes.

Naic disentangles herself and turns on Che. "Go away!" she shouts. "Leave us!"

"Mother Earth!" Che breathes. "She is willing."

Sickened, she falters. To her utter dismay, one of the hunters motions to her to join them in their rutting. Vomit rises in her throat. Turning she stumbles back along the game trail to the camp.

What will I do? I can't even tell our hunters. My maidens would be punished, not those Stonefish pigs!

But why? Why? Are my maidens so desperate? Are they that frightened of being left without mates? I have failed them. I didn't even think to ask. Artisan knew. He understood. I'm a fool! But one thing I can do. I will insist upon the building of marriage huts if my maidens wish them. And if our hunters do not support them, I shall call down the wrath of Noha upon them. Noha won't put up with this!

To her relief, the Stonefish hunters begin the construction of the proper mating huts without her interference. They want to take the maidens with them for they, too, are isolated in a strange land. Nevertheless, Che, realizing what a life awaits her maidens, is having second thoughts. She confronts at the entrance to their hut Tina who is the shrewdest of the three.

"I would speak to you, Nimi."

Tina, her face a pale, obdurate mask, replies, "Speak."

"I fear for you," Che begins.

"Why?" Tina glares into her clan mother's amber coloured eyes.

"I am afraid you'll be treated cruelly by these Stonefish. They don't respect females. They would pass you among them. I'm sure of it. And probably to others as well. Don't you see how cowed their mates are? If you wish it, you and your nimi need not go to them. I'll speak to Artisan and the hunters and to my Napima when he returns. I promise . . ."

"You?" It is almost a snarl. "You shall do nothing!" Tina's mouth is twisted, her eyes desperate. "I will not live one more sun without a mate. We go further and further into this spirit-forsaken land! Perhaps we'll never again see our kind. And it is forbidden to mate with our hunters. I will not spend all of my days as a mere carrier of burdens!"

Che wants to cry, "But you aren't . . ." The words stick fast in her throat for *carriers of burdens* are exactly what her maidens are.

She says instead, "The Stonefish are unseemly and cruel. I have seen their hunter strike the females. You must have seen this, too."

"Unseemly? Cruel?" It is a sob. Tina makes an effort to control herself. "Ninga!" she wails. "I am lonely. So are the other maidens. Each sleep time we listen as you and Whea moan and cry out in pleasure in your huts. But for us, there is no respite for the hot coals that burn between our legs. We have no recourse but to satisfy ourselves and each other. Do you really want us to continue like that?"

"No!" Che cries. "But these Stonefish are beasts. Wait for another clan, other clean hunters."

"I shall not wait! There will be no other clan!"

Berick and Naic come from the hut's doorway and range themselves on either side of Tina. Che steps involuntarily backwards.

Tina says bitterly, "Besides, in the dark, one male shaft will be the same as the next."

At the dismay on Che's face, she relents a little. "We aren't like you, Ninga. Don't you see? Understand us, I beg you. We are only lonely maidens and you . . . you are CHE!"

Sadness cuts through Che. What more can I say? And who is Che to judge?

"Forgive me. I have failed you," she murmurs.

She turns her back on them and retreats into silence and she has to admit that as the days pass, the three maidens seem content enough and the Stonefish females make much of them. Furthermore, despite her disgust, she is forced by custom to treat the newcomers hospitably.

She cannot help telling Lara what she saw Naic doing in the woods. And Lara is just as upset as she. "How could they? I find these Howwaydosey males repulsive and smelly. How could our Nimi go with them and in such a manner?"

"I have pleaded with them but they are as granite. I should have seen this coming."

"There's nothing you can do. Anyway, perhaps they'll be treated well. They are certainly more attractive than the Stonefish females. They are fat, dirty seals! I don't know how Megi and Tuk can stand the ones they chose."

"Some are slim enough" Che says and can't help smiling. Lara is not above being vain of her beauty. But then what else has the poor thing got?

There is more trouble to come.

The maidens are mated and lionized by the Stonefish females and Che has begun to accept the inevitable when the Howwaydosey introduce the Fox to a new game. It is played with four mackisins and four rabbit foot bones, one of which is marked. The play consists of opposing teams guessing under which mackisin the marked bone is hidden. One points at the mackisin with a willow rod. Score is kept with wooden tallies. The winner claims some possession, weapon or piece of clothing owned by the loser.

Artisan, though he obviously doesn't approve, again chooses to ignore this new problem. He sequesters himself in his hut and keeps Rin and the other Fox cubs with him, away from the boisterous, often savage play of the Stonefish young.

The twins, Megi and Tuk play the gambling game at every opportunity and, being novices and not overly intelligent, they are stripped again and again of their possessions by hilarious Stonefish. Unperturbed, they order their fat new wives to make more clothes for them, make new spears and knives for themselves and gamble them away at the very next opportunity. Diminutive Fuum wisely refuses to play the games, and because he does, Quork also refrains, although he watches with glittering eyes.

"This will lead to nothing but misfortune! If only Noha were here to put a stop to it!" Che says desperately to Whea and Lara.

She is particularly angry when a Stonefish hunter claims the right to take Megi's new mate into the bushes when the latter has no possessions left to lose. She is glad when Megi, seeing Che watching, refuses the challenge and sends the female instead to borrow a beaver-tooth knife from Lara.

Since these are indeed unusual times, Megi and Tuk have each taken two Stonefish wives, jolly girls with slanted eyes. Che had stipulated only that the girls bathe in the river before mating. She and her nimi present them with new, clean tunics.

Lara says to Che, "Don't you think we should ask for a mate for Dinkka? There are three Stonefish maidens left."

Che hesitates. Surely Lara isn't afraid that Fuum might take one of them and cast her off. Che, herself, is now convinced that Fuum has no interest in maidens. Indeed he consistently ignores them. In fact, he spends little time with Quork now and has chosen as an almost constant companion a comely Stonefish stripling. They often go into the forest together and return late with no game. She has heard the Stonefish call things to them on their return, laughing suggestively and making gestures which she refuses to understand.

Steeling herself, she decides to become friendly with the three remaining maidens and see if she can pick a half suitable one for Dinkka. After all, it is not fair that he go without even a second-rate mate when it is likely that he will otherwise be lonesome.

It takes awhile to realize and to be ashamed of the fact that she hadn't considered this when thinking of the Fox maidens. I have so much to learn about being clan mother, she decides despairingly.

Megi and Tuk prevail upon the Stonefish to remain in the valley for the rest of the year, as the marsh grasses are already turning to golden brown.

"If you stay," they say, "You shall meet our Ogima."

Noha and Dinkka return from their scouting journey late in autumn when the snow is already in the woods, the shallower lakes frozen over and the caribou returned to the mountain valleys. They come with news which is to galvanize the clan.

CHAPTER 25

Discovery

This must be the Grandfather of Rivers!" Noha breathes, almost frightened by its grandeur.

Dinkka says, "Yes, Ogima, we have come beyond the high mountains. Is your dream now fulfilled?"

"Perhaps," Noha replies doubtfully.

Dinkka is silent.

Noha remembers standing before a fire in the old land's cold mountains where he said, *"In time, the Eyo will come to a new land where no hunter dwells, and he will claim it and people it, eat of its many animals, and travel very far. There will be great lakes, wider than the eye of the Eyo can see, great plains of grass thick with bison. Do not hesitate. Manitou speaks."*

I must not hesitate, Noha silently vows.

This is indeed a mighty valley. But is it truly the Valley of the Dream? Where are the plains? The bison? And the wide lakes? And why do I see mountains marching endlessly to the south along the river? Couldn't this be just another path placed here for us by Manitou to lead us to the new land?

Before finding the magnificent Grandfather of Rivers, Noha and Dinkka had scouted to the east of the mud flats and discovered a place of spruce, cedar, and hemlock trees. The mountains through which rivers carved paths were ancient, rounded, silt-covered masses looking like giant sand-dunes. Close up, the slopes displayed alpine tundra gently rolling down to drowned muskeg on wide plains.

They descended to the flats and halted on a riverbank. Noha had no intention of stopping there. Moved by some primeval evolutionary surge, he chose unerringly one of the passes that would lead him directly across the mountains. Bypassing an inviting valley which probed to the north, he followed a tributary river and then a second tributary that rose between the bald mountains. After many sun's trek, they emerged on an alluvial plain and saw the palely glistening, snaking water of another river which mirrored an empty sky as it led them to a junction with the most impressive river and valley of all, which they now overlooked.

"We must hurry to the clan before the warm time is gone," Noha says.

They don't stop to explore the Grandfather of Rivers but set off at a run back the way they came. They race like spirit animals, no rock, ravine or precipice an obstacle. They leap from place to place, agile as mountain sheep, Noha always in the lead with victory fire in his eyes; Dinkka, his shadow, content to place his mackisins in his Ogima's footprints. Their manitu exult with the news they carry to their people.

When they rest after one sun, Noha looks out over the blue waters of an inner river with bands of yellow ochre shore and moss green forests standing reflected against the sky. Two caribou are swimming the river, their antlers sticking up from the water like curved arms embracing a patch of blue, their brown and white backs and stubby tails skimming behind them.

I wonder what sends the caribou on their yearly migration, Noha muses. What manitu whispers in their ears? Do they, like I, receive a message from the ancient Totem of their family? Do they think about the morrow or wonder what is beyond the mountains? Are there Ogima among them?

He knows there is no use asking his companion for the answers to these questions.

There are no answers.

He sleeps.

When they wake, they don't break their fast but run once more. They eat the ground and consequently it doesn't take them many sleeps to reach the camp on the inner flats. They stop to bathe in the icy river before entering the camp and stride nobly toward the huts, ignoring the cubs's squeals and the females' scurryings but nodding toward the hunters' spears which are raised in greeting.

Noha suppresses a grin. *Wait until they hear*!

But what's this? There are more huts than before and new figures move about my camp!

His heart leaps. Maybe Ecakik . . .

He scarcely controls his disappointment when he reaches the two hunters who stand in the centre of the hut circle. One is Quork and the other is a stranger, a hulking, slant-eyed man who wears a bear pelt about his waist and whose hair is hacked off above his ears. He is very dirty. He stinks.

Who is this creature who looks at me with such crafty fearfulness? Noha stares haughtily at the stranger. Behind him, Dinkka poises on the balls of his feet, ready for anything.

"Greetings to you, Nidjkiwe," Quork says.

Noha answers and belatedly remembering the laws of hospitality, says, "I see that our camp is honoured by the presence of a great bear hunter."

The contours of the stranger's face relax and his spear, which had been hovering just off the ground, settles into the dirt in a peace gesture.

At least, he doesn't intend to make trouble just now, Noha decides. Though he spoils with his smelly presence the telling of my great news.

The Stonefish are quick to learn and already they can speak a little of the Assinbo tongue. The stranger hunter says, "I am Ogima of the Howwaydosey. We are new come to this land and have journeyed here through the mountains in the north."

Hope rises again in Noha. This stranger could have seen Ecakik or Kraac! For the first time, he realizes how much he misses his nidjikiwe.

He refrains from interrogating the Stonefish ogima because it would be discourteous to do so immediately. Instead, he leads him to his hut, where Che is scurrying about, readying a spot for them to squat before the door. To Noha's relief, she doesn't start asking questions but keeps her eyes downcast and her mouth closed. She prepares food for them and remains in the background while they talk.

In the meantime, Dinkka has gone to his bachelor hut to find that Che has sent no less than three stranger maidens to serve him. Dinkka remains outwardly impassive while his heart bangs against his ribs as it never has during the chase. A deep flush swells from the edge of his breechclout to the roots of his hair. He sweeps imperiously by the maidens and squats on a beaver blanket at the hut door.

"Manitou, help me!" he mutters.

The three maidens vie with one another in attentions to this small but desirable hunter who bears himself like a sky manitu. Dinkka, for his part, is surreptitiously examining them and realizing that they are eager to please him. It is obvious that he must choose one of them as a mate and he had better be sensible about it. He forgets his embarrassment and smugly contemplates the problem.

When he has eaten, he has noticed that all three of them prepare food well, but their beaver foot coverings are rough, and he doesn't like those heavy pelts about their waists. Nevertheless, he can't help noticing that above the waist they wear nothing at all except very long, very course, very dirty black hair hanging loose on their shoulders and through which brown nipples peek.

To distract himself, he mutters, "They should tie their hair neatly back with thongs as the Fox females do." Then at the enticing picture this idea presents, he blushes again.

He tries once more to concentrate on practicalities. His bride will have to be taught tailoring. Che will see to that. And his bride will have to make bear-paw mackisins and cover his hut with snow in the cold times and . . .

His determined manitu is wandering once more.

Their sloe eyes are intriguing and the one with the tremendous shoulders and melon-like breasts smiles a lot. Dinkka likes females who smile a lot. He sniffs. The second one is the most comely of them but she moves listlessly and she obviously doesn't bathe. How would he manage to make her wash herself? He will ask Che or Lara. He contemplates the last maiden. She is too young and bony and small. She looks like an emaciated songbird, and her breasts are no more than infant swellings. And she moves awkwardly.

Just then that very maiden trips over the edge of Dinkka's blanket, almost falling on top of him and spilling a skin of boiled meat over the ground. She recovers quickly but cringes as if expecting a blow, and tears wet her eyes when she moves away and nervously tries to clean up the mess. The tears are enough to melt Dinkka's soft heart and furthermore, when she was near, he had noted how smooth and creamy brown was her skin. She is clean. She smells of berries. She stirs his loins.

"What is your name?" he asks kindly so as not to frighten her.

"My name is Kal," is the soft reply. Now it is the girl whose face is crimson. He likes that.

As it turns out, Dinkka might have saved himself the worry, for he has to take all three of the maidens as brides or cause mortal insult to the Stonefish clan. This is not an Eyo custom but their own clan will grow faster and extra wives be given to stranger hunters, should they ever meet more. So, he squares his shoulders and builds three marriage huts to which he brings three brides on three successive nights. He spends the first night with Kal and the next two with the others whom Che has rubbed down with wet sand and dunked in the river and scrubbed mercilessly. The sounds which come from the marriage huts prove that Dinkka need not have worried at all.

On the fourth night, Che sees him nonchalantly entering Kal's hut once more. She chuckles and says to Whea, "This will make Kal first mate. I approve of her. She shall soon outgrow her awkwardness and become a fine companion for Dinkka. She's too meek, though. I'll have to change that." For once Che and Whea are in agreement.

Dinkka suffers a great deal of good natured tormenting from Tuk and Megi who feel that they can handle only two mates. They are solicitous of his health and offer to help him with his tasks.

"Here, poor fellow," Tuk says, "let me help you lift that rock. You must be exhausted with so much sleep time work to do."

Dinkka grandly ignores the teasing and in two moon's time, he has succeeded in impregnating all three of his mates.

At the council fire on the night after his return, Noha tells his people and his guests his wonderful news.

"I have seen beyond the mountains a valley plain upon which wanders the Grandfather of Rivers. It rises I know not where in the south and flows to the north and, I am certain, feeds the Endless Lake. This may be the land beyond the mountains of my dream."

Dinkka looks up, surprised at this misleading statement, but says nothing.

So great is Noha's pleasure that his clan cannot help being enthusiastic and curious. Besides, going across the mountains might rid them of the Stonefish problem. Even Tuk and Megi are getting tired of being cheated of their belongings. There is one Fox hunter, though, who agonizes. Fuum changes from an exhilarated hunter to one in misery as soon as he divines Noha's intention. One day, he disappears into the forest with his stripling friend and doesn't return for some time. When he does, he goes straight to Artisan's hut and remains there for a full sun. He comes out a subdued, gaunt-faced shadow of himself. Noha is put out that both Artisan and Fuum ignore him, but he has no other suspicions. It is Che who worries.

Surely, Fuum cannot prefer the company of that stripling to his own mate, his own people!

An insight that has been knawing at her knowing place comes once more to her.

I don't understand this but I can't ignore it. I must go to Artisan!

It is almost as if he had expected her.

"What troubles you, Nimi?" he asks gently.

"It's Fuum. I think . . . I suspect . . . It doesn't seem possible but . . . Lara told me . . ."

Artisan raises his hand. "Don't say any more," he commands. I know you will never rest until you find out so I'll tell you this much and then you must forget what I've said. Do you promise?"

With sinking in her belly, Che says, "I promise."

Artisan takes a deep breath. "You must understand, Nimi, that all the world is not as you see in your clan or even as you saw among the Omeeseh. Surely the Stonefish have taught you that."

Che nods.

"Good. Did you know that some clans will even war one upon the other?"

"War?"

"Kill each other out of anger or greed or lust or some other excuse."

"It can't be."

"It is so!"

She struggles with it but finally says. "Yes?"

"If such can be, then you must realize that there is much more beyond your ken. For instance, understand that not all hunters or all females, for that matter, have the same bodily desires in their manitu."

"I . . ."

Artisan thunders, "Don't interrupt!"

Che starts.

Artisan softens. "I'm sorry. I didn't mean to be harsh but there are times when you believe that *only you* feel things, know things, understand things. That is perfectly good in itself but not enough, Nimi.

"There are those who are different. Different in important ways. Time and place and events and, perhaps, their very manitu have made them so. This is as Mother Earth meant it to be. I don't know why. But it's enough to know that it is so. Often these different ones find in their hearts the feeling for which there is no word . . . but it's for one of their own kind."

"You mean a hunter . . . and a hunter?"

"Yes."

"But . . ."

"For the sake of Mother Earth, be still for once!"

Che's eyes round rebelliously but she grabs her bottom lip with her top teeth and bites down hard.

"Do you understand what I have told you?"

She stares still biting her lip.

"You can answer when I ask," Artisan says, shaking his old head and smiling tiredly.

"I don't. I mean, yes, I think so."

"Then let that be enough. And don't let me catch you bothering Lara or Fuum with this!"

"I won't."

"Good. Now leave me. I have had enough trouble for one day."

Fuum tells Noha that night that he will follow him to the Grandfather of Rivers, and Che, watching his face as he does so, begins to feel as sorry for him as she does for Lara.

"Mother Earth. Grant me wisdom!" she prays.

To add to her confusion, Che also has doubt about Noha's latest enthusiasm, for his dream has already brought a lot of hardship into her life.

She sits with her head in her hands. I hate to leave the mud flats but the Stonefish are here now and I would be rid of them. One more trek won't kill me. And I would like to see the Grandfather of Rivers. Anyway there is fire in Noha's eyes! I'll go without complaining but this is the *last time!*

CHAPTER 26

The Water Vessel

Happily the Stonefish decided to remain on the flats when Noha led his people over the mountains and into the new place.

When Che looks from a mountain slope upon the Grandfather of Rivers, she says to Lara, "I can see why Noha was so excited."

In the maze of plaited, alder fringed streams, muskeg, lakes, ponds, and sloughs which form the Grandfather of Rivers' delta, there are three channels. There is the main mile-wide middle channel and a second, narrow, twisted channel to the east. Finally, there is the western channel. It is along the third channel that Noha leads them. South of them spread vistas of coniferous forest and grassland. They make camp at the joining of the western branch and the Grandfather of Rivers. Here the great river lies broad and placid between low banks where the forest marches to the water's edge. This is taiga land, limitless deep green forests of jack pine, black spruce and splashed among them, white birch. In the area around the camp, there stand mostly spruce, not crowded together but standing individually in beds of soft green reindeer moss.

"There will be no lack of animals and fish in such a country," Che says to Lara.

"Ogima somehow always seems to be blessed in his choices," Lara replies.

The river is here three quarters of a mile wide and it is lined with ramparts from which one can look far down or upstream. Che isn't surprised when Noha sends Dinkka up there to watch for animal herds or when he takes his hunters and sets off to explore to the south.

"Now he's off with the hunters leaving us to set up camp as usual. He had better let us remain here for a time," she mumbles crankily to herself. For, no matter how annoyed she gets with her mate, she never criticises him to the other females.

She wonders if Bara had ever gotten angry with Kiconce.

Noha and the hunters are able to follow the banks rather easily, keeping to the sandy shore in some places but more often trotting along tall escarpment rims. They make sleep camp on shore away from the mosquitoes of the brush land above them. The second day, they sight a small herd of woodland musk oxen and give chase. The beasts form their protective circle and fall easy targets for the clan's spears. They slaughter them on the spot, carrying the dripping meat back to the main camp. Their laughter precedes them.

The smiles fade when Noha, at the customary feast, reveals his actual plan. "I wish to move gradually south along the river and set up temporary camps at likely spots. We shall dry meat and carry it with us and no food pits will be dug until Pepoon comes; then we shall select a place for winter camp."

Che sees big Quork start to protest, but for some reason Fuum puts a hand on his thick arm to stop him.

I guess he's finally beginning to understand the futility of opposing Noha, Che thinks bitterly. One would think that Artisan at least would stand up to him. Artisan chips quietly at a bone needle as if he has no opinion at all.

Che might have been even more upset if she could have heard what her mate said to Dinkka after the others had gone to their sleeping platforms.

"You are always faithful, Nijkiwe," Noha says.

"You are my Ogima," is Dinkka's diplomatic reply.

"And you are my companion. And it is to you that I entrust the decision of my heart. Or, if I should be unlucky and go to the land of the spirits, I wish you to follow my dream to its completion."

Dinkka whispers, his voice breaking, "Your wish is my wish."

"If only the others saw so clearly," Noha says.

He continues, "It is my private plan to lead my people ever southward until Keewatin never again keeps them captive in their huts and they dwell forever in a land of light and warmth. But first I want to find a narrow place on the Grandfather of "Rivers to cross with our best swimmers to explore the eastern country."

"You have spoken."

Noha doesn't go to Che that night. The dawn finds him squatted on the high headland, keeping watch in all directions for musk ox, caribou, and mammoth. It is a bewitching autumn morning. Sleep time's damp mist rises in grey layers from the river, allowing Sun to spread warmth over the land. Far to the north, He shines yellow-white on the delta beginnings where the river shatters into a thousand scintillating infant tributaries. Looking that way, Noha sees a dark splotch along the western riverbank, a mark which he takes at first for an outpost of spruce trees. When next he looks, the dark area has moved.

"Perhaps it's a small herd of oxen making its way along the water's edge."

He stands, shading his eyes to see better; but as yet he can make out no definitive shapes. He remains there patiently until Sun has cleared the horizon and behind Noha, the camp is stirring. Che emerges from their hut to add wood to the cook fire embers. Cubs awaken, complain, and are fed. Hunters follow the warm bodies of their mates to the cook fires and soon are chewing on crisp broiled meat, the juice dripping down their chins. Still Noha gazes puzzled to the north.

He does not dare at first to believe the evidence of his eyes; at last, with a whoop, he gallops into camp and hauls a startled Dinkka away from his food.

"Come!" he shouts. "There are men to the north!"

"People?" Dinkka's face lights.

"Come! We must run to meet them!"

Che, overhearing them, says to Rin, "It will probably be more of those dreadful Stonefish," and then looks guilty.

In no time, eight Fox hunters are trotting along the shoreline, grinning at one another and shaking their spears in the air. They haven't realized until that moment, that despite the time spent with the unlovely Stonefish, they are desperately lonely for the sight of their kind.

They draw up finally in a ragged line on a moss covered hillside, with Noha at their center. Far below them, the strangers halt. Noha can see now that it is not just a group of hunters but an entire clan on the march with females and cubs in the rear. A tall, youthful figure steps from the clan and begins to climb the hill. It must be their Ogima. He comes naked but for his breechclout, carrying not even a spear.

Noha quickly strips himself of weapons and says to his followers, "Wait for me here."

He strides down the hill.

He has gone only forty paces when he falters. Taking a deep breath, he quickens his pace. Thirty strides more and he has forgotten all dignity and is leaping over the ground, shouting at the top of his lungs.

It sounds to those on the crest of the hill as if he is crying, "Eyo! Eyo!"

Noha takes the last few yards in a flying bound and grabs in a bear-hug the leader of the clan.

"Nidjikiwe!" he cries, and unashamed tears of joy seep down his cheeks as he embraces his cubhood friend, Laf.

"But where is the son of Kiconce? He cries, casting about him for a sight of Ecakik. Nowhere can he see his eldest brother.

Inik tells Che the tragic story of the Wolf Clan. They sit together in Che's hut because the females of Inik's clan are weary and Che has insisted that her friend not attend the formal council called by Noha.

"You must take food," Che urges, noting how thin Inik is and how her shoulders droop even though she has put aside her burdens. Their cubs snuggle closely together on Che's sleeping platform as the two ningas talk quietly.

Inik will take only a little herbal tea.

She has a burden to share and I must help her bear it, Che realizes.

She says simply, "Tell me."

"I knew you would understand," says Ink and begins her long and sorrowful tale.

"At first, our clan prospered. The Long-Faced One and my mate worked well together."

Che nodded, realizing that Laf, because of his arid relationship with Jag, would have had to channel all his energy into the hunt and would have spent more and more time with Ecakik.

"The Long-Faced One was so successful in the hunt that the elder hunters began to look to him for guidance when my Napima was not available to them. The two striplings made much of him. To my Napima, he was always respectful and loyal."

Che wondered. Why does she feel she must explain Laf's popularity? Surely he had nothing to do with . . . She refrained from asking.

Inik continued. "The Long-Faced One's mate spent more and more time wandering the land, collecting roots and communing with the manitu of rock, hill, and sky, and making offerings to them. She mixed strange potions in her hut and sang songs and shook her turtle rattle. In the treatment of wounds and broken bones, she became even more adept than Boog."

Che was beginning to suspect why Inik spoke so long about Jag and Laf. She knew that Jag would have done her duty and lay with Laf but her body would have been a dead thing under his.

As if to confirm the direction of her thought, Inik said, "Her belly did not swell. And she did not tend properly to her mate. I saw to his clothing and cooked his food. As for my Napima, he got stronger every day. He was a bear in the hunt and when not busy with his duties would sit long time on the shore, watching for sea animals and replenishing his supply of spear-points . . .

Ecakik summoned Laf to the shore of a river which flowed into the Endless lake and said, "I guess you wonder why I make the striplings carry the whale carcass bones from camp to camp. I want to make a water vessel from them."

Laf stared at him, puzzled that such a good idea should come from this predictable leader of his, but his puzzlement was soon replaced with a flicker of interest and then with fire as he realized what an excellent notion it was.

"Shall we try it now?" he asked.

"Not yet."

That summer, Inik gave Ecakik a boy cub, a red, squalling fighter with the roundest face and the blackest eyes ever seen.

"We'll name him Pu," she told Ecakik.

Ecakik nodded his agreement and Laf, who was eating with them, said, "He is a fine cub, worthy of the name of Wabimakwa's small hunter."

Inik smiled at him. She felt sorry for Laf who had once been so full of laughter and now seemed so empty. He was content only when working or hunting with Ecakik or sitting quietly with them by their cook-fire.

The Wolf Clan journeyed along the tundra shores until they came to a muskeg swamp, a place of shifting sand and gravel where streams and rivers wandered madly and there were countless lakes. It was the delta of the Grandfather of Rivers. It was early in the time of Nerockamink and their bellies were full. Ecakik was displeased because of the barrier which the wandering streams presented. He had hoped to move further toward the rising sun. Now they would have to wait until the time of darkness froze the waterways so that they could walk on them.

"The clan will not like that," he said to Laf. "They will surely refuse to travel in the dark."

Laf, who admired his ogima but didn't share his desire to wander always to the east, confided in Inik. "I think that a mighty river, or even two or three rivers, feeds this place and for the first time, I wonder if we might not do well to follow Noha's example and lead our clan to the south."

To agree with him would have been a betrayal of her napima, but in her heart Inik felt the same as the Long-Faced One. At the same time, she hated to see her Ecakik wander listlessly about the camp, poking into female things and being a nuisance. Even in their hut, he seemed suddenly too big.

"You are bored," she said. "Perhaps this would be a good time to make your water vessel."

She was delighted to see Ecakik's unhappiness disappear immediately. He sent five hunters back to the west for caribou and kept Inik, Laf, and the females at his side. The females constructed fishing weirs on the edges of the twisting waters, using driftwood which they found near the Endless Lake. In the weirs, they caught the sweet fish who came at that time of year to feed on the small ones who pastured in the shallows. Jag wandered off as usual to commune with her familiar spirits and to collect roots.

It was time to build the water vessel.

Ecakik's face was wreathed in a big, cublike grin as he and Laf arranged the whale bones on the sand, copying as best they could the shape of a fish. They fastened the bones together with caribou thongs which had been soaked in resin but they had difficulty in making a cover to keep out the water.

"I'll go for Inik" said Laf.

Inik laughed at him but she left her nimi to fish and came to sew for the hunters a large caribou skin blanket. Meanwhile the hunters shaped their water vessel and with many mishaps and finally with Inik's help, they constructed a strange, long, heavy raft with curved sides and flattened ends.

Inik watched amused as, with the exuberance of striplings, they dragged the heavy thing into the water and struggled with it across sandbars until they found a stream deep enough to carry it on its back. And it did sit on the surface, though it was very low in the water and wobbled crazily. Ecakik crawled in, shouting and rocking back and forth as he tried to balance on the bones and avoid putting his foot through the skins. Laf attempted to steady the thing and keep a straight face at the same time.

Ecakik climbed out, almost upsetting the vessel and announced, "I shall take it on the Endless Lake."

Inik was suddenly frightened and she could see that Laf was also alarmed, for a cool wind was blowing from the east and the sky had darkened. One of the sudden squalls which live in the east might descend upon her napima.

Laf said, "It might be better to wait, Ogima."

"What if the lake monsters were to drag you beneath the water?" Inik asked.

Ecakik scoffed at their warnings. "I do not fear the lake creatures."

Inik looked helplessly at Laf because it would have been unseemly for her to disagree with her mate in front of the hunter.

"Let's float on that big stream over there," Laf said, trying for compromise.

Ecakik divined his strategy and said, "This water leads to the Endless Lake. We shall guide the vessel upon it!"

There was nothing to do but acquiesce. "You have said it, Ogima . . ."

Inik falters and pushes at her lips as if to make them continue the tale.

"I watched them from my place on the shore. I wanted to call another warning, even if it did shame my Napima. But it was too late. Ecakik was in the vessel and the current had set him drifting low in the water toward the Endless Lake.

"Then I did call out," she whispered. "I did. They did not hear me nor did they see me run along the shore. The vessel was drifting fast and my Napima's hands gripped the sides. The Long-Faced One was running alongside but his feet kept sinking in the sand and he fell to his knees. The vessel outstripped him."

"Don't go on," Che says in dread.

Inik pays no heed.

"The rivers long finger pointed out on the lake and the vessel slid along as if it were alive. The Long-Faced One screamed an alarm into the wind but my Napima would not listen. I raced to the shore and watched helpless as Wind swept the vessel out on the lake.

"I yelled, *Jump out!* while he was still close to shore. He didn't jump. I don't know why. Perhaps he didn't hear. Perhaps he would not leave his precious water vessel to the mercy of the lake monsters. Perhaps he was as a stripling who forgets how vulnerable flesh is."

Like Pu.

Che wants to weep. Can Inik have lost both of them, Pu and Ecakik?

Inik says, "The Long-Faced One was shouting, too, and he leaped into the rising waves and began to swim to the vessel. I wept with relief as napima turned to see his head in the water. He called something and stood. The vessel jerked wildly and Napima's arms clutched the air. He fell backwards into the water . . . he couldn't sss . . . swim."

Inik slumps forward, tears spilling down her face, but her voice goes on and on in a drowning whisper as if she will never stop, cannot stop.

"The Long-Faced One dove on the spot where Napima disappeared for a long time; he could reach neither the bottom of the lake nor his ogima. My Napima floated ashore the next day and I gave thanks to the Spirit of the Endless Lake for allowing me to bury him as befitted his rank and to tend the four-day fire at his grave."

Che stares in horror at Inik. *I have done this thing!* She wails in her heart. I, in my pride and stupidity, put the evil notion of building a water vessel into Ecakik's head. He would never have . . .

Inik is saying, "Laf was chosen Ogima."

Che notices the different appellation, *Laf* not the *Long-Face One.*

"And he took on his task with a heavy heart. He was lonely for his friend and he is not one who enjoys such honour. As for Jag, she came no more to his hut, preferring to wander the hills and shout incantations to the sky. Our people went to her with their ills and injuries, begging her to drive out the evil spirits which inhabited them. And she helped them. One day she constructed a hut apart from us and spent her days there fasting and lying often in a trance. I am in awe of her, for it is said that her powers are even greater than Boog's.

"Many sleep times after my Napima's death, Laf visited her hut. No one knows what passed between them but upon leaving her, he came to me. He said that he knew that I had lost the only one for whom I could hold the feeling for which there is no word, just as he had when Miira died; but that it was useless to dwell alone in misery. In the end, He asked me to come to his hut."

Inik looks straight into Che's eyes and says, "The clan must grow. And he was as Nidjkiwe to my Napima." She glances over at little Pu who lies secure in sleeping Rin's arms. Her tears have stopped and she is calm as she says, "I told him that I would be honoured to be his Ninitegamagan and to follow him into a new life."

Despite her pity for Inik and her own dismal guilt feelings, Che is dismayed. Without a murmur of revolt, Inik accepted all.

If Noha were to die . . . If Noha . . .

Why isn't Inik angry? Why doesn't she curse the Manitou of the Lake? Why doesn't she curse me? I was the one who got this terrible idea in the first place. Poor, big, gentle Ecakik!

It is too much. Che sobs. "Forgive me."

Disconcerted, Inik says, "Don't weep. Your tears will not bring back my Napima from the spirit world."

"It isn't that!" Che gulps. "It's . . . It was I who told him to gather the bones. I was the one who thought first of the water vessel. I am an interfering fool! I am unworthy of my clan! I presume too much!" Che's head swings from side to side as if looking for escape.

Inik kneels beside her and puts her thin arms around her. "You are not to blame, Nimi. I always knew that it was you who thought of the water vessel. My Ecakik could never have devised such a plan. It changes nothing."

"But . . ."

"No! Still your lips and don't let words escape them. We are what we are. You are strong. You are not like the rest of the females. You are a staff upon which I shall lean."

Che sobs even harder, overwhelmed with this amazing female's simple goodness and wanting at the same time to protest that she is tired of being strong, that she, too, needs support. Together they rock back and forth and, on the sleeping platform their cubs sleep and dream, and beyond the hut, the hunters sit in council . . . where Noha listens to Laf and tries not to blame him for his brother's death.

And so it is that the People of the Wolf throw in their lot with the People of the Fox to become once more the *Eyo*. There is no news of Kraac, and Noha and Che realize they will never again see him. Laf, who bears unwillingly the title of *Ogima*, with the consent of his people gives the leadership over to Noha.

It is, strangely enough, Fuum who first suggests that they send the Wolf Clan maidens over the mountains to the Stonefish. "Who knows now, if ever we shall meet more people," he says.

After consultation with the hunters, Noha agrees. Exhausted Meg and Tuk need no urging to present their superfluous brides to the unmated Wolf hunters.

Che is with Dinkka when Noha says to him. "You are the only hunter who has three mates. Why not give two of them to our nidjkiwe?"

Dinkka's head, which is bent over the spear point he is chipping, looks quickly up. His eyes are wide.

Che knows he is thinking about the cubs in his mates' bellies. And because it is Noha who asks, he will not protest.

And he doesn't at first.

He says only, "I shall keep Kal."

"Of course," Noha agrees, completely oblivious to the pain on Dinkka's face.

Che cannot stand it. She says quietly, "What about the cubs?"

Noha looks annoyed, then contrite. "I didn't think of that. Would you like to wait until the cubs are born and then keep the males for yourself?" he asks Dinkka.

It is then that Dinkka comes as close as he ever has to criticism of his ogima. He says firmly, "Kal is with cub. This one shall be mine. Besides, I would not want to separate the females from their young. Whatever the cubs are, male or female, their new nuse must agree to take care of them as they would their own. This is a condition I make."

Noha is surprised but he replies, "You have said it, Nijkiwe."

"Good for you, Dinkka," Che murmurs.

Dinkka keeps little Kal for himself.

As for Che, she takes up the burden of her days, comforted by the constant solace of lying with Noha and by Inik's renewed friendship. And it was well for her that she has found once more a kindred manitu.

CHAPTER 27

Nahanni

"How grand he is!" cries Noha.

The golden eagle is perched on a cliff's rim, tearing to pieces some hapless prey.

Che notices Dinkka glance over his shoulder at Kal and seeing her loving smile, hears him whisper, "How solitary he is."

Noha has once more prevailed upon the clan to journey south. The further they go, the more heavily wooded is the land. At first, the river is low lying, its banks clothed in willow and spruce and coloured crimson by fireweed and wild roses. But they have now come to a place where it narrows and enters a canyon. Crenellated, clay ramparts rise two hundred foot-lengths into the air. Here, on narrow cliff shelves, nest raucous, slatey-backed peregrine falcons. They don't appeal to Che as much as had the birds of the seacoast and marshes but she has no time to think about her reactions. After sleep, the people are once more on the move. They come to salmon coloured, limestone cliffs where alder and willow line the banks. Beyond the cliffs, they see a black bear swimming the river with her two cubs. Noha leads the hunters to waylay her but, when she spies them on the bank, she turns tail, and soon her large rump and the cub's smaller ones disappear among the opposite trees.

Jag, who seldom speaks, mutters, "It's a good omen."

Che can see that Noha is frustrated. "He hates to be confined to one side of the river," she says to Inik.

He cheers up, however, when Dinkka spots a woods buffalo herd in a meadow beside a silver lake.

"Perhaps they are precursors of the herds in my dream," says Noha to his hunters. No one answers.

They set up camp at a spot where the river is warm and forested islands sit on the water. Whea immediately begins building a fishing weir. When Che, Inik, and Lara come to help, she moves deliberately away to join the other females.

Che bites her lip. Can she be jealous of the intimacy which grows between us three? I must give her more attention.

She notices, too, that Kal often glances wistfully their way. They are struggling with a stake that refuses to bite into the riverbed. Remembering the long ago day when Bara had called into the Eyo females' midst a heartsick Omeeseh maiden, Che shouts to Kal. "Nimi, will you help us here?"

Kal runs up eagerly and seizing a rock from the bank begins to strike the head of the stake with more zeal than accuracy.

"Take care," Che laughs, and flushing Kal begs pardon and begins once more to pound on the stick.

This time her aim is accurate and Che feels the stake take hold.

When it is firmly embedded, Inik suggests, "Let's rest, nimi." They clamber up the bank to the spot where the cubs play in the brush.

Rin, who has been patiently watching Ra, asks, "May I go into the forest, Ninga?"

"Don't go far. Not all of the animals are your friends."

"I shall stay within sound of your call."

Lara watches him go with a smile. "Though he has only five summers, he's a stout little woodsman."

"I think he would rather speak with the animal manitu than hunt them," Inik says.

"That's true," Che agrees. "And there will be time enough when he is a little older for Ogima to teach him woodsman's secrets. For now, he must simply wander and absorb because his spirit is of the forest."

"Do you like this place?" Kal asks shyly.

Che looks about her at the river, the islands and the trees. "I like it very much."

"Do you think that Ogima will allow us to stay here?"

Inik and Lara glance anxiously at Che because they suspect that she and Noha are in profound disagreement upon this point. They, too, are weary with travelling and would prefer the clan to establish seasonal camps and move only when hunting demands it, like the old days. But they also know that Che will not openly oppose Noha.

"Che's tone is harsh as she says, "I don't know."

But she does know. Noha will move on no matter what. He will never allow them to join their spirits with the manitu of a single place, to rest in peace for more than a short time.

In the meantime, Noha and his hunters prepare to swim the river. All are to go except Fuum who can't swim and fears the water.

"Take the little ones into the forest and teach them," Noha tells him. And so Fuum takes a band of boys, including the twins but not Rin, into the forest and initiates them into the art of setting a snare. Che makes some excuse to keep Rin by her. The Artisan sees this and frowns at her but she pretends not to notice.

Noha grins happily. It's almost like old times! I have eight fine hunters with Laf on my left and Dinkka on my right. If only Ecakik, Kraac, and my Nuse were here, all would be perfect!"

It is a seasoned group who swim the river, holding to trees which they had knocked down after firing their bases and then trimming their branches. They slide through the opposite forest in single file. They kill forest deer and cache the meat to be carried back later but the primary purpose of their expedition is to find out if this is the land of Noha's dream where the grassy plains will be thick with bison.

Instead, they find the land gradually filling with icy streamlets all of which flow from the east and they see that the trees are thin and stunted, and that a cold wind blows. After many grim days, they come unexpectedly to a narrow emerald green lake's edge and see that, instead of an opposite shore treed with spruce, pine, aspen, and larch, there rises into the sky a sheer wall of ragged, clear blue ice. They halt. The water from just such a glacier barrier had killed Kiconce.

Laf cries out, "Shall we never reach the new land?"

Noha is staring at the glacier. He has been reliving the wild search for his nuse and his skin is grey with suppressed anguish as he says, "Don't worry, my hunters. We shall find a way around this new barrier. Isn't it true that, as we travel ever south, the day, though it is interrupted by time of darkness, returns always to our eyes even though autumn is due?"

"It is so," Dinkka says dutifully, though the other hunters look at one another and are silent.

"Aren't our bellies and food pits always full?"

"You have said it," Quork, who is a voracious eater, grunts.

"Let's then return to the River, carrying with us the fruits of our hunt and wait once more for the caribou's return. For when the Grandfather of Rivers turns to ice, the Eyo huts must be well dug into his banks."

Laf later approaches Noha. He finds him alone on the ramparts on a mild and sunny winter's day.

"You look always to the south, Ogima," he says.

The tone is the old one of diffident friendship and Noha recalls the days of their youth when they were inseparable. He sighs. Laf has something to say.

He's a good hunter and my friend, and he gave up his clan to me without a murmur, for the good of all. I shall listen to him.

"To the south lies the path of the dream," Noha says.

"It is extremely important to you, isn't it?"

"It is important to the People."

"I agree. But don't you sometimes wonder if the Giant Reindeer truly meant for the dream to be fulfilled in one generation? It seems to me that the ways of Manitou are much slower. I tend to believe that the dream will be accomplished by the the sons of many, many future sons."

Noha turns to stare.

"Let me finish."

"Your people are tired, my friend. They will follow you, as shall I, but they have already come very far from their home. Don't you think they need a belonging place for a time at least?"

Noha sighs. "I hear what you say Nikdjkiwe, but I must do what I must do. Even if I am forced to go on alone. If my people disobey and stay behind, I shall not stop them. And what about you? You once chose my Nisages over me. Which way will your heart take you, if the people won't follow me?"

Laf looks out over the big river. He takes his time answering but in the end, he says simply, "You are my Ogima."

Noha puts his hand on Laf's shoulder.

Just then, Dinka races up from the camp. "Ogima! The twins have spotted a lynx in the woods. Will you hunt with us?"

Noha's hand drops from Laf's shoulder. He grabs his spears from where he had stuck them in the shallow snow. "I'm coming!" he shouts.

He begins to run down the hill, pauses, turns and calls belatedly, "Will you accompany us, Nidjkiwe?"

Laf grins. "Not this time. Good hunting!"

However, when Noha turns away, the smile slowly fades from Laf's mouth and he contemplates the horizon with worried eyes.

For a time, it seems that Laf's words have been heeded and that Che's wish for a lasting home is realized. The Eyo spend three winters on the Grandfather of Rivers, and they see many wonders. There is on the opposite bank of the River a place of burning where pinnacles of black, shiny, easily broken rock send up smoke spirals, as if far beneath the ground a gargantuan campfire burns eternally.

"We'll leave offerings of spears and pelts to the terrible giants who must dwell beneath this ground," Noha says. Che gladly sacrifices her best ermine robe for the purpose.

"But who will take the offerings across the river?" asks Fuum.

Noha looks about him. Fear marks the faces even of his hunters. But on one face there is contempt.

"I shall take them," Jag says. "Build me a raft and I shall take the offerings across." In this land of many trees, it hadn't taken the Eyo long to learn to fashion rude rafts.

"It is not necessary," Noha says. "I shall do it myself."

"It is not for you to do," Jag snaps.

Everyone is suddenly very still.

Whea whispers, "I wonder if he will stand for that."

Jag continues. "I am the shaman." It is the first time she has made this claim aloud and not even Noha dares gainsay it. "It is for me to go. Besides," she says, "I wish to speak with these underground giants."

There is nothing Noha can do but give in and the smug looks on some of the surrounding faces worry Che.

The clan watches as Jag floats across the river and wanders on the smoking hillside. Che gathers her cubs close, expecting to see giant hands reach out of the ground to grab the shaman. However, Jag returns safely and even has the temerity to bring with her some smooth black rocks from the giants' camp.

"Some day that one will go too far," Che confides in Inik. "Not even Boog had dared show such disrespect to the spirits."

When Rin would approach Jag to examine the rocks, Che snatches him back. "I do not want you near her," she says.

"Why, Ninga?"

"She doesn't like cubs."

The idea of anyone not liking cubs is so foreign to Rin that he almost protests, but then he looks thoughtful and in his deliberate way says to Che, "I am not afraid of her, Ninga, but I shall stay away from her if that is your wish."

Once again, the Eyo move south, fishing for pike, jackfish, and walleye; scrambling along cliff tops where falcons and swallows nest, and perfecting their forest skills. They arrive finally at a confluence in the Grandfather of Rivers. A fork swings to the east towards the permanent ice and another swings to the west towards the mountains. They have no choice but to go west. However, the River's mood has changed. It is full of swirling currents and large, flat islands. A mysterious tributary, an icy grey river, leads even further to the west.

"We shall call the tributary, *Nahanni, River Somewhere Over and Beyond*," Noha says.

Che looks at the river and a presentiment seizes her but she contains herself until she and Noha are alone in their temporary hut and the cubs are asleep.

"I would speak with you, Napima," she begins. Though she tries to keep any complaining tone out of her voice, she sees Noha's face stiffen.

"Speak then," he says grudgingly.

"I don't like this place," Che blurts.

He turns angrily upon her. "You don't like a lot of places. Why should this one differ?"

Pain shoots through her. Why does he so resent me? I seldom speak out. It's not fair.

She gets control of herself and in as reasonable and friendly a tone as she can muster, Che continues, "Couldn't we find a spot further to the south in the land of the summer nymphs and build there a hut with a stone base? We could remain safe and happy there until our cubs are grown and must look for mates."

She holds her breath. Surely, he can't find fault with that. This place is dangerous! I feel it in my bones!

Noha shrugs impatiently but she can tell that he is at least listening.

"My Nimi grow weary of endless journeys," she coaxes. "The young are thin and need to put fat on their bodies."

"Have you and your nimi forgotten the dream?"

"We do not forget, as I have told you many times. But it may be that one hunter can't find the land of the dream in the days allotted to him. Better, perhaps, to entrust the dream to young hearts and be satisfied with the riches in our hands."

"You have been talking with Laf behind my back."

"No!"

"You are a foolish female! What do you know of dreams?"

"You wrong me."

Noha's eyes soften. I didn't mean to hurt you, Ninitegamagan." He moves closer to her. "Don't be upset." He slides his hand along her inner thigh. "Come to the sleeping platform and I shall pleasure you and you will forget your nonsense."

Instead of moving into his hand, Che jumps up and stalks from the hut. His mouth a round of surprise, Noha stares incredulously after her. "This female puts herself forward," he cries.

Che's talk with Noha has the opposite effect to what she wants. Noha, who had intended to avoid the dangers of the mysterious tributary at whose mouth they sit, now seeks out Dinkka and Laf and tells them, "After sleep, we three shall explore this River Somewhere Over There and Beyond."

Even Dinkka has misgivings this time, but he will not gainsay his Ogima when he speaks with such determination. It is up to Laf. He tries.

"It is the time of Nerockamink," Laf says. "And the river isn't friendly."

Indeed, the river's entrance is a backwater, sliding between islands of swamp grass and leading to a channel where it runs swiftly and dangerously;

however, Noha, unhappy with the estrangement from Che and unable or unwilling to heal the breech, needs action to still his aching loins.

"We will go," he snarls.

They set out the next morning. The rampaging river has stripped trees whole from its banks and tosses them about like twigs. Water white as females' milk streams from the silt covered mountains, canyons, and gorges.

Laf whispers to Dinkka, "Fear fills my gut. This river holds evil for me. It is stupid to go on, especially at this time of year. But how to convince Ogima?"

He says to Noha, "We should wait for summer when hunting is good and there is no need for our presence in the camp. It is not too late to turn back."

Noha looks at him and then at Dinkka. Even his younger friend's eyes are glazed with foreboding.

To their amazement, Noha halts. "Perhaps you are right," he says. And leads them back to camp

Laf feels as if released from some terrible doom. However, if he expects Noha to forget the project, he is wrong. Che continues to be cold to her mate and he, too arrogant to try to win her, waits until one hot, sticky day when the mosquitoes are thick in the woods, to insist once more that the journey be undertaken. This time Laf and Dinkka have no choice but to obey without argument.

As they are leaving the camp, Jag stalks from her hut. "You! Former mate!" she calls in her high pitched, squeaky voice. "Do you dare challenge the giants?"

Laf hesitates and looks back at her.

"Come on," Noha laughs. "She's just jealous."

Even Dinkka looks shocked at this disrespect to a shaman. She will surely wish ill luck upon them! But Noha has already strode on and looking ruefully at one another, his friends follow.

The river's first miles are low banked and easily trod. They cross a wide, flooded plain dotted with sandbars and treed islands and they wander in a maze of shallow channels. Stopping at the base of a twisted mountain, they hear a mournful wind blowing along the cliffs, and even Noha shakes his torso as if to rid himself of creeping matchee manitu.

They wade through low rapids, avoiding the powerful eddies and piles of tangled uprooted trees, to where swallows nest on a hot cliff bordering the north bank. Then the river narrows and vomits from a gorge. Here they find sulphur springs not far from the banks. Into these, they plunge naked, splashing and shouting like cubs.

"See how silly your fears are, Nidjkiwe," Noha laughs.

The laughter is infectious. With a grin, Laf says, "Let's teach him a lesson!" They circle their ogima who flees from them in mock terror. They catch him and dunk him soundly before letting him go.

Since the river is now turbulent and made impassable by white water, they are forced to climb above the sombre canyon's sheer ochre walls to the fir clad brink. They are relieved to be in the sunshine once more, hot and bug infested as it is. Laf kills a young deer and they eat well before sleep.

The next day, they find that the canyons widen and they enter a long valley of undulating, pine covered hills and meagre streams. In the valley grazes a small mammoth herd. To the west mountains loom. They don't tarry but cross the valley at a trot, ignoring the hot sun and the elephants, and find the river again. They then follow it up a series of serrated limestone canyons which plunge two thousand strides to the churning river. Far beneath their feet is a narrow flume of water, and towering over it on the sharp curve of the opposite shore is a lonely black sentinel rock. They gaze into the gloomy gorge.

Laf whispers, "I sense an unseen *matchee manitu* watching us from the trees, from the river, and even from the sky. "Perhaps we should not pass the sentinel rock."

"I must see where the river goes," Noha insists.

They continue more slowly now as they fight their way through the cliff-top forest amid a welter of game trails. At no point are they again able to climb down to the river which tosses and threatens, whirling in pools and gouging caverns in the cliffs. One day, they hear a distant booming that doesn't abate but becomes even louder as they move west.

Laf, always so brave, is seriously frightened. He tells Dinkka, "I am certain that a malevolent manitu haunts this river and that to go on is to court disaster. But I must not again fail an ogima. Like I did Ecakik! I must protect Noha." Noha is moving steadily through the forest toward the thunder; Dinkka follows. Laf swallows his fear and trots behind, gripping his spear tightly.

The roar is deafening and they cannot speak to each other even if they wish. They emerge at a high cliff's edge and stop, their mouths hanging open. Before them stretches an immense cavity in the mountains, and in front, across and below them are gigantic buttresses over which wild cataracts leap and plunge to the river far below, there to dissolve into misty rainbows. They stand awed at the beauty of the place and Noha, in a grand gesture to the fall's manitu, breaks his spear in two and casts it far out to plunge to the river below.

On the way back to camp, they find the giant's footprint.

It is, in fact, no bigger than a mammoth's print, but the horrifying thing about it is that it has a humanoid shape. They don't tarry near the find but hurry back the way they had come, stopping only to rest in darkness, too terrified to build a fire. Laf stands first watch while the others sleep.

It is at the blackest time of night that *Nahanni* calls to Laf from the darkness and Laf is not surprised, nor is he any longer fearful.

"I come," Laf says. "But this you must grant me. You must leave my Nikjkiwe in peace."

They find him in the morning, not far from the camp. His head has been torn from its shoulders and carried off by some creature as powerful as Wabimakwa. Around his body are the strange, giant humanoid footprints.

Many suns have passed when Noha staggers into the Eyo camp with Laf's headless corpse wrapped in skins and slung across his back. Dinkka walks behind him, his face as white as the water from which they have returned. Jag stands by the campfire, smoke circling her tangled hair. Inik creeps from her hut. She doesn't speak. Artisan is behind her. Che runs to her and supports her as Noha places his pitiful burden at her feet.

His face is wet with tears. He says, "I don't ask your forgiveness, Nimi. I don't deserve it. But I promise this. I shall take care of you and yours all the days of your life."

When what has to be done is done, he goes to Che in their hut.

"Come lie with me," he says humbly. "I need you."

It is too much. Che cannot.

And he allows it.

Unfortunately, even the guilt over Laf's death is not an emotion that Noha can harbour for long. He now fears that only Dinkka, and perhaps Quork and Artisan still support him. And his mate? The one who should follow him without a murmur, flesh of his flesh, fulfiller of his needs, she has betrayed him.

Often he takes the one-horn from its pack and sits smoothing it before the fire. There is no consolation in it. So when Che continues to refuse him, there comes a night when he drags her to the sleeping platform and throws her upon it and thrusts his knees between her reluctant thighs. As he forces his shaft into her, Che, too stubborn to cry out in pain and too obstinate to respond to his need and her own desires, turns her face from him in loathing. Noha shouts his triumph as he fills her, but his hazel hued eyes are empty.

That night, Che dreams of the day long ago when Noha had found her scratching in the sand on a beach far away and asked her to be his mate.

How kind he was then! How gentle!

She awakes, her head and body aching and her throat stiff with unshed tears. Leaning on her elbow, she gazes down at the open, cub-like face of the sleeping hunter beside her.

"I didn't mean it to come to this," she whispers.

BOOK IV

CHAPTER 28

Maunk – Loon

"See the moss on the side of the trunk?" Noha, who has stopped beside a tall pine, says to Rin.

"Yes, Nuse."

"Moss usually grows on the side of the tree which points to Pepoon's country. The opposite side shows the way to the land of Summer. Use this knowledge to guide you."

"What if there is no moss, Nuse?"

"Then you must look at the tree branches. The side where they are thickest and clothed in full green is the side of summer."

Noha strides suddenly off.

"Come. Let me show you how to avoid going around in circles in a strange forest and coming always upon your own footprints."

Rin, who can find his way in any forest by instinct alone, follows and listens.

The band is growing yearly and is almost fifty strong. Rin is a rangy stripling. Noha has taken upon himself the boy's training and Che has not objected because she is now certain of Rin's nature. He might follow but he will follow no one blindly. Noha teaches him to set a snare, to build a deadfall, and to raid a beaver stick hut. He takes him often into the forest where he tells him the secrets which any hunter in a new place needs to know. The boy, a sensitive striplilng who has noted and worried about the lack of true communication between Noha and Che, listens patiently and intelligently to Noha's instructions and tries to make his nuse proud of him. For, although he loves his ninga deeply and with a stripling's inarticulate wisdom, understands her embattled spirit, he also loves and admires Noha. He also knows he will never be like Noha except in his special kinship with animal manitu.

Noha chooses another tree. "Here, stand beside and a little behind this tree." He tugs his ogucen into place. "Now use your eyes and place the three trees in front of it one before the other in your sight."

Rin obligingly squints and lines up the trees one in front of the other.

"Now let's go to the second tree. "See now, if you once more do the thing with your eyes, choosing a new tree further on, you will not stray from your true path."

"I understand," Rin says patiently.

"But," Noha shakes a finger at him, "be careful always to take your sighting from first one side of a tree and then from the opposite side of the next tree."

"Yes, Nuse," Rin says, though he knows that he will never need to use this woods lore. He is thinking that he could teach it to Pu and the twins.

Warming to his task, Noha says, "Let me show you how a hunter on the trail of a moose or caribou who changes direction tells the hunter following where he has gone."

He quickly gathers some sticks and props one against the other, pointing them in the direction he intends to take. "If you place two sticks side by side like this, your hunters will know that you have gone toward a camp. But if you place a short stick thus," he places a twig upright at the lower end of the slanted stick, "It means that you are close by."

Rin smiles at the ingenuity of this practice. This he will use.

"Also," Noha continues, "If you put the same upright stick at the high end of the other, your companions will know that you are gone up over and beyond. Even more amazing, if you place two twigs this way, they will know that you will be gone two sleeps."

"And if three, three sleeps?" Rin cries.

"You speak true, Ogucen." Noha places an affectionate arm across Rin's shoulders and gives him a squeeze with his hard hand.

Rin isn't the only one who has grown; however, his sister, Ra, has changed only in size. She is a sweet girl cub who still tries to follow her brother everywhere and often has to be chastised for this by Che who can't forget how Drilla used to shadow the first Pu. Rin's friends, Whea's twins, are lively cubs, favourites of the adults, especially of Megi and Tuk, and a source of great satisfaction to their ninga. In the cold times, Whea herself sits now with the former Wolf females and avoids Che's hut. On the other hand, Che and Inik are closer than ever. Inik laughs and jokes less than she did before but otherwise seems unchanged by the tragedies that have dogged her.

She confides to Che, "I am content enough without a mate."

Che nods thinking, Inik wraps her manitu around her male cub and for her it is enough.

Inik's second Pu, born on a barren arctic shore and without nuse, is a chunky, happy cub of five summers, proudly bearing his first small spear. Kal has born two babes for Dinkka and there are many other brown babes in the camp; the people don't waste long winter nights. Kal and Lara are Che's other two special companions.

Poor Lara is yet barren and has finally been cast off by Fuum, who prefers to be without a mate. Che sympathizes with his decision, but her loyalty is to Lara. Fortunately, it is a time of plenty and Che has seen to it that Lara is allowed to build a hut and travel with the clan. She hasn't argued against Noha's ruling that Lara must snare her own food because she can see that Noha doesn't like enforcing the custom. She simply sees to it that the striplings and maidens secretly provide Lara with any extra food needed. Noha pretends not to notice.

"In some ways, he's like Kiconce," Che tells Inik.

She is proud of Rin who is especially generous to Lara partly at the instigation of his ninga and partly from his own good nature. Artisan also befriends Lara. He teaches her his entire herb lore because Jag now depends more and more on shaking rattles, dancing, chanting, and painting her face to drive trouble from her people. The smaller cubs are quite frightened of her. In the meantime, the minor ills and accidents have to be treated, and Lara proves a good pupil. In this way, Artisan makes a respected place for her in the clan.

He is now an old hunter whose face is so seamed and cracked that it threatens to crumble. He has confided to Che, "I feel near to the time of passing into the spirit land. Lara is a sensible female. I hope she will take my place in some measure as the clan's solace."

Che assures him, "You'll be with us for many more summers." She convinces neither him nor herself.

Jaf makes no outward objection to Artisan's arrangement, although Che often sees her staring malevolently at Lara. Indeed, Jag rarely speaks to anyone and her disappearances from the camp become longer and longer

Che is no longer frightened of her. She tells Artisan, "I think it would be wise to let the shaman go her own way."

"A good decision. Otherwise you shall make an enemy of her."

Che toils as usual and is glad of Lara's help in caring for her new daughter, Vine, an ugly infant with wise eyes. Che, who has now lived twenty-five summers, is aging fast, as the Eyo females often do. She is much thinner and her thick hair is grey streaked. She has returned to Noha's sleeping platform though there is little pleasure in it, and her relationship with him is still strained and unhappy. She hates this but doesn't know how to remedy it.

She tells herself, "In this, I have failed both him and myself."

Who am I anyway?

What am I?

The hunters, with the exception of Artisan and perhaps Dinkka, think of me only as *Ogima's mate*. True, I am honoured among the females. And I am the one who came back from watching two bear cubs slide on their rumps down snowy hillsides, and with the help of Artisan and Rin, constructed the land raft!

Che had been excited by the idea and her cheeks had glowed rosy with both cold and enthusiasm. Ever since Ecakik's death, she had suppressed her creative thoughts, but now the will to build surged in her.

Who can drown on the land? She reasoned and ordered her ogucen and Artisan about in her old, imperious way. Artisan chuckled and obeyed with all the alacrity his old bones allowed.

Together, they took down a spruce tree by burning through its trunk. They hacked off the branches with stone axes and painstakingly split boards from the log, with stone wedges. The boards they planed with beaver knives until of a small finger's thickness and ten feet lengths. They smoothed the planks' edges with skin scrapers so that they would lie snug together; the ends were tapered. They then secured the boards together with battens attached to the upper side with caribou thongs. Artisan strung the thongs through holes in the boards and slid them along hollowed grooves on the underside of the raft to avoid scraping and wear on the ice.

Che was aware that Noha watched their activity from a distance, a sneer on his lips but curiosity and admiration lurking in his eyes.

Artisan and Rin soaked the ends of the boards in tall birch bark containers, into which Che had put water and hot stones. The front supple batten was then secured to the softened board-ends, which were gradually rolled up and back and tied to the second batten. This made an effective, curved front for the land raft. It skimmed lightly over the snow.

"A female on snowshoes will pull heavy loads on the raft with much less effort than it takes to tote a pack on a tumpline!" Che said, grinning.

Noha, on seeing the land-raft completed, demanded use of it and dragged it into the forest. Che shrugged and glanced sideways at Artisan. Their lips twitched in suppressed laughter.

Che said, "Such a slow pace will soon bore my Napima."

Sure enough, Noha brought back the raft and bestowed it upon Che as an object fit only for a female.

The birch bark containers used to soften the planks had been a long ago idea of Lara's. Artisan used a piece of winter bark, which Lara had found lasted well, was pliable and could be folded very easily into a drinking cup, much easier to make and more useful than the woven grass cups of days gone by. They heated the winter bark and it bent without cracking and was fashioned into a seamless, leak proof trough with ends creased and tucked into shape. They had also made taller containers by sewing birch bark with willow root thread and coating the seams with pine pitch to keep liquid in. These pots or baskets were used for cooking and could be suspended to heat over a fire as long as they were full of water. They were the prized possessions of the females, who made winter excursions into the forests to find scattered stands of birch and to strip the bark.

Noha had made a point of complimenting Lara on her invention but said not a word of praise to Che for the land raft.

One late day of red and yellow leaf time, Che is weary and has wandered off alone along the shore of a small, shallow lake. She enjoys being by herself but she is distracted from her reverie by *Maunk's*, Loon's, mournful cry and stopping behind a tree, she watches a small drama unfold upon the lake.

The air is cold and already thin ice sheets are forming at the lake's rim. Most water birds have already flown south in honking skeins, so Che is surprised to see on the water, a black-faced loon and with her, a young chick. Not far away, the she-loon's mate calls frantically and pumps his wings in preparation for a long takeoff across the water. Che knows, just as the male maunk knows, that if the pair are to survive the winter, they have to move to a nearby river or lake that won't freeze. There they can winter safely among floating ice.

The she-loon will not leave her chick who, try as it might, cannot yet fly.

Che's manitu reaches out to them. The chick must be a late hatchling nested in rotting vegetation after the maunk's eggs were taken by foxes. It is too young and frail to climb to the clouds. Surely the maunk won't leave it.

Again and again, the she-loon's mate calls. She strains toward him her long, slim neck with its white necklace and calls him back with a plaintive cry. He succumbs to her entreaties for some days, and every day Che comes to watch. But there comes a time when his survival instinct becomes overpowering and the he-loon disappears into the sky vault never to return. Still the she-loon remains with her chick, encouraging it, protecting it with her body, feeding it fish which are becoming harder and harder to catch.

Day by day, the air grows colder and the she-loon is forced to peck ice from her chick's body. The ice free circle of water grows smaller and smaller as seven suns pass, and finally there is not even enough launching space left for the she-loon herself to leave for safety.

Che finds her there one morning in the very center of the frozen pond, her starved body stuck fast in the ice, one wing extended across the frozen corpse of her chick.

No!

Crawling on her belly, Che smashes the ice away from them and snatches the she-loon to her own body. It is too late to save the chick but Che wraps the mother in a lynx pelt and carries her through the woods for many miles to a big lake which is still free of ice.

As she stumbles along the brown leaf choked, frozen game paths, she thinks bitterly, I prayed every day to the manitu of the little lake to let the she-loon and the chick go free. My prayers weren't heeded.

I defy you, *Manitou*!

She releases the she-loon on the big lake's open water and watches anxiously as it flutters helplessly and finally, with a supreme effort skitters across the water and soars into the sky.

"Go. Find your mate!" Che cries.

Che turns wearily back in the direction of the camp. It will be a long slog home.

Noha, who has been aware of Che's many absences from camp and has surreptitiously walked the nearby forest, agonizingly convinced that she will not return, sees her come quietly into the clearing, her stride faltering and her face stricken. For once casting away pride and oblivious to the hunters' stares, he runs to her. The old tenderness wells unbidden from its hiding place in his heart.

He says, "You are sad, Little Ninitegamagan."

She stares into his eyes, searching for she knows not what.

"Will you speak of your sadness to me?" Noha urges.

"I cannot, Napima. I do not know its roots."

"Surely you know that I wish you happy?" Noha asks humbly.

"I have always known that."

"Forgive me for the past and come with me to our hut," Noha begs, his breath quickening.

Che glances about and the old mischief rises in her eyes. "What will the hunters think if their Ogima dallies away the day on the sleeping platform?"

Noha laughs. "Perhaps they will be wise and do the same."

When they are naked together, Noha fingers the gold amulet on her breast. "I am glad that you wear it always," he says.

Their mating is long and gentle, and there is great comfort in it. That night Che awakes sobbing in her mate's arms and, though Noha asks her, she cannot tell him why.

CHAPTER 29

Scouté—Fire

Scouté, Fire, begins his terrible work in the east.

At first, he smoulders harmlessly in dry grass near the edge of the Lake of Trout and is almost extinguished in the sand; but a transient, western breeze swoops down upon him, plays with him, and flies on, trailing sparks. Scouté licks his way up a bank and nibbles at a small tree's base. Soon he is swallowing the forest. In two suns, a holocaust marches in a line thirty miles wide toward the Eyo camp.

It is high summer and hot and Scouté's heat waves roll far ahead of his flames, baking the forest until tinder dry. The air becomes so torrid that the trees reach flashpoint long before the flames have reached them, and when vagrant sparks touch them, they rip skyward and explode into huge torches. When this inferno reaches the forest roof, it skips across the treetops, a wind of flame. Below, streams and small rivers boil and shrieking animals flee, their frantic feet no match for the conflagration's speed.

The Eyo camp sits on a spit of land that reaches into a shallow tributary river.

It is dawn and all are sleeping.

Che is the first to wake and stumble sweaty from her hut. She goes to the river and drinks, plunges her hands into the water, splashes her face and neck. She stretches langourously, looking out over the mist scarved water to the tree-line beyond. Her eyes widen. There is a muted glow in the morning sky, as if the sun shines orange upon it. As she watches, it darkens until the rising sun is hidden. She sniffs the air and an acrid, almost pleasant odour invades her nostrils. As she turns to run to the camp, grey ash flakes drift to the ground around her.

She screams, "Scouté!" all the way to her hut and before she reaches it, figures are straggling dazed from other hut entrances.

Noha emerges abruptly into view. Dodging around her, he races to the camp's center yelling, "Hunters! To me!"

Che whips into the hut. Rin has crawled naked from his skin bed and is shaking Ra awake on the opposite side of the hut. Vine whimpers from her mother's bed. Che snatches up the infant and orders the older cubs to follow her.

"Bring skins."

She hurries them to the spot where the hunters and others have assembled, a frightened group. Noha silences with a curt order their murmurs and wails and then he speaks to them.

"What say you, my hunters?"

Dinkka steps forward, neglecting in this emergency to ask permission to speak. "The wind blows from the east, Ogima. The fire will come here."

The hunters' dark eyes search the sky. Tuk sniffs and nods.

"Soon!" is the verdict from all sides.

Che has never experienced a forest fire and has seen only fires set by hunters in grasslands to drive prey; however, she has heard many tales of the horror, the power, and the speed of Scouté.

Noha looks to old Artisan.

"Speak!"

"There is no escape," Artisan says flatly.

"Can we outrun Scouté?"

"Not even Noha can outrun Scouté."

"What shall we do?"

"Take refuge in the river and pray that Manitou does not allow Scouté to suck away our breath and cook our lungs and boil our bodies."

"You have said it. To the river! Take skins to cover your heads!"

The Eyo swarm to the river, ninga clutching babes to their breasts, striplings and maidens holding the hands of the young, the hunters shepherding in the rear, most moving calmly and with their courage quieting the timid.

Noha is the last to enter the water. He wades only as far as little Che can while holding the baby. He drapes wet skins over his family's heads and directs Rin to stand near him, lifts Ra in his arms and kneels on the river bottom. He looks into Che's amber eyes and smiles and then he begins to chant a song of supplication to the Great Spirit of the River, to the Spirit of Fire, and to the Great Manitou.

He begs, "Spare the lives of my people!"

Che stares about at the Eyo. Artisan is quiet, eyes closed, a wet rabbit skin over his ancient head.

He knows that Scouté can leap across two-mile-wide rivers in minutes and once the trees on both banks are burning, the surface of the water will heat and then bubble. He looks around at the cubs and despair stands stark in his old eyes.

The air is becoming grey with smoke. The people cough and choke. Their dark eyes run caustic tears. Jag shrieks one imprecation to the sky and is silent. They remain thus for a very long time, struggling to breath in the scorching, oxygen starved air. Some have all but given up hope and weep and groan in helpless panic. Mothers pour water over the heads of whimpering cubs. The weaker cry out in terror.

In her heart, Che shouts, *Not now! Not yet! Not my cubs!*

A sudden stillness. Wind, which has been getting stronger with each minute, veers sharply to the north and gradually, as the Eyo gasp, the air begins slowly to clear. By mid-day, nothing remains to remind them of the near holocaust but the smouldering opposite river bank, charred twigs, ash that floats on the water and the stink of smoke in the air.

Scouté has swung off to the northeast before it reached and crossed the river.

The Eyo are spared.

That night, cavorting, relief crazed figures leap in silhouette against firelight. Artisan doesn't join the dancing and Che finds him lying grey faced and breathless in his hut.

"Nuse!" she cries, calling him *Father* in her fear for him. "What is it? Are you possessed of a matchee manitu?"

The Artisan tries to answer but instead chokes and grips his concave chest in agony. Che leans over him.

"I'll get Lara!" she says. "And Jag."

"No. Not yet," Artisan gasps. "Stay with me."

"But they can help."

"I am beyond help, Little One."

Che disobeys him and races for Jag. The shaman comes and fills the hut with her chants and spells. Under her ministrations, the Artisan grows worse. It is Lara who gives him some respite with hot herb drinks. Despite this and the power of their love for him, Scouté claims Artisan. In the hour before the rising sun, he dies in the arms of the females and with the cubs and striplings standing in a ring around his hut.

The grief of the females and the young cannot be assuaged. The hunters gather about in knots and murmur darkly among themselves. When Noha seeks to join them to console them, all but Dinkka turn their backs on him.

Big Quork finally voices their accusation to Noha. "Always we wander endlessly," he snarls. "And for what reason? Manitou is surely angry and has sent Scouté to scourge us. For this madness of yours, first Laf and now Artisan have died."

"He speaks the truth!" Tuk cries.

"We shall wander no more!" shouts Megi.

Noha staggers under their battering words, which injure him as no angry blow or thrown dart could. He looks into Dinkka's face, and although his friend stands resolutely by him, he cannot meet Noha's eyes.

Noha loses his temper.

"The caribou and the forest beasts have left this place. You'll starve if you stay here!" he screams.

"Then we shall leave and find a better place and stay there!" shrieks Fuum.

Soon everyone is yelling and gesticulating.

A quiet voice breaks into the melee. A sudden shocked silence.

"I am shamed. My nimi and I hide our faces in the necks of our cubs to hear such words from our hunters' mouths. Artisan would have wept to see you like this!"

Noha whirls.

Che.

"Have you forgotten the Ogima of the Reindeer Clan?" Che snarls into the stillness. "Have you forgotten the dream? Have you forgotten the words of your revered shaman, Boog?

"*Where my Ogima goes, I will follow,*" she vows. "*And with me will come my Nimi and our young. We will go. We will persevere. We will find the Valley of the Dream!*"

Astounded, they watch her as she calmly turns and marshalling the females and cubs, begins to set the camp to rights.

One by one, the hunters lower their heads and shamble away.

Noha breathes, "My hunters listened to her and not to me. Never shall I understand this amazing mate of mine."

CHAPTER 30

Rin's Dream

It is in the land of trembling aspens and white birch that Rin comes of age.

He is a compact stripling, slim and wiry-muscled like his nuse and short in stature like Che. He has an aristocratic, oval face with a high bridged, narrow nose and serious, yellow-brown eyes that light when he occasionally smiles. He likes to wear his straight, black hair chopped off at the shoulders and controlled at the forehead by a soft leather band.

Noha often tells him, "You look like your long lost uncle, Kraac."

Che sees that Rin is like Kraac in other ways also. Unlike most of the Eyo striplings, he often goes off alone into the forest, hunting and trapping and always returning with a bundle of furs which he has scraped himself.

Inik says to Che, "He speaks the languages of all animals, and the beasts come to him without fear, and he can call down the birds from the sky."

"I am proud of him," Che confesses.

Despite his solitary ways, Rin gets along well with others. Whea's twins, though younger than Rin, are already bigger than he. Unfortunately, they have inherited Whea's argumentative ways as well as Quork's strength so they do a lot of wrestling and squabbling; however, they adore Rin and followed him about like two gangly, young bears. The cub closest to Rin is his little cousin, Pu, who now has nine summers.

Everyone loves Pu, just as they once loved his namesake. He is bright and quick, and his round face and merry, slanted eyes show a happy nature. He and Rin enjoy swimming together as they both are like trout in the water, an innovation in the clan. Little Pu never oversteps friendship's bounds, respecting Rin's need to go by himself into the pathless forests, although he doesn't clearly understand that need.

When the time comes for going apart according to the custom, Rin builds himself a hut on a forest lake's edge. The lake is almost perfectly circular and the pines whisper and lean in a deep green belt around its yellow shores. The trees are so thick that they blot out all but an overhead circle of blue sky.

"This is the place," Rin says.

He fasts for fourteen suns, taking only occasional sips of water from the lake. On the fifteenth day, he is weak and his hunger pains have faded to a kind of pleasant torpor. He is lying on his back in the lakeshore sand, eyes closed, when a voice from the sky calls his name.

"RIN!"

He starts, dizzy with sudden apprehension.

"*Have courage,*" says the voice, "*for you have been chosen to father a great race. Do not tremble. You shall lead your people across the endless plains. The pesheshkey will come in their millions to feed your people.*"

Rin protests. "I am a boy of the forest. Its creatures are my brothers. There are no plains here and I do not know this word, *PESHESHKEY.*"

"*You shall indeed come to the plains. And your skill shall strike terror into the heart of giant bison who shall stampede in anguish at the sound of your name.*"

"I am deeply honoured, O Spirit, but shall I never return to the forest which I love?" Rin asks sadly.

"*Never.*

"*Take courage, little buffalo hunter, for in time to come, the sons of your son's sons shall come to a Great Valley. It is a fabled valley far, far to the east. It is cut by a mighty River into ancient rock, rock as old as Mother Earth herself. There in that ancient forested place, the Eyo shall dwell forever, People of the Forest, the Valley, and the River.*"

The voice fades.

"Is it the Valley of the Dream?"

"*You have said it.*"

The voice disappears and comes no more and Rin falls on the ground in a faint. As he sleeps, the small furry things of the forest came to lick his face and hands and, when he wakes, they ministered to him and he tells them about the spirit message. Before he leaves the sacred place, Rin takes a handful of golden sand from the shore and wraps it securely in a tiny pouch which he shall always wear on a thong around his neck.

When he has returned to the Eyo camp, Rin tells only that he has dreamed but he does not tell of what. Jag is angered by this and demands of Noha, "Force him to relate his dream!"

Noha trusts his ogucen and haughtily refuses. Jag creeps to her tent, muttering imprecations against him.

"Don't anger her, Napima," Che begs.

Noha swings to face her. "What say you, woman?"

"I fear her powers," Che tells him anxiously. "I am certain that she consorts with demons and could bring ill happenings to the people."

Noha laughs. "Be silent, woman; don't tell me your fears."

Che shrugs and is silent. She anxiously watches her ogucen and mate as they go about their daily tasks, hoping to shield them from harm with the fierceness of her love.

Finally she notes, Noha may bluster but he's now more careful in his treatment of Jag, and is comforted.

CHAPTER 31

Peshekey — Bison

Ra is always by Che's side. She is growing into a lovely female with dreamy ways. Vine, the youngest, is a different type. Her face is as wrinkled as a walnut and her sparse hair hangs light and fine. Though still a toddler, she has an indomitable will and stalks about on short, bowed legs afraid of nothing and no one. Even a scowl from Ogima, himself, doesn't cow Vine, and she will stand before him like a little old fury and kick fiercely at his ankles if he tries to move her out of the way. Che loves this independent spirit in her. Only if Vine puts herself in danger does Che scold her.

"Let her enjoy these few years of happy innocence," she says to Inik . . . and thinks, For now I'll indulge Vine. Let Mother Earth teach her as she did me.

So Noha leads and the Eyo follow and, in the fullness of time, in the time of Menokemeg, they come to a dry land, the plain of Rin's vision. At first it seems a barren place of parched grasslands where the sun beats down relentlessly and there are only small patches of fertile hill country. They move to the west, once more searching for the mountains and the melt water lakes and rivers so that from wooded slopes, they might venture out to hunt the flatlands. They follow a narrow twisting river bordered with cottonwoods, and it leads them over short-grass prairie to the Rocky Mountain's foothills.

As Che gazes awed at their magnitude, her inner voice says, *"They have waited our coming for a million years."*

"We shall find no people here," Che murmurs sadly and for an instant, Kraac's dark eyes flash into her knowing place.

The air is dry and hot. The Eyo move slowly, savouring a special feeling for this new land. Noha strides in front. Che watches him. He's still strong and agile despite the silver streaks in his long hair and the aches which assault him in the early morning.

With him, as always, is Dinkka, looking older but keeping up nicely with his leader. They are trailed by the elder hunters and finally by Rin, Pu, Whea's twins, and the striplings in a group. Che and the females and babes bring up the rear. Jag walks off to the side, a dirty figure with hare pelts hanging untidily from her emaciated frame. She mumbles incessantly to herself and her eyes are vacant and indrawn, lost in another world. When she focuses them on those around her, the look is malevolent and crafty.

"Jag is more than a little mad," Che tells Kal, Inik, and Lara. "But since she is spirit visited, we must continue to care for her even though we fear and avoid her."

"She scares me," Kal says.

"I know, but she is special and must be judged by different rules. We run to her quickly enough in emergencies, don't we? Such as the time when you almost developed the rotting greenness in an injured leg," she reminds Kal.

Che thinks privately, I wonder if Kal would not have recovered just as well without Jag's chanting and gourd rattling. Che sometimes suspects that Jag had caused the infection with spells, but she dares not voice her suspicion even though Kal is partly lame because of it. These things must be borne. Like many things.

Noha is nervous and excited. Rain and cooler air have come and the grasslands thrive. His scouts have sighted bison herds on the prairie, and he can scarcely wait to get the clan settled so that he might begin the chase.

"Nuse," he prays to Kiconce's manitu, "the journey has been long. *Let this be the place*."

A bowed river leads them into one of the most beautiful valleys he has ever seen. Its rolling foothills are covered with spruce and pine and promise good trapping, while on every side, giant, tree clad mountains encircled and protect them with gargantuan arms. The riverbanks are wide and flat and cut by many streams. The nearby hills slope steeply but are climbable and present magnificent views of the winding, blue-green river and the mountains beyond.

Noha says, "We'll camp here on the finger of sand at the river bend."

He takes Che aside and tells her, "This could well be the Valley of my Dream. I hope, Ninitegamagan, that we shall stay here for a very long time."

Her eyes glisten golden brown as she replies, "I thank you, Napima."

And Noha looks deeply into her eyes and says, "And I you."

Rin is just as pleased as his parents. He will be able to continue his beloved trapping here in this peaceful valley and also be initiated into chasing peshseshkey on the open plain as is his fate. He can see that his nuse thinks this to be the Valley of the Dream, and perhaps it is, for Noha. Rin has told no one of his own dream in which the spirit has talked to him of a Valley far, far to the east. The vision is a part of his cubhood and he prefers to forget about it and live for the quiet joy of the moment.

Let Manitou arrange the rest.

The first close sighting of pesheshkey strikes wonder into the Eyo hunters' hearts. The bison are powerful beasts with brown, woolly coats, stupid bovine faces, and lethal horns that sweep straight out in six-foot lengths. Behind the pesheshkey's neck is a large hump, and the beast's height at that point is often seven foot lengths. The animals travel in herds of fifty to three hundred, cropping the grass and then moving on. There are countless of these bison on the plains, a seemingly inexhaustible meat supply. Added to these are scattered mammoth herds.

"It's a paradise!" Noha says to Dinkka.

The bison, like the rhino which the Eyo previously hunted, have a keen sense of smell but are handicapped by bad vision. Unlike the rhino, they are gregarious animals who close ranks when frightened and stampede in insane charges, ignoring all obstacles and building implacable momentum until exhaustion or disaster brings them to a halt.

"Anyone who gets in their way will be trampled into blood, flesh, and bones in seconds," Noha warns his people.

In the badlands, Rin, Pu, and the twins have scouted an arroyo whose northern tip has a sheer drop of a hundred strides. When they report this to Noha, a plan is made at council and the striplings sent out again to locate a herd in the vicinity of the arroyo. This they do, being careful to stay upwind of the bison grazing peacefully and myopically on the short, stubbly grass. There are almost two hundred bison in the herd.

"It's a large herd," Rin tells Noha, reluctance in his tone.

"Have you scouted a smaller herd in good position for the hunt?" Noha asks. For he, too, dislikes hunting a large herd. It is not fear but pity for the beasts that moves them.

"I have found no such herd."

"The Eyo must eat."

"It is so, Ogima."

"We hunt!"

On the day of the hunt, Dinkka and Quork make a wide circle and approach the herd from the north. There is very little wind but what there is blows from that direction. Rin, Whea's twins, Pu, Megi, and Tuk, and two of the younger hunters formerly of Laf's clan are stationed at intervals in a long corridor on the left flank. The rest of the hunters, under Fuum's supervision, take the right flank on the mile-long path to the arroyo. All are equipped with loose skins and wooden rattles as well as their leaf-point spears.

The day is clear and as they wait, the wind from the north strengthens.

Noha wishes he had more hunters.

He gives the signal. He, Dinkka, and Quork leap from their bellies and run pell-mell downwind toward the distant herd.

As his feet fly over the ground, Noha's heart sings and a cry of blood lust spouts from his lips. Dinkka and Quork are also howling and the startled herd, catching their scent an hearing their distant cries, begins to mill and stumble about. Finally, an old bull darts to the south away from the screaming, yipping men and the rest of the herd wheels to follow him. Calves bleat in fear and try to keep up with their mothers as their flight's momentum increases. The old bull, his red veined eyes rolling in dread, tries first to steer to the east and then to the west, only to find his way blocked by cavorting, shouting men who make another terrifying, rattling sound and whose skins flap crazily in the air. Mindless with panic now, the bull steam-rolls directly south.

When the herd's monarch reaches the edge of the arroyo, he tries in vain to halt, bellowing in anguish, but the weight and velocity of the bunched animals in the rear propel him screaming and kicking over the edge, where he bangs and bounces down the side of the arroyo, lands on his back and is immediately pinned by the threshing bodies of a half dozen of his herd. As the heaving mass struggles to free itself, he becomes more firmly wedged and his spinal column is wrenched into an unnatural U-shape. The other beasts are no more fortunate in their last agony. Some are wedged head down with hindquarters pointing to the sky. Some sit on their ends like begging dogs. Long, threshing horns cut into neighbouring flesh. Calves die quickly under their elders' immense weight.

The hunters run to the arroyo's lip to gaze down at the carnage they have wrought. Rin gulps back vomit and closes his eyes.

"Never before have I seen so many animals die, and die so horribly," he says to Pu.

Pitiful screams pierce the sky and the huge mass writhes like a single, expiring giant. In less than an hour, two hundred animals have been annihilated. The elder hunters' faces are stiff.

Rin looks at Noha. My Nuse is upset, too.

"Go for the females," Noha gruffly orders Pu.

The merry stripling, now solemn and pale, turns on his heel to trot back and bring forward the females, who are waiting with their choppers, flint scrapers, and beaver tooth knives some miles away in a cottonwood clump's shade. Jag and Lara remain on the oasis with the youngest cubs and Inik and Che lead the others to the killing site.

Che is horrified at the mountain of dead and dying beasts, but there is no escaping the task ahead. She watches as the hunters drag the carcasses into slaughtering position. They begin at the top of the pile, first dispatching with clubs and spears the animals that live and then tying leather cords to their different parts and dragging them down the side of the bison pile to the ground. It is wrenching toil. When they have managed to separate three animals from the pile in this way, they are forced to rest and the females take over.

Fighting off nausea and a sudden strange weakness of lungs and limbs, Che does her part.

At first, they butcher in an experimental way, trying the techniques that they would have used on any large, grazing animal. By the third bison, they are expert. They roll the animal on its belly, legs splayed, and cut through the hide along the backbone. They then methodically scraped the skin downward from the sides and stretched it out on the ground. On this mat, they will place the cut meat. First, they strip away the tender flesh of the back then hack away the forelegs. This leaves them free to work on the hump and the body cavity. As they cut into the internal organs, they chop away choice pieces and give them to the hunters to suck.

Rin refuses his share.

And I don't blame him, Che mutters, noticing how pale her ogucen's face is. She herself is having difficulty breathing.

Whea and Kal slit the bison's throat, pull the tongue out through the slit, and slice it off. With the striplings help, they sever the spinal column and cut away the pelvis meat and the hind quarters. From the first bull, they preserve the head and the horns for a feast dance but every other useable ounce of meat is taken from the rest of the three carcasses and wrapped in skins.

Che tells the maidens, "Place the bones neatly along the ground in the order in which they are secured. Remember that the bones are the resting place of the bison's manitu and must be treated with respect." She is proud of the way Ra leaps to the task.

She's not afraid of hard work!

They set up camp nearby and light bison chip fires. Over these, meat strips are smoked and dried. Of course, there is no way in which such a small clan can hope to slaughter all the bison but they take as much meat as they are able. The greater part of the kill is left for scavengers.

"The birds and little meat eaters of the prairie will be glad of our coming," says Che to Inik. And it is a consolation.

CHAPTER 32

Sheshin — Song

It is autumn before a sufficient supply of meat has been prepared for the winter and dragged back to the mountain camp to be stored in pits or made into pemmican. The wearying task done, Che seeks seclusion in her hut.

Inik seeks her out there. "Is something wrong, Nimi?"

Che looks up at her with feverish eyes, "I don't know. My body and my knowing place seemed no longer to obey me and I want only to sleep."

"You are just overtired," Inik says. "Rest, now. Kal and I will take care of Vine."

She leaves the hut and hurries off to find Lara.

"I think our Ninga is possessed of a matchee manitu," she says breathlessly.

Lara pales. "Not Che!"

"Yes. Prepare some of your remedies quickly. I must go to tell Noha."

For many days and nights, Che tosses in fever and, though Lara and Inik nurse her faithfully, and

Noha refuses to leave her side, and even mad old Jag comes to drape her with charms and screech into her deaf ears, Che is lost in the land of dreams.

The days of her life march before her eyes. She is once more the passionate woman cub fighting to possess Noha. Once more, she meets the great grizzly; once more she lies in Kraac's arms; once more she rescues the she loon. But nowhere in these visions does Che find the answers which she has sought over the years.

In her delirium, she opens her eyes. Above her, the faint outline of Inik. Che sees not her nimi.

"Who are you?" she asks and hears no answer.

"What creature are you come to steal my manitu?" Che demands. But the figure melts and comes together in a new form and the face is Che's own face and then again not her own.

"Who are you?" Che cries again. "You wear my visage. Where do you come from? Where do you go?"

The stranger gazes down on her in wonder and in recognition and in love.

"Who am I?" Che cries.

"You are Che," says the vision. "We are Che. I am what I am. I am the offspring of your spirit, the one who comes after you."

"Remember me!" Che cries. "Remember me!"

Her fever is breaking!" Inik grabs Noha's arm. "Che will live! Che will live!" She turns sympathetically away from the spectacle of her ogima on his knees sobbing like a cub.

When she recovers, Che doesn't remember the vision, and she knows no longer the strength of her former days.

All these things Che bears and once more she rallies. Noha is kind and she finds solace in her friendship with Inik. She and Inik consider themselves elders now, since their hair is grey and already their teeth are beginning to loosen; they stand proud and revered among the others. Even Whea has finally succumbed to Inik's sweetness and Jag leaves them alone. Also, their rank has earned them certain privileges. One of these is to leave the camp occasionally to go for rambling walks together in the mountains.

On these walks, they speak very little to each other but commune in their manitu and delight in pointing out particularly lovely scenery or in standing quite still on a hillside to listen to the call of geese or watch a golden eagle soar in the domed sky. To salve their consciences, they usually bring along bark baskets into which they gather berries and roots and often, for their own sake, flowers.

One day, they follow the river to its source in a haunting, aquamarine, melt-water lake at a mountain glacier's foot. There they climb to an alpine meadow dotted with blue forget-me-nots and look out over the lake. Che is panting and white from the climb so they sit down on a carpet of light green moss and gaze down at two moose wading through a glacial stream and Che wonders what the stately animals think of these two helpless female creatures who look down upon them.

Across the lake, a glittering glacier climbs skyward in a perpendicular, indigo cliff, and from under its blue-green topmost edge, cascades of melt-water tumble and glide to the lake below.

Che gets to her feet and sings a song of joy and resignation.

SHESHIN—SONG

Remember me, O ye waters!
I remember
The flowers soft beneath my mackisins
The birds that sang to me alone
Though only a woman
The brown eyes of the cubs
The hands of my mate
The bear who didn't eat me
The snowshoes
The land raft
The Endless Lake
The hut of bones

I remember the loon

Never more shall I write upon the sand
A dark cloud is on my path
I am weary
I would see what is beyond the clouds
Remember me!

On the way home, they come face to face with two bighorn rams with a ewe in tow. The animals stand still to curiously examine them before swinging on sure, dainty feet up a side canyon. The two friends laugh, for this day, even the simplest things fill them with joy.

Two nights after that peaceful day, Che dies quietly in her sleep.

There is no time to run for Inik or even to summon Jag to dance and chant around the small corpse. Noha is inconsolable, turning furiously from anyone who dares to commiserate with him. Rin is wise enough to leave his nuse alone and let him prepare Che's grave himself. Noha permits only his own Rin, Vine, and Ra to approach the grave while the rest of the Eyo stand mute outside his hut. Dinkka defies Noha and comes slowly inside followed by Inik with an armful of forget-me-nots.

"I would speak," Dinkka says.

Noha looks up at him from grief swollen eyes. Dinkka goes on, "She was a good female and my friend. The world will be empty without her."

Noha doesn't reply.

Dinkka trys again. "Her manitu will bring much joy to those who have crossed over to the land of the spirits before her. I ask permission to place some objects in her grave."

Noha does not reply.

Dinkka says, "She was beautiful!"

Finally, Noha says in a hoarse whisper, "Do as you wish."

At a signal from Dinkka, Inik leaves the tent and returns with a miniature toboggan which the Artisan's knarled old hands had once painfully fashioned. This she places in the grave along with a small fish carved of ivory and a bundle of sweet smelling herbs and loon feathers. She spreads the forget-me-nots over her friend's deerskin tunic where they form a frame for the dear, plain face and the gold nugget which lies on Che's breast.

At this gesture, Ra begins to weep quietly and little Vine stares fiercely at the wall of the hut as if memorizing its surface. Rin looks at his nuse and speaks for him who is beyond speech.

"In the name of Ogima, I thank you, Great Hunter. I thank you also, Friend to my Ninga."

The aging hunter and the middle-aged woman nod and solemnly leave the hut.

EPILOGUE

It is Inik who first notices that Lara is with cub. Not believing her eyes, she calls her aside. Lara is still lovely, although her dark hair is silver streaked and she is thin except for the swelling beneath her tunic.

Inik is blunt. "Are you *mooshkey,* Nimi?" she asks. Lara nods.

"How? You have been cast aside by your mate these many years."

Lara refuses to answer, for to do so would be to accuse her former mate, Fuum, of impotence and everyone knows that only females can be *matchee waybegun.*

"You shall surely be strangled and your cub with you!" Inik cries in anguish. She is fond of the quiet, unassuming Lara, just as Che had been.

Dinkka comes upon them as Inik persists in trying to learn the name of Lara's aggressor. She is so worried that she has forgotten to lower her voice.

"Be silent, female!" Dinkka says angrily to Inik, who is startled and hurt.

"She is mooshkey!" she whispers fiercely.

"I can see that."

"But she will die!" Inik says. "And the hunter who abused her will go free!"

"Have you thought that perhaps Lara will bring forth a son?" Dinkka asks gently. "Surely one of the hunters will take her as a mate."

"Who?"

"I shall take her if no one else steps forward."

"You?" Inik's mouth quivers at this ludicrous idea, for it is an old joke in the clan how Dinkka had gotten rid of two mates and how he worships his Kal, lame though she is. He has never once cast his eye on another nor has he shown more than friendly interest in the offspring of his former mates.

Dinkka puts his arm protectively around Lara's shoulders. He doesn't ask who the cub's nuse is, for he thinks he already knows. It is not Lara's former mate, Fuum, who has mellowed with age and now leads a singular but contented existence. It could be one of the younger hunters, who, deprived so long of release for their natural cravings, might have turned to one of Lara's beauty. After all, she is not of blood relationship with the clan, being a former Mahantanis.

He says, "I shall take her to Ogima to see what can be done for her."

Lara goes along meekly and Inik follows. They find Noha in his hut, smoothing the one-horn.

"We would speak with you, Ogima," Dinkka requests.

"Enter."

They do so, trailing a subdued and reluctant Lara who keeps her eyes trained upon the ground. Inik, too, stands uncertainly, knowing that she has no business here but hoping she might help Lara in some way.

"What do you want?" Noha asks impatiently.

Dinkka speaks. "This female," pointing to Lara, "is mooshkey."

Noha's eyes widen in surprise and something stronger.

He's angry! Inik thinks despairingly. Lara will be strangled!

Noha's voice is flat when he asks, "Is this true, female? Look at me!"

Lara raises her head and her eyes meet his. "Yes, Ogima."

"How many hunters have you taken to your skin bed?" he asks imperiously.

"Only one since I was cast aside."

He has to believe her, for a member of clan would not lie.

His next words clap like a thunderbolt on the air. "Then, I shall build a marriage hut for you. You shall be my mate, for the cub is mine."

Rin is flabbergasted when he hears the news. If the truth were told, he himself has looked with hungry eyes upon Lara, as have all the young hunters.

But to think that my Nuse has taken to his bed a barren female! After Che!

Not matchee waybegun indeed, he thinks ruefully.

Could it be that Fuum . . . ? No. Surely hunters are never impotent in these things. The manitu of fertility must have descended upon the female and rendered her mooshkey.

This explains the lessening of grief I noticed in my Nuse over the past months. There has been new spring in his walk though he is an old creature of forty summers. Rin grins. How my Ninga would have laughed! He thinks suddenly, "And she would have approved."

Rin chuckles, but in his throat and chest and loins, there is a terrible ache and he knows that all his hunting, trapping and quiet sojourns in the forest will never assuage this ache.

MAYWISHER, LONG TIME AGO, it was in the spring of the fifth year of the time in the grasslands of the new country, the Rocky Mountain foothills and the Sweetgrass Mountains. Rin was a slim man with an arresting air, dark of skin and eye and the natural center of every group of which he was part.

Noha was older, milder. He guided his people with wisdom and kindness and no longer took part in the chase though he led every hunt. Inik had died, much loved and much regretted, while crazy old Jag sill lived, though she spent her days wandering, howling in the mountains. Rin pitied her and left in secret near her ramshackle hut on a mountain lake, meat. Lara and Whea kept the females and maidens busy and content. Lara and Noha dwelt together amicably. There had been no starvation, although the winters were often severe and Fuum had frozen to death in a prairie blizzard which caught him far from camp.

Rin was standing on a knoll on the plain waiting for Noha who had sent him on a scouting mission and promised to meet him at this spot. The old, wandering fever had struck Noha for one final time, and he had talked the council into moving the clan across the tundra which bordered the southern edge of the ice ocean, to explore the grasslands beyond.

There, they were to find . . . but that's another story.

"When Noha finally climbs the knoll, he is breathing heavily.

He's old, Rin thinks.

"Did you see the movement to the north?" Noha asks.

"I saw it."

"What do you think, Ogucen?"

"It is not the movement of bison or mammoth."

"Those are my thoughts also."

Noha has gotten back his breath and suddenly he smiles and the old light sparks in his eyes. Not all the suffering, the unfulfilled promise, the never quenched yearning, the loneliness which he feels for himself and for his solitary people has been able to stifle that which is the strength and the beauty of Noha.

"Let's run!" He laughs. "Let's run on winged feet to the north. Let's together see what new thing Keewatin blows through the ice corridor."

And so down the long slope they fly, an old man at the end of his days and a young man about to set out on the pathway of a dream. And from somewhere, perhaps from the manitu of her ogucen, Che looks on. Thus, on the tenth year of their sojourn in the land south of the ice, two hunters of the Eyo, the first men to inhabit North America, welcome the forerunners of those who are to come after them to the New World.

NO LONGER ARE THE EYO ALONE